JULIA DU VAL

NELDA HIRSH

GREEN ROCK BOOKS, BOULDER CO

PUBLISHED BY GREEN ROCK BOOKS LLC

ISBN: 978-0-9829650-0-9

Printed in Canada

Design by Nick Pirog

First Paperback Edition

DESCENDANTS OF MAREEN DU VAL

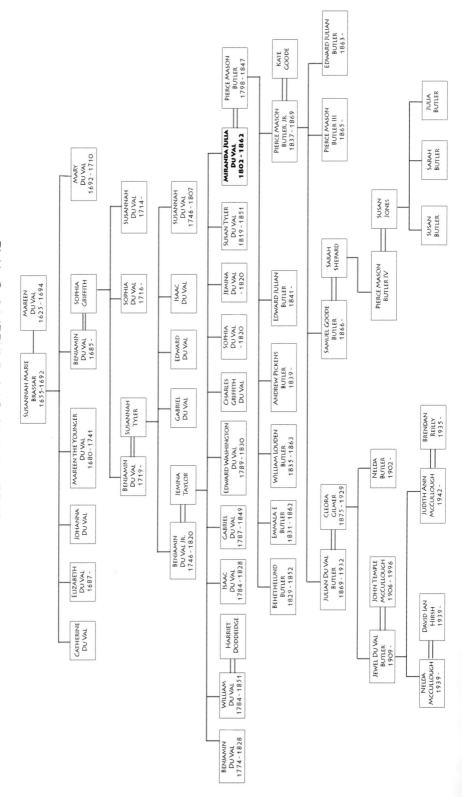

PROLOGUE

THE FOLLOWING tale is based on the life of Julia Du Val, who journeyed to the Indian Territory (present-day Oklahoma) in 1826 and remained there for three years. Early in the 19th century, it was unheard of for an unmarried and affluent woman to undertake such a dangerous adventure. I became curious about her and began to research her life as she was my great-great grandmother.

Remember that women of that time, even those from fine homes, lacked our modern comforts --- no refrigeration, screened windows and doors, or most important, no indoor toilets or running water. In that sense, life on the western frontier, as opposed to the east coast, was probably not as different for Julia Du Val as the contrasts would be for Julia and a woman today. Still, her life on the frontier would have been arduous and at times, very lonely.

We often think of American pioneers as either the first New England settlers in the 1600s and 1700s, or as travelers to the West during the wagon train days of the Gold Rush, or as homesteaders in the post-Civil War era, when the railroads were completed. But there was another frontier period before the Gold Rush, which is less often treated and that is when Julia Du Val began her adventure. During this time, women became more active in public affairs and certainly more outspoken as particular causes, such as abolition and suffrage, seized their spirits. Women were also becoming aware of the "Indian problem", although the tragic Trail of Tears was still a decade away.

It is difficult to learn much about women of America in the 1820's, at least outside their purely domestic settings. One must resort to tracking material about the women through the men in their lives. Since Julia's husband later became Governor of South Carolina, there were documents to be found, both in the Indian Territory and at the South Caroliniana Library at the University of South Carolina. With a little conjecture here and there, this is what I found.

TABLE OF CONTENTS

SUMMER WHIRLWIND

AUTUMN CHILL

FIRST WINTER

THE FRUIT OF THE SWEETGUM TREE, UBIQUITOUS IN THE
INDIAN TERRITORY, IS UGLY TO SOME AND ATTRACTIVE TO
OTHERS. I USE A DRAWING OF ITS HARD, PRICKLY HUSK FOR
CHAPTER BREAKS BECAUSE IT BECAME A SYMBOL OF JULIA'S
DIFFICULT LIFE ON THE PRAIRIE. YET ITS PERFECT CIRCULAR
FORM ALSO HOLDS A CERTAIN CHARM AND THE PROMISE OF
EVERY YEAR'S CYCLICAL RENEWAL.

FREDERICK TOWN, MARYLAND

1825

CHAPTER ONE
A Formal Dinner Party

"WE'RE ALMOST there, Mother," Julia crowed with delight.

Jemina Duval shared her daughter's anticipation. Their groomsman steered the horse-drawn carriage onto East Church Street and came to a halt before a white brick Federalist-style home. The women paused to admire handsome gray shutters accenting the façade's wide windows glowing from the light within. Holding their gowns clear of the brick sidewalk, they mounted the marble steps leading to a paneled front door. Their gaze was drawn above the door where fan-shaped crystal added to the sedate elegance of the house. Before either lady could raise the brass knocker, a butler opened the door to welcome them into the grand foyer. Their stoles were whisked away as they entered a generous reception room, where whale oil lamps shed a gentle glow on bare shoulders and the gentlemen's starched white shirts.

The dinner tonight was planned in honor of General Lafayette, who had returned to Maryland for the first time since the Revolutionary War. Julia Du Val thought such an important person's presence made it imperative that she wear her finest Empire-waist gown of pale green velvet. She had piled her black hair on her head, allowing one wave to drop above her right brow in a style she imagined stressed her large eyes.

Julia spied Judge Tawney with his daughter, Elizabeth, and Francis Scott Key, his former law partner, chatting by the grand stairway newel post. Justice Tawney beckoned Julia over to his conversation, welcoming her warmly by kissing her hand. The judge's position carried great respect for Julia, but it was more his intellect and strong personality which won her admiration. At this moment General Lafayette and Judge Tawney's wife, Ann, who was Francis Scott Key's sister, joined their little group.

"General Lafayette reminded me, just before you arrived," the judge addressed Julia, "that he was only your age when he first came to Frederick to fight in the Revolutionary War. As I am sure you know, he spied on the British to help the colonies' cause. But I am shirking my manners. Allow me to make the introductions first. May I present Miss Du Val to you, General? She is one of my favorite young ladies."

The judge gazed rather tenderly at Julia. Looking at the world from wide-set dark green eyes, she projected a look of honesty and interest in the world. A high forehead and long straight nose gave her face a rather strong demeanor that was tamed by soft rounded cheeks. She wasn't given to smiling often, but when she did, her whole face brightened, and her usual seriousness, somewhat a strain at times, would be forgotten and forgiven in a flash.

General Lafayette bowed and kissed her hand. "*Enchanté, Mademoiselle.* What a long time ago that now seems, and it was embarrassing because I spoke so little English." He smiled pleasantly at Julia. "*Regarde* how the town has prospered since then!"

"We are so honored to have you with us again," Julia responded. "I learned some French from my father, who enjoyed maintaining a connection with his European roots." She pointed to the first column of the wide stairway. "Speaking of prospering, did you know that many folks here call this newel post 'the mortgage post' because the loan documents were always stored in the column under the ivory button on top until the loan was finally fully paid. Then the document was taken out, burned and the ashes put back under the ivory button. I imagine there are ashes under *this* button!"

While General Lafayette laughed, Judge Tawney shook his head in disbelief at her choice of topics. Thinking she had better be more proper, Julia continued, "The country owes you a great debt, Sir, in helping us become a free nation."

"Indeed, we do," echoed Judge Tawney.

"But presently we are fighting very different wars on the western frontier," Julia said. Impressed with the general's erect posture and finely drawn features, she became suddenly very earnest and focused her comment toward him, "The Indians are constantly harassing the settlers and my brothers are there to help maintain the peace." She turned back to the judge, unabashed by his reputation or stately presence. "I have been considering going to visit them as soon as the time is right for travel. What do you think of my idea?"

"Altogether too bold is what I think." He gestured with his whisky glass, sloshing the amber liquid alarmingly. "Now why on earth would a lovely woman such as you want to venture about in the wilderness? Great Heavens, what an extraordinary idea!" the justice exclaimed.

Mrs. Tawney's hand rose to her throat in distress. "I think it would be foolish, Julia! It would be most unsuitable for an unmarried woman and dangerous to your health, I'm sure." Ann Tawney was usually a pretty, cheerful woman but the frown she now wore plunged her eyebrows into a dark "V."

"Actually, I am perfectly serious. When I was only ten, my father gave me the Lewis and Clark Expedition reports to read, and I have wanted to visit the frontier ever since. Now that my brothers are there, I think I have an even better reason to go." Both Judge Tawney and Mr. Key regarded the intense young woman with affection and some wonder.

"But how on earth would you travel, *ma chere*? Certainly not alone! *S'il vous plait, pas toute seule,*" interposed General Lafayette in a fatherly tone. He seemed tempted to break into French whenever emotion colored his speech.

"Well, to tell you the truth, I haven't spoken to my mother

about this yet," --- she glanced across the room to assure herself that Jemina was not in ear shot --- "so please don't mention it to her this evening. But I did talk about it with our plantation overseer, and the next time he takes supplies out to William and Edward, he suggested he might chaperone me." Julia couldn't resist adding with a wink in Elizabeth Tawney's direction, "And perhaps Elizabeth could come too."

"Harrumph," said Justice Tawney, as clearly as Julia could decipher, which she correctly imagined to imply doubt and disagreement. Their hostess, Ruth Ridgely Baltzell, saved Julia from further explanation, as her magenta taffeta skirts rustled with her approach.

"How beautiful you look tonight," she told Julia, embracing her friend.

At the last minute, Julia had tied together a few sprigs of herbs from their garden for Ruth, and she now presented her with the small aromatic packet. Ruth was a city girl from Baltimore and always seemed pleased with Julia's country gifts.

"I brought a little sweet woodruff for repelling insects, a bit of horehound for colds and yarrow for treating fevers and dyspepsia. I hope you will need none of it, but these items may be a beneficial addition to your medicaments."

"Why thank you, my dear. You are always so thoughtful."

Julia took her hostess' hand. "I have been admiring the new portrait of you here in the foyer, and now I see you were posing in the very dress you are wearing tonight. The deep wine color becomes your dark hair perfectly."

"Indeed, one thinks of wine, roses and happiness," agreed the debonair General Lafayette. They all admired the portrait of Ruth in the dress with big puff sleeves and a flowing pink scarf. Her hair, parted in the middle, was more elaborately done in the portrait, pinned in three waves down each side, forming soft scallops around her face.

"So lovely," Judge Tawney beamed at her.

"No more flattery," Ruth laughed. "It's time for you all to

move into the dining room. The wine steward has related to me that dinner is served."

As Julia glimpsed Dr. Baltzell slipping his hand around Ruth's waist to steer her protectively toward the table, she experienced a vicarious thrill of hope. When the doctor married three years ago, there were rumors that Julia was a disappointed aspirant for his hand. But she had never entertained romantic dreams for him; Dr. Baltzell was a kind man but a little formal and too old, already exhibiting a deeply receding hairline. She wished Ruth happiness and enjoyed having her for a friend. Tonight, as Julia quickly reviewed the guests taking their places, she was disappointed not to find a new and exciting gentleman among the group. She had to admit some envy, not that Ruth had such a beautiful house, but that she had someone who loved her. Sometimes Julia felt as though life were passing her by.

The mahogany table, unfolded to its full extent, glistened with silver, crystal and French Limoges china in honor of General Lafayette's visit. Julia found herself seated with her back to the imposing King of Prussia marble fireplace between Mr. Key and Mr. Brien of the Catoctin Iron Foundry. The latter was a successful munitions manufacturer for the Revolutionary War and the War of 1812. Judge Tawney sat opposite while her mother was seated down the table on Dr. Baltzell's right.

They had barely taken their seats when the Judge announced to the group at their end of the table "Julia's harebrained plan." Julia turned her head just in time to witness her mother's startled and pained expression. If only she could plow ahead with her plans without worrying her mother. Tonight Jemina looked very pretty, her round eyes bright and plump cheeks rouged. But she had aged quite a bit since her husband died and often seemed pale and listless. Julia thought the way she wandered around the house lately without a sense of purpose seemed the most aging and worrisome behavior of all.

"Oh, Judge Tawney, you are truly exaggerating," Julia replied, with a slightly embarrassed laugh. "Of course I don't really know if it will be possible. But it does seem like the frontier is an interesting place to be and things are all too quiet on the plantation without my brothers."

"You should be grateful things are calm after so many wars at the birth of our nation," said Mr. Key. "I still tremble at memories of 1812. Can it be already a dozen years ago?"

Ruth spoke from the head of the table, "And we have you to thank, Mr. Key, for the beautiful poem you wrote in Baltimore during the terrible bombardment of the harbor. How terrified we all were!"

Francis Scott Key bowed his head to her in recognition of the compliment. "It still makes me shiver to think of it," interposed Julia. "And now I understand there's a movement afoot to make the poem our national anthem. Are you not proud you had the chance to do something so brave and wonderful?" she questioned with such ardent expression, Mr. Key had to repress a smile.

"Perhaps," he admitted. "But I still prefer today's peace and quiet."

"But what about the Indian problem and the frontier? I do not think it is quiet out there," pursued Julia, her cheeks already bright from the wine she had drunk. "I am sure you know that Thomas Jefferson believes the Indians should be assimilated. He really thinks they could become part of the White Man's society, but others take it for granted that they are all wild men who cannot be tamed. What do you think?" she asked the group at large.

Judge Tawney spoke up. "Oh, my, Julia, this is nothing you need bother yourself about. It is a very difficult question and one that will trouble our country for a long while, I fear. However, I must say, I believe the Indians are entirely too primitive to understand our culture."

"I am afraid I disagree, Justice, with all due respect," said General Lafayette. "There is some evidence that some of the tribes wish to learn agricultural techniques and settle down. And if they are not taught, how do you expect to achieve peace on *la frontière*? You are aware, I know, that the descendents of the

French colonialists have similar problems with the Algonquin around *le Lac Champlaine* and ..."

Ah," said Mr. Key, "Surely there is enough land to go around now that President Jefferson has completed the Louisiana Purchase. Good Lord, Sir, he doubled the size of the United States in one grand sweep. We only must persuade the Indians to move further west and there shall be no more problem. Have no more fears on that score."

"I don't think they want to move," Julia rejoined. "At least that is what I perceive from my brothers' letters."

"Enough politics," Ruth called from the other end of the table. "I want no problems at my dinner table tonight."

"Julia started it," teased Mr. Key.

"As she always does at home," said Jemina with a note of resignation, but more than a touch of affection in her voice. "And be careful, she can honeyfuggle you into anything she wants." Julia was relieved to hear, in just those few words, if not a veiled acceptance, at least her mother's willingness to consider her surprising plan. The conversation turned to other subjects, like Judge Tawney's new wine cellar and the increased prices the farmers were getting for their tobacco.

"It's good for the economy, but you know, it will bring more folks into the area, and it's already getting too crowded," Mr. Brien commented. "I would hate to see our beautiful thick forests cut down and tilled."

"Oh, they won't be soon," Dr. Baltzell interjected. "Prices are too high. Indeed, in 1715, our 178 acres of tillable land, complete with a house and farm buildings, cost about 50 pounds sterling with 2000 pounds of tobacco as a bonus. It's hard to know equivalent prices now, what with British sterling, tobacco and paper money all being viable currency."

Mr. Key chimed in. "I'd say the gentry are still putting their income back into land. That is still the prime source of wealth. Of course, agriculture is not my business, but these scalawag moneylenders raise my ire, demanding loans at six percent! Now that's hard on any new inhabitants coming into town and we attorneys welcome their arrival."

Growing sleepy from all the wine and stimulation as the men talked on, Julia began to think of the comfortable, four-poster, lace-canopied bed upstairs. The ladies had packed a few things because the Baltzells thoughtfully had invited them to stay overnight, saving them a cold and dark ride home. The gentlemen's dismissal of her plans rankled, and she knew she would have to discuss her proposed trip with her mother tomorrow. She realized she had shocked her neighbors this evening, but she felt as jumpy as a grasshopper sometimes. She just wanted to *do* something. In the hall the grandfather clock chimed half past ten o'clock, and Julia and her mother discreetly slipped upstairs soon after the gentlemen retired to the study for their segars and clay pipes.

CHAPTER TWO
THE RIDE HOME

JACOB, WHO had spent the night in the servant's quarters, duly turned up with their carriage the next morning. It was considered unladylike for a woman to drive a conveyance herself, but Julia ignored this rule much of the time on the farm and in their immediate neighborhood. For such an outing as this, however, the ladies depended on Jacob as their escort and driver. He had been one of the family's slaves since he was young and in their minds, he was considered part of the family. Jemina fussed with plaid blankets, tucking herself and her daughter into the family's two-wheeled chaise for the five mile, hour-long ride home.

In Frederick Town's center, large stand-alone homes with wide covered front porches, bay windows and turreted corners, hugged the red brick streets. As their carriage passed the Huguenot Church, Julia felt a twinge of guilt that she had not attended last Sunday. When Jemina didn't press her to come, she always chose other activities. Yet most of her friends attended several services on a Sunday, seeing the dressing up and discussing sermons more as entertainment than worship. Her father had often reminded her that just a century ago this church had been a haven for French Protestants fleeing discrimination in Catholic dominated France. As they passed through the outskirts, the houses became more modest attached structures, and toward the end of North Market Street, the red brick suddenly changed to a packed dirt road.

Mother and daughter both knew the conversation could not be avoided. They had finished discussing what everyone wore last night and all the delicious dishes Ruth had served. Now the subject of a possible frontier trip loomed so large in both their minds that Julia knew exactly what her mother meant when Jemina blurted, "It's just not something young ladies *do*. In fact it would be considered downright *odd!*" she said as though that were the crowning argument to a long discussion.

"People already think me odd, I imagine," Julia responded. "If I were normal, I would be married and have children by now, at this *advanced* age of twenty-three! But I haven't wed, Mother, and let's face it, the gentlemen left in the neighborhood know I am not destined for them, nor they for me."

"Pshaw! Anyone would be lucky to have you."

"Of course that's what you think. But you forget, I don't want them either. I refuse to get married just because everyone thinks it's the right thing to do," Julia said stubbornly. "You have said practically the same thing yourself! I would rather spend an evening alone than have to sit up straight and talk to a dullard!" How difficult it was to explain to her mother her occasional urges for freedom or the feeling that mute submission to a man she didn't fully admire was impossible.

Julia remembered all too well how a few years ago there had been a young man whom she found interesting, and she had believed he thought her charming. Indeed, he had said so. She was disappointed, even shocked, when he gradually ceased calling upon her and then married someone quite out of their circle. She had not been deeply hurt, but she had expected and wished for the friendship to grow. On reflection, it probably was more her pride than deep feelings which had been wounded. She still grew cold with embarrassment when she thought about it. And for quite awhile afterward, she sensed people whispered behind her back about her having missed a great opportunity. Her mother knew she felt awkward meeting him and his new wife socially, and Jemina, in her intuitive, quiet way had managed one day to casually say, "Well, we don't get married to satisfy other people now, do we?"

Jemina's complaint interrupted her reverie. "I wish your father were here. Perhaps he could talk some sense into your head!"

Four years had passed since her father, Benjamin's death, yet Julia still missed him. Especially his calling her "Juliette" when no one else did and the way his deep voice engaged the company with clever stories at events in town like last night's party. Having often ignored her daddy's advice when he was alive, she now wondered whether he would think her plan to visit her brothers on the frontier was too outrageous. He might have refused to let her go—not because he thought it too wild, but because he loved her too much. Julia sensed both reasons were prompting her mother's negative reaction.

"Oh, Mother, I don't want to leave you all alone, but I do want to visit Edward and William and see the rest of our country. It must be absolutely stimulating, and I may rest assured knowing you will be well taken care of here by Mrs. Paddington and all the staff."

"But women stay at home, Julia. I can not imagine how you conceived of such an injudicious plan." She shook her head as though to say "no" "And there's so much to take care of here on the farm!"

"Mother, please try to understand. I just feel I want to know more about the world, and I am sure I shall be safe."

"Well, we shall see," Jemina said. "It's out of the question for the present at any rate." Clearly she hoped her imaginative daughter would abandon this preposterous idea.

Soon the ladies' buggy bumped along beside lush shamrock meadows, interrupted only by neat white fences, clearly delineating the property lines of gentlemen farmers. As far as the eye could see, easy and gentle slopes rolled to the horizon with occasional small woods punctuating the landscape. Thoroughbred horses and woolly sheep grazed here and there, naturally mowing the verdant sward.

About half way home the carriage crossed the Monocacy River, which emptied into the great Potomoc River just west of their property, thereby describing the southern boundary of new Frederick County. Julia smiled, "Do you remember, Mama, how we all thought the Monocacy was the perfect place to learn to swim?"

"I do, indeed. How it used to frighten me!" Then, as she always did when taking this route, Jemina commented on the Schifferstadt's house and how there were "simply too many Prussians living in the neighborhood these days." Then as she always did, Julia answered, "Yes, Mother, but the Germans here are no longer Prussians or mercenaries. The revolution has been over for a long time, and they are good citizens now."

"Well, General Lafayette might have some thoughts about that! You know he is a marquis," Jemina responded. Being accustomed to her mother's habit of speaking with non-sequiturs, Julia was able to follow her pattern; she knew Jemina would always see the United States as an outlying colony for English, Scots, Irish and French settlers. She could never quite fathom why her mother drew the line there, believing other nationalities inferior, and imagined she had just sensed a whiff of snobbery.

Hawthorne and hickory trees crowded the edges of the road leading toward their tiny community of Mt. Pleasant, where Benjamin Du Val had decided to settle down. He always said it reminded him of the ancestral northeast of France. Her parents would always look back toward Europe, she thought, while perhaps her generation was beginning to look westward. Julia was very glad when the horses turned into their drive, providing an excuse to abandon the discussion.

THE JOURNEY

1826

CHAPTER THREE
LEAVING MT. PLEASANT

SUNLIGHT FILTERED through the branches of giant white oak trees on the Du Val family's plantation dappling the forest floor, and just as she had as a child, Julia Du Val jumped and danced from one puddle of light to another. Slowing to a ramble, she bent to touch the Maidenhair fern, too beautiful to be real, she thought, and always her favorite amongst the plants her father had revealed to her because of its pretty name and feathery leaves. More exotic greenery, which he had carefully brought from France, grew closer to the house. She opened the low gate in the fence separating the forest from the well-tended lawn of their home. Entering the yard, she admired the old wheelbarrow, piled high with pumpkins and brightly colored gourds, propped decoratively by the back porch. An old red sleigh festively guarded the back door. How could she leave this place?

As it turned out, her mother had been right that her "harebrained scheme" was out of the question for the present. In fact, it had taken almost a year to bring her plan to fruition, giving her ample time to review her decision. Some days she would feel sure of herself, and on others, when she gazed at her mother's face, a *frisson* of panic would strike. How could she selfishly ignore how much her mother needed her at home? And how much she took for granted at their farm! --- the comforts provided by the dairy, the outdoor privy, the smoke house, the wine cellar and more.

Yet, since all her brothers had left home to pursue their

active lives, the house often echoed with emptiness. She longed for the boisterous presence of Edward and William, who wrote her fascinating letters from the Indian Territory about their experiences as army officers and keeping peace on the frontier. Now only her mother and herself were left at home, two spinster sisters having died the same year as her father. What a terrible year that had been, and she doubted whether her mother had recovered from the triple blow. *She* certainly had not. Another sister of Julia's, Susan Tyler, had married and moved with her young husband to South Carolina. Even though Julia was the youngest of ten children, her unmarried years were beginning to add up. Julia hated admitting to herself a wish to marry. Why was a man so necessary for her happiness? After all, she didn't want someone telling her what to do and how to do it. "Oh bother!" she heard herself say out loud sometimes. She didn't want to think about it. Except she was bored much of the time.

With all the men away, Julia had taken over some of the business duties of the family plantation. She'd become accustomed to being her own guide through her day, and she generally felt adequate to the tasks presented by her daily life. Always good with numbers, she derived a great deal of satisfaction preparing the order lists for the farm and adding up the profits from the tobacco and cereal crops at the end of each month. Still, she often felt restless and impatient with the monotony of her days. Somehow she expected more out of life than a placid lake reflecting back upon itself.

"Wild as a March hare." That's how her father sometimes described her. And perhaps she was, for she had always loved the sense of freedom that running gave her, her knees pumping, her arms swinging rhythmically, and the wind in her hair. Sometimes he would also call her "headstrong as a two year old," even as he beamed over her intelligence. Though assured by her family that her small stature and tiny feet were fashionable and appealing, Julia often wished she were taller and stronger. Actually she was unexpectedly strong for a small female and secretly prided herself on her physical abilities. Growing up with the rough and tumble of her brothers, and with parents who didn't seem to mind when their daughter returned from outside as dirty as their sons, had prepared her for an adventurous life. At least, she liked to think so. Her father had drawn the line when she would slip and say, "Gol, darn it!" which he allowed the boys to shout. He would remind her that ladies never spoke in such a coarse manner.

The opportunity to persuade her mother about her proposed trip finally arose when Edward wrote of his need for a number of items from the farm. Military provisions, while adequate, left much to be desired for men accustomed to a comfortable plantation life. Julia thought the estate steward, Mr. Paddington, could very well chaperone her while seeing to it that a shipment of wine, cheese, whiskey, a few slaves, and other essentials were safely delivered to Cantonnement Gibson.

Mr. Paddington had been a family retainer since before Julia was born, and his wife also lived and worked on the estate. Jemina Du Val had to admit she could not place her daughter in more trusted hands; he would watch over her like his own blood. Indeed, he had worked alongside Benjamin Du Val with the loyalty of a brother, but the two men had always preserved the formality of employer and employee. Mr. Paddington invariably wore a rumpled tweedy jacket, wool in winter and cotton in summer, neither of which ever quite buttoned over his broad stomach.

At last, Jemina, appreciating that ennui could be as harmful to her youngest daughter's health as the unknown dangers of the frontier, agreed to let Julia go. The unselfishness of this conclusion made Julia feel all the more guilty about her desire to leave home and see the rest of the relatively young country. But she suspected her mother understood she couldn't abide the *status quo* any longer. It wasn't exactly that she was embarrassed about not being married, but rather that she felt some small sense of failure.

As Julia strolled around the garden, she wondered if it were a problem that she had no particular ambition. Because she had always exhibited an interest, her father and her older brother, Edward, had taken the time to teach her more than most females. How much easier life would be, she thought if only she possessed a strong talent--- in art or singing for instance. Well, her natural intelligence and active mind would just have to do.

CHAPTER FOUR
THE STAGECOACH

AT DAWN, on the day of departure, all of Julia's doubts rushed back, like a strong tide after a storm. When the frontier scheme was only in the planning stages, how invigorating it had been to make lists of all she would need in the Indian Territory, to make her purchases in town and stow everything in two large wooden traveling trunks. Since Edward occasionally wrote of heat, mosquitoes, dust, and mud, she had wisely decided on only two petticoats, two pairs of sturdy ankle boots and one pair of dancing shoes. A sensible nature also counseled her to pack her simplest frocks, her riding habit, and several bottles of perfume in case she couldn't bathe as often as she would like.

She tried to brush away the cobwebs of vacillation by reviewing her supply list. She had thought to bring many items for a garden in the Indian Territory. She imagined most herbs were hardy and remembered hyssop would be good for its strong scent if there were unpleasant smells about. She added the plants she'd taken to Ruth, remembering that yarrow would be helpful to treat wounds, and lamb's ear, a soft and woolly herb, could be used for bandages. Then, for her cooking, she put in a paper some thyme and lovage, which gave a celery flavor to many dishes. Her mother had taught her that the seeds made a tea for the treatment of indigestion and the canes could be dried and used as drinking straws. What essential items was she forgetting?

She reminded herself that in mid-March the timing was

exactly right because the spring rains raised the water level of the western rivers to the appropriate grade. By late summer the big boats would not be able to pass again until the next spring. Edward had written that construction at the fort was moving along quickly, and he thought there would be living quarters for a few women by the time Julia arrived.

The trip in the abstract, however, had seemed like a much better idea than it now appeared. Surely she would miss her mother as much as she had missed her brothers these past months. Why hadn't she realized this before? Why on earth had she pressed for this crazy scheme? She had let her imagination run wild with thoughts of seeing new birds, exotic flowers and most exciting of all, Indians. How utterly fascinating these red skinned people seemed, their faces both strong and sad. Was their skin really red, she wondered? She had pasted in her Daily Book the words of Thomas McKenney, President Madison's Superintendent of Indian Trade, who had urged that "Indians be looked upon as human beings, having bodies and souls like ours, possessed of sensibilities and capacities as keen and large as ours, that their misery be inspected and held up to the view of our citizens, that their trophies of reform be pointed to."[1]

She was not the only one concerned with the plight of the Indians as it had even become a cause for the female parishioners at her church. They urged everyone to send used clothing to nearby eastern tribes. When she'd read *The Last of the Mohicans* by the great James Fenimore Cooper, she'd wept over the nobility of Uncas and marveled at his sympathy, love even, for the white girl, Alice. Cooper had made it seem so right and so real that the Indian brave and the aristocratic female could understand and respect one another. With these thoughts, she had added a few items to give to the Indians when she met them.

These earlier impressions now seemed like gossamer imaginings and her mother's tears tugged at her compassionate conscience. But hating any sign of cowardice in herself, she hid her own watering eyes and stepped up into the family wagon, which was essentially an English coach modified for the American rough roads. An iron railing at the back and on both sides allowed one to strap baggage that didn't fit on the flattened roof. Jemina flapped her hands in front of her face, as though to wipe away tears, to say don't worry about me, and wave goodbye, all at once.

"Give William the unguent for his chapped skin as soon as you arrive," her mother called from the steps. "And don't forget to always wear your bonnet against the sun and be sure to tell Eddie about the new filly!"

"I will the first, I won't the second, and I will the third," Julia smiled as she waved. As her mother's lone figure quickly receded from view, she tightly gripped her hand valise and felt some comfort in knowing the bulky friendly form of Mr. Paddington, wearing his Benjamin, a long all-weather coat to shield him from the elements, shared the bench outside with Jacob. Since her brothers said she would have little space to put her things, she had not brought too much. Now she already regretted leaving behind her soft blue shawl, only bringing her sturdier gray one and a flimsy bit of organza for an evening dress. "Oh dear," she murmured to herself. "Oh dear, oh dear."

As they turned left out of their long driveway onto the main road, the sight of two huge luxurious magnolia trees made her breath catch. Would there be anything on the prairie nearly so beautiful as these dark shiny leaves surrounding white waxy blossoms? An easy swell of broad hills began to rise just west of Frederick Township with a view of the Catoctin Mountains to the north. Julia knew that was the most popular area to reside, yet she believed her father had chosen well, preferring their large tract of land with a gentler slope northeast of town.

Julia recalled the family lore --- how her ancestors had tended to be quiet farm people and Du Val literally meant "from the valley." The first arrivals settled in the hills of Virginia, where the fertile land seemed friendly and the people welcoming. It didn't take long, however, for the best land parcels to be snapped up, prompting descendants of Mareen Du Val of Normandy to move on to Maryland, where they believed they would encounter less competition than in Virginia. They planted tobacco and made a fine living shipping thousands of dollars worth of "hogsheads" of the dried leaves back to Europe. Pushing a bit further westward into Maryland in search of the best arable land, the Du Vals subsequently became proud founders in Anne Arundel, Carroll, Montgomery, Frederick and eventually Cumberland counties. Family legend had it that Mareen Du Val's first land had been patented to him by Lord Baltimore. As their families grew and new opportunities arose, their plantations proliferated, often becoming self-supporting, rudimentary villages. Why had she felt she must leave this land where her family had invested so much? Well, it wasn't forever!

In just one hour, as the carriage left Frederick and familiar sights fell behind, new vistas and the prospect of the journey quickened Julia's interest. Sometimes she believed herself as curious as their calico farm cat, who more often than not found herself in trouble for poking her nose where it didn't belong. Every day of sameness or idleness could not satisfy her; this Julia knew.

Hagerstown, only fifteen miles away, already boasted 4000 inhabitants and many important new buildings. How much more modern it seemed than Frederick Town, Julia observed with amazement. They passed through Braddock Mountain and Middletown Valley, rather dark and gloomy with dense overgrown vegetation, but then a flock of four or five hundred wild turkeys in the brush by the road made her laugh, so noisy and awkward were they.

Reaching South Mountain Inn late that afternoon, more than ready to stretch, Julia jumped down from the confining conveyance. She didn't want to complain but sincerely hoped that tomorrow the new fangled stagecoach they called a "flying machine" would be more comfortable than the family carriage, which Jacob would return to Mt. Pleasant. The innkeeper welcomed their party with hot toddies and suggested they meet in the dining room in an hour for supper. Pleading fatigue, Julia requested a small repast and hurried to the privacy of her room.

THE NEXT morning Mr. Paddington spread a large map on the breakfast table between them. She'd studied this map before the trip but it had acquired more importance and reality since they were on the road. "Best you review our itinerary, Missy. We'll be taking the new National Road to Cumberland, then across the state of Pennsylvania for about 200 miles in all, until we meet the Ohio River just past the state line at Pittsburgh. Once there, we'll board the first steamboat headed south. The Ohio River winds through Virginia, Ohio, and Indiana and joins the Mississippi River at Cairo, Illinois. You'll be seein' a mighty lot of our country.

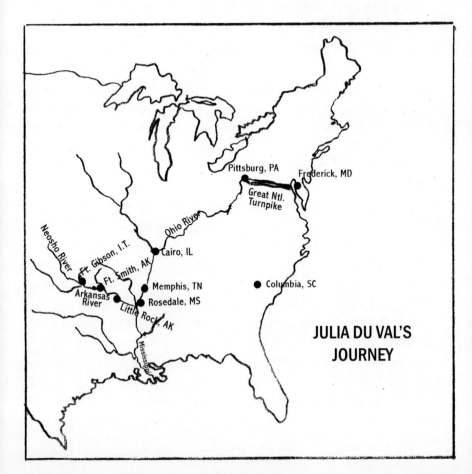

Appearing rather pale and tired after a restless night in a strange bed, Julia smiled with more bravery than enthusiasm. "I suspect I need to find my traveling legs."

"Not to worry, my dear. Not to worry. You're doing fine. Just fine."

Julia found his heartiness encouraging until she spied the stagecoach which drew up to the door. It looked no finer to her than a Conestoga wagon, though it was billed as a Concord Coach, built by the new wheelwright shop in Concord, Massachusetts. Designed to hold twelve persons, including the driver, it offered upholstered plank seats, the most comfortable, by far, being the rear where one could lean against the back wall of the wagon. Since Julia was the only woman, she was offered the back middle seat. The only protection between the passengers and the elements were leather curtains to be drawn down to cover the sides when necessary. When it was warm, one had to choose between dust and heat, and Julia quickly decided she preferred heat, but most of the men chose dust. When it was cold and rainy, all agreed to lower the curtains, but the dank smell of humanity and wet wool immediately made her feel squeamish, though she didn't want to admit it.

The newly invented carriage boasted "springs", long strips of leather stretching from rear to front axle that held up the body of the coach. Still, by afternoon the hard seat and rough road made Julia conscious of every bone in her body. She thought of the dancing paper skeletons the children hung on the door at Halloween and envisioned her limbs jumping and jiggling haphazardly with the lurching wagon. She welcomed the smooth stretches where the great new National Turnpike was finished. Julia began to wish for another woman to talk to as two traveling salesmen chattered away together about popular items they would be offering to prospective clients in Ohio and another pair of farmers had their heads together over the trials of spring calving.

To be fresh and safe, the six horses and the drivers where changed every 10 to 15 miles, but by evening, having covered about

60 miles at the rapid gait of 8 miles per hour, the good humor of all eight passengers was strained. Clearly, to vent his spleen, the one Julia had privately named "Mutton Chops" ventured,

"So, young lady, what are you doing lollygagging about the country?"

"I hadn't thought of it as 'lollygagging', Sir." She tried to sit up straighter. "I'm on my way to visit my brothers who are soldiers out in the Indian Territory."

"Well, that's a damned fool thing to do if I ever heard it," the gentleman grumped. "What were your parents thinking of to allow such behavior?"

Trying to keep her irritation out of her voice, Julia explained, "My father died a few years ago and my mother felt I was adult enough to make my own decision."

"I say, it sounds like a mighty dangerous thing for a girl to do. I cannot imagine there isn't enough to keep you busy at home."

"Of course, there is, but I have long been curious about the West."

"Curious or not, I certainly wouldn't allow my daughter to travel by public conveyance in wild country."

"How else would she travel, Sir?" Julia asked as politely as she could muster, hiding a mischievous smile.

"She wouldn't, my dear. That's the point."

"I'm here to watch after her," Mr. Paddington, now seated inside, finally interceded. "Miss Du Val is helping me on plantation business."

"Well, I never," Mutton Chops harrumphed again and Julia hoped that would be the end of it. If everyone were going to disapprove of her, she knew this would bother her much more than the physical hardships of the trip. With that thought, she began to very much look forward to the next inn where they would stop for the night when she could nurse her bruised bones and enjoy several hours of privacy. She was loath to complain as this whole expedition had been her idea, and there was no need to get in a pucker over this buffoon, she told herself.

Suddenly the novel *Rob Roy* popped into her mind. How she'd loved that book! In fact, she never could wait for Sir Walter Scot's latest tale to appear at Frederick Town's bookstore. But at this moment, Scot's depiction of highwaymen and bands of robbers preying on innocent travelers, in particular upon the hero Frank Osbaldistone, disowned by his father and sent to Scotland to mature, seemed all too *apropos*. Despite the risks, how envious she had been of Frank who, as a young man, had the power to act as a free agent and the liberty to cultivate his own talents in whatever way his taste determined. Now her over rich imagination had placed her on an unknown path. "Thank you, Mr. Paddington," Julia whispered, glaring at Mutton Chops with renewed resolve.

CHAPTER FIVE
THE STEAMBOAT

AFTER THREE days of lurching along corduroy roads, sleeping in lumpy beds and eating in pump rooms at dark taverns among boisterous and dubious company, Julia rejoiced at the sight of a finer hotel in Pittsburgh, already a bustling city due to the commerce on the Ohio and Monongahela Rivers. Mr. Paddington told her they had been lucky not to have a single accident with the stagecoach--- lost wheels and turnovers being not uncommon occurrences. Still, she sighed with grateful relief as the lobby's gaslights drew her indoors. Plush chairs and settees adorned the reception room and she noticed finely dressed men and women conversing in soft tones in the dining room nearby. She might want to spend more time here on her return home, she decided.

Awaking early the second morning, she felt greatly restored, one day in bed having quickly cured her worries and fatigue. She wandered down to the wharf, delighted to be on foot rather than in a cramped coach. The cool fresh air caressed her cheeks while she watched the river turn from deep gray to a foggy white. As the sun climbed higher, the water glinted in the light reflecting in her amber and green eyes, and a skinny cat brushed against her skirt, his meow reminding her it was breakfast time. Upriver a bit, she spied a steamboat tethered near an old cottonwood along the bank. Perhaps they could leave today; she had no important reason to stay on in Pittsburgh, although she knew Mr. Paddington had been very busy fulfilling more requested purchase orders for the fort.

The weather remained bright but cool, and Julia pulled her shawl more tightly around her shoulders. She stood as straight as she could in an attempt to ward off prying curious eyes with her rigid posture. Amidst this loud and chaotic scene, she let her bonnet partially hide her face and pretended not to hear all the blasphemous and rough talk as she watched the boat being loaded, mostly by slaves and a few free men hired for the voyage. "Shut pan," shouted one stevedore to another. "Watch your arse," was the quick return.

Mules pulling carts and wagons and horse-drawn drays lined up one after another, pushing their way toward the waiting boats. Sailors bellowed orders, porters pushed hand carts offering help with bags, harridans hawked food and boys, wearing sandwich placards, advertised good deals at nearby hotels while one fellow on stilts, towering above the din, handed out leaflets touting a seamy show for the evening. The hull sank deeper into the water as the lading continued through the afternoon. And sure enough, by dusk Mr. Paddington and Julia were directed up the gangplank by stevedores gawking as though they'd never seen a woman before. As two firemen stoked the boiler with wood, stacked high below, the ship's tall chimney began to belch smoke, and with long poles, the crew pushed away from the underbrush along the bank raising a trail of bottom sand.

"Best we not tarry," said Mr. Paddington with satisfaction.

The "Rose Marie" was only a small packet with a handful of staterooms. After the bustle of departure, the quiet of the river surprised and enthralled Julia as she stood on the single passenger deck, enclosed by a white railing, watching the huge wheel churn and splash in the murky dark water. At first there were noxious odors from all the slops tossed into the river near the harbor, and so Mr. Paddington, gently guiding her by the elbow, suggested she install herself in the ladies' saloon situated aft. Alone in the rather dingy room, she felt the grumble of the boilers under her feet and the constant vibration of the paddlewheel. The few available windows were grimy with soot and shut tight, making the room stuffy and airless. Well, once properly underway, she could always take a stroll on deck when she liked.

Removing her bonnet, she chose the largest of the four chairs in the small room. In a short while she grew accustomed to the gentle rattle of the boat and began to wonder if she were the only female aboard. She pulled a small book from her pocket before realizing it was too dim to read and there were no oil lamps provided. So, her reading would have to be done outdoors in daylight hours.

It wasn't long before Mr. Paddington came to fetch her for the evening meal, and just in time he was, for when the dinner bell rang, a crowd pushed them like pebbles in high tide toward a double door. At the table she found another young woman already seated and shyly keeping her eyes upon her plate. The clatter of cutlery and dishes drowned out any hope of conversation and the choice victuals disappeared all too quickly. Nevertheless, there was plenty to go around, and Julia saw she would neither starve nor particularly enjoy meal times.

Having come from a large family, Julia had never needed to put herself forward much to make friends and now found herself relishing the challenge of presenting herself to a stranger. When one of the men at the table was especially ill mannered, Julia and the young woman chanced to look at one another and smile. What a relief to find someone of like mind!

After the meal Julia rose and walked around the table to introduce herself. "My name is Abigail Abernathy," was the reply.

"What is your destination, Miss Abernathy?" Julia asked.

"I am on my way to visit my sister in St. Louis," the young woman explained. "Her husband is a Moravian, and they have started a Moravian school there. They both wrote and begged me to come and teach. They say there are many children, white and Indian, but no teachers. When our mother died last month, I decided to join them."

"That sounds exciting --- and brave too," Julia said encouragingly while thinking that Abigail, tall and wispy in frame, with thin blond hair and dark chocolate brown eyes, did not appear strong enough for such an undertaking. Julia had noticed, however, that Miss Abernathy ate quite a lot during dinner and seemed energetic in her demeanor.

"And what about you?" her new friend inquired.

"I do not have such a clear mission. I am just exploring, I expect. And going to visit my brothers." She felt some discomfort that her answer sounded rather spoiled and irresponsible, even like an admission of failure. "Please call me "Julia"," she added. "I hope we shall be friends."

"I am sure we shall. And I am Abigail," she smiled.

After dinner Mr. Paddington escorted her to her quarters, and as she should have realized, she and Abigail would bunk together. Indeed, they were extremely lucky to have a separate room as most of the other passengers simply folded down berths from the walls of a single large cabin. There seemed to be some sort of lottery to determine who got the berths and who got the chairs and tables, but Mr. Paddington instructed her not to fret over it. He would get along just fine.

The Ohio River wound westward, gently looping like bric-a-brac through the countryside. The easy meandering along the brown river road could be peaceful or boring, depending on her mood. Sometimes, especially when the water ran faster making her restless, she longed to raise the dark green curtain of trees hiding the interior and hurry downstream toward the rest of her life. At other times, she found herself completely content with the confinement, contemplating wading waterfowl or reading by the deck's railing seated in a rusty metal folding chair. Mr. Paddington always seemed to be hovering nearby and so the rougher element didn't bother her when she dared sit on a coil of rope to attain the view she wished for a watercolor. She had stopped drinking so much water because privacy was such a problem and the smells of the night soil and the odors of close quarters on the boat sometimes made her queasy. She wished she had better control of her body.

Julia smiled inwardly at the irony of her constraints here, how she had thought to escape the predictable boredom of her life on the plantation, and now it was equally as difficult to tell one day from another. She must find entertainment within her own mind, and she liked to think of her imagination looping and turning like the Ohio River, with unexpected discoveries at every turn. Would she see this new world with the veil of her past over it or without the scrim of hardened opinions? Surely she was young enough to welcome all the good that would come her way, even if it first seemed strange.

Frequently she and Abigail would chat about their young lives as though each of them had had a long history. It did seem to Julia that she had much to tell, about everyone in her family, the farm and the growing importance of Frederick, Maryland. Abigail was quieter and Julia admired her greatly for her desire to be of service with teaching. She felt some shame at her own instinct to take all that life offered rather than first considering what she could give.

The river seemed to run faster as they proceeded west, and on the third night out, not long after she fell asleep, Julia was startled awake by a thump. The steamboat shuddered to an undignified halt. Fearing she knew not what, Julia leapt from her bunk and donned her shoes. Going barefoot was a fate to be avoided due to the slick of tobacco juice on deck, the occasional spittoons apparently more for decoration than actual use. Grabbing her dressing gown, she pulled it on as she stuck her head into the corridor.

"We have run aground, Missy," Mr. Paddington appeared, looking grizzled and disheveled. "If we can not dislodge by daybreak, I expect we will all have to get off the boat to lighten her. Might as well try and get some sleep for the present."

"Try" became the operative word as sailors' shouts and occasional rocking and banging serenaded her throughout the long night. A soft mist enveloped the crippled hull when day broke, and the captain ordered all to alight to a jolly boat to shuttle them to a small island midstream and immediately adjacent to the sand bar which had caused their present predicament. Julia shivered in the damp dull morning, pining for her warm bunk and hot tea. Abigail came to stand beside her until one of the passengers put his coat on the ground for them to sit.

And a long morning it was, watching the hull rock back and forth and wondering if they were essentially shipwrecked. The sight of the riverbank only thirty yards away dispelled that notion, but when a snake, disturbed by all the commotion, slithered by and slipped into the water, Abigail and Julia squealed despite their brave intentions. Julia startled again when a huge flock of migrating ducks rising from the water made a flurried, whooshing sound like a storm whirling around a chimney. By noon the steamship got underway again with talk among the passengers as to whether Capt. Maconnaghy was incompetent regarding running aground or brilliant regarding the rescue. Having no experience to make a judgment, Julia preferred to think the latter.

AFTER SEVEN and a half days the Rose Marie pulled into Cairo, Illinois where Robert Fulton's new steamship, the Clermont, rocked gently in the harbor. This would be the vessel to take her down the Mississippi River to Memphis and finally to the mouth of the Arkansas River. But her excitement was tinged with regret, for she and Abigail had to part ways at this juncture. How appalling this thought now appeared!

The two young women had enjoyed one another's company on the boat and had subtly bolstered one another's courage. After all, they both had chosen such an adventure with the confidence they would not only survive but learn from it. Having to leave such a new but firm friend disturbed Julia. Until now, friendships were for life in her small town while growing up and she had no experience with such a fast moving attachment.

"We will see one another again, I know," Abigail assured Julia, assuming an elder sister's mien.

"Of course we shall," Julia agreed. "But I shall miss you." The girls clung to one another while Mr. Paddington looked on, smiling like a doting uncle.

Julia watched pretty lasses with petticoats and parasols strolling along the wharf with their gentlemen in order to gaze at this relatively new invention bobbing upon the water. Bunting hung over the tall sides of the steamship displaying the colors of the states they would pass along the river. So thrilled was Julia with all the bright hullabaloo that she grabbed Mr. Paddington's large paw of a hand and exclaimed, "Oh look, look, how big the paddlewheel is!" When she saw Abigail standing aside, she put her arm around the girl's meager waist and hugged her again.

Indeed, this ship had twelve individual staterooms and a mid-ship side wheel. Mr. "P", as Julia had begun to call her kindly chaperone, had revealed last night that a first class passage for her would be $10. When they boarded ship in the late afternoon, a school band blared trumpets, piped piccolos and pounded drums while curious crowds waved below. How very lucky I am be enjoying this expedition, Julia thought, and glad she had found the courage to leave.

After the excitement of departure and tears upon leaving Abigail, who was headed upstream to St. Louis, time slowed down. It seemed they crept down the Mississippi. Indeed their speed was only twice as fast as walking most of the time although the steamship company advertised a velocity of 12 ½ miles per hour. The river marched southward like a lumbering brown animal, sometimes sleek and quiet, sometimes furry and sonorous, and occasionally odoriferous. Julia quite liked the animal's more placid moods, but found its darker, stormy, rumbling periods upsetting. But even on these days she preferred to be outside pacing the deck rather than cooped up in her cabin, sometimes making her feel like she was covering the entire route on foot as the scenery slowly slid by. Frequently they passed flatboats carrying raw materials and produce downstream. She knew the river boatmen, wearing loose shirts and broad-brimmed floppy hats, were considered a disreputable lot, but she enjoyed seeing them playing cards on the decks, their faces open and friendly.

As they neared Memphis, Julia espied dogwood and crape myrtle ashore and experienced a pang of disappointment on learning she would not have a whole day to tour the city. She would have liked to linger awhile. Late in the afternoon a jolly group boarded the ship and immediately asked her to join them for eggnog and pound cake. Compared to her gentle-natured Abigail, their rowdy and loud manners certainly would change the tone of her floating home, she realized. When Julia mentioned that she had expected Memphis to be a bigger place, one of her fellow passengers, recognizing her as a tourist in his neighborhood, took on the job of instructing her.

"Let me remind you, little lady, that only a while back this area was still a part of the Chickasaw Nation. It was just about five years ago that the Indians around here signed a treaty ceding the western part of Tennessee to the U.S, and that is when our Andrew Jackson named the settlement "Memphis.""

When the friendly fellow took to following her about the ship, she stayed in her cabin until his group debarked downstream a bit. She felt uncomfortable with his over-familiar style and found his loud pedagogy suffocating. Why could she not be more relaxed and amiable, she wondered.

On and on they meandered. Would they ever arrive? She knew Mr. P. sat up late at night, drinking brew with the other male passengers and discussing livestock and feed prices in the various states, the weather and probably, women. Most nights, she retired early, usually more than ready for the privacy her little room afforded.

The river looped back and forth so many times that Julia began to fear they were constantly retracing their steps. Gradually the scenery changed, becoming greener as they spiraled downstream. Also, the days began to lengthen as the river slowly uncoiled and the sun burned hotter. She noticed more Negroes on the riverbanks and bales of cotton piled up on the wharfs. One night a group of minstrels came aboard and performed for the passengers singing haunting melodies about corn and cotton and Moses. The plaintive voices made her a bit homesick and she longed to arrive, wherever it was she was going. In the moonlight, she pined for a man's arms around her and wondered if it would ever happen for her. Alone on the ship's deck, a superannuated sisterhood suddenly seemed appalling, if not downright frightening. Even if she felt strong and capable most of the time, having someone to share the joys and vicissitudes of life would be a great comfort. With a broad and unfocused longing, she gazed upon the dark waters, wishing for something or someone significant to fill the hollowness inside.

ONLY ONE more river to go --- the Arkansas. They landed at the wharf in Rosedale on the Mississippi-Arkansas border two and a half weeks after her departure from Frederick Town. The village was a sad affair; odd, she thought, for the confluence of two great waterways. Once again, all their baggage was transferred to another steamship while they spent the night at the most pitiful lodging yet. The "hotel" encompassed one large room below for eating, drinking, and doing business, while upstairs there were two rooms for sleeping, one for the men and one for the ladies. Otter spears, fishing poles, fishing nets, and old paintings dimmed with smoke covered the walls of the multipurpose room downstairs. To escape the dingy reeking interior, she hurried upstairs immediately after dinner, and then to avoid talking to the strangers with whom she was sharing a bedroom, she curled up on her hard little bed and wrote to her mother.

> *Dearest Mother,*
>
> *I expect this may be the "low point" of our trip. I'm trying to laugh at the situation but being so tired at this*

moment, it's hard. Such a miserable set of people I never met – regular vulgarians from Cincinnati and Pittsburgh – regular half-cuts.[2] I hate to sound snobbish but it's really shocking.

I thought my heart would die within me when I saw what we were to eat for dinner --- dirty bread, tough chickens with lard poured over them instead of butter and no sugar for our coffee. They say we must eat one peck of dirt before we die and I think I consumed a great deal of my share tonight. I'm afraid of catching some horrid disease, sleeping in such a bed and in the room with such disgusting looking people but there was no other choice. [3]

I doubt I will get much sleep because there is a coon chasing chickens on the roof. I am not joking. At least it is a warm, starry night --- I know because I can see the stars through holes in the roof. Heaven help us if it rains. I can't wait until morning when we can leave this awful place.

With love, Julia

THE NEXT morning she gave her letter to the captain of a steamboat going upstream on the Mississippi, greatly doubting his assurances of its proper delivery. Only when she'd franked the envelope with twenty-five cents did she realize they'd covered well over 1,400 miles from her home.[4] If the rivers didn't loop and turn so much it would be about half that!

As they steamed upstream on the Arkansas and westward, she decided this river was the most picturesque of the three she'd traveled, perhaps because it was the least inhabited. She had never seen beavers before and laughed at them, busy building a dam. How silly they looked with their giant teeth, big whiskers and strong flat tails, rather like a bucktoothed overgrown squirrel.

Dense foliage shadowed the wide waters' edge with lacy, lat-

ticed patterns, and in some spots, high banks were thickly overgrown with flowering vines and large trees or dense canebrakes.
When the steamship reached Little Rock, she beheld a truly southern city, handsomely built of brick, with all the southern trees
like wisteria, magnolia and pecan in profusion. Their ship edged
into the harbor and again, welcoming band music lifted her spirits. She found the cleanliness truly astonishing with every street
regularly swept, washed and brushed and no litter and scraps
lying around to produce offensive odors. Quite an improvement
over the state of affairs in Pittsburgh, she thought. However, they
were not to stay long, which suited her just fine. Upon leaving the
very next day, she imagined the water's path ahead was a tightly
wound party streamer tossed out before her. She had so much to
look forward to. Only three more days to go, Mr. P. told her.

CANTONNEMENT GIBSON

CHAPTER SIX
THE FORT

WHEN THE weary wayfarers reached the convergence of the Arkansas and the Neosho Rivers, their cargo was transferred yet again to a flat-bottomed boat which could forge the shallow waters up to Cantonnement Gibson. It was only a distance of three miles but the larger vessels could not navigate the narrower and shallower rivers.

These last miles seemed to drag on interminably. The boat crept alongside the river's border, where an extensive canebrake formed an almost impenetrable barrier, two miles wide in some places. At last, they pulled up to a natural landing formed by a rock ledge on the eastern bank of the Neosho River. High reeds and cattails hid much beyond the immediate shore from view.

Julia knew she should not expect her brothers to meet her since they could not know when she would arrive. Yet how she longed at this moment for a familiar face. Suddenly, from the reeds, a ragged line of Indians appeared, shamelessly staring at the new arrivals. Not knowing what a proper greeting would be, she produced a smile and received one in return from one of the young girls.

Mr. Paddington began shouting orders to the crewmen to gather their belongings together, and taking Julia's elbow, guided her across a makeshift gangplank to the flat rock and then the muddy embankment. Holding her skirts up to avoid the slippery shore, she managed to pull herself up to level ground as a group of mounted soldiers rode into view.

After so many days among river rats, their neat appearance, shining brass buttons and clean jackets looked as brilliant and exotic as a stage show. One of the men broke rank and shouting "Juliette," descended from his horse, and in just a few running strides reached his sister. As he whirled her around in his arms, tears of relief and weariness slid down Julia's sunburned cheeks.

"Oh, Edward, Edward, how happy I am to see you!" she cried. "I swan,[5] I thought we never would arrive."

"And I you, little sister," he beamed. "I must admit, I was getting a little worried, but perhaps you didn't make such bad time after all."

"I have no idea. But now that I am here, it doesn't matter. What I need most is a bath and a bed that doesn't move."

"We'll see what we can do about that," Edward said, putting his arm around her waist. Edward, being a little over six feet tall, towered over Julia's five feet, two inches. With his loose and lanky frame, he took long steps wherever he went. Deep crow's feet radiated from the corners of piercing indigo eyes under dark straight brows. His hair, black like Julia's, always looked unruly except when covered by his army hat, which he now wore at a cocky angle. "Here comes a pony cart. Would you like a bumpy ride back to the fort in the wagon or do you prefer to ride pinion with me?"

"With you, of course. Do you mind, Mr. P., going in the cart?"

"Of course not, my dear. I'll wait for our valises and join you shortly."

"Hello, Paddington. Glad to see you both safely here." Edward shook the plantation steward's hand.

"And I am glad to see you, Sir, and glad to deliver your sister. She has been no trouble and fine company."

"I'm not surprised," Edward said.

At this moment Julia noticed the rest of the soldiers still on horseback staring at her like a rare species. Edward noticed too and laughed. "We will follow," he announced, helping her up onto his mount. "That will save you from twenty eyes upon you for the whole trip."

How wonderful the familiar long arm of her brother felt encircling her waist as they walked the horses away from the river. On the plain the rough logs of the fort soon rose before them, forming a square barricade, with a partial second level. A broad blue sky framed the dark and simple buildings. In single file Julia and her cortege of the 7th United States Infantry passed under a heavy lintel to find themselves within the fortress walls.

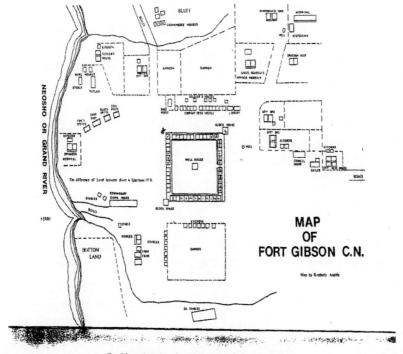

Fort Gibson, about 1835, adapted from a drawing by Lieutenant Arnold Harris, Seventh Infantry.

Key to Map 4, Fort Gibson about 1835:

-a — Magazine
-b — Acting Assistant Adjutant General's Office
-c — Officers' Quarters
e, f, g — Officers' Quarters, upper and lower room
h — Officers' Quarters, lower room, Quartermasters's Office
i, k, l, m — Officers' Quarters, lower room, Soldiers' Quarters

Having long imagined this moment, Julia's shock silenced her completely. Probably a good thing, she thought, when she recovered. At least she had not revealed her total dismay. She stood on a dusty parade ground, undecorated except for a stone well and a single flagpole. As there was no wind, the flag hung rather limply from its lonely perch. Everywhere she looked was identical, with the continuous interior log wall broken up about every twelve feet by single low doors, most standing open for the air, revealing stingy rooms with dirt floors. She was reminded of the stables at home. Each chamber held two cots or a double bunk. The lucky ones had a single small window with a view to the empty prairie. Wooden benches perched against the outside wall of a few rooms and at regular intervals, a slatted water barrel or wooden bin stood on a flagstone walkway. The heavy logs were chinked and daubed with mud, and all would have been very drab without the red barrels.

"Tonight at supper we will present you to Colonel Arbuckle, our commanding officer --- we call him the CO --- but for now, we'll let you wash up and rest."

Julia hoped Edward did not notice her silence. She seemed completely unable to think of anything to say.

He led her to a lineup of log cabin rooms on a low bluff a short distance outside the stockade and forming a line under a stand of live oaks. "Thank you, Edward," she murmured. Perhaps everything would look less dismal with some rest, she hoped. He pointed to the officer's mess hall back down the little hill and advised her to join him there at the next bugle. Giving her a quick salute and a grin, he hurried off.

When Julia stepped into the room, she gasped. All her joyful excitement carefully stored for so many weeks leaked out like air from a party balloon. How could she possibly live here? Her father built finer houses for his hogs! The interior resembled a jail cell, with a dilapidated single bed with woven ropes suspending a thin mattress, a spindly chair, a side "table" and barren walls. Realizing she was still standing paralyzed at the door, she took a few more steps into the bleak space. Her footsteps and the rustle of her skirt startled several creatures and sent them scurrying.

"Oh," she wailed. Halting, she took a deep breath and tried to regain control of herself. Spying a pottery pitcher and bowl, she rushed over to the little stand made from a packing crate and with shaking hands, poured water into the chipped bowl. She hastily splashed water on her face and the back of her neck. "Ah," she cooed, "Aaah." Finding a small cotton towel tucked next to the bowl she dried her face and hands and fell in a heap on the bed.

She began to feel a little angry with Edward and William. How could they think this was a proper place for her to live? It might be all right for a man, but not for a lady. She closed her eyes to blot out the offensive sight.

"Oh, Lord," she said out loud. She must have lain there for a half-hour feeling too discouraged to move. Perhaps she even momentarily dozed off for suddenly she heard the clomping of boots and men's laughter nearby. Then there was Mr. P. thumping on her door.

"I have brought your belongings, Missy," he announced. With some embarrassment she quickly roused herself and opened the screen door. Two enlisted men carried in her two trunks, a box with books and gifts for her brothers, and her toiletry satchel, all the while sneaking frequent looks at this lovely specimen of womanhood who had suddenly landed amongst them. Their admiring glances boosted Julia's spirits momentarily, and she assured Mr. P. she would be fine --- for one night, at least, she told him, hoping she sounded ironic.

It's really not so bad, she told herself. She could probably fix it up. Going to the ewer, she washed again, this time with the coarse soap the army had supplied her. She picked up a small pewter candleholder, frowning at its dusty pocked metal and the stubby candle. At least an oil lamp perched on a crate next to the bed. No further amenities in sight. Peeking under the bed, to her immense relief she found a chamber pot. At least she wouldn't have to use the outdoor privy with the men. Maybe her brothers had not been so lax after all. She brushed her hair vigorously, pulled it high off her neck and wound it into a chignon at the back of her head.

Edward and William awaited Julia outside the officers' mess hall and William immediately enveloped his sister in a brotherly bear hug. He and Edward didn't look much alike with William being fair and a few inches shorter. Having a sweet red mouth and a head of wavy blond hair, William generally was considered the more handsome of the two while Edward appeared more rugged.

The brothers led Julia into the low-ceiling eatery, graced only by a long plank table and four paned windows which cast squares of late daylight onto tin plates. The thick log walls were whitewashed and the ceiling, also made of logs, had been left its natural color. A now cold wood fireplace resembled a little cave at the end of the narrow room. Edward and William introduced their sister to several other captains, Bonneville, Cross, Williamson and Philbrick. They all bowed over her hand without kissing it as was the custom in the army.

Everyone remained standing until Colonel Arbuckle strode in. He inclined his tall gaunt figure toward Julia and asked her to be seated, then directed all to sit. She found his hawk nose and crane-like neck a bit daunting but he did not appear unfriendly. Long benches were attached to the tables so one had to step over the bench to sit down, which Julia found tricky with her long skirt.

Julia laughed, a delightful sparkling sound, when everyone spoke to her at once. "How was your trip?" "How long did it take?" "Did you get sick?" She tried to answer everyone as all attention was upon her. When the babble and confusion died down, she said, "I was very interested in the Indian women at the wharf. One even smiled at me."

"Don't be easily fooled," William cautioned. "The Indians are never to be trusted."

"I think that is an exaggeration, William," Edward said.

"No, it is not," William said abruptly. "Mark my words. They are all savages. And do not forget it."

"Certainly there are some violent tribes," another soldier commented. "But I believe the Cherokee and others around here can be educated. In fact, I would say they seem eager to learn."

Drawn to the voice of the man across from her, Julia studied him. He sported long dark sideburns but his cheeks, upper lip and chin were smoothly shaven. His eyes were bright, clear, and intelligent, yet an inexplicable air of boyish mischief defined his overall demeanor. Perhaps it was the thick dark hair brushed back almost like wings which gave him a somewhat rakish look.

"That is what Mr. Jefferson thinks," Julia interjected, "and I believe it makes sense. But I have not spent time among the Indians as you men have."

"Of course it makes sense," the gentleman with the sideburns replied. "And let me introduce myself, Miss Du Val. My name is Pierce Mason Butler and I am most honored to know you."

Some of the men lost interest now that the mild conflict seemed to have blown over, and others turned away when Julia began to speak more quietly with the handsome soldier across the table.

"What is your job out here, Mr. Butler?" Julia inquired. "Oh, excuse me! I imagine I should have indicated your rank, but I do not understand the insignia."

"Oh, you will get used to all the military folderol before long," he smiled. "I have just been promoted from lieutenant to captain. And I do agree. In general Mr. Jefferson is right, at least regarding the Indians around here. They learn quickly and seem good natured, especially the women."

"But my brother," she hesitated and nodded toward William who was engaged in conversation with the soldier on his other side, "He thinks of them all as a nuisance. Well, more than a nuisance. I think he sees them as a barrier to the white man's expansion. He seems to think it right and necessary to push them into the Pacific Ocean just because they are blocking our way."

"I am afraid that because many are primitive and violent, it makes an easy rationale for such bullying behavior," Pierce replied. "But the Indians have not been given much time to adapt to us or learn from us. Of course, one could ask why they should have to when they were here first. But that is already water under the bridge, I must allow. The White Man is here to stay and moving further west. And also, as I said before, different tribes react differently to us."

Julia listened intently, then nodded. "That is very interesting." She smiled at him. "Where do you come from, Captain Butler? You probably already know our family lives near Frederick Township, Maryland."

"Yes, so Captain Du Val told me. My family has a plantation near Columbia, South Carolina, and my brothers and I all went to South Carolina College. When I decided on a military career, our family friend, John C. Calhoun secured a commission for me as a 2nd Lieutenant in the U.S. Army."

"And then you became a First Lieutenant?"

"That is correct. I was first promoted a few years ago and transferred to Fort Smith in the Arkansas Territory. Then next thing I knew, I was sent here to build and garrison a new army outpost within the frontier region known as the Indian Territory. We call it the I.T. around here."

"It must be terribly hard work," she observed.

"It is. But I like the challenge. In the beginning we were all housed in tents. We set to work hacking back the cane and undergrowth, felling trees and sawing and hewing logs. In a year and a half, from May 1824 until January of this year, I am proud to say, we managed to house most of the garrison. But as you can see, it's still an ongoing project."

"I can also see it can not be easy to deliver all the supplies by poling upstream in a keelboat."

"You are certainly right about that!"

Julia sometimes found it difficult to hear this rather soft-spoken man above the din of cutlery on tin plates and the loud male voices around them. Shortly, Col. Arbuckle in his double-breasted jacket with gold buttons and epaulettes rose to signal the end of the meal, and the scraping of boots as everyone stood made any further conversation impossible. She left the mess hall thinking that perhaps her first negative reaction had been too strong. The dinner hour had been most enjoyable.

"Sleep tight and don't let the bugs bite," William said, leaving her at her room and quoting their father's frequent words when he tucked them in as children --- the "tight" referring to the laced ropes in the bed's wooden frame which could be screwed tightly (or less so) with a special tool for a firm or soft bed. Julia was too exhausted to try or even to wait while William did it for her. She lay down on the meager mattress tossed on top of the ropes. Tomorrow would have to do.

CHAPTER SEVEN
FIRST MORNING RIDE

THE SOUND of reveille jolted Julia from her cot. Yesterday she had been too confused to truly assess her new surroundings but this morning she would have to learn the lay of the land. She had found the chamber pot the night before but now realized the immediate need of water for her morning wash. She could not just walk about outside in her nightgown, but the cistern she had spied was about three rooms to the left out back. Slipping on a pinafore over her nightdress, she picked up the heavy earthenware bowl and pitcher supplied for her use last night.

There being no exit to the back, she stepped out from her room by the front door and found she had to walk in the grass along the row of rooms to reach the cistern. The wild grass, though scythed, prickled under foot, and she hurried lest she be seen before completing her toilet. Tomorrow she would wear shoes and plan ahead for her water supply.

So much for not being noticed! Many eyes peeked at her as she tried to pump the water with the cistern's handle. There is absolutely no reason to be embarrassed, she told herself, yet she felt conspicuous and awkward. Not a drop came. She pretended to ignore her interested audience, but Julia felt like she was on stage with folks laughing at her when a young Indian woman appeared around the corner of the building.

Smiling at Julia, she took the pitcher from her hands, set it aside, then placed the container directly under the pump's spout.

Then with two hands, she cranked the lever hard and a gush of water splashed directly into the ewer.

"Oh, thank you, thank you," Julia grinned with relief. "You are very good."

The girl smiled again and scurried back from whence she'd come. Carrying her precious water back over the stubbly ground, she managed not to spill much and mercifully, attained the privacy of her room. A grimy rug made by sewing together gray army blankets covered much of the dirt floor. Her trunks were stacked in one corner and objects she'd pulled from her hand valise lay jumbled on the single chair in the room. Knowing she could face the day more clearly once she had eaten, she brushed her hair cleanly back and tied a bow around the thick black tresses. It seemed her dress would certainly need to be simpler here than at home. Predicting the day would be warm, she donned a blue cotton skirt with a voile blouse and replaced the pinafore she had first worn with her nightdress over the practical ensemble.

At the sound of the bugle, she headed again to the mess hall, wondering how long she would be invited to share the officers' meals. Platters of fried ham with red-eye gravy, pans of beaten biscuits, heaps of scrambled eggs and pots of extremely gritty boiled coffee welcomed the men and Julia. Although this was a much heartier breakfast than she was accustomed to, she found she was extremely hungry. Captain Butler appeared at her side before either Edward or William reached her. "Good Morning, Miss Du Val. How did you sleep during your first night at our fine fort?" he inquired.

"Well, I certainly felt protected. I have never had my own private army guarding me throughout the night." While she spoke she studied the man with large dark eyes and even features who had charmed her last night.

"That's our job, you know. By the by, this morning I must ride over to the Three Forks settlement, where the Verdegris, Arkansas and Grand Rivers converge, to visit the Chouteau's store. They are fur traders who have been in the area forever. Perhaps you would like to take a ride with me? It looks like it is going to be a particularly fine April day."

The invitation surprised and pleased her. How wonderful it would be to get some exercise after being cooped up for so many weeks. And she welcomed the chance to get to know this man better. "That sounds very nice," she agreed.

"There are several stables here at the fort, but let us agree to meet at the one by the kitchen gardens," Capt. Butler instructed. "If you reach the oxen stables, you'll know you have gone too far."

As SHE tried to dress quickly, Julia found her fingers becoming all tangled in the long row of tiny buttons on the jacket of her riding habit. All the way up to her neck they went, and the sleeves buttoned tightly as well to protect her arms from sun and dust. She wore her pantaloons under her long skirt.

"Oh, fiddlesticks," she cried with exasperation as one pesky little button hit the floor. She would find it later. She wondered if she should have told her brothers where she was going, but she would not expect them to be her constant chaperones.

Hurrying toward her meeting, she passed one of the latrines and thought she would swoon from the odor. Quickly she pulled a perfumed handkerchief from her sleeve and held it to her face. Locating the stable was easy. She just had to follow her nose to the nearest barn, where she found Captain Butler awaiting her.

"Can you handle a frisky mare, do you think?" he asked. She noted his slim but strong physique and confident way with the horses.

"I have ridden since I was five, so I should be capable," Julia replied.

The captain led out a lovely palomino, complete with side-saddle and a left slipper stirrup shortened for her leg length. The saddle also had a large skirt meant to keep a woman's clothing free of horsehair and sweat. "The CO's wife sometimes rides and I am sure she will not mind your use of her saddle," he explained.

With help from Captain Butler, as he cupped his hands to give her a step up, she perched herself upon the saddle, settling her right leg between the security horn on the right and the smaller leaping horn to the left. When the mare made a few skittish motions, Julia skillfully balanced herself on the centerline of the horse, all the while sweet-talking the mare and maintaining her weight with the thigh of her right leg.

"Well done!" exclaimed Captain Butler, launching himself atop a tall chestnut. Julia guided her horse to follow him down the road leading to the Neosho River, that local folks, her guide explained, sometimes called "The Grand."

Turning left, they rode along the bottomland next to the water. Willows, live oaks and sweet gum trees lined the muddy bank, and a few squirrels scooted out of the way of their horses and up the tree trunks, scolding them for interrupting their foraging for acorns. A mockingbird then fussed at the squirrels. Porcupines also lived in the cottonwood trees along the rivers, Capt. Butler told Julia. "The Indians hunt them for their flesh and their quills, which are pulled from the hide and stored in pouches made from buffalo bladders. The quills are then used to decorate dresses, moccasins, baby boards and other items. It is extraordinary what these people can do with the materials at hand."

"I will look forward to seeing their work. You seem to admire it."

"Indeed, I do."

Julia regarded Captain Butler's straight back in the saddle, his suntanned hands as he gentled his mount, and his deft horsemanship. She remarked on a bit of early morning fog, still floating upon the river like thick cream on coffee.

"Yes, this low-lying site has its problems for us. It's essentially a swamp down here, and the miasma bringing us a lot of malaria."

"I am sorry to hear that," Julia commented. "Unfortunately, I know many people back east who live with the ague. There seems little one can do for someone when they have an attack of the shakes." The thought of it so persistent and nearby caused her a small *frisson* of alarm but Captain Butler had dropped the subject.

COLONEL PIERCE M. BUTLER

Beyond the canebrake a prairie drained by Bayou Menard extended to the northeast. The bayou's valley was densely wooded with oak, ash and hackberry bushes and heavily overgrown with nettles and tall weeds where Julia imagined numerous snakes hiding.

"You see," Butler pointed out, "the area does have its benefits. There is plenty of timber nearby for our building and stone to be quarried for the foundations and chimneys."

"So, that is why you need the oxen," she discovered aloud.

"Yes, and by the by, I would advise you not to walk down by the river on Tuesday, Thursday and Saturday, immediately after retreat. That is when the enlisted men bathe."

Julia laughed. "I shall remember," she promised.

Captain Butler spurred his horse and together they broke into an easy canter. As the motion brought a light breeze to her cheeks, Julia squealed with pleasure. "This is marvelous," she called to him, and the smile he returned, turning in his saddle, warmed her even more.

Pretty groves of trees appearing as if planted by man's hand broke the expanse of prairie, where bluebonnets and flax bloomed profusely. Unlike eastern wild flowers the prairie flowers heavily scented the morning air. She would have to collect some seeds, she thought. Even the canebrakes, with their feathery evergreen tops on the fertile bottoms of the rivers, were fetching. Capt. Butler explained to her that they provided pasturage for cattle all winter. The open plain, resembling an ocean of tall grasses, stretched as far as she could see with hints of palest green rippling here and there like foam atop a wave. Lonely hawks rode the breezes until their sharp eyes caught a movement, and down they would plunge into the yellow flaxen sea to seize their prey in sharp beaks. In some places huge herds of bison had trampled or grazed the six-foot high grass to a low and placid legume lake. The massive hunched shoulders of these dark wooly animals were a fearsome sight to behold, Butler told her, and their movement across the flat land could be like rolling thunder.

Feeling pert and happy, Julia called, "It's all more wondrous than I imagined! Thank you so much for bringing me along." She drew her horse closer to his. "I have been wondering, how many men do you oversee?"

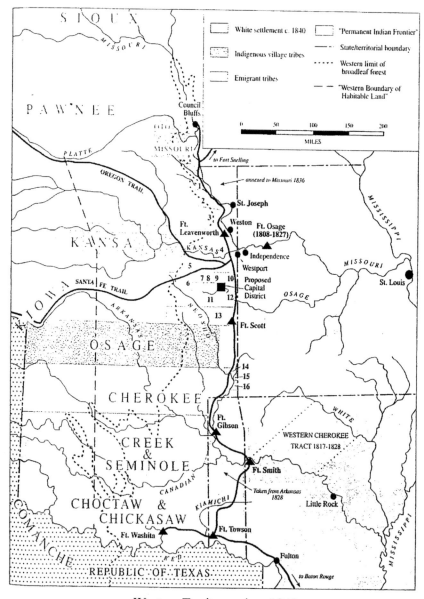

Western Territory, circa 1840

"My command includes three sergeants, two corporals, twenty-five privates and two musicians, one a fiddler and one a piper." Julia rewarded him with a little giggle. "We make up company B, which numbers forty-six men in all, and all of the companies are under the direction of the Quartermaster."

"So how many in all are there at the Post?"

"It varies from time to time. I would say there were about 150 of us last August and now there are close to 200 and still growing. There's a lot of work to do."

"My Goodness!" she marveled.

When they reached the Three Forks Trading Post on the bank of the Verdegris River, which divided the Cherokee and Creek settlements, they dismounted and tethered their horses. The door of the store stood open to a floor that needed sweeping, litter lying about everywhere, and complete disarray on the shelves. All quite a contrast to neat army life. The man she assumed must be Chouteau wore his hair pulled back, Indian style, and he clearly hadn't used the river for a bath in a long while. Yet the man was polite and bowed a bit when he took her hand.

"Mademoiselle," he said. "How fortunate for all of us that you have come."

Capt. Butler seemed a little put out with the attentive look Chouteau gave her and immediately distracted him with business.

"Our sutler has instructed me to buy more candles and soap," he declared. "The ration is four pounds of soap and one and a half pound of candles per soldier per month,[6] but it seems they need more lately. I don't know where it's all going. Perhaps everyone is reading and washing more, but I doubt it. And we also need more salt. You know," he said, turning to Julia, "the Indians gather salt from salt deposits on the prairie and sell it to Chouteau. Then he increases the price for us."

Chouteau winked at her as though acknowledging his guile. Julia ignored him and began to poke around the store, finding only necessities and nothing very pretty. Until she came upon a pile of Indian baskets. How handsome they were, she thought. One day she would come back and choose one. Also, there were fur hats and vests which she found amusing. Maybe Mr. P. would like one to take home with him; she would check with him before purchasing the gift.

With their saddle bags full to bursting they prepared to head back to the fort. Obviously having heard of their presence, a few Indians arrived to view the visitors. Though only loitering and looking, Julia found the men's demeanor regal and imposing but felt uncomfortable staring back because of their skimpy dress. Several of the men wore only breechclouts while others were a bit more modest with leggings of deer hide and their bare chests glistening in the sunlight. Their skin certainly wasn't red, but she thought rather of pale chestnut or burnished copper.

"The Indians at the settlement did not seem hostile," she commented to her companion when they left. "They just seemed curious."

"That is true," Butler replied. "But we should not ignore real problems and differences. The tribes do not want to be a part of the U.S., even if offered such a possibility. Their sense of the world is very different from ours in that they believe in communal land. The Indian simply does not understand the concept of private ownership."

"Well, it seems like a very romantic if difficult concept for me."

"Exactly. And it just will not work, but perhaps, if given land and taught to farm, they will adopt our ways. It is an uphill battle, however, because the Whites have inflicted some real damage while claiming we are here to help. The Indians have been hit hard by smallpox, and they are more restricted because of incursions of hunters, trappers and finally settlers. No matter if they stood and fought or slowly succumbed, the result is the same --- loss of land, loss of their traditions and loss of dignity."

"That is all so extremely sad. What a terrible situation! Now that I witness it first hand, it seems more serious somehow. What can be done?"

"Do not ask me! It's all more your brother's problem as Indian agent. My charge is to build the fort and the roads."

"Is Monsieur Chouteau married?" Julia asked, changing the subject.

Butler laughed. "As a matter of fact he is, to a half-breed woman and that is one reason all the Indians around here accept him as one of theirs, I expect. She is quite a beauty, by the way."

Julia wondered what kind of woman he found beautiful and now was very curious to meet Mme. Chouteau. In no hurry for the outing to end, they allowed their horses to amble along. Nearing the post, Julia realized how formidable it appeared from the outside. The tall pointed logs called "pickets" formed a high and sturdy block, protecting everything inside the square. Admittedly, there were many service buildings outside the stockade, like the sutler's store, the stables, the corncrib, and the gardens, but with even a short warning, everyone could reach the fort's interior quickly.

"Perhaps we can ride again later in the week," ventured Butler when they brought the horses in. "I am too busy for the next few days receiving lumber which has been milled upstream. A big supply will arrive by keel boat tomorrow and so..."

"I understand," Julia replied, giving him her hand. "When you have the time, I'll gladly accept your invitation."

WHEN JULIA returned, energy and delight were still dancing around inside of her like spring lambs, and the drab appearance of her room seemed particularly nettlesome. Throwing her riding crop aside she searched at the bottom of one trunk with feverish haste and pulled out her quilt from home. Composed primarily of blues, greens and white in a "china plate" pattern, she arranged it across her bed, it immediately perking up the small square space. Wisely, she had brought her favorite pillow with which she replaced the grimy, hard object supplied by the army. She hung her dresses on a wooden rod behind a curtain in the corner and kept all her folded clothes in the trunks, there being no where else to put them. Dashing back outside, she picked a few wild asters and black-eyed Susans and thrust them in a tin cup she'd found discarded on the floor of the "closet." What an improvement! Wishing for company and curious about her neighbors, Julia decided to walk the short distance to the place she had heard the soldiers refer to as "Suds Row."

Steam rose from huge black laundry kettles where, at the moment, four women with red arms bent over washboards scrubbing a grey mass Julia assumed were men's undershirts.

"Howdy, Miss," said one, as Julia neared.

"Hello," said Julia in her usual friendly tone. "I hope you won't mind if I visit. I only just arrived yesterday. My name is Julia Du Val."

"Yep. We know. I'm Minerva. This is Clem. Short for Clementine, you know. And that's Mary and Eliza." She smiled at Julia, revealing several missing teeth.

The sun was lowering in the sky and the afternoon heat was dissipating a bit. Still, beads of perspiration rolled down the women's faces and damp hair clung to their necks. The tubs were placed out under the trees but Julia longed for a cool drink.

"I'm glad to meet you all," she said. "Have you lived around here long?"

"No, Ma'am. We kind of go where the soldiers go. We've come up from Fort Smith. It's pretty good pay and there's always the chance one of us will find a husband."

They all laughed loudly at that and Julia joined in. Their honesty certainly was refreshing. Two dirty children, a boy and a girl squatting on the ground, halted their play with a corncob doll to stare at Julia. It reminded Julia of her old doll, which she had saved to hand down to her own children one day. The doll still lay in a tiny crib by the fireplace in her room at home.

"I was wondering where I might find the Indian girl who helped me with the cistern this morning. I'd like to thank her again."

"Oh, her," said Clem. "You needn't pay them Cherokee no mind. They don't talk much English and the ones around here mostly jes sweep out the officer's cabins."

"I see," said Julia. She wandered over to a sheet of paper tacked up on the tree.

Recet for Washing Clothes

1. *bild fire in back yard to het kettle of rain water.*
2. *set tubs so smoke won't blow in eyes if wind is peart.*
3. *shave 1 hole cake lie sope in bilin water.*
4. *sort things. Make 3 piles. 1 pile white, 1 pile cullord, 1 pile work briches and rags.*
5. *stur flour in cold water to smooth then thin down with bilin water (for starch).*
6. *rub dirty spots on board. Scrub hard. Then bile. Rub cullord but don't bille just rench and starch.*
7. *take white things out of kettle with broom stick handle then rench, blew and starch*
8. *pore rench water in flower bed.*
9. *scrub porch with hot sopy water*
10. *turn tubs upside down*
11. *go put on a cleen dress, smooth hair, brew cup of tee, set and rest and rock a spell and count blessings.*[7]

She wondered if the last line was meant to be humor or realism. Well, she wouldn't apply for that job.

"I'll see you tomorrow," called Julia as she waved goodbye.

EDWARD CAUGHT up with her as she returned to her room. She expected a hug but instead she received a scolding. "What were you doing, talking to the laundresses?" he asked with clear consternation in his voice.

"Why, just introducing myself," Julia said.

"You should know, Julia, there is a clear social hierarchy on the base. You should not be talking to them. You are the sister of an officer."

"Well, that's the most ridiculous thing I ever heard!" she exclaimed. "They are the only women I have seen around here and I think I should be able to speak to them. And *they* said I could talk to *them* but not to the Indian girl."

"Well, they are right about that. It could cause all kinds of problems."

"Heavens, what kind of a problem? She was very kind to me this morning."

"Hell. --- Oh, excuse me, I haven't been talking to many ladies lately. I don't know. Then they would all expect to be your friend or something."

"And what's wrong with that?"

"Well, for one thing, it's not the way things are done around here, and for another, it might create difficult expectations."

"Oh, Edward, honestly, sometimes I think you men create problems rather than solve them. I really don't understand. You have never been a snob before!"

"I am just telling you, Julia. We have to be careful. That's all. And you don't understand. Why some of the laundresses are. . . " he paused. "You know, I should not even be speaking to you about it. But you must learn, I guess." Another pause. "Some of them are prostitutes."

Julia blushed but then said, "Well, they seemed perfectly friendly and nice to me."

Edward shook his head. Having his sister here might be more complicated than he'd counted on.

EARLY THE next morning Julia paced in her room --- seven steps across, seven steps back. Edward's scolding the day before was still bothering her quite a bit. Where was she supposed to fit into this strange community? Here on the frontier she had not really expected to find class divisions, there being no "society" to speak of. Yet now she had no real lady friends and she could hardly fraternize with the soldiers. And why not? Partly because she had brought along many little barriers of "civilization" of her own with her.

Being a "lady" counted for a lot in Mt. Pleasant, Maryland, and to be honest, she realized she did not want to give up all that reputation and class afforded her. Yet why couldn't she just extend the boundaries a little, do more than had been allowed before. What harm could there be if she knew herself to be honest and good? The problem was, she had found, that being a lady largely depended on what others thought of you.

So what was she going to do all morning long? She paced the seven steps back and forth several more times. She dare not walk too far from the fort, feeling it would be neither proper nor safe. If she should stroll around camp too much, it might look like she were flaunting herself. The idea made her cringe with embarrassment. She could walk looking straight ahead, minding her own business. But that might look unfriendly and snobbish. Oh, bother! She was being an absolute ninny. She would just be herself and suffer the consequences. Her brother had made her nervous over nothing, she suspected.

Julia gathered together the seed packets she had brought from home and set out for the gardens. There were two large plots, one to the north and one to the south of the stockade. She thought she might prefer the one to the south because it was farther away from the prying eyes of the laundresses and the officers' quarters.

It was perhaps a bit late in the season to be planting but she decided she might as well try and hoped she would find a few empty furrows for her herbs. After so many aimless weeks on the river, she craved some sense of purpose. She knew she would like to make some contribution to life at the post, earn her keep a bit, and the garden seemed like a good place to begin. Besides it would just plain feel good to dig about in the dirt for a while. When she arrived, a soldier on garden duty was kneeling down busy weeding, and as she let herself in a little wooden gate, he stood up, wiping off his hands,

"Ah, you are William's sister. I am Lieutenant Munro." As he unfolded from the ground, she realized what a tall man he was. He had a thin straight nose, prominent eyes, and crooked teeth, but a friendly grin brought the whole face together in a pleasing way. He wore a beard as many men did to protect their faces against sunburn and windburn.

"I am very pleased to make your acquaintance, Lieutenant Munro. Is there any chance of planting some seeds in your garden?"

"Certainly! We welcome most anything we can find. And what you might call a weed-- a hollyhock for example-- is a flower to me."

"What are you growing?" she asked.

"Well, we have to supplement our meat and starch diet with any vegetables we manage to grow. You see, the Army provides only pork, flour, beans, vinegar, salt and whisky when we're lucky. We have here zucchini and cabbage and pole beans," he pointed to various furrows. "You know, you should always make sure to plant your pole beans when the horns of the moon are up. Oh, and over there I have planted some lettuce. Not many around here are so keen about salad though."

He showed her where she might find some free space and supplied her with a trowel.

"We don't have many tools," he explained. "The War Department commands us to make gardens and excuses the gardeners from military drill, but the only supply requisitioned is a book called *The American Gardener*. I am not complaining. I would rather dig here than at the road site any day."

"That makes sense to me!" Julia said. Good dirt had clearly been brought into the garden – there was none of the limestone outcropping she was constantly tripping over on the grounds of the fort --- and she discovered the soil was easy to work. With the background of their common and enjoyable labor, she found it easy to converse with Lieutenant Munro. He wore a floppy old straw hat and she was glad she had donned her big brimmed bonnet. It seemed unusually warm for spring to her but then she knew nothing about this climate as yet.

"Where does your family live, Lieutenant?" she asked.

"Maryland, ma'am. Like you, or so I've heard." He looked embarrassed for a moment as though he had realized he should not admit everyone was talking about her. Apparently deciding there was nothing he could do about it, he continued. "But from around Cumberland, where the Allegheny Mountains begin. I guess my Scots ancestors were looking for something like the Scottish highlands."

"Oh," she said. "We passed through there on our way here." She did not mention she'd found it somber and claustrophobic compared to the open meadows in eastern Maryland. "Do you like it out here in the I.T.?" she chatted as they continued their companionable task, feeling a little like she already belonged, using the local lingo.

"It's all right, I reckon, though it sure seems awful isolated sometimes. The work is important, I would say," he observed.

"Yes, I think so too. With this Indian problem becoming more and more complicated all the time. Do you think it is possible to become friends with the Indians here?" she asked him.

"Well, I don't know ma'am. I wouldn't say so for the men --- but it could be different for the women. They seem kind of sad, lost even."

"I know what you mean," Julia agreed. "I do not want to cause trouble but I thought I might try--to make friends, I mean."

"Don't see how it could hurt anything," Munro replied. "But then your brother might not agree. If we are tryin' to help settle these Indians, seems like bein' friends is the right thing to do. Though I must say, most of the enlisted men consider most of the Indians darn lazy. Can't say I am of like mind."

"Are the enlisted men happy with their work here, keeping the peace and all?"

"I would not go so far as to say they're happy, but it's a livin'. The CO reminds us all the time about how important it is what we're doin' out here. And I guess it is."

Julia hated it when her trowel cut an earthworm in two, and there were many of them in the rich loam. She worked quickly, making herself a location key for her planting and marking her rows with crossed sticks.

After thanking Lt. Munro for his help, she purposefully headed over to the commanding officers' quarters where she had learned the Indian girl might work. As she crossed the post's grounds, she noticed numerous globes of mistletoe hanging high in all the trees like lanterns, appearing rather eerie to her eye. Sure enough, there was the girl on the porch of the commanding officer's cabin with a straw broom in her hand. She wore a straight soft suede dress which fell to mid-calf and beaded moccasins. Her thick black hair was plaited in a single braid down her back and tied with a strip of red cloth at the end.

The CO's cabin was raised about two feet off the ground on stone piers with wooden steps running up to a front porch and stone chimneys abutting both ends of the log structure. A walk-through divided two rooms, one for living and one for an office.

Julia waved and called "hello." The Indian girl watched her progress, leaning on the broom handle. "Hello," Julia repeated. "I wanted to thank you again for your kind help yesterday." Unsure if the girl understood or not, she pointed to herself and said, "My name is Julia. Julia Du Val," she repeated. "What is your name?"

"I am called Walela," she answered clearly.

"Walela. How pretty! What does it mean?"

"A bird," answered Walela, with a little shrug of her shoulders, as if to explain she couldn't say what kind of bird.

"Will you come and see me one day?" Julia asked. "I have many questions which perhaps you can answer."

"One day," Walela said and carefully resumed her sweeping, which Julia guessed was a signal for her to leave, and the lunch drum was sounding as well.

Edward and William had preceded her at the mess hall, and she wedged herself between the two. "This outdoor life makes me hungry," she admitted, tucking into the bowl of soup in front of her. One bite, however, brought a not-so-pleasant reaction, and she leaned over to William to ask, "What *is* this?"

"We don't know, exactly, but we all know the general recipe from kitchen duty." He assumed a pompous, pedagogical posture and continued. "To make the *soupe du jour*, you put into the vessel at the rate of five pints of water to a pound of fresh meat, or not so fresh," he winked. "Then you make it boil, skim off the foam and moderate the fire. Salt is then added according to the palate. Add the vegetables of the season and cook for one or two hours, adding sliced bread some minutes before the simmering is ended. When the broth is sensibly reduced in quantity – about five or six hours, the process is complete. Delicious, *n'est-ce pas?*"

Julia giggled. "Well, luckily I'm hungry enough to eat it. It's actually not so bad when you get used to it." But she could see she would take good care of her garden for future meals.

CHAPTER EIGHT
STICKBALL

THAT EVENING, after the bugle call and flag lowering ceremony for retreat, William came to visit Julia. She thought he looked especially handsome, obviously just cleaned up after one of the tri-weekly river baths. It really was like living on the farm, she realized, with all its buildings for different purposes and all the various jobs to be done. She felt quite at home in a very short period of time, largely, she imagined, because she had two brothers close by. She had not had much time to dwell on any discomfort, and so far, though life here was rustic in the extreme, it was not too frightening. There had been a centipede or two and a daddy longlegs, but so far no scorpions or tarantulas, which she'd been told to look out for, had come her way.

William was stronger and stockier than Edward and had always been the shyer of the two. Yet here, she'd observed, William seemed to be equally outgoing, and she should not forget that William was the married one, his wife still living back east with several daughters. Munro had dubbed her as *William's* sister just today. Perhaps it was the equality of their lives on the post that had evened things out a bit.

William had inherited sandy blond hair from Jemina's side, unlike the Huguenot Du Val dark coloring. His skin was also fairer, and his cheeks always appeared flushed from either exertion or heat. For a man, he had a rather curvaceous mouth with bow lips, making it irresistible for various aunts and other women to pinch his cheeks.

"I saw you talking to the Cherokee girl today," he said.

"My, there is certainly no privacy around here, is there? Why? Are you going to tell me I should not have."

"No," he answered. "Not at all. I just was wondering if she were nice. She is very pretty, I think."

"Yes, I guess she is. And she seems to speak some English. I wonder how long she has lived around here."

"Not long, I expect. There are more Creek than Cherokee but Arbuckle says more Cherokee are on the way soon. Oh, here comes Captain Butler." Julia thought she detected a note of disappointment in his tone.

"Good evening, Lieutenant. Du Val. Hello, Miss Du Val. I just dropped by to see if I could interest you in accompanying me to a Cherokee stickball game tomorrow afternoon. As you can see, there's not much to do but work on a weekend here, but this might be fun. Perhaps you would like to come along too, Du Val."

"As far as I can tell, the only Indian sports are hunting, warfare and stickball. But I have heard it is quite a sight," William said. "Yes, let's all go."

"I am already looking forward to it," Julia agreed with enthusiasm.

And it would appear more proper, she thought, with her brother as a chaperone.

ON THE south side of the fort lay a plain, about 400 feet distant and fifty feet below the acreage of the post. Captain Butler held Julia's elbow as they traipsed over the uneven ground to a field crowded with Cherokee Indian youth.

Walking on Julia's other side, William spoke. "I am told these Indian boys must not eat rabbit before a game because the rabbit loses its wits under stress. The tendency might carry over to the ballplayer."

Laughing, Julia replied, "I don't know. That does not make much sense to me."

The game quickly got underway while more spectators continued to arrive. Julia wondered how much attention was paid to bath day because as more enlisted men pressed close to the field for a better view, the stronger the stench around them. Feeling self-conscious but unable to resist, Julia pulled her scented handkerchief from her sleeve to hold close to her face. She spied Walela on the opposite side of the field and saw that William had seen the girl too. In fact, he was staring at her.

Bringing her attention back to the game, Julia commented, "Goodness, it looks very difficult. Look at them throwing that tiny ball with what looks like a little spoon on the tip of a hickory stick."

"That's exactly what it is," Capt. Butler explained. "The spoon is a loose webbing of Indian hemp or thongs made of twisted squirrel skin. Also, the players have entwined bits of bat wing into their stick and the net to instill swiftness."

Julia counted ten boys on each team and the field looked to be about 100 yards long and almost as wide. In the center was a tall pole, maybe thirty feet high, she estimated, with a carved animal head on top. They would toss the ball in the air with the sticks and try to hit the head, then catch the ball again if the attempt failed. A team would earn three points if one of their members managed to hit the head. A group of Indian spectators across the field were growing noisier and noisier, thumping one another on the back and jumping high in the air, until their boisterous merriment caused everyone to smile.

William seemed to grow restless and wandered off after a short while. Despite her early interest in the new game, Julia's concentration began to flag as well. She noticed that she and everyone around her were swatting at the myriad insects delirious over all the warm flesh in the field. "It's not even dusk and the gallanippers are out in full force, I am afraid," Butler commented.

"I guess we cannot blame them," she answered. Searching for a topic of conversation which might interest the captain and genuinely curious, she inquired of him, "Do you have a big family?"

"Smaller than usual, I guess," he said. "I have only two brothers, both older, one named William and another called Andrew Pickens. We were all born at Mount Welling Plantation in the Edgefield District of South Carolina, and all went to Moses Waddell's Academy for our schooling, then on to South Carolina College. Since my brothers did so well, I had a challenging time upholding the family name."

"I expect you are being modest. Are your parents still living?"

"My father died five years ago," he explained. "And my mother shortly thereafter. There is a rather remarkable tale about my mother which I will tell you if you promise not to say I am bragging."

"I would like to hear it but will have to save my true opinion until afterward," Julia smiled.

"Her name was Behethelund, which already sounds daunting, does it not? When we were children, we were told that during the American Revolution, Behethelund went out one night in a canoe all alone, determined to warn the American soldiers about the presence of the British nearby. She managed to find them and return home under cover of darkness. Her warning saved the Americans."

"My heavens! What a brave lady she must have been."

"It's the most exciting bit of family lore," he told her with a beguiling grin.

"Edward told me you army fellows do not always get along with the Indian agents," she enjoined.

"Well, now, I don't know if I would go that far. But it is complicated. The Indian agents, including your brother, Captain Du Val, sometimes think they can give the army orders about Indian policy since they are appointed by the President. But Colonel Arbuckle pretty quickly disabused him of that notion. Obviously, the agents and the army do not always see eye to eye, but they have got to work together."

"But how do the Indians feel about the Indian Agents?" Julia wondered aloud.

"I would say it depends on the particular agent. I imagine the Indians are waiting to see if Agent Du Val really has their best interests at heart, and I think the army believes he is doing a respectable job. To his credit, there have been no major problems keeping the peace so far."

Julia nodded, absorbing the information and quietly approving his thoughtful and serious manner. "Edward wrote me that the Indian tribes actually fight more amongst themselves than against the white settlers."

"That is a true but little recognized fact," Butler admitted. "You seem to be quite an enlightened young lady --- and a very pretty one too," he added with a smile.

Julia thought she was past the age of blushing but felt her cheeks burn. "You are most kind, Captain, but this Oklahoma sun is certainly hard on a lady's complexion. I fear my skin is already beginning to look like an armadillo."

"Far from it, Julia," he responded, using her Christian name for the first time. This would have been forward on the east coast, she thought, but did not seem impolite here. "But you should talk to some of the Cherokee ladies and perhaps they will share some buffalo grease with you."

"Ugh, I am glad to say I still have some lotion from England I brought with me."

"Buffalo grease is better." She wasn't sure if he were teasing or not.

Lieutenant Munro hailed them and hurried over. "Have you seen William?" he inquired.

"Not for a while," Butler answered.

"Why?" Julia asked, sensing some tension in Lt. Munro's manner.

"Arbuckle is asking for him. Says he should report to the CO's office immediately."

"I wonder what the dickens for," Butler mused.

The game showed no sign of drawing to an end, and they decided to take a stroll along the river where pecan and cottonwood trees grew in abundance. He took her hand as they walked, ostensibly to guide their way. The warmth of his fingers entwined in hers shocked her into silence and she suddenly felt too shy to look at him.

So much seemed to be happening so quickly. Whereas life at home had dragged, here there did not seem time to think about something important before another serious matter occurred. This was not what she had expected of "life in the middle of no-where" as her friends in the East had called the frontier. Rather than watching from the sidelines like she often did in Mt. Pleasant, where rarely did anything seem interesting enough to become engaged beyond observation, she realized she felt very involved with everything here.

"Is life always so busy at the fort?" she asked her companion.

"Well, it probably seems so to you because everything is new. But I would also have to say that life definitely has become more interesting since your arrival, Julia. Is your stay to be of some while?"

This time she forced herself to look at him and found admiration and affection in his eyes. She felt flustered but managed to reply modestly, "I think you have just missed the company of women."

"I don't think so," he said and drew her hand more closely into his. And I think you should call me 'Pierce'.

"I think so too," she smiled. "And I am not yet sure of my future plans."

CHAPTER NINE
WILLIAM

BY EVENING the news had pervaded the fort like smoke from a campfire. William Du Val was being held by the Quarter Master for questioning. Too upset to eat her supper, Julia told herself there must be some mistake. Coyotes howling near the fort gave her the jitters and she went outdoors and began pacing in the grass in front of her room. Finally, just before tattoo --- the drumbeat signaling the soldiers to return to quarters --- Edward appeared. He looked worried and his dark hair stood on end more than usual.

"What could it be, Eddie? What on earth could it be?"

"I don't know yet, Sis. But I'm sure everything will be all right."

"You don't look so sure! Have you been able to see William?"

"Not allowed to until tomorrow morning. Maybe old Arbuckle just needs some time to check out Willie's story or something, but I honestly don't know what the trouble could be."

The story continued to blow around the post with the morning's bugle call. William was being brought up for selling liquor to the Indians. Since Chouteau's place was fairly far away, William and another soldier named Peter Carnes evidently had become enterprising and set up their own store nearby.

Pierce arrived shortly after breakfast and Edward turned up momentarily as though by mutual understanding, Julia's room had become a meeting place.

"So you've heard," he commented grimly.

"William knows it is against the law," Julia said with conviction. "He would not do that!"

"Of course he knows it," Pierce said. "Only just recently the Indian Intercourse Act of 1802 was amended, making it a requirement of all military commanders to confiscate any unauthorized whisky in the possession of Indian Traders. There was a lot of talk about it around here at the time."

His tone didn't sound accusatory, rather it expressed a desire to clarify, which pleased Julia. "I wonder if he even has a license to trade with the Indians," Edward mused. "That is the first question. The Indians want the stuff badly now and they have been known to steal cases from Chouteau's store."

"Well, that could be the answer," Julia said with relief. "Perhaps that's how they got hold of it. Please, hurry, both of you, and try and talk to him." She had a burning desire to do something, but feeling as helpless as a fly in lard, wanted to at least spur others on to remedy matters.

By afternoon, they knew the bad news; an Officer Wilkinson had discovered five barrels of brandy, rum and wine at their store. Col. Arbuckle demanded the lot be seized and brought inside Cantonnement Gibson as evidence and for safekeeping. Julia suspected the contraband might very well have come to William in the delivery accompanying her and Mr. Paddington. How could he have been so foolish --- and dishonest? She shouldn't blame herself, but she could not help feeling somewhat responsible.

NOW THAT the novelty of a new woman on the post had diminished somewhat, Julia found the men wore pretty much what they wanted when dress code was not mandated by a special event. Also, since the water in the area was highly impregnated with lime, everyone's clothes usually looked like they had been dipped in ashes. Everything was so chalky, she sometimes wondered if there were not something wrong with her eyes.

Then there loomed the pesky problem of bathing and washing her hair. Since the water was so hard, at least the soap rinsed out easily. Just getting enough water to wash was the difficult part. All the officers hired "strikers," enlisted men whom they paid extra for taking care of their needs, like cleaning their boots or currying their horses. But Julia needed a woman to assist her, which probably meant asking one of the laundresses for help. Though friendly enough, their toughness put her off a bit. So, why not Walela? It would help solve her bathing problem and she had to admit, she was just plain curious about the girl.

Julia was on her way to find her when she ran into William just leaving the commanding officer's office. Instead of looking sheepish or sorry, which she would have expected, she thought he appeared belligerent.

"Hello, Sis. Look, it's all a big ruckus over nothing," he immediately said.

"Is it true, William? Were you selling liquor to the Indians? You know it's against the law and it only creates more problems for the white settlers and the army. Especially for Edward as Indian Agent," she added.

"Whoa! They don't know for sure I was selling it. And besides, everybody is forgetting the Presidential directive which allows Indian traders to transport whisky into Indian country for their personal use," he dissembled.

"Oh," she said, unsure now if he were telling her the truth. "Well, please be careful. We were all very worried about you, you know." She doubted if he would heed her warning. Turning around, she saw Walela watching them from Col. Arbuckle's porch.

"I'll see you later, William. I need to talk to Walela." Julia felt William watching them for a few minutes; then he walked away.

Walela wore the same dress she'd had on yesterday but so did Julia. Class distinctions not withstanding, the difficulty of everyday life became a great leveler, Julia thought.

"Good day, Walela," she greeted her.

"Hello, Miss Du Val," the girl smiled.

"I'm wondering if you might be able to help me out. Do you have any free time? Would Col. Arbuckle allow you to assist me too with cleaning, cooking and especially carrying water? I could pay you the same amount he does," Julia almost pleaded.

"I would prefer to work for you," Walela responded with her eyes cast downward. "I could send my aunt to Col. Arbuckle."

"If that is really all right, let's begin right away. Just come over as soon as you can." Very pleased with her arrangement, Julia's step was much lighter as she headed back to her room. Still, something bothered her about William's manner with her. It was so easy to be fooled by his angelic looks, which only made his dishonesty more glaring.

JUST AS she had suspected, the William debacle was not to disappear as easily as the ubiquitous wisps of dandelion that blew away with the slightest breeze. The next day Julia learned that William and Peter Carne had been unable to produce a document licensing them to trade with the Indians. After a few days, the issue seemed buried for the moment, like the seeds in her garden. But she had a feeling William's problem would reappear like a recalcitrant prickly thistle.

When Pierce invited her for another ride, this time to a Creek Indian village, she agreed with delight, glad for the distraction and excited he had asked her.

CHAPTER TEN
WALELA

ON THE morning of the ride Walela arrived early to help Miss Du Val bathe. Julia admired the girl's basket decorated with a geometric chevron design in a darker brown against a natural background. She spied something wrapped in leaves inside which she imagined must be Walela's lunch.

Together they carried a big tub of water from the cistern into her room. Then they transported pitchers and bowls of boiling water from the laundress's kettles. When the water reached a comfortable temperature and Walela had several rinse pitchers at the ready, Julia removed her robe and stepped into the tub, quickly sitting down in the warm water.

Walela was shocked at the young woman's pale skin. She had never seen a naked white person. The white men at the fort, when they removed their shirts to work in the summer, were all suntanned and weathered, but this whiteness gleamed. She thought Julia looked very beautiful but very fragile, almost like a ghost. Paralyzed by this unearthly beauty, she gazed at the woman in the tub. Julia's voice jolted her from her reverie,

"Quickly, quickly, Walela, I'm shivering. Please pour some warm water over me."

Both women laughed as they washed Julia's hair, and Julia squealed when soap got in her eyes and purred when the warm water slid down her shoulders. By the time they had finished, the little room resembled a small pond. Finally, dressed in her riding habit and feeling exhilarated over her bath and the prospective ride, she whirled in place, twirling her riding crop above her head. Walela smiled and said, "You look lovely, ma'am."

"I appreciate your help, Walela. Thank you!" Julia called, practically skipping as she left.

Viewing the mess in Julia's room, Walela's shoulders sagged a bit. She set to work, dragging the wet gray blanket rugs out into the sun. Heavy with water, they made a sorry soggy sight. She was struggling with the largest one when Edward strode into view.

"Here, let me help you," he quickly offered.

Walela stood still, not knowing whether to accept an officer's offer of aid. Thinking she might not have understood him, he came over and took the heavy rug from her hands, hanging it over a fence rail.

"Now we need a broom," he announced. Understanding perfectly, Walela retrieved a broom from Julia's room and began to beat the rug. Edward dragged a second carpet from the room and hung it to dry. He took the broom from Walela and whacked the rugs energetically. Stopping his exercise, he gazed at Walela. Her copper skin and dark eyes seized his attention and her high cheeks appeared brushed with radiance.

"Thank you most kindly, Sir. Thank you."

Her shy smile, so fresh and bright, made his breath catch. He wanted to stare at her but knew he must not.

"Please tell my sister I need to speak to her," he said rather gruffly and rushed off in confusion.

Walela watched him go, surprised both at his kindness and then sudden growl. He was tall and lean, and unlike some of the other soldiers, she had noticed he was always working. Leaving the blankets outside to dry, she returned to Julia's room to clean up. She carried the bed linens out to Clementine, whom Julia had hired to do her wash. Walela wished she could earn as much as the laundresses did, a full $1.00 per month from each person whose laundry they washed and ironed, which she knew was even a higher monthly wage than an enlisted man received. Maybe that's why many soldiers married the washerwomen, she thought. Of course there weren't any other women around, but it certainly couldn't hurt that it considerably raised the family income.

Walela then dusted the single chair and trunks and picked fresh flowers for the tin cup. A gold bracelet from Julia's mother gleamed on the trunk top by her bed. Walela couldn't resist picking it up to admire it more closely. She rubbed her fingers over the smooth design cut into the yellow metal and slipped it over her hand. How lovely it was, like the gold of a sunfish flashing in the sunlight. She removed the bracelet and carefully replaced it on the trunk. She had better hurry to the CO's cabin to help her aunt get started, and then she could finish making Julia's bed after the sheets dried on the line under the tree.

CHAPTER ELEVEN
THE CREEKS

AT THE stable Pierce led out their mounts, already saddled and dancing with energy at the anticipation of exercise. As always when leaving the fort, Pierce wore a pistol at his belt and a rifle was sheathed from the saddle near his leg. He was trained never to leave his horse without a gun on his person.

New green shoots feathered the fields and the soft morning air remained momentarily free of the scent of wood smoke. As they set out together, their horses in tandem, Julia felt both excited and at ease. The horses' slender legs, eagerly stretching out upon the open expanse before them, delighted her, suddenly giving her an exhilarating sense of promise, freedom and hope. She loved these little adventures, but admitted to herself she also needed and enjoyed the security of a soldier at her side. His knowledge of the territory felt extremely comforting.

Wild prairie grass grew rank and heavy making the going tough at times, and the ground was chinked here and there with limestone. To protect the horses' feet, they had to go at a walk or an easy trot for much of the way. No wonder the farrier at the post always seemed busy.

"Edward asked me to have a talk with the Chief of the Creeks regarding the arrival of more of their people soon," he explained, turning in his saddle. "We signed a treaty with the Creeks this year for their removal from Alabama to land here on the Arkansas River near the mouth of the Verdegris. It's beautiful and plentiful country --- you will see shortly. An advance contingent has just arrived, and already there are some arguments as to the boundaries of the Cherokee's land and the Creeks' allotment. That will need to be settled presently."

"Do they know we are coming today?" she asked, even while distracted by the sun highlighting his smoothly shaven cheek and the metal insignia sparkling brightly on his cap.

"No, but their scouts will let them know we are on the way, I am sure. Are you worried?" he expressed his concern.

"A little," she admitted. "I have never visited an Indian village before."

"I understand, but you need not fret." He offered her a warm and encouraging smile. "Edward asked me to assure the Creeks that their lands are secure. The Cherokee are supposed to occupy the land between the Verdegris River and the Red Fork of the Arkansas River. The parcel for the Creeks is just south of the Cherokee, between the Red Fork and the North Fork of the Canadian River. The Osage are farthest north, up the Verdegris. Edward is visiting the Cherokee Indian villages with the same task this week and he needs help with other tribes. I presume the government has not gotten around to sending out agents to all the different tribes yet. He knows I enjoy this kind of work when I'm not too busy with the building of the fort."

Coveys of prairie hens fluttered with alarm when they passed and Julia spied a herd of deer in the distance, their coats a leonine yellow with white tails accenting their rumps. The graceful animals bounded further off, then stopped, turning to look back at them. One morning's ride on the grasslands certainly explained a lot about all the venison in their diet. Tall reeds waved like a honey gold flag, rippling or flat out as the winds changed, and the grass bent low became threads of golden silk covering the rich ground. With occasional patches of brightly colored wildflowers, Julia thought the land resembled an embroidered medieval tapestry or an elaborate enameled bowl like the one her father had brought from France one time. It wasn't an empty prairie at all;

rather, it was full to bursting with life and beauty. As though to punctuate her thought, a fat bunny burst from the grass, startling their mounts and making them laugh together. When everyone had settled down, Julia asked, "Who in the government is making these treaties?"

"Let me think. The year I came out to the Indian Territory --- that was in 1824 --- a new Bureau of Indian Affairs was set up within the War Department to regulate Indian matters. The legal and administrative treatment of all the tribes goes through this new agency," Pierce explained.

"I see. So, what do the Indians think of the arrangement?"

"Now that you ask, I'm not sure. The Indians seem to call all Kings and Presidents 'The Great White Father,' but it is hard to know what is in their minds when they say that. One thing I know it means is that they expect gifts, like from a father to a child." Julia smiled at his interpretation.

The pungent persistent aroma of wood smoke indicated they were nearing the Creek village and almost immediately, they sighted log houses nestled among the trees. The encircling forest held the small community in its protective palm. An advance party of young men came out to greet them and seemed surprised at Julia's presence. Julia tried to mask her equivalent astonishment, as several of the braves showed off ornate tattoos of swirls, dots and bands all over their bodies. Pierce explained to her how using either fine flint points or brittle pine needles to make little holes in their skin, they then rubbed black soot from burning pine into the raw flesh, so that when the punctures healed, a series of black dots remained.

While he spoke, Julia sensed that her presence made him see the Creeks' wild appearance with different eyes, giving him second thoughts about bringing her along. He had told her it would be a sign of peace, but now he seemed worried he had foolishly put her at risk. She had hoped he simply wanted her with him, and pledged to compose herself in order to soothe his sudden alarm.

The young bucks directed Julia and Pierce to follow them

into camp where the scent of smoke became even stronger. Perhaps its intensity was a good cover for other odors, she thought. Pierce helped her to hobble her horse, fettering their fore legs with leather straps to prevent their wandering far from the camp. When all had dismounted, Julia couldn't help staring at the lithe bodies of the Indian men, noting their skin color was darker than the Cherokee, more like mahogany. When they began to speak, the language sounded musical although punctuated by guttural breathy breaks. The village centered around an open dirt area in the middle of which was an open sided house, called the summerhouse. A platform about two feet off the ground served as a community seating and activity area. Some women squatted there, apparently busy with weaving baskets and several naked children played in the dirt near the platform.

A squaw took Julia by the hand and led her aside where another group of women stood. The men then sat down in a circle under the trees, and a pipe of kinnikinnic[8] was lit from the fire at the center of the group. The smoke rose like dancing ghosts above the scene.

The Chief stood up and spoke first, welcoming the visitors, his interpreter at the ready to convey his words to the visitors. The Chief wore a spray of red feathers atop his head and a single braid, with a long white feather attached to it, fell in front of and below his shoulder. He was bare-chested with a string of bear claws encircling his neck and a red blanket over one shoulder. In his left hand he held a staff, its full length dangling with coon and foxtails.

The meeting of friends gladdens the heart. Our countenances are bright as we look on each other. We ought to thank the Great Spirit who has taken care of our lives. When first we met we were taking the red path. We waded in blood until the murders of our women and children had ceased. War is no more heard in our land. The mountains speak peace. Joy is in our valleys. [9]

When the Chief finished speaking, Pierce took this as a signal to explain his mission. First, he presented the Chief with a gift of coffee from the garrison, knowing this was a beverage as much prized by the Indians as by the Whites. After a proper thank you from his host, Pierce began, "I thank Chief Roley McIntosh for his welcome and hospitality. As you acknowledge, I have come in peace and to further peace among your people and mine. The area around Cantonnement Gibson," he said, "has been designated by the Federal government as a place to allow Indians an opportunity to adjust gradually to the culture of white society. The army is here to guard this place where Whites are not permitted to settle permanently, or to displace the Indians."

The Chief, after listening carefully to his interpreter, shook his head in understanding and approval. But what about the Plains Indians to the West who had been constantly harassing them, he wanted to know. Especially the Delaware and the Osage.

"Yes," Captain Butler replied, "This is a concern, and the role of the army is also to protect the displaced Eastern Indians from any hostile Indians."

"I notice," said Chief Opothleyaholo, visiting from a group called the Upper Creeks, "that the white man who is our agent is so stingy that he carries a linen rag in his pocket into which to blow his nose. Is it for fear he might blow away something of value?"[10] he asked curiously.

Pierce stuffed his handkerchief back in his pocket with embarrassment and seemed at a loss for words.

While the men were talking, the women stood in a group at the back of the circle. Julia watched a papoose strapped to a baby board and swaddled in deer skin on the back of one of the women. The baby's jet black hair stood out in all directions like spokes on a wheel and yellow mucus drained from his nose. When Julia smiled at him, he grinned back.

Growing tired of watching the men's meeting, the women beckoned to Julia to follow them into one of the houses. Just outside the low door she saw they were drying a buffalo skin, which she had noticed was often used by soldiers as well as the Indians to make a large carrying trough or sack by punching holes at the corners and tying it up with leather strings. She found the home very neat inside and was astonished to see a spinning wheel set up by the fireplace. A pot of hominy stood in the chimney corner, and a squaw dished some out offering it to Julia. The smell was not particularly appetizing, but she felt she shouldn't refuse. Smiling, she accepted the bowl. Next time she came she would bring some medicine for the baby. But perhaps they wouldn't accept white man's medicine. She must find out.

Julia glimpsed a few colorful blankets, primarily red and black, stacked in another corner. Going over to them, she stroked the rather coarse but strong wool. Especially fetching was a shoulder bag hanging on the wall, made of soft hide with an abstract pine needle design. "Very handsome," she said admiringly. The women brightened with her praise.

Pierce soon came to fetch her, and Julia thanked her new friends for their warm hospitality.

"I am so happy I came," she told him on the way home. "The Chief's speech was very impressive! I must admit, they do not seem like savages to me. In fact, they display great subtlety of understanding, I think, and can be as quick to laugh as to anger."

"Many of these old men are great orators," Pierce replied. "It's as though the forces of nature are speaking through them, the wind and fire. It's often a powerful experience. And I am very glad you came too."

Julia thought he colored a bit with this admission and happily loosened her grip on the reins. She allowed her horse to lead her home, relaxing into his gentle gait. As they crossed a small stream, she spied an abandoned beaver damn. What an extraordinarily interesting day it had been.

CHAPTER TWELVE
FOOLISH

THOUGH JULIA saw Pierce at most meals, all of a sudden it seemed he didn't seek her out or ask her to accompany him on his errands. At first she thought it must be her imagination, but then he always appeared extremely busy or a little distracted. Was he trying to avoid her? Did he regret his earlier advances? She found herself adopting a new reserve when speaking to him and worried she had appeared too forward before. Perhaps he had been offended by her natural and informal manner with him.

The rough edges of the fort began to bother her more. Her chapped hands irritated her and the grime under her fingernails appalled her. Splinters seemed to lurk everywhere like insects ready to bite and her stomach resisted another spoonful of the *soupe du jour*. In her giddiness over Pierce, she had foolishly overlooked how difficult the smallest chore could be. And the noise! Constant bugles and drums and men whistling or yelling orders or talking loudly or rudely guffawing! How could she have even contemplated living in such an uncouth place?

Had she been so besotted she couldn't see how primitive this land was? Just thinking about the smells of the Indian village suddenly made her stomach lurch again. And even more disgusting, on warm or windy days the whereabouts of the privies were all too evident and untended chamber pots proclaimed their presence as well. She didn't know if the stench was worse in the mornings or in the evening when the men would return from work, their clothes stiff and stained with sweat, dirt and dribbles of tobacco juice.

She noticed that Edward drifted over to her room every day, and she welcomed his company. But then she realized it was always when he knew Walela would be there. At first she didn't realize his pattern, but after a week when he came by, she asked him if he did it on purpose.

"Aw, Julia, don't be daft," he laughed, but he looked confused. He could not deny how much he looked forward to just watching her. She carried herself with a natural grace unlike anything he had ever seen. When she swept the floor, her body and the broom swayed together in a lithesome and sensuous dance. When she helped Julia brush her hair, he watched the rise and fall of her breasts. Good Lord, he better get control of himself. Here lay real trouble. And he appeared even more bumbling when Walela shortly arrived for work.

"Where do you live, Walela?" Julia asked when the Indian girl stroked her hair and Edward watched from his seat on her bed. "Were those Cherokee men I saw at Chouteau's from your tribe?"

"I believe so," she answered. "Our village is just up the Verdegris River a little way."

"And how do you reach the fort every day?" Julia inquired.

"My uncle, who is too old to be a warrior now, brings me on his horse. Most days he fishes and hunts while I work here and then he takes me home."

"I hope there is no longer a need for the young men to be warriors," Edward interjected.

Walela stopped mid-stroke, looking surprised. "But then how would you know who would be your Chief?" she asked. "Our men prove themselves in battle and hunting. Then we know who is a true leader."

Edward thought the breathiness of her speech was enchanting. "Well," he smiled, "perhaps that will change one day, Walela. The men would still prove themselves with their hunting skills and perhaps farming could replace warfare."

She listened carefully but still looked genuinely puzzled.

"What are you doing today, Sis?" he asked.

"I'm afraid I must face the music." She made a grim face. "Mr. P. has warned me he plans to leave next week, and I may return with him if I like. We have been here now for three weeks and he has no more reason to stay. He probably will not be coming back for a year, if then, and so my chance for a chaperone home would be problematic for quite a while." She turned on the three-legged stool to face him. "Oh, Eddie, am I crazy to think I might stay here? It has seemed much more difficult this past week, which surprises me a bit because I was so happy at first. But I don't like giving up easily, and I think I would like to stay for a few months at least."

Edward burst out laughing, the crow's feet crinkling at the corners of his deep blue eyes. "That's why you came, isn't it? Not to stay for just three weeks. I would say from your expression it's pretty clear what you *want* to do, and there's no urgent need for you to go home. Sure, I know Mom misses us, you especially, but she will be all right. Why do you think you should leave?"

"Well, I don't want to get in the way. And of course, I did not know what it would really be like here. I have been busy, but I don't know what I would do for a great length of time."

He guffawed. "That's easy, is it not, Walela? There's always *too* much to do around this darn place."

"Yes, Sir," she politely replied, reminding him he had just engaged a servant in their social conversation.

"So, to answer your question more directly," Julia said, "I was thinking, what I would like to do today is create some window covering. Walela tells me it is possible to dye some muslin with beet juice, and I will have beautiful red curtains by tomorrow evening." She paused and laughed at herself. "I sew quickly if rather sloppily, you know."

Somehow she had gotten away with not mentioning the most important reason for staying. She wasn't ready to say it out loud for she needed to be sure herself before inviting anyone else's opinion. And she certainly did not want to endure the humiliation she had before when her beau had chosen another over her.

"All right, Walela. Let's get started with those curtains. We shall ask Clementine if we can borrow one of her tubs." And to Edward she called as he left, "Just wait 'til you see this place. Maybe I *can* make a purse out of a sow's ear!" Getting busy again was already helping to pull her out of the doldrums.

CHAPTER THIRTEEN
THE DANCE

IT'S NOT to be a formal affair," Pierce explained. "But more a party to bid Mr. Paddington goodbye, to thank him for bringing us so many useful articles, and a celebration of your decision to stay with us."

"What a wonderful idea!" Julia exclaimed.

"It seems Colonel Arbuckle agreed because we haven't had a frolic around here in a long time." He took her hand. "I am truly glad you are staying," he said, looking into her eyes. He appeared so handsome to her then, with his straight nose and softly curving mouth, she just kept staring at him. When he moved closer, she quickly squeezed his hand, replying, "Me too, Pierce, me too." Then she pulled her hand away, feeling overwhelmed.

"But I thought you . . . well, . . .you haven't seemed to want to talk to me very much recently. So, I am a little surprised." Here she was, just blurting out what was uppermost in her mind and heart with him when she probably should have been coy. But from the start, he had not seemed to deserve or want such behavior. She grew more alarmed when Pierce looked discomfited.

"I'm sorry. I have been a bit beastly", he said. "I was afraid of rushing things and didn't want to scare you. And to tell you the truth, I have been a little scared too." He gave a small laugh, as though to say she could take him seriously or not.

"Is the party this evening?" she asked.

"No, we do a lot of things quickly, but this will take a few days of preparation. The privates will lay down canvas and wax it for dancing. And of course, there's the famous Army punch which must begin to ferment."

"No!"

"You're right. I'm fooling. But watch out, come Saturday, it's potent stuff. I must get to work. You are an all too pleasant diversion."

As she watched him go, she reflected that Pierce seemed the busiest of her three men, always at the river overseeing the unloading of supplies or organizing the ongoing building of the fort. Edward disappeared for days at a time visiting various tribes in the area. Besides the Cherokee and the Creek, there were Crow, Choctaw and Seminole that she had heard of so far. William worked with Pierce as a supervising officer for the building of the fort, but his somewhat laconic temperament led him to take life more easily. Though she should not forget his enterprising little store which he had opened with his friend, Peter Carne. She needed to visit the place, ask him some questions and do a little investigating about the liquor issue. She had heard no one mention it for a while.

She had been wishing for a dressing table and now, in anticipation of the party, seemed the right time. As she wandered over to the sutler's, she realized how her life took place mostly away from the heart of the post. She had watched the men gather on the parade ground at tattoo the day after her arrival, but since then, she'd felt no need to visit the barracks or officer's offices above.

A soldier chewing tobacco sat on a stool behind a counter already nicked with heavy use.

"Good morning," she said. "My name is Julia Du Val."

"Yes ma'am, I know. Pleased to meet you. I'm John Nicks. What can I do for you?" Nicks was a stocky, sturdy man with a lantern jaw and thick graying hair. One thought of the strength of a bull but his eyes were exceedingly friendly.

"I am wondering if you might have a large packing box, some planks and a pork barrel. I need to 'buy' some furniture."

Nicks chuckled. "Yes, we sure do, Miss Du Val. Have all those things. I reckon you'll be needin' some nails and a hammer as well."

"Well, yes, possibly, but even better, if there were a soldier who would like to help me, I'd be glad to pay him."

"How about me?"

"I don't see why not. I would appreciate that, Mr. Nicks."

"Well, then I'll be bringing things by about 4:00 o'clock, when I finish here. We can get started right away."

She continued to be surprised at how friendly and helpful everyone was here. Perhaps it was just the lack of social graces and formality, but she generally felt quite comfortable with these exchanges. Julia hurried home to write a letter to her mother, feeling terribly guilty she had waited so long.

Dearest Mother,

I do not know where to begin! There is simply so much to tell and I wish you were across the table from me so I could relate it all to you in person. I hope you received my letters from the rivers. I tried to send you something from every major stop, from Pittsburgh, Cairo, Memphis, Little Rock, and Fort Smith.

Edward and William both look well and seem to be liked by their men. Perhaps that's not so important to a man, but I think it's a good thing. Edward certainly has his hands full with the arrival of more Indians from several different tribes every week. I hadn't realized how different one tribe is from another until I came here. I've only seen the Cherokee and the Creeks first hand, but they are very different in skin color, language, dress and culture. Apparently this is even truer of the far Western Plains tribes, like the Sioux. Honestly, the Eastern tribes seem as different from the Plains tribes as an Indian and a White Man. That is probably somewhat of an exaggeration, but I think you would be very surprised.

I have become friends (somewhat) with a Cherokee girl who is helping me with daily chores. She is amazingly "civilized" and eager to learn. In fact, her English is remarkably and surprisingly good.

You see, I've used the word "surprised" in the last two paragraphs. I think this is one of the reasons I've decided to stay for a while and am sending this letter home with Mr. P. That way, I'm sure you will receive it. I love all the surprises, all the unexpected happenings each day, though I admit some of the events aren't entirely welcome, but then I'm surprised at how I react. I'm amazed, for instance, that I haven't been more frightened of the Indians. Their culture is so foreign to us. But the tribes nearby do not seem the least bit ferocious --- only rather sad and confused. The Cherokee, especially, appear hard working, and a group of Creeks, recently arrived, are already busy planting corn and building houses. I think it's inspiring.

Inspiring --- that's another reason I think I'm staying. You just don't have any idea, Mother, of the vastness of this country until you travel, the great width of the rivers, the height and density of the forest, and the breadth of the fertile land. It seems truly inexhaustible and it takes my breath away to see it all. I try not to feel too small amidst all this bounty and vastness, and it is astonishing how much good work the Army has already done. The prairie is so much prettier than I expected, like a soft watercolor with washes of yellow and blue wildflowers waving in the breeze. And so many rivers! There are more waterways than roads, a truly potomic environment.

Writing it down now makes me realize how thrilling it really is. As far as the eye can see, there is boundless land, covered with honeyed grass, plentiful with herds of deer and bison and so much sky often filled with flocks of birds I've never seen before. There is a gorgeous bird, bigger than a crow, they call a "magpie." He is startling to see, a bright iridescent blue and black body with white commas on his wings, a long black tail and a truly terrible call.

I admit my "quarters" were a shock when I first arrived. I don't know what I expected but certainly more than four walls and a roof over my head. Well, that's what I've got but it's an interesting challenge to "decorate." How spoiled I've been!

There is one gentleman whom I find charming and he has invited me to a dance tonight. His name is Pierce Mason Butler and he comes from Columbia, South Carolina. It sounds like his family has a good-sized plantation there, and I think they grow primarily cotton, indigo and rice.

I regulate my life now by drums and bugles instead of by the clock. First there's reveille or wake up. Then the breakfast drum, followed by the guard mounting at 9:00 a.m., the fatigue drum for working parties to come in, the dinner drum and finally tattoo.

It takes two to three weeks for your letters to reach me and I am so hungry for news of home. I'm well, if a bit thinner (probably a good thing). Do not fret, Mother. I have two strong brothers to watch over me and so much to learn here.

With much love, your, Juliette.

Not wanting to worry her mother, she had not mentioned William's trouble.

By evening of the next day she had her dressing table, constructed of a plank laid over two small packing crates, and what she named her *fauteuil* made from the pork barrel. Its rounded back made it too fancy to call it a "chair" she thought. The pillow the army supplied for her bed became a seat cushion and she knew one day soon she would cover it with more dyed muslin.

Gazing out her single window she watched long black shadows gather under the trees and listened for the crickets opening chorus. She concentrated on how alone she felt sometimes in this vast land, how small and inconsequential. But then she thought, she just had time to lie down and rest for an hour before the party.

Her mind raced with anticipation, hardly restful. How keyed up she felt, much more so than before the fancy dinner party for Lafayette, the evening she had announced her scheme to make this trip. The rough walls of her log cabin room no longer seemed so strange but actually rather charming.

JULIA BEGAN to hear the music a half-hour before Pierce arrived to escort her to the festivities. She could pick out the sound of drums, a clarinet, fiddles and of course, the ubiquitous bugle. Her feet itched to dance as she checked herself in her little mirror for the umpteenth time.

With so many men around, she hoped the low square neckline wouldn't be considered too revealing. The pale peach, gauzy fabric of her dress shadowed a darker silk slip underneath, and puffed sleeves covered just the top of her shoulders. The bodice gathered under her breasts with one long stem of peach and green floral embroidery falling from the center of the bust to the floor. Quite fancy for a frontier outpost but she had brought so little to choose from. She felt a little flutter in her abdomen when she heard his step by the door and, picking up her shawl, she rushed to open it for him.

"You look exquisite," he exclaimed. "A wonderfully charming confection!" She could tell he really thought so as he held her by both hands and just kept looking.

"You look rather dashing yourself," she smiled.

"Shall we go?" he rejoined, guiding her close to his side.

Evidently, Colonel Arbuckle had decided everyone needed to blow off some steam. Sawhorses with planks across them made fine trestle tables for the party fare, and the busiest spot without question was a big basin of "Shotgun" punch at one end of the table. Tantalizing aromas wafting around the post all day had everyone chomping at the bit for a taste of the suckling pig specially roasted for the whingding. The suckling, with a mouth stuffed full of crabapples, now held the place of honor at the other end of the table. Bowls of potato salad, plates of pickled cucumber and cauliflower, cole slaw, and thick slices of bread and butter weighed down the makeshift table. Desserts would follow later after the dancing.

Julia knew little fraternizing between the laundresses and the officers' wives ever occurred, but tonight the barriers had been temporarily lowered. She spied Clementine, Minerva and Mary, all dressed to the nines, ---- at least in their own eyes. Certain to evoke attention, each had given particular attention to their hair dressed with feathers and ribbons abounding. The soldiers and officers all wore their dress jackets glittering with epaulettes and gold buttons, sure to scratch a lady's cheek if held too close.

As Julia might have guessed, the dances in evidence were not the minuet nor the quadrille. The musicians played loud and fast, with all the energy and disorder of a school band. Pierce seized her around the waist and off they went, down the floor, heel and toe and stomp, stomp, stomp. "Yahoo," yelled one soldier. Stomp, stomp, stomp was the cocky reply.

Everyone poured youthful exuberance into the steps. The fiddle took the lead and several soldiers from Tennessee jumped to the floor, doing a quick jig. Then the full group burst into a polka, a galloping dance recently brought over by German immigrants. Julia bent over and held her side, trying to catch her breath. Pierce laughed with her, wiping the perspiration from his brow with a large handkerchief.

"Oh!" she cried. "That was delightful!"

Holding her hand, Pierce directed her to the punch bowl, where a soldier ladled generous amounts into mugs for the thirsty guests. William and Edward each stole Julia away for a spin and brought her back to Pierce's arms. She couldn't remember when she had ever been so happy.

Pierce introduced her to several officers' wives. One called Anna, was a particularly fetching lady. "You must join us at our sewing bee," she said with enthusiasm. Julia learned from some of the married men that their wives were visiting family back east, having found life at the post drab and too rigorous. A few would return soon for a visit, now that the rivers were high. Finally, she was to meet the commanding officer's wife, called the "COW" by the soldiers, Pierce told her. Julia thought this cruel since the poor woman, except for a weight problem, bore no other bovine characteristics. She seemed perfectly friendly when they shook hands and Julia promised to visit her one day soon. Where had she been keeping herself, Julia wondered, since her cabin was only a sort distance from her own room. She too would only stay a short while she led Julia to believe.

At that moment John Nicks approached. "Good evening, Miss Du Val, how lovely you look tonight," he said with a friendly grin.

"So, I see you've met Captain Nicks," Pierce said.

"Oh, dear," Julia's hand flew to her mouth. "I am so sorry, Capt. Nicks. I did not realize you were an officer! Pierce, I let him build my furniture after buying the materials at his store."

"No way you could have known, dressed as I was. Serves me right. We officers get a little sloppy out here in the I.T. Also, I usually eat at the store or at home instead of in the officers' mess. And I enjoyed the task immensely, I must say," his deep voice boomed above the din.

"Well, tonight you look very much the handsome officer," she offered, hoping her gaffe would be genuinely forgiven. Indeed, he did, with epaulettes, gold buttons and a high winged collar framing his formidable chin.

"Flattery always wins me over," he rejoined. "You must come over soon and visit my wife, Sarah. I've told her about you and she would welcome a new friend. She was very disappointed to miss tonight's festive affair, but she is still keeping home after the birth of our daughter Eliza. Our little one was born on April 19."

"How wonderful!" Julia exclaimed. "Congratulations to you both and of course, I will visit mother and baby very soon." She must remember to ask Pierce where the Nicks family lived.

Mr. Paddington joined them, his cheeks even more florid than usual from the punch. When he asked Julia to dance, unbidden tears sprang to her eyes. "Oh, Mr. P., I really don't want you to leave."

"I know, Missy, but you know I have to go. It worries me, leaving you without a proper chaperone. It's not the best situation by a long shot."

"Well," Julia said, "I guess it's not 'normal' that I am here at all. But Edward and William promise to watch over me."

"Hmmm. Maybe. Guess I don't set much store in young men taking on that extra responsibility. But you have a good head on your shoulders and that's the best assurance I can give your mother." He beamed at her over spectacles that rode low on the wide bridge of his nose.

Mr. P.'s paunch made dancing a bit awkward but he seemed not to mind. Taking both of Julia's hands, he managed a little sliding two-step with her. His gnarled hands engulfing hers spoke of all the security he had provided over the past few months, and again, she questioned whether she were brave enough to be left alone here in the middle of the prairie.

When she looked across the dance floor filled with young soldiers and a very odd assortment of women, she caught Pierce watching her and Mr. P's odd dance. Yes, she would have to take whatever risks staying here called for. Still, when Mr. P. excused himself early for tomorrow's daybreak departure and she bade him goodbye, Julia felt all the weight of her inexperience and female vulnerability. She threw her arms around him, saying tremulously, "Thank you, Mr. P., so very much and stay well."

After her kindly chaperone left, she felt off balance and subdued for a little while. Yet as the dancing and feasting continued, Julia wanted it to go on and on. She danced with more abandon as she let the music pour through her limbs. When the pace slowed and Pierce's warm hand pressed the center of her back, she allowed herself to sway with him, utterly content.

One sour note occurred when one of the men asked William about the possible court-martial over the liquor issue. Julia thought her brother exhibited undue arrogance, feeling there probably was more to worry about than he acknowledged. "We'll be exonerated," he said, too flippantly and bombastically for her comfort.

Strolling slowly home, his arm around her waist, Pierce suddenly stopped under a tree and pulled her to him. When she melted against his body, he tipped her face up to his and kissed her gently. Her response awoke a passion in both of them, and they clung to one another tightly.

"Oh, Julia, will you be my love?" he asked.

"It seems I will," she smiled, looking into his eyes. There was no moonlight, the frequent river fog having crept in, but they welcomed its screen, drawing further into the trees.

"Every time I see your smile, it seems like a blessing," he murmured, stroking her cheek.

She could not resist brushing the wings of dark hair away from his cheeks. "You are the answer to all my dreams," he continued. "I believe I have been waiting for you for a long time."

"And I for you," she whispered.

She pulled her shawl more closely around her.

"We cannot stay out here all night," he laughed. "I should take you home."

"Home," she thought. The little room with the army blankets for rugs and the pickle barrel for a *fauteuil* did seem a little like home, she thought.

CHAPTER FOURTEEN
MORE TROUBLE

SHORTLY AFTER reveille, the sound of tapping, then William's voice, rudely awakened her. "Julia, get up!" he called from outside.

"Go away, William," she called. "I don't have to rise with the bugle like you do."

"You need to get up for *this* news," he called.

To keep everyone from hearing what he had to say, she stumbled out of bed, pulled her dressing gown around her and opened the door to her brother. He barged in like a young buffalo.

"Your boyfriend has been arrested," he announced without further ado, and Julia wondered if she didn't detect a note of satisfaction in his voice. For a moment she thought she might be dreaming, but of course, she was not.

"What on earth are you talking about, William? Pierce and I were together until late last night," she countered angrily.

"I know. I know. Believe me, there are rumors about that too! But it seems he ran into a bit of trouble when he got home."

"What kind of trouble?" She now was feeling quite distressed and disoriented.

"I'm not exactly sure --- some kind of fight with a soldier he doesn't get along with so well, I think."

"I don't believe you!" Her brother just stood there watching her confusion. Julia took a deep breath. "Well, thank you for letting me know. Really, I appreciate it. Now, please, William, scram and let me get dressed." Mercifully he departed, slamming the door behind him.

She splashed water on her face and jumped into her clothes. Too upset to care about appearances, she headed in a not very ladylike trot straight over to Pierce's room on the parade quadrangle. She could barely restrain herself from breaking into a run. The cloudy morning threatened rain, which she knew meant fog down by the river. With vexation she shook clinging grasshoppers off the bottom of her skirt and walked even faster. As she neared his door, her courage began to fail, but remembering his words last night, she raised her hand to knock.

No answer. She tapped again, harder this time. No answer. She pushed the door open --- no one locked doors around here. Empty. Here in the officers' quarters, he had a single bed like hers whereas she knew the enlisted men's rooms each held bunk beds. When she saw one of the soldiers standing outside watching her, she became horribly embarrassed. What a sight she must be, a woman knocking on an officer's door!

"They arrested Captain Butler last night," he offered.

"Oh! Do you know why, please?"

"Not exactly," he answered. "But there was some kind of ruckus here."

"Oh dear." Her hands flew up to her cheeks.

By now, everyone would be heading to his assigned work for the day, and she hadn't the courage to address Colonel Arbuckle himself. As she walked slowly back to her room, she tried to push away the panic welling up inside. She had known Pierce for only a few weeks and yet had come to trust him. What could have happened? Just this morning, very early, Mr. P. must have left for home. If the fog hadn't delayed him. And she had elected to stay behind, largely because of a man supposedly now in jail.

In her room she found some cake wrapped in wax paper she'd brought from last night's party and ate it absent-mindedly. Realizing she was still very tired from the previous evening's revelry, not to mention the shock upon awakening, she lay back down on her unmade bed and closed her eyes. She heard a light rain begin to fall and wished she could go back to sleep.

Why was everything suddenly so complicated? First, William selling liquor to the Indians and now Pierce in the lock-up. She would talk to Edward this afternoon. Surely, he would know what had happened, and she just could not and would not believe Pierce had done anything wrong. But she wished he were here to tell her himself that everything was all right.

LATER THAT morning Edward found Walela loitering in front of Julia's room. "Is she not here?" he asked, wondering why the girl seemed unoccupied. "Miss Du Val is sleeping, Sir," she whispered. "I did not want to disturb her."

"You are right, Walela. I imagine she is very tired after last night's party. Let's allow her some beauty sleep, shall we? If you have no more work here today, I could give you an escort home because I need to pay a visit to your village anyway."

Walela looked down, not answering immediately. "My uncle is still here, Sir. And I am not sure my people would allow this."

"Of course, Walela. I am sorry to have embarrassed you."

Edward hurried off, flabbergasted at himself. Why had he suggested such a thing? Surely he had not been thinking.

AT NINE o'clock the next day, since Pierce had not shown up the previous evening, Julia wandered over to the Parade Ground to watch the Mounting of the Guard. Though she had worried a great deal, her day in bed had gone a long way toward recovering her strength, and she felt hugely comforted when she spied Pierce calling out his orders to Company B. It must not be so bad if he had not been further detained, she decided, basking in his glow when he caught sight of her out of the corner of his eye. He didn't smile but his demeanor immediately became more energetic. She recognized the feeling --- just like the end of sewing class, she thought.

As soon as the guard ritual ended, Pierce dismounted and led his horse toward her. The relief just to behold one another was evident in their eyes and it was difficult not to embrace before everyone. She gave him her hand which he held tightly. "Do not worry, Julia. All will be right soon," he assured her.

"But what happened, Pierce? Tell me."

"I have long had an argument with Lt. Newell. It goes back to our time together at Fort Smith. He and a few others have been "gunning" for me, and a word fight erupted last night. They accused me of misconduct. It is a long story and I don't want to bother you with the details." He shook his head as though in wonderment. "They are hotheads and I expect it will blow over."

"But they arrested you."

"Yes, they certainly did. The Quartermaster held me in detention all yesterday while my accusers drew up their specifications against me. I am extremely angry but will be glad to have it settled." His grim tone worried her more than his words.

"I do not always understand the way the army works," she replied.

"I know. There may even be a court-martial, but do not worry when you hear this. May I come and see you this evening?"

"Of course," she answered, reluctant to let him out of her sight until then.

Upon returning to her room, she found Walela cleaning up. The girl seemed quiet and out of sorts, and when she slammed the tin cup down with unusual force, Julia asked, "Walela, what's the matter?"

"Nothing, Miss Du Val. Perhaps I am just a little tired."

Julia laughed nervously. "There is a lot of that going around, I think." She gathered together her trowel and garden gloves, hoping to find some comfort tending her plants. Shortly after she left, Edward arrived for what had become his steady morning visit.

"Hello, Walela. My sister isn't here?"

"No, Sir. She went over to the garden, I think."

"Oh. Well. Look, Walela, I'm sorry about yesterday. I did not mean to offend you."

"Thank you, sir. You did not," she whispered.

"I just would like to talk to you more. It would help me with my work, I think. Perhaps you could be my interpreter sometimes." He watched her expectantly.

"Perhaps," she said.

He bid her "good day," and when he turned to leave, she watched his tall, determined figure stride back to his office.

PIERCE TURNED up at Julia's room shortly after supper. When he removed his hat, she could see how tan his face had become from working outside every day, and the white skin near the hairline looked very vulnerable and tender. His ruddy cheeks and imposing physique exhibited health and vitality, giving Julia a strong and sudden urge to reach out and touch his face.

"Would you like to take a walk with me?" he asked. "It's a lovely evening."

"What a wonderful idea! Just one minute while I find my shawl. I find the spring breezes still a little cool."

Pierce gently guided her, holding her elbow as they strolled down toward the river. When they reached the trees close to the water's edge, he took her hand and held it tightly. Julia found she liked his seriousness compared to the easier manner of her brothers. She sensed it was not just that her siblings were more comfortable with her; it was a real difference of personality which made him more cautious and careful with his speech and manners. She didn't think it shyness but stemmed rather from a need to choose the right words and a deep desire not to offend.

"I am so sorry all this brouhaha has happened right now," he began. "I sincerely hope you are not entirely repelled by what occurred."

"I don't think so." She gave him a reassuring smile. "But I am not really sure what *has* happened."

"I shall try and explain. Here, why don't we sit right here by the water?" He took off his coat and laid it on a flat rock for her to sit upon. She made herself comfortable, and he sat beside her, propping his arm behind her back for her to lean against. As darkness descended the branches above cast long black shadows like fingers grasping the earth and the crickets began their chorus.

"Lieutenant Newell has brought a number of charges against me. I know I am not guilty, but he could make real trouble for me and my career."

When Pierce stopped speaking almost before he'd begun and with such a worried look in his eyes, Julia felt more apprehension than she had earlier. But not knowing how to help him, she remained silent until he decided to continue. "I am certain it goes back to my arresting him in March of last year at Fort Smith. You see, I had ordered him to load provisions onto a public boat and to accompany them from Fort Smith to Cantonnement Gibson. There were perishable items, including lamb and pork, as well as non-perishables, such as vinegar and flour. I directed him to proceed to Cantonnement Gibson immediately because of the perishable goods. Then, for reasons I cannot fathom, Lt. Newell failed to obey this order. I arrested him, believing that was the proper course to take, with the stipulation that he be held until I heard back from Col. Arbuckle at Gibson as to whether he supported my action. Again, for reasons I don't understand, -- or remember to tell you the truth-- Col. Arbuckle failed to respond to my letter, and Newell festered in jail. After not hearing from the colonel, I released Newell several weeks later. I believe he has borne me enmity ever since this incident and has abided a desire to get even with me."

"I see," said Julia. "I can understand how that might happen. But then what occurred last night?"

The moon suddenly slipped behind a cloud turning the river from dark brown to an inky black. The waters at this juncture of the riverbed were quiet, and only the croaking of frogs and the sibilant slurp of water among the reeds would have warned a stranger of the river's presence.

"After leaving you last night --- and you must know I was certainly not in a hostile mood, in fact, quite to the contrary! --- I repaired to my quarters. Then, I heard a loud commotion and saw a large group of men milling around outside my room. I called to them, ordering them not to enter my quarters or the quarters of Company B."

Julia turned so she could better watch Pierce's face. He continued. "It turns out that the leader of the group was Lt. Newell, who was serving as Officer of the Day. Apparently, they were trying to find and confine, or arrest, a Private John Peasly and others who had been in a fight --- even a riot perhaps --- who had escaped from the Corporal of the Guard. Of course, as soon as I entered the room, I could see that Peasly was not in my quarters, but Newell refused to take my word for it. He now accuses me of addressing him and his men in an unofficer-like and ungentlemanly manner, claiming I thwarted him and his men from carrying out their duties in their search for Peasly. I was extremely angry with his belligerent demeanor, but I believe I behaved properly."

"I am sure you did," Julia encouraged him.

"But that is not all. Newell kept adding on grievances against me to the Quartermaster. He has a long list of specifications that while I was at Fort Smith, I degraded myself as a commanding officer by engaging in play and wrestling publicly with Tom, who is the Negro servant of the sutler of the troops there. He claims also that I disobeyed army regulations by re-enlisting a man named Higgins, who had once been a deserter, and on and on.

"The truth of the matter is I didn't know Higgins had been a deserter when I re-enlisted him. That must have happened when I wasn't there. And as for Tom, nearly everyone treated him differently from other Negroes. And what a disgraceful and irrelevant thing to bring up against me! The business about obstructing their search for Peasly is true in one sense --- I did refuse their entry, but they, especially Lt. Newell, were the violent ones and he was itching for a fight. It was ludicrous to think Peasly could be hiding in a box in my room that Newell wanted to open. A man couldn't even fit inside it.

"So, Julia, I don't know what else to tell you. The whole affair seems ridiculous and trumped up to me, but Newell has managed to make me answer to all his charges."

"Oh, Pierce, I know the army is a stickler for regulations, but these courts- martial sometimes seem blown up out of all proportion."

"Yes, perhaps, but when there is contention, it is a thorough if laborious way to get to the truth of it."

As if to highlight his words, the moon popped out again, casting a pearly luster on the water and suffusing the couple in its soft shimmering glow. She felt like they could rise together and dance and glide down the river's opalescent path.

"I knew you could have done no wrong, Pierce," Julia solemnly said.

"Did you, Julia?"

"Yes, of course. I think I have trusted you from the moment I met you. Perhaps it is not comely or modest for me to me so frank, but this stripped down life here seems to bring out this tendency in me."

He tilted her face up to his and kissed her lips. His mouth felt soft as velvet and when she slid her arms around him, he crushed her tightly in his embrace. "Oh my darling girl." Pulling back a bit so he could see her better, he continued, "Admittedly, your freshness and beauty are an unusual and welcome sight compared to our daily scene. So it is no surprise I was delighted to discover your bright and intelligent countenance across the table in the mess hall the night you arrived. But never has the smile of a woman taken my breath away like yours did. I welcomed all the commotion so you did not notice my confusion."

"And I noticed you above all the others," Julia confided. "Your voice, your reasonable arguments, and especially this hair," she giggled, stroking the dark wings back from his temple which she always wanted to do.

"Well, if you are going to continue to trust me, I had better return you to your room." Standing up, he offered his hand to pull her up. They stood in a warm embrace for a while, neither wanting to let go, but finally she stepped away and turned to walk back.

"I shall have to just be content knowing you are so near," he added when he left her.

"Good night, sweetheart," she said, the word falling naturally from her lips.

SPRING STORMS

CHAPTER FIFTEEN
EDWARD

"HELLO, SIS," Edward boomed. "Could I steal Walela away today to help me with a visit to the Cherokee village. There is trouble brewing over an incident with the Osage and I have a feeling her advice could help immeasurably."

"It's all right with me. I can manage alone here today. What do you want to do, Walela?" Julia asked.

"I will go with Captain Du Val if he needs me," she replied softly.

"You may ride one of the army's horses," Edward offered. "You could then ride him back tomorrow morning. Please, meet me at the stable in half an hour."

When they met, Edward carried a brace of veteran brass barreled pistols, which looked as though they were well broken in. He noticed Walela studying them and explained, "Just in case we come upon some buffalo. I've heard there are several herds in the area and these are best if one can get up close. Rifles are awkward to discharge from horseback."

"I see. But I think bows and arrows are better."

"Yes. Of course."

As their horses headed for the Cherokee settlement, Edward attempted to engage Walela in more conversation.

"I am truly grateful to you for agreeing to help. These are tricky times, for both our people, don't you think?" Walela nodded in agreement. He wanted to subtly persuade her they were two intelligent people who could work together on the same side. He ploughed ahead.

"You know, an important part of my job is to mediate --- uh, do you understand? --- that is, settle, intertribal disputes. We are quite proud that there have been no clashes between the Indians and the soldiers at Cantonnement Gibson." He paused. "What do *you* think, Walela? Can our two people learn to live together?" His tone, with no hint of patronizing, indicated he sought real understanding.

"I do not know, Sir. There are many differences in the way we think. The Cherokee believe a mysterious but real power dwells in nature --- in mountains, rivers, rocks, even a pebble. White people may consider them only objects, but to the Indian, they are tangled in the web of the universe. Every object is pulsating with life and potent with medicine."

Her little discourse left him momentarily speechless. "That is wonderful, Walela. Surely we may learn from one another. As a matter of fact, it seemed to me recently that your tribe is beginning to understand and enjoy private property."

"You may be right, Sir. But we still do not think of ourselves as owning the land as you do, rather that we are temporary caretakers."

He chuckled. He thought the smile she granted him was beatific, but she jumped off her horse before he could hold her hand and help her down. At least she had just spoken with him in a very open and frank manner.

A number of young braves held turtle rattles in their hands, which looked suspiciously like clubs to Edward, even though he knew they were not. These rattles were used in their dances and actually made a rather pleasant sound.

The matter at hand proved to be ugly and dangerous. A Cherokee named Red Hawk had apparently been murdered by an Osage brave. Chief Jolly hotly warned Captain Du Val that in retaliation, the Cherokee would attack the Osage in revenge and the sooner, the better. A group of young warriors stood by listening to their leader name this threat. As they shuffled their moccasins in the dust, Edward could not help but think of a field of angry bulls pawing the ground.

Edward was not surprised either over the incident or the reaction. Still, he ardently hoped to reverse the negative chain of events and scrambled to think of some clever way to avoid the impending disaster. He dissembled with platitudes while he desperately searched for a solution, despairing over a certain forfeiture of all that had been secured with the Indians if he didn't think of something quickly.

Deciding to take a risk, Agent Du Val offered to Chief Jolly that if the Cherokee would agree not to attack, Col. Arbuckle would arrest and incarcerate the Osages accused of the murder of Red Hawk while all relevant facts pertaining to the case were assembled and presented to President John Q. Adams. It would be Adams who would then decide the murderer's fate. With considerable passion Edward urged them to maintain the peace, begging Chief Jolly not to break the previously agreed upon truce. By the end of the meeting, the Indian Council agreed, at least, to wait a short while before retaliating and to think about Agent Du Val's offer.

After the meeting with the tribal elders and the obligatory peace pipe, Edward thanked Walela for her help. "Since your people trust you, and you are my friend," he said, "it goes a long way to further our negotiation."

"This is true," she replied, "but I am doubtful whether it is possible for this truce to last. Even though the elders have agreed to wait, there are many young warriors who believe revenge is the only path. It hurts them to look weak to the Osage. It is not their way."

"I understand that," he assured her, "and I will return, with you, I hope, next week to report assurances from Cantonnement Gibson. And please, Walela, let me know immediately if you sense trouble brewing."

"Of course."

Since Indians did not shake hands, he wondered what to do and finally gave her a rather awkward bow. She smiled and waved goodbye when he hurried away to report to Col. Arbuckle. Having made promises to the Cherokee in his commanding officer's name, he hoped the colonel and President Adams would agree to his plan. Perhaps he had ventured beyond his mandate but it had been a precarious and potentially explosive moment.

Immediate events left him less than sanguine. All along the frontier events confirmed imminent conflict, with tribes stealing livestock from one another and general unrest. Only a few days later an Osage was killed and scalped within a few paces of the trading house near Three Forks. The Cherokee, however, claimed innocence. The two-to-four week mail service from the Fort to Washington City would prove too slow and cumbersome for this hot issue, and Edward doubted if he could keep the fire tamped down for such an extended period. He thought grimly of the new expression recently made popular by a Sir Walter Scott novel -- no Indian tribe could be expected to "let sleeping dogs lie" for long.

EDWARD DID not wait out the week before asking Walela for her assistance again in translating at a conference in her village. Arbuckle had supported Edward's offer to the Cherokee, and Edward needed to relay Arbuckle's assurances to Chief Jolly. He wanted to convince the Chief that the Army would do all in its purview to hurry along President Adams' intercession and to maintain the peace between the Osage and Cherokee. He hoped he successfully covered his surprise at her ready acceptance.

Walela always refused a saddle and her natural grace on the horse astounded him. The woman and animal moved as one with the rider making the pony appear more lithe and beautiful. As their horses stepped smartly along together, Edward mentioned recent problems the post had been having with wolves attacking the spring calves. Taking advantage of the abundance of good grazing land, the Army maintained a few livestock for milk and beef. The cattle pretty much roamed free because the commanding officer elected not to take manpower from the building of the fort for cowboy duty.

"Recently we've had to maintain a night watch to shoot these critters raiding our herd," he complained.

"The Cherokee will not kill a wolf," she said, with some consternation in her tone.

"Why on earth not?" he asked, genuinely surprised.

"Because wolves are messengers to the spirit world. We believe we must not interfere in nature's ways of communication."

"Humph," he said. They rode in silence for a while and then Edward mused, "I like the idea, Walela. I just don't think practically I could live with it. I'm not willing to sacrifice my cattle."

"Perhaps you could deter them another way, Sir."

"Well, I certainly don't know what that would be."

The prairie sparkled in the early light, the morning dew glistening on the opening blossoms like brilliant sapphires, topaz and rubies in a crown upon the dome of the earth. Scissor-tailed fly-catchers darted hither and thither, intercepting insects in the fresh glow, while magpies somewhat marred the ethereal atmosphere with their raucous calls.

"How can such a dramatic and beautiful bird have such an ugsome voice?" asked Edward in a companionable tone.

Walela laughed. "I expect it's just another example of nature's balance."

The riders made a point of circumventing a Prairie Dog "town" so that their horses would not step into one of the holes which served as the critter's front door. These little social animals, about the size of a small rabbit, fascinated Edward, who found their scampering and gossiping among one another almost human. He could imagine their sidewalks below, leading from one burrow to another in order to facilitate interaction. When they arrived at the Cherokee village this time, everyone appeared busy with their chores and paid little attention to the Indian Agent's arrival.

"Sir, if you would not mind," Walela said with a tentative voice, "before your conference, my mother has asked to meet you. She is my only parent as my father was killed many years ago in a skirmish with the Delaware." How little they really knew about one another, he realized.

"Oh, I am so sorry. I did not know. Certainly, I would be most happy to meet your mother. It's my understanding the maternal line is very important in the Cherokee society. Is that correct?"

"Yes," she acknowledged. "The women within a lineage own common property and have special rights. They live with their husbands, who by law must come from other clans, and with their unmarried children. Marriages within the same clan are prohibited. The families that make up a clan may be scattered among several villages, yet clan members must always offer hospitality and assistance to one another as well as avenging the killing of another clan member."

"I see," he replied. "So, it seems the women have most of the power here."

"Not really. Although the cornfields, houses and other family possessions belong to the women, men hold the majority of tribal government positions. They direct the life of the tribe."

They approached a small cabin and a middle-aged woman came out of the house. She wore a soft deerskin dress like Walela, a leather string necklace with brightly colored beads sewn in a corn design on a circle of suede, and several shell bracelets on her wrist.

"Captin Du Val, this is my revered mother of the Bushyhead clan."

Again, not knowing the proper greeting, he inclined slightly at the waist. "I am most honored to know you." The crow's feet at his eyes crinkled engagingly, winning a return smile from Mrs. Bushyhead. "The Bushyheads are a big clan, are they not?" he asked. "I know I have heard the name frequently."

Walela explained a little more about her clan while Mrs.

Bushyhead, not understanding much English, studied Edward seriously and raised her hand to them when they left her for the conference with Chief Jolly.

All went as well as could be expected with a general agreement between the Cherokee and the Army and with promises made by both. Mercifully, the absence of the Osage at the meeting of course made accord much easier but consequently, less secure.

CHAPTER SIXTEEN
BROTHERS

THE NEXT morning dawned overcast and raw, requiring flannel shirts and ponchos for everyone, an odd occurrence so late in the spring. Julia nursed a slight headache and fussed at her brothers when they tromped in, bringing mud and a blast of unusually damp chilly air behind them.

Having hung their wet wraps on pegs by the door, Edward and William immediately began roughhousing for the right to occupy the *fauteuil*. William pushed Edward aside, Edward grabbed William by the arm and tried to unbalance him by knocking one leg out from under him, William then tried to pick up Edward and throw him on the bed.

"Hey, stop it. Hey! Boys, how old do you think you are? Stop! You're acting like twelve year olds. STOP!" Her voice became louder and louder. The stool went over and the *fauteuil* rocked.

"What's gotten into you two?" she scolded, slipping into the fauteuil herself.

"The weather, I guess," Edward said. "It's making me restless."

"You!" said William. "You should be as happy as a jackass eating prickly pears, as they say around here, cozying up with Walela everyday."

"Don't be ridiculous!" Edward barked.

"Hey, I'm jealous. I saw her first, you know," William complained.

Julia interrupted. "William, hush! What are you saying? You're *married!*"

William flung himself onto the bed, his head in his hands. Julia jumped up and came over to him, putting her hand on his head. "Willie?"

He raised his head, brushing angry tears from his eyes. "This place is getting me down, I guess. It's been almost a year since I've seen Harriet and the girls. Too damn long!"

"William, why not ask for some leave?" Edward asked.

His brother shook his head as though to clear his mind. "My partner, Peter Carnes, finally produced the license authorizing our firm to engage in trade with the Indians. Now let's see them accuse me of whipping the devil around the stump![11] Colonel Arbuckle has referred the matter to the U.S. attorney at Little Rock for prosecution. But Heaven knows how long that will take. I'm confident I'll be confined here for the duration."

"My Lord!" Julia gasped, worried anew by the seriousness of it all.

"That doesn't necessarily mean you would not be granted some leave," Edward said. "Maybe Arbuckle would be happy to have you out of the way for awhile. Get you calmed down."

"Maybe," agreed William in a dispirited voice. "I guess there's no harm in asking."

"Let's go," said Edward, taking his brother's arm and pulling him up. "See you later, Julia."

Julia rubbed her temples and lay down on the bed, closing her eyes. She thought a visit home would be a lifesaver for William. She had overlooked, in her own joy and excitement, the loneliness this army life could bring. She chided herself for her egocentric behavior and wondered what she might do to help him. Perhaps putting in a good word of her own with Arbuckle would be a good idea.

AFTER THE mid-day meal Julia took herself off to the commanding officer's headquarters, full of resolution though mixed with a pinch of trepidation. In the best of times, the erect, tall, and steely figure of Colonel Arbuckle appeared daunting, but she felt she must try and do something for William. Besides, Mrs. Arbuckle had only recently invited her to drop by sometime, though she probably had not meant so soon. Well, no time like the present!

Presenting herself at the door of the CO's office, she asked the Adjutant for permission to speak to the colonel. And then there he was, just on his way out, his long body as thin and sharp as his sword. She determined to suppress her nervousness.

"It will take just one minute, Sir," Julia managed in a tremulous voice.

"What is it? I can only give you a moment, Miss Du Val." His voice rasped somewhat, suddenly rendering him more approachable.

"Sir, it has come to my attention," she thought that sounded rather military "that my brother, William Du Val is suffering from a great deal of stress and anguish at the moment, and I feel it would restore him greatly to have a home leave. Only for a month perhaps."

She paused for breath and noticed he was staring at her in what looked like disbelief. She rushed on.

"He has not seen his family for almost a year and he is not well." She ran out of courage.

"Young lady, I am running an army, *not* a social camp. Your brothers already petitioned me earlier today. I recognize your concern for your brother, but in army life, especially as an officer, he must meet the challenge. He should seek the attention of the army doctor if he is unwell. As you know, there is also this matter of selling liquor to the Indians, which has yet to be resolved."

"Yes, Sir, with all due respect, I understand that, but only one month, I am confident, would mend his spirits, and I hoped you would consider it."

"Miss Du Val, I am very busy. Capt. Du Val will continue his duties here. Good day." He strode off, his sword hanging straight at his side, leaving her feeling foolish and angry. No wonder William had a problem. She couldn't deal with this intractable kind of authority. It's a good thing she didn't have to make a life in the military. She would see Mrs. Arbuckle another day. Thanking the Adjutant, who had watched the unusual scene, she strode angrily back to her room.

Grabbing her trowel, gloves and bonnet, despite the cool weather, she headed once again to the garden to work out her fury and frustration on the weeds. At least the moisture was good for her vegetables. A flock of chattering cedar waxwings perched on a yaupon bush lightened her heart somewhat and the garden began to work its soothing magic.

CHAPTER SEVENTEEN
DOUBTS

JULIA HURRIED to the Guard Mounting in order to catch William. She wanted to tell him about her interview with Arbuckle and her miserable failure to secure a leave for him. He slumped upon his horse, hardly a proper military bearing.

"I'm so sorry, Willie. I thought I might be able to help."

"I appreciate your trying, Julia, but I could have told you it was a pretty damn fool thing to do," William said grumpily.

"I am not so sure. And I thought the man totally lacking in compassion, and he was rude to boot!"

William laughed. "I guess I'm not surprised. He was probably dumbfounded by a woman meddling in his affairs."

"I know you must have heard the latest news. Oh, William, Pierce is to be brought before the Court-Martial too." Saying the words somehow made it more real and her voice trembled with anger and dismay.

"I have heard. But don't say "too," William warned. "It's not definite about me. I'm hoping we will avoid that. Carne and I have protested to the Secretary of War about the seizure of our goods. We are contesting the Army's position that the few barrels of liquor found at our store constitutes a violation of the Intercourse Act. "

"I must say I am surprised you are feeling so confident about it. You can be a little too cocky sometimes, William. It scares me a little and you might offend others with this attitude. Nevertheless, I hope you will be successful."

"Of course we shall," he boasted, then quickly changed tack.

"Actually, it worries me a little --- no, a lot, that Captain Butler is courting you. I've wondered if I should not write Mom about it."

"Why on earth? What are you talking about?" Julia stammered.

"Why don't you walk with me to the sutler's place? I need to pick up a few things there and we can talk as we go."

She trotted along beside him, taking many short steps to his wide strides.

"First, it seems to me things are moving too quickly," William said, holding up one finger in the air. "I'm afraid you have really set your cap for him. You and he looked pretty serious at the party the other night and I couldn't help wondering what was going on. Second," up went another finger, "he is a military man with a life out in this God-forsaken Indian Territory, and I don't think it's a place for a well-educated young lady like you, or a woman used to the comforts of a fine home. And third," finger number three, "just like Edward, you have the wrong idea about the Indians. I can't understand why you are both so blind. These plans to teach them and assimilate them into White society will not work. No chance in Hell of it. I'm sure."

Julia stopped dead in her tracks. "You can stop right there, William!" She felt like she was on fire, or was going to fly apart. "I do NOT want to hear anymore. And don't you dare write Mother about Pierce! I plan to do just that --- to tell her what a wonderful man he is."

"Aw, Julia, don't get so huffed. You know now how hard it is for Harriet and me to be apart for so long. It's not a healthy way of life. You are my little sister and I only want the best for you."

William always seemed to take her up and down like a whirly-gig. Suddenly, all his belligerence had disappeared and a sweet smile asked her to forgive him.

"I know. But I mean it. Do NOT write Mom about Pierce."

"All right. But you better agree to take things a little more slowly," he rejoined seriously.

"I shall try," she wryly agreed. "Now I should let you get to work."

BUT WHAT would *she* do today? It rained the entire afternoon and evening. Julia's room remained dreary and dark all day, becoming oppressive and claustrophobic to her. With her typical resolve of finding something to do if threatened by bad humor, she seized paper and pen, tucked her legs under her, at the ready to write to her mother. But what had happened to all her hurry and excitement to share everything? Jemina and her life in Mt. Pleasant seemed so remote. After fidgeting with the pen for a half hour, she found the light too dim to continue and her eyes ached with the strain of staring at the blank white paper. Putting the writing materials away, she lay down.

Could William be correct that this type of life would be too difficult for her? Was it a total flight of fancy? She had only been here a short time, and what was she going to do with herself beside ride horseback and garden? She had never liked feeling useless no matter where she was. She pulled a light blanket over herself as the day remained cool. Early summer on the plains seemed to flip like a pancake on a griddle, hot, cold, wet, dry. Maybe she was getting sick, or maybe it was just a bad case of the collywobbles. She lay still, curled up in a tight ball. Last night she had felt everything was perfect and now she fought tears. What was the matter with her? Maybe William was right about how the isolation of this place affected you.

Floating, suspended in a gray papery cocoon, she couldn't wait to break open its confining ellipse and fly out. Perhaps she dozed for a short while for when she turned over, the room had become filled with encroaching dark shadows. She thought about her long trip out here and her desire to see the frontier. So, now she had seen it. The question loomed whether she could make a place for herself here or not.

Recalling her journey prompted her to remember her friend Abigail who had discussed the Moravian's mission of teaching with her. She sat up in bed and tried to remember what else Abigail had said. What tools did they use? What exactly did they teach? Perhaps she should write a letter to Abigail and ask how events were unfolding for her. She rummaged amongst her books and found where she had written down her traveling companion's address. Again, she pulled out her letter paper and pen and despite the waning light, quickly wrote a note to her friend. She hoped it would not be too long before she received a response.

CHAPTER EIGHTEEN
MYTHS AND SURPRISES

EDWARD ACCOMPANIED Walela home one evening a few days later, giving the excuse that he needed to deliver a document to Chief Jolly. It could have waited, he knew, but dammit, he so enjoyed being with her. He liked the way she explained the world to him, even if he sometimes thought her ideas extreme or foolish. There was something comforting about the Cherokee world-view, and the lilt and breathy quality of her language continued to enchant him.

Walela seemed quite at ease with him now and readily answered his questions without embarrassment. She spoke directly and honestly, even at some length, as though she hoped he would understand her ways. The sun, sinking rapidly, set the western sky ablaze with fiery pinks and reds. For a brief moment, the earth seemed to stand still as all held their breath awaiting the final descent. Even after the crimson globe disappeared, the plain continued to pulse and glow with opalescent light and Walela pointed out a hungry fox, his fur a deep magenta in the twilight, already abroad searching for his evening meal.

"Would you like to hear about how Grandmother Spider stole the sun?" she asked Edward.

"Of course." He slowed his horse so they could walk side-by-side easily. "All right. Here is the story. In the beginning there was only blackness, and nobody could see anything. People kept bumping into each other and blindly feeling around. They said: 'What this world needs is light.'

"Fox said he knew some people on the other side of the world who had plenty of light, but they were too greedy to share it with others. Possum said he would be glad to steal a little of it. 'I have a bushy tail,' he said. 'I can hide the light inside all my fur.' Then he set out for the other side of the world. There he found the sun hanging in a tree and lighting everything up. He sneaked over to the sun, picked out a tiny piece of light, and stuffed it into his tail. But the light was hot and burned all the fur off. The people discovered his theft and took back the light, and ever since, Possum's tail has been bald."

Edward gazed at Walela, enraptured with her storytelling as she continued.

"'Let me try,' said Buzzard. 'I know better than to hide a piece of stolen light in my tail. I'll put it on my head.' He flew to the other side of the world and, diving straight into the sun, seized it in his claws. He put it on his head, but it burned his head feathers off. The people grabbed the sun away from him, and ever since that time Buzzard's head has remained bald. Then Grandmother Spider said, "Let me try!" First she made a thick walled pot out of clay. Next she spun a web reaching all the way to the other side of the world. She was so small that none of the people there noticed her coming. Quickly Grandmother Spider snatched up the sun, put it in the bowl of clay, and scrambled back home along one of the strands of her web. Now her side of the world had light, and everyone rejoiced.

"Spider Woman brought not only the sun to the Cherokee, but fire with it. And besides that, she taught the Cherokee people the art of pottery making.[12]"

Edward smiled. "That is a charming story, Walela. But do you believe it is really true?"

Her mount stumbled and she appeared to use the distraction to assemble her thoughts. "I know you have different explanations, but many of our legends make sense to me. They are one way to think about what we cannot understand. But since we do have several different myths about one idea, I see no one as absolutely true," she mused.

"Well, that's incredibly broad minded! So, you would be willing to hear some of my myths?"

"Certainly. Where do *you* think the sun came from?"

"Well, like different Indian tribes, different white people have various ideas. My people --- we are called Protestants --- believe a Superior Being, whom we call God, created Heaven and Earth in six days and on the seventh day, He rested. That day, Sunday, is our holy day every week. The sun, the moon, the stars and the earth are all part of His Creation. But like your people, there are many interpretations of this story and some think it is only symbolic."

Walela listened raptly. "Tell me more stories," she said.

"One day soon. But here we are and I must speak with Chief Jolly. You are very good company, Walela."

A young brave wearing three eagle feathers in his hair approached them. Edward knew the eagle was regarded with extreme veneration by the Cherokee and only a man with warrior status dared wear its feathers.[13] Walela hailed him in Cherokee and then introduced them, telling Edward this was her elder brother whose name was Red Fox. Edward extended his hand which Red Fox coolly ignored while addressing something abrupt and harsh sounding to Walela. She looked upset and glanced quickly at Edward, who gave her a questioning look.

"What does he say, Walela?" Edward asked.

"He says I should not ride with you."

"I see. We shall talk tomorrow then. I shall go now to see Chief Jolly." Edward inclined his head to Red Fox and left them, with an unpleasant churning in his gut. He tried not to allow her brother's unfriendly countenance to disturb him, but the brave's blank glare had made him profoundly nervous. Reflecting on the interaction, he hoped he had masked his discomfort and met the challenge.

THE RAINS continued for two days, swelling the rivers to a dangerous stage and getting on everyone's nerves. Angry churning waters carried broken branches and tangled vines, pulling up bushes
on the bank and drowning small animals while persistent thunder
boomed overhead like terrible threatening curses.

The four walls of Julia's room seemed to shrink around her.
Even if this suffocating feeling was her imagination, the mud and
mold were all too real, as was the dim indoor light. All of her
clothes felt damp and sticky, and the constant drip, drip, drip
from the eaves became more and more irritating. In this gray and
soggy world, it stretched the mind to recall the glorious painted
sunset of just a few days ago.

Walela appeared grumpy too, eliciting reluctance on Julia's
part to talk to her. The girl seemed to plod instead of moving with
her usual grace and kept abnormally quiet. Finally, figuring it was
just the weather, she broached the subject on her mind.

"Walela, do you think the children in your village would like
to learn English and perhaps even other subjects?"

Walela considered before answering. "I wanted to learn and
therefore, I feel others would like to do so also. I am not sure how
the village elders would feel about such a thing. However, I think
they would welcome it, mainly because I believe Chief John Jolly
is interested in promoting the education of his people."

"That is my understanding," Julia brightened. "I have been
thinking; perhaps I might help with this. I would like to teach if
my efforts would be appreciated."

"I will ask," said Walela, smiling for the first time in several
days. "Have you heard of a Cherokee man called Sequoia? His
English name is George Guess."

"Yes, I think so. But please, tell me about him," encouraged
Julia.

"His mother is a full-blooded Cherokee but his father was
white. He was raised entirely among the Cherokee and I don't
think he ever spoke English when he was young. However, he understood the magic in the written word and how it could preserve

the spoken language. The Indians call a written page "the talking leaf." Sequoia is a very intelligent man and he began to think
about this magic. At first he made a mark with a piece of bark
on a stone for every word. But there were too many words and
he quickly realized this must not be the answer. He worked for a
very long time, gathering all the sounds in the Cherokee language.
He broke the language into syllables and finally came up with 86
sounds to which he assigned a symbol. They say the work took
him 12 years and it is called the Cherokee Syllabary."

"What a remarkable story!" Julia said. "I would like to meet
him."

"You can. He lives on the military road being built between
Fort Smith and Fort Gibson. He is responsible for making the
Cherokee literate and with the help of Dr. Worcester, a mission-
ary, he is trying to set up a Cherokee newspaper to be called the
Cherokee Phoenix.[14] It is Sequoia who encouraged me to learn and
Dr. Worcester taught me my first English."

"I had no idea! How wonderful! So, please, Walela, if you
think I might be of some help, speak to Chief Jolly and let me
know what he thinks."

This conversation seemed to make them both feel better and
they set to work peeling potatoes and chopping onions for a soup
they would cook in the kettle hung above a fire outside, planning
to eat at home instead of attending the officers' mess. Soon, Julia
was crying from the onions and laughing at the same time. Walela
laughed with her, making their chores go more quickly. Julia suddenly realized that throughout the whole day, through her own
impatience with the rain, behind her conversation with Walela,
provoking her tears and laughter, Pierce had constantly been in
her mind. Thoughts of him were a background chorus, alternately
soothing and exciting. She held him close in her memory and
rejoiced he had taken her over. It seemed entirely natural rather
than odd that she should love a man she barely knew.

CHAPTER NINETEEN
POLITICS

EDWARD FINALLY succeeded in persuading several Cherokee chiefs to meet at the garrison with the chiefs of the Osage to discuss a complaint about stolen horses. Preserving the peace between these two tribes, especially with the Red Hawk murder issue still simmering, was proving to be a constant battle. He looked upon the day the representatives from both tribes assembled at Cantonnement Gibson as a sign of hope and accomplishment. He invited Walela to be on hand as translator and when her brother Red Fox arrived with Chief Jolly to speak for the Cherokee, he was not surprised.

The weather promised to be mild, prompting Edward to hold his meeting outside. They pulled a long table out onto the Parade Ground and placed it near the flagpole. Soldiers stood on either side of the entrance to the stockade, supposedly as a welcome guard when the Indians rode up. The extraordinary sight attracted Julia and other members of the cantonnement community who unabashedly gaped at their appearance. Julia thought it truly resembled a parade of royalty as the colorful and exotic entourage arrived.

The Osage Chief, Clermont, appeared the most daunting, wearing a huge medallion on his chest and feathers atop an otherwise shaved head. Large ear spools framed his wide face and he carried a long shield dripping with feathers. Wide bone bracelets encircled huge muscles on his upper bare arms and deerskin leggings flared widely at his ankles. Several Osage braves wore "roaches" on their shaved skulls. These head decorations were made of feathers, deer and horsehair, and stood up down the middle of the crown like a short horse mane. Shamefully, Julia acknowledged she would have gasped with fear at the menacing spectacle if soldiers had not been all around her.

The two parties were escorted inside the barricade. Offering the Cherokee and Osage opposite ends of the table, Edward placed himself at the center, requesting Walela to stand behind him. He then commended both tribes for accepting his invitation, saying their presence alone went a long way toward establishing peace.

"It is extremely important," he told them, "that the Cherokee, Osage and other tribes in the area find a way to communicate with one another."

Chief Jolly then indicated he would like to speak and amazed Edward by extolling the virtues of accepting change and acquiring property. He recounted how his people's lives had improved and invited the Osage to come to the Cherokee settlements to observe how far the Cherokee had advanced from their "former poverty and wretchedness." Another of the Cherokee chiefs attributed their progress to the "good advice of the Whites for the acquisition of his present property by which he could live comfortably."[15]

The Osage chiefs listened but said most Osage were not ready to settle down to a life of agriculture. Yet observing how avidly they listened, Edward believed such advice might be making subtle inroads. Better that the suggestion should come from another Indian than a pale face, he suspected. Chief Clermont, however, still refused to admit any Osage warrior had stolen the horses. Edward decided to let the issue rest for the moment, for he had a harder nut to crack.

"Now," said Edward, "to the more difficult matter of the murder of the Cherokee brave, Red Hawk." He told them that General Gains of the U.S. Army had authorized Col. Arbuckle to arrest and hold the Osage(s) accused of the murder of Red Hawk. But still, the murderer(s) had not been turned over by the Osage. This urgently needed to happen while all pertinent facts in the case were assembled and while President Adams made his decision. The Osage remained stony faced but did not openly contradict.

At the end of the meeting the Indians were served cake and "virgin" punch. They gobbled up the cake, making sounds of satisfaction, but the punch was not so popular, and several spat it out upon the ground. As the last Indian departed, Edward said to Walela, "I think we might have accomplished something today."

"You are a good man," she replied.

Red Fox, watching Edward with glittering sharp eyes throughout the conference, had not uttered a word, his manner making Edward extremely uncomfortable. At least, for the moment, he wasn't actively belligerent, he told himself.

EDWARD APPEARED at Julia's door at twilight, an unusual time for him to call upon her. "I need to talk to you," he said with urgency in his voice. Her first thought was that she must have committed some folly, but she quickly revised that impression when she realized his distraction and emotional state.

"What is wrong, Edward?" she asked, taking him by the hand and leading him to the *fauteuil*.

"Oh, Julia, I cannot believe what has happened."

"What, Edward, what?" she asked nervously.

He put his head in his hands and groaned.

"What?" she asked more harshly.

He looked up. "I believe I have fallen in love with Walela." He searched her face as though to find an answer to his conundrum there.

"Oh, my Lord!" she said, sitting upon the bed. "Oh, Edward, no. How stupid of me. I didn't realize."

"Do not scold me, Sis," he begged "I am suffering enough on my own. I am appalled at the situation in which I find myself. I think of her constantly. She is *so* lovely. She is intelligent and worthy. Do you not think so? Oh, Julia, what am I to do?"

Julia stared at him in shock. What, indeed? She should have known something was afoot with his constant visits. Enjoying his company herself, she had been blind to his main attraction.

"I cannot say I do not understand," she said slowly. "As you have probably guessed, I have fallen in love also, and I believe my love is returned. Although there are questions as to the wisdom of these feelings, I do not believe there are insurmountable barriers. But Edward, as you surely realize, there *are* insurmountable barriers for you."

He shook his head as though in a daze. "I know, Julia, I know all too well. But these feelings will give me no respite. I want to be with her all the time."

She glimpsed fireflies twinkling by the little bush at her door, fairy lights she'd called them as a child. How very complicated life becomes, she thought, wishing at this moment for the simplicities of youth. And what strange surprises this Indian Territory, the Army and the Indians held for her and her family. She felt totally unequipped to cope with this new dilemma handed to her.

"Edward, I will not be the one to tell you what you can and cannot do or what you should or should not do." Her voice rose a little though she was trying to control it. "However, I see no earthly way this could work out! I am sure her family would block such a thing even if the Army did not. As painful as it seems, I think you should try not to see her for a while. Oh, dear, I just realized, this probably would not have happened if I had not come out here." She laughed with some irony. "It sounds like you and William both need to go away for a time. And maybe you should take me with you!"

Edward jumped up, nearly knocking over the chair and began pacing back and forth across the little room, his head almost reaching the low ceiling.

"Even if my feelings would allow it, that's impossible. She comes to the post every day. I can't wait for her arrival and wish I could keep her here every night."

"Oh, Edward. Do you know how she feels?"

"No, but I suspect she may return my affections. But her brother, Red Fox, is unfriendly, to put it mildly!"

"So, the Indian Agent will be the one to cause hostilities! Have you told William?"

"Of course not! He would have apoplexy. You are the only one who knows."

"I think you had better keep it that way for now. And Edward, perhaps just some time will make this problem disappear." Even as she spoke these words, she heard their false echo. For now she clearly understood herself, if he were truly in love, time would make little difference.

He looked at her in mute disbelief, shook his head and left.

JULIA NOTICED that Edward came by less often and Walela continued to droop like a wounded bird. The rains and mud subsided as the week progressed, and so she could not blame the dark moods on the gloomy weather any longer. Indeed, overnight the grass all around the fort began to look like the green baize atop the gaming table at home, and as gentle sweet breezes wafted across the prairie, many of the denizens of Cantonnement Gibson began sneezing.

Living in such close quarters made it seem like someone was *always* sneezing or scratching. Edward came over one day to report that the Osage still had not turned over Red Hawk's killer.

"I know," Walela said. "Red Fox and others discuss going after the murderers themselves nightly. Why should they wait on the White man's procedures, they ask continually."

"Please, Walela, tell them, *remind* them that 'to keep the peace' is the reason. It's the only way to a more secure future. But I do understand their frustration. Also tell them that I will ride over to talk again with the Osage Chief early tomorrow."

"I will," she said, but without her usual warm smile.

"Is there any chance you could go with me?" he asked. "It is a much longer trip, as you know, than to your village, but you could be a great help."

"No, Sir," she said very softly. "I am sorry."

"I, too, Walela, I too. Good-bye then." He left feeling like he wanted to weep.

FOR JULIA it seemed a lyrical time, with sunny days in the garden, reading, or riding horseback with Pierce. She had brought with her several works of Sir Walter Scott and James Fenimore Cooper. As she picked up the books to choose, she thought how strange and far away the European and New England worlds described in the novels now seemed. Surprised, she realized the frontier scene felt more normal to her than the formality of the eastern seaboard described in her novels. She hadn't shown her brothers her copy of Fielding's *Tom Jones*, which had an illicit reputation. They would most likely be shocked that she expected to read it and had brought it with her. Even with wearing a bonnet or a broad brimmed hat, her face and hands were becoming as brown as an Indian's. She no longer thought such a natural healthy glow unattractive and hoped Pierce found her new look appealing. It was a pretty good assumption he did as he sought her company whenever he had a free moment and easily persuaded her to join him on all sorts of errands.

In order to help Edward once again, she and Pierce planned a ride out to visit the Creeks. This time Julia decided to bring along several items for the women. She looked forward to taking them a few medicinal herbs once her garden began producing, but for now, all she had to offer were some cosmos and nasturtium seeds she had brought from Maryland. She would advise them they could eat the nasturtium blossoms. Pierce carried several chickens in his saddlebag as a gift of friendship.

He brought no official message; the Indian Agent simply

wanted to reassure all tribes that the army and the Federal Government were present to help them in whatever ways they could. The Plains Indians continued to be a source of worry to the newly settled Eastern tribes and the Army considered it their duty to protect the recent arrivals. Also, as official reports needed to be filed from the frontier to Washington City regarding the status of each of the settlements, so periodic inspection visits were required.

Julia recognized several of the women she'd seen before and presented her seeds wrapped in paper. One woman, appearing quite agitated reached for Julia's hand and began to pull her toward one of the houses. Willingly she followed and found a little girl lying in a tight ball on a mat upon the floor. The woman gently put her arm under the girl's head and pointed to her jaw which was grievously swollen. Coaxing her to open her mouth, Julia saw how inflamed were the gums and tears ran down the child's cheeks.

Understanding the woman wanted her help, Julia smiled assurance and motioned she would come back. She would have to find someone who could understand what she needed and then she could offer her family's recipe for toothache. After some time and with Pierce's help, she assembled the necessary items and went to work, boiling together gruel of maize flour and milk. While the mixture was still over the fire, she added some hog fat and stirred it all together until it was mixed equally and very hot. She then spread the gruel upon a handkerchief and applied it as hot as possible to the swollen cheek until the cloth had cooled. After doing this several times, the girl appeared to relax some and the mother tightly held Julia's hand. She seemed to understand she should repeat this through the night, and Julia waved goodbye, extremely happy to have helped.

On the way home, Pierce informed Julia he had received a letter only yesterday from his elder brother, Andrew Pickens Butler, who lived near Columbia, South Carolina. "I am sure you would like him," Pierce said, "and he will like you too."

Julia couldn't help but wonder if Pierce had told Andrew

about her. Pierce continued, "Andrew wrote that people are calling this time in our country 'the Era of Good Feelings'".

Julia chuckled. "Yes, they are. You've been out here too
long if you had not heard that yet. President Monroe was quite
popular, as I'm sure you know, but I'm not certain how much he
actually had to do with the good times. I must admit, however,
with the Monroe Doctrine, we are not likely to become involved
with foreign entanglements. At a dinner party in Frederick not so
very long before I came to the I.T., everyone was commenting how
they welcomed the peace and quiet after the rough times of 1776
and 1812."

"Yes, but you see, at the moment, there are no pressing in-
ternational problems and so it's easy to enforce the Doctrine. Having thrown out the British for a second time with the War of 1812,
our shores seem safe. There is plenty of land and jobs for everyone. It appears we can keep expanding the country all the way to
the Pacific Coast with riches and abundance for all. However, I am
afraid the folks in Washington City don't realize how complicated
things are out here at the edge."

"How right you are!" Julia exclaimed. "Heavens, if they only
knew how tentative and primitive everything seems here. But
Pierce, I think the Army has done so much, and everything is less
chaotic daily. Do you not think so?"

"Perhaps. In any case, I like your optimism. You might just
make me believe in this 'Era of Good Feelings'".

"Honestly, Pierce, I know you missed the last election but
you must not have received much news out here. The election
stirred up such a ruckus, Mother said she thought our "Era of
Good Feelings" had gone right out the window. It was more like
four pugilists in the ring."

"To my mind, John Quincy Adams was the only choice[16], but
he is such an aloof and icy man," Pierce commented.

"Mother wrote me that all the others seemed like such ruf-
fians --- Mr. Jackson of Tennessee, Mr. Clay of Kentucky and Mr.
Crawford from Georgia. She said if they were representative of the

people I would be with on the frontier, it was doubly worrisome."

Pierce laughed. "Well, next time you write to her, be sure and comment about my good manners."

They managed to hold hands for a short time across the width between their two horses. Any space separating them seemed too much these days, and she wondered at how free and easy she felt with this man.

CHAPTER TWENTY
INJURY AND INDIANS

JULIA AWOKE at dawn with a flaming pain in her ankle. Throwing back the sheet, she beheld a foot swollen up like a hard orange gourd. She swung her legs over the side of the bed and tried to walk, immediately discovering she could put no weight on the throbbing extremity. What to do?

She hopped over to her dressing table where she kept a first aid box. Pulling off the top of the tin, she found a bottle of castor oil, physicking [sic] pills, a little bottle of rum, dried yarrow for coughs and colds and a small vial of peppermint essence which many believed could cure anything that ailed you, from colic in newborns to the aches and pains of old age.[17] Poking around further, she discovered some senna for use as a purgative but saw nothing she thought might help her foot.

Tears of pain and frustration began to run down her cheeks. What could it be? Probably a scorpion or spider bite but it could have been a snake. She began to get very frightened and hopped to the door to see if anyone was out and about. Nary a soul in this quiet area of the post.

She struggled back to the dressing table stool and tried to open the rum bottle. The cap was screwed on very tightly and at first, she was unable to budge the lid. Panic and anger must have afforded her sudden strength for the screw top moved, and she quickly sloshed some of the rum on her foot, hoping it might alleviate some of the pain and work as an antiseptic if one was needed. She remembered seeing one of the older Indian men wearing a snake mask, used to scare evil spirits out of the sick. She'd been told he was one of the magic people who could pick up a rattle-snake. People could go to such a person to find out how long he or she had to live. As many times as the magic person could pick up the snake, it meant that the other person could live that long.

Hobbling back to the door, she looked outside for help. Her foot was becoming more swollen and more painful by the minute. When she opened the door, the pearly dawn cast an amber patch of light upon the floor, and there lay a huge scorpion, his long seg-mented tail with its venomous tip grotesque in the spotlight. Julia froze and then started to scream and holler for Clementine. She heard the door next to her room bang open and Clem and Mary appeared in a jiffy.

"What has happened, Miss Du Val? What on earth is the matter?" Seeing no intruder, her hysteria seemed mystifying.

Julia pointed to the scorpion while limping back to her bed. In no time, her rescuers killed the insect, propped up her foot and scurried away in search of a piece of raw beef to draw out the poi-son. Julia wept with the pain, but shortly began to recover some equanimity. When Clem returned and placed the slab on the of-fending ankle, Julia began to wish for tea and for the company of Pierce. She was embarrassed to ask the woman to fetch him for her and knew it would look improper besides. She would just have to wait for him to turn up. She did request some sassafras tea, which she thought would help the fever, and finally collapsed back on her pillow.

As soon as Guard Mounting was over Pierce appeared, full of concern. Apparently, the rumor drums of the Fort had readily alerted him of her mishap. "So," she said, slightly pouting, "now I can't even make a drama out of it for you." Still, he tenderly em-braced her, saying "my poor darling" several times, consoling her greatly.

He poked her foot and told her she should stay in bed for the rest of the day. "These bites can be very nasty. You know the scorpion is related to a spider and some people have quite severe reactions."

"How do you know that," she asked him with some doubt in her tone.

"Just country boy stuff, I imagine,"

"I feel silly now for being so frightened," she apologized. "What a noise I made. I was afraid it might have been a snake."

"Well, luckily it was not. It will smart like the dickens for awhile, but you'll be bright as a button soon enough."

When Walela arrived, her surprise and genuine concern warmed Julia as well. She downright giggled when Edward and William simultaneously charged in to find out how she was getting along. Although she was sorry to have her moment's privacy with Pierce invaded, it was gladdening to know they both cared enough to run over right away.

"Good morning, Captain Butler," said the brothers, almost in unison. "Hello, Walela."

"Good morning," she replied, immediately moving outside.

"It looks like my mishap was announced at Guard Mounting," Julia joked.

"Practically," William said. "Everyone seems to know. So, how is it, Sis? Not too bad, I hope."

"I am better now that I know it was a scorpion and not a rattler. I think my fear was worse than the bite."

"Scorpions are bad enough and there's no need to apologize," said Edward, moving toward Julia and displacing Pierce. "I am not sure, Julia, that it is appropriate for you to be entertaining gentlemen at this hour and in your state," he said quietly, alluding to her nightclothes, but of course, Pierce, who had politely moved aside for Edward, heard him.

Julia colored instantly and instinctively pulled the sheet higher. "Edward, Captain Butler called to inquire if I need anything, which I greatly appreciate."

"Well, do you?" asked William.

"Do I what?" asked Julia.

"Need anything?" asked William.

"I imagine some peace and quiet wouldn't hurt," Julia replied rather grumpily. "It was good of you all to come and see me, but I think I would like to try and sleep now. The tea must be helping."

"Be sure and keep your foot up," counseled Pierce, giving her a distressed look.

"Call for us if you want for anything," Edward offered, kissing Julia on the brow.

"Thank you all," said Julia, still feeling a combination of mortification and anger at Edward's criticism. The door banged with their departure, and she truly was glad to be left alone.

ONLY A few steps away William, appearing to be in a high dudgeon, said to Edward, "I think this situation is getting out of hand. Julia does not belong here! She should be at home with Mother instead of gallivanting around the country. She is a cultured, sheltered, young woman and has no idea how to take care of herself in this vulgar society!"

Edward watched the color rising in his brother's face. "I don't know, Will. I think she seems all right. There is certainly a more independent and free spirit out here but I would not call it vulgar."

"Well, I don't know what else to call it. Look at most of the women here --- laundresses, whores, Indians! My God, Edward, the ignorance and lack of good manners around her are appalling. I'm truly worried and have no doubt she should have gone home with Paddington."

"Simmer down, William. Look, she has us to protect her and now Captain Butler, as well." He grinned at his fuming sibling.

"Ah! What a bundle of thorny twigs that is! I admit he is from a good family but he's a military man. She cannot stay out in the I.T. forever for God's sake, Edward, and so she should NOT marry him!"

The two men walked quietly for a few minutes in the mutual

understanding that they were headed for the coffee pot on the hob at Sutler Nick's store. Besides offering supplies, the small cabin had become a gathering place of sorts. Today it appeared empty except for the sutler himself, but it was a good place to sit outside on the bench and sip an extra morning cup.

"Your concern may be too late, William. I believe our sister has fallen in love with Captain Butler."

"What a sorry idea it was for her to visit us out here," William complained, kicking the dirt with the toe of his boot. "I just didn't realize how free the society was until I witnessed Julia's behavior in contrast. She is so refined and intelligent. The classless society around us may be good for those at the bottom, but for a woman like Julia, it's a real danger. Edward, look at the women around her. They have no moral standards and are totally uncultivated. We are beyond the civilized boundaries out here."

"Aw, William, I think you are exaggerating. For crying out loud, the officers' wives are fine enough ladies. Sutler Nicks' wife, for instance, is a good woman. I think we have to find Julia another place to live and get her off the post. She shouldn't live in such close proximity to so many men."

"Perhaps. But then we wouldn't be able to keep a close eye on her. Some of the enlisted types can be violent and that alarms me."

"Why don't we talk to her tomorrow," Edward suggested. "And whatever you do, don't alert Mother yet. You will worry her unnecessarily."

Upon leaving William, Edward felt conflicted and unsettled. How could he possibly tell Julia what to do when he, himself, was in such an imbroglio of his own design. Yet William seemed so definite about what was right for their sister and so clear with his reasons. Then again, perhaps the situation wasn't as simple as William portrayed it. Perhaps, also, he and Julia had been more open to the life the frontier offered --- allowing the people and the land to speak to their hearts and minds and seep into their skin. Understandably, a man with a wife and children back home would be less porous to a new existence.

The sweet song of a robin redbreast awoke him to his surroundings, and he hurried off to clear his desk of paperwork. He didn't make it up the stairs to the second floor offices before a commotion at the gate demanded his attention. The guards were blocking the way to a mounted party of Indians. Charging over as fast as his long legs could carry him, Edward beheld an amazing sight --- a band of Osage bringing in the accused murderer of the Cherokee brave, Red Hawk. His heart clapped with joy for here truly was evidence the truce was working and a clear indication of the Indian's desire for peace. He then spied John Hamtramck, the new Osage agent, who must have had a hand in making this happen. Well, it was good to know he would have some real help in the area now.

He asked one of the soldiers to hurry over to Julia's in search of Walela. She did not speak Osage, but he understood her presence at this kind of affair would bring a tranquil note to the proceedings. He dispatched another to fetch Colonel Arbuckle and an interpreter, another to the kitchen for refreshments. Posting a guard of several Indians and several U.S. soldiers with the prisoner outside, he welcomed Chief Clermont, his accompanying braves and Mr. Hamtramck into the post's only meeting room.

The room held a heavy oak table with eight chairs. Edward gestured that all could sit but his guests were crowding to the walls to look with curiosity at drawings of the area, with rivers and towns delineated. The waters were painted gray, the fields green and yellow and the sky blue. They talked excitedly among themselves, pointing to various places on the maps.

Colonel Arbuckle's boots could be heard on the wooden steps, other men's shoes clomping up too and then Walela appeared with no sound at all. Edward simply spoke to her with his eyes, assuming she knew he wanted her nearby. She nodded slightly in return.

Even to Edward, the Indian's bare chests somehow seemed more exotic indoors than out. The room felt oppressive to him with all the exposed muscle and sinew, bone, horn and feathers touching the ceiling. He bid one soldier to open the window and again urged everyone to be seated. All did so with the exception of their leader, who remained standing, as did Col. Arbuckle and Edward.

The tall figure of Indian Agent Du Val certainly cut some authority as did the commanding officer, but both paled next to the proud determined carriage of the Indian braves who cast a daunting presence. For good reason, he knew, the Indians thought of him as a "paleface," but he pulled himself together and addressed the group.

"I welcome you today and commend you for your brave act. Your Cherokee brothers now will have no reason to seek revenge and attack the Osage. We have worked long and hard to achieve what you have made happen. Violence has been averted today and we may all look forward to many days of peace. I and my colleagues are honored to hear the words of Chief Clermont who has come to speak to us."

Edward sat down as all eyes turned to the tall and muscular chief. Edward couldn't help but wish his own body, revealed to all eyes, would be as strong and handsome as this man's. Strangely, the voice was rather reedy, high, and disconcerting at first but quickly the music of his words riveted his listeners. It was a shame, Edward thought, that they always had to have interpreters.

"Friend and Brother! It was the will of the Great Spirit that we should meet together this day. He orders all things, and he has given us a fine day for our council. He has taken his garment from before the sun and has caused the bright orb to shine with brightness upon us. Our eyes are opened so that we see clearly. Our ears are unstopped so that we have been able to distinctly hear the words which you have spoken. For all these favors we thank the Great Spirit and him only. . . . .

"Brother! Listen to what we say. There was a time when our forefathers owned this great land. Their seats extended from the rising to the setting of the sun. The Great Spirit had made it for the use of Indians. He had created the buffalo and other animals for food. He made the bear and the deer, and their skins served us for clothing. He had scattered them over the country, and had taught us how to take them. He had caused the earth to produce corn for bread. All this he had done for his red children because he loved them. If we had any disputes about hunting grounds, they were generally settled without the shedding of much blood. But an evil day came upon us.

"Your forefathers crossed the great waters and landed on this island. Their numbers were small. They found friends and not enemies. They told us they had fled from their own country for fear of wicked men, and had come here to enjoy their religion. They asked for a small seat. We took pity on them, granted their request, and they sat down amongst us. We gave them corn and meat. They gave us poisonous spirituous liquor in return. It was strong and powerful and has slain thousands. The white people had now found our country. Tidings were carried back and more came amongst us. Yet we did not fear them. We took them to be friends. They called us brothers. We believed them and gave them a large seat. At length their numbers had greatly increased. They wanted more land. They wanted our country. Our eyes were opened, and our minds became uneasy. Wars took place. Indians were hired to fight against Indians, and many of our people were destroyed.

"We have scarcely a place left to spread our blankets; you have got our country, but are not satisfied; you want to force your religion upon us.

"Brother! Continue to listen. You say that you are sent to instruct us how to worship the Great Spirit agreeably to his mind, and if we do not take hold of the religion which you white people teach, we shall be unhappy hereafter; you say that you are right, and we are lost. How do we know this to be true? We understand that your religion is written in a book; if it was intended for us as well as you, why has not the Great Spirit given it to us? . . . . You say there is but one way to worship and serve the Great Spirit; if there is but one religion, why do you white people differ so much about it? Why not all agree, as you can all read the book?

"Brother! The Great Spirit has made us all; but he has made a great difference between his white and red children; he has given us a different complexion and different customs; to you he has given the arts; to these he has not opened our eyes; we know these things to be true. Since he has made so great a difference between us in other things, why may we not conclude that he has given us a different religion according to our understanding; the Great Spirit does right; he knows what is best for his children. We are satisfied.

"Brother! We do not wish to destroy your religion, or take it from you; we only want to enjoy our own.[18]

"Brother! We have brought you your prisoner. We have taken this opportunity to address other issues. If you understand us, this will lead to peace in this great land. This is all we have to say at present.

Greatly moved by this speech, Edward wished other white men would have the opportunity to hear these words from this wise man. It was a powerful moment where all present sensed something of significance had happened, even if not fully understood. The men all regarded one another solemnly and Edward felt as he never had before the magic of the peace pipe tradition. Clearly, this was what was needed to seal the truce and mark this historic moment. How sickly signatures on parchment would look in comparison to a beautiful pipe with feathers dangling from the long stem. Nevertheless, Edward and Col. Arbuckle produced and signed an agreement and asked the Osage to make their mark, which they dutifully did. When one of the braves asked that the paper hang on the wall with the maps, Edward gladly consented. Yet, he mused, for the Indians, the peace pipe would have been as binding as the document was for the army.

"Next time you visit," he announced, "you will find your truce framed upon the wall." The meeting was declared over and the prisoner led away to be secured by the Quartermaster.

WALELA ARRIVED early carrying a pitcher of water as she did for Julia every morning. One could never have enough water, it seemed, for washing, drinking or cooking. The hand pump out back saw almost constant use, serving everyone's needs. The post collected rainwater as well, and this spring fortunately the barrels were usually full.

On this particular morning Julia was feeling melancholy, missing her mother and for some unknown reason, pining for certain foods she'd not had for a very long time. And if she weren't careful, she would soon be saying she had a 'hankering' for something, like the folks out here did. How delicious a *crème caramel* would taste, the smooth custard whispering on her tongue, or a *poulet au estragon*. The Huguenot ancestral traditions persisted at the Du Val family table and good food with a French flair was the norm. If only she had her own kitchen, she could remedy some of the problem.

"I have good news, I think," Walela announced.

"Tell me, tell me," Julia urged, ashamed of her gloomy mood.

"Chief Jolly says he would like for you to teach English to some of the children. You could begin next week and if it is agreeable to you, you could come two times per week, on Tuesday and Friday afternoons."

"That is wonderful! Perfect! Oh, thank you, Walela. I hope it will go well. What do you think? What should I teach them first?"

"Probably just some phrases. But they will need to learn your alphabet because they know only Sequoia's Cherokee alphabet."

"Perfect! I can't wait to get started!" Julia exclaimed, while simultaneously hoping she would hear soon from Abigail, perhaps with some instruction tips.

Edward and William tapped on the door, their approach unheard over the women's spirited conversation. The brothers asked Julia to take a stroll with them and she quickly agreed, letting the door bang behind her. Walela knew it was unreasonable, but she felt excluded from the usual morning chat. The tension in Captain Du Val's manners toward her since Red Fox's interference upset her greatly, and she longed for their former easygoing exchanges. She did not want to counter her brother's wishes but neither did she wish to live under his restrictions. She was proud of helping Edward at the peace conference and knew he had come to depend on her presence.

She had been treated so naturally, so much like one of the Du Val family. She treasured Captain Du Val's respect for her, delighted in his company and, she must admit, found his gangly physique and cornflower blue eyes most appealing. With disappointment, she watched the three Du Vals walk away and turned reluctantly to her daily chores. How foolish she was to expect otherwise, she told herself.

Edward, William and Julia headed together over to the Sutler's "coffee shoppe" and settled themselves with fresh tin mugs on the bench outside. A cherry tree by the little dirt patio in front of the store seemed just about to burst into bloom, unusually late this year due to the cool weather. Tight brown buds had given way to green knobs, clustered densely on each branch and twig, and today, a froth of pink peeked from each green cup.

Julia loved the early mornings and evenings best here, she decided. Every day the mourning doves' call gently awakened her, even before the blast of reveille, and the light on the grass cast their world in gold. A pair of these doves tamely pecked their way through seed scattered in the gravel next to the store, their soft gray feathers a paean to all that is fragile and gentle on the earth.

William abruptly broke her reverie. "Listen, Julia, Edward and I are worried about you. We think this place may be too rough for a young lady. Perhaps you should have gone home with Mr. P."

"What are you talking about? A little scorpion bite is not much to be alarmed about!"

William had taken up his habit of digging the toe of his boot in the dirt, chunk-chunk-chunk, making dust scatter on her skirt.

"And stop that!" she demanded in a sisterly tone, putting her hand on the offending leg.

"I know. But it's the company, Julia. There's really no good company for you here," William persisted.

"I am not sure about that! I know I have not sought out any of the ladies who live off the post yet. Although I don't think there are many. But I have been so busy with you two, Walela, my garden, and of course, Pierce."

"Yes, that's another issue, Sis," Edward took up the thread. "I don't feel as strongly as Willie about these matters, but have you thought about what your life would be like out here? How long could you really stand it?"

Julia remembered her longing for missed luxuries just this morning, and she also knew she occasionally wished to see pretty china instead of her chunky earthenware bowl, or a silver or crystal candlestick instead of pocked pewter. But she knew she would not give up on her adventure yet.

"I do not know, Edward. I miss the comfort of home, but I am not ready to leave. I like the feeling of freedom here. I like my independence. I find it all so exhilarating." She paused for a moment. "You know, it seems a little funny. I feel freer here and you seem less so. Building this fort around you. Shutting yourselves off." Her brothers stared at her, bemused. "And you are right. There *is* Pierce. We have confessed our sentiments for one another, but he has not asked me to marry him."

"The Devil!" Edward exclaimed. "This is all worrying me more now than before!"

"Well, I am not worried," Julia said with more courage than she actually felt. William's boot, chinking again, indicated his emotions pretty clearly. "I found a promising and exciting occupation only this morning," she continued, telling them more about teaching English to the Cherokee children.

William looked like he would explode, so red did his face become. "And just how do you plan to go over there two times a week, young lady? You cannot ride over and into an Indian village without a chaperone!"

"Oh, dear, I had not thought of that," Julia moaned.

"I am afraid you haven't thought of a lot of things!" Edward sounded alarmed. "William may be right that the way of life here is making you too independent and unladylike." He pointed at her arms. "And look at your skin! What would mother say?"

"I don't care," Julia fairly shouted, then tamed her reaction. "Really, I don't. I *like* riding and gardening and going to the Indian villages with you, Edward, or with Pierce. And furthermore, I don't see why I should do only what's expected of me. I can do more than that! You are both talking nonsense."

"I understand, Julia, I really do," Edward replied. "But I share some of William's concerns. Let's just think about it, shall we, and maybe we can come up with a chaperone for you. After all, I am the Indian Agent," and he gave her an encouraging smile.

"I hope so," she said, giving them both a quick hug before almost running home, not wanting them to see tears which she didn't fully understand. Just when she had been so happy thinking she had figured everything out, at least an occupation, more criticism and doubts came from out of the blue. It's not reasonable, she thought. Their lives are not so perfect right now and so why should they expect more of her? It did not seem at all fair. For all she knew, William's store was no more than a front for a groggery. By the time she got home she had become angrier. She felt like she needed their approbation but resented doing so. It also seemed like they were punishing her for being a girl. Dash it all. That wasn't exactly right either, but whatever their motive, she knew she would not budge for now.

CHAPTER TWENTY-ONE
A QUESTION

DURING THESE early June evenings the extended daylight prompted everyone to stay outside longer to enjoy the balmy weather. Robins bounced along the ground looking for worms and squirrels chased one another in silly circles. Frequently now, Julia found herself pining for more privacy, feeling many curious eyes upon her when she would drag her spindly chair outside to sit and read in the twilight. More than occasionally she would sense another person close by, even if she saw no one.

On one such evening Pierce came by, and when she raised her large contemplative eyes from her book and saw him, she felt a fluttering sensation in her stomach. "Hello," he said, sitting down in the grass next to her chair, extending his legs out in front of him. He wore his regulation army pants and a cool civilian cotton shirt open for two buttons, revealing his tan neck and his wavy hair growing over the back collar. It was all she could do to restrain herself from stroking his hair so close to her hand. He began combing the grass with his fingers.

"Ah, ha!" he whooped, having spotted a patch of wild clover. "I bet I can find a four leaf clover before you can."

"I'll bet you can't," she responded gamely, jumping up from her chair to join him on the ground. Purposefully, his fingers kept finding hers, and when he stroked her wrist, she looked into his eyes.

"Your gorgeous eyes haunt me day and night," he whispered. "They are the color of clover with flecks of gold."

"I am glad," she whispered back, "but I am sure there are many inquisitive eyes upon us right this moment."

He grinned. "How about we go for a little stroll?" he suggested, getting up and extending a hand to help her up as well.

"Good idea." She took her book inside while Pierce, following her, carried her little chair. They didn't dare embrace here either because of the open window and door, and it would look indiscreet if she should close either. Carrying on a courtship among a company of soldiers was proving more difficult than under the noses of parents, she thought.

They took their usual path down toward the Neosho River, and as they meandered along, she recounted for him the teaching idea and a little of her conversation with Edward and William, leaving out their explicit reservations about him. When they reached "their" rock by the water's edge, they sat down close together, and he slipped his arm around her waist. The rock was still warm from the day's sun and a few rambunctious perch were jumping in the shallows as though to entertain them.

Julia leaned her head upon his shoulder, breathing in the warm earthy scent of him. His arm tightened around her waist as they drew together. He kissed her deeply and profoundly, and when her lips parted, he moaned aloud. Her fingers sought the tendrils of hair on his neck she had wanted to touch earlier, and he pulled away to stroke her cheek.

"My precious girl," he breathed.

The fire of the descending sun in the West mounted one last flame edging the rippled clouds with pink and gold. The strokes of light appeared very broad on such a huge canvas of prairie sky.

"Julia," Pierce said quietly, "I want to be with you always. Will you marry me?" She inhaled quickly with surprise. Even though she had wanted this, she had not been sure it would happen and certainly not so soon.

"Always seems right to me too, my love. Of course I will." The answer escaped before she even thought about it --- a most unusual reaction for her, she realized.

They hugged one another tightly while she laughed softly, saying "Yes, yes, yes!"

She drew away, becoming more serious. "But Pierce, how? When? Where? And where would we live? Everything is happening too fast!"

"I have been thinking about all these things. There are no restrictions in the Army to officers marrying, so no problems there. However, I wish I had more to offer you right away. But God knows, you understand the conditions out here. When we return to my plantation in South Carolina, I am sure you will be very happy, but I do not know when I shall be able to return. It could be a few years, Julia."

She nodded, encouraging him to continue, although the words "a few years" had caused a little tremor of fear.

"Building things is what I do out here, so I don't see why I cannot build us a house right outside the post, nearby, where some of the other officers' homes are. Perhaps we can find a place to stay until then, because I think we should schedule the ceremony as soon as possible. Next week even!"

Julia gasped. "Oh, Pierce, I don't see how that would be possible. And my mother! How can I be married without her?" She watched the river flow by, growing darker as the reflected light of day faded away. The rocks too morphed from mounds of sparkling mica into flat gray slabs as a few frogs began their evening serenade.

"You would have Edward and William with you."

"Yes, but I must tell you that they are very concerned about my life out here. They --- especially William --- do not think it's a proper place for me at all. But maybe if I am safely married, they would relax a bit." She grinned with hope.

"There is a mission not far away," he continued, growing excited. "I know the priest. He performs functions here sometimes when we need him. We could ride over tomorrow or the next day, and if you like him, perhaps he could marry us."

She looked up at this man she had just agreed to marry.

How handsome he looked, how kind and capable he seemed. "I have only known you for a little over a month. Everyone will say we are moving too quickly. How is it possible that I am so sure this is what I want? I do not understand but it is, Pierce, it is! But I must write to mother. She at least must know before it happens."

"Tell her I want to take care of you and hold you close every night."

"My love," she kissed him once more.

"I will speak to Edward and William first thing in the morning," he offered. "I understand their concern about you, and I would like to contact your mother and request her permission as well. Perhaps our marriage will solve more problems than it causes."

"Now you are the optimist," she kidded.

"I will make it happen," he promised.

JULIA COULD hardly wait to get out her letter paper and pen to write to her mother. Of course, Jemina wished for her daughter's happiness above everything, but this news would be a shock. Most certainly she would expect Julia and her fiancé to come home for a full and proper wedding, she would send out the bans and enjoy designing a wedding gown or modifying one of her sisters' dresses. Also, she would think it unwise as well as improper to marry so quickly. Jemina surely would advise more time to get to know her future husband; it just would not look right at home, and Julia regretted putting her mother in this position. Her letter would be happy but disappointing news for Jemina if that made any sense.

In fact, to be honest, Julia agreed with what she knew would be her mother's reaction. Normally, she would think it foolhardy to rush into marriage. She had always been more practical than romantic, more level headed than flighty. Yet here she was about to take the plunge without much testing of the waters. Her heart, however, insisted this was the right road for her, and she could not help but think she had journeyed a third of the way across the entire continent just to find Pierce. The rivers had flowed straight to him, and she was not about to tempt the fates and refuse the gift life now offered. Bending her head to the paper, she began to write.

Dearest Mother,

I received a proposal last night from the gentleman I told you about in my last letter (how quickly events are unfolding!), and I have accepted. His name is Pierce Mason Butler, and I am sure you will find him as wonderful as I do. He is a good man and I believe he loves me. What a joy it is to write those words!

My sadness though is that we plan to be married very soon, here at Cantonnement Gibson, and I will not have you with me at my wedding. I never could have imagined such a thing and I know you will feel as devastated as I. But I truly do not see any other way.

As William and Edward will attest, it is difficult for me to remain here unchaperoned and do all I wish to do. If I am married, I think it will solve a lot of the problems posed by my "gallivanting around the countryside," as William puts it. In fact, those were the very words of a pompous old gentleman sharing our stagecoach on the way out here. Edward and William have qualms about keeping an eye on me, and a husband may just be the answer to all the propriety concerns. Of course, that is not why I am marrying!

I must say, I really don't know what all there is to worry about although I do understand it just doesn't look right. Every soldier has been extremely courteous and proper and although some of the women around these parts have a hard exterior, they are kind enough. Perhaps my brothers are afraid I will forget my good manners and become brassy and tough. I seriously doubt it!

Loving Pierce as I do, I now understand how difficult

*it must be for you to live without father --- and all of us, for
that matter. But because you have loved, I hope you will
understand my new and unwavering desire to be with the
man I love. I cannot imagine being far away from him, and
my love feels as broad and wide as this vast prairie. You
always made me feel needed at home, Mother and I have
missed that. Perhaps now, I will feel needed again --- and
loved. How very happy I am and only your presence (and
father's) would make it perfect.*

*I will write you again when we have decided on the
date. I expect Pierce is speaking with William and Edward
at this very moment and I am a little nervous about that. I
hope this letter finds you well and that you will share my
happiness.*

Your loving daughter, Julia

She was not to see any of "her" men until evening, after the
bugle called everyone back to the fort. Perhaps the hours to reflect
had muted her brothers' reactions for when they called on her,
they seemed gracious enough if not pleased. Or, perhaps one had
made the other see reason. She felt some reserve in their manner,
which she should have expected, but her shimmering delight inside masked all other qualms after having written her mother.

"Julia, Pierce told us that you and he wish to marry," William
said in an almost accusing tone.

"Yes, is it not wonderful!" she said exuberantly.

"Well, I hope so," Edward seriously replied. "I know how you
feel about him, Julia, but we are worried because you have not
known him for long. Not long at all. We understand he comes
from a fine family but there is this outstanding court-martial for
charges which could be meaningful. You realize he is being accused of unofficerlike and ungentlemanly behavior. That is hardly
what one would wish for in a husband."

"But Edward, they are false charges!" she replied hotly.
"From a man who has been angry at Pierce for a year and who was

looking for a way to get back at him."

"Yes, this may be what Pierce has told you but the trial has not occurred and we don't know what will happen," William said, taking up the gauntlet.

"Nothing will happen," said Julia. "I know he is innocent of this vile attack."

"Sis, you are in love with him. Of course that is what you think," William responded, the familiar flush of anger suffusing his fair face.

At this moment, Julia burst into tears. "How can you say these things? You must see what a good man he is and how awful that Lt. Newell is. Besides, I trust Pierce implicitly. He just would not behave in the ways Newell has suggested. You must support Pierce in this. You really must!"

Edward came and put his arms around Julia. "All right, Juliette, all right. Calm down. We'll stand behind him on the trial matter, but that doesn't mean it is right for you to hurry up and marry him."

Her tears ceased as quickly as they had begun and she became sharply angry, breaking away from Edward. "Oh yes, it does. I had not realized it before but it cannot hurt his cause for everyone to see I believe in him. And I do. And there is simply no reason for us to wait. It is not going to change anything and it will mean everything to me to have you two beside me at our wedding. It will be very sad not to have mother here, but I had believed the two of you would totally support me. I need you so much." She fought off tears again.

"Goodness!" she laughed. "I am coming apart at the seams. I admit I am not acting very mature at the moment, but I am quite sure this is the right thing for me." She gripped each elbow, hugging herself as she shivered slightly and then straightened up, recovering.

"Please, you are my older brothers, but I do not think I can defer to you on this. Do you understand?" Her eyes beseeched them both.

Edward again embraced her and said, "I understand, Julia, I really do. But you should listen to your family on this occasion. All we are doing is to ask you to wait a little. Just think about it for awhile."

When they left, Julia felt angry and helpless. She would need their approval to marry out here. She had no other family. Yes, she had always been impetuous. But she knew she was right about this matter. They would make her wait indefinitely and her brothers had a point about the difficulty of maintaining the status quo with Pierce. The old rules just didn't fit in the Indian Territory, and yet her brothers expected her to still live by them here. What could she do?

JOINING JULIA for breakfast in front of her room, Pierce appeared flustered and unsettled "Dearest," he began. "I know Edward and Williams have not acquiesced yet to our plan but I would like to proceed as though the wedding will take place. It takes so long to arrange anything out here; I think any delay would be a mistake. And, I don't know what I was thinking. Old Dwight Mission is entirely too far for us to go to visit Reverend Washburn. The settlement is on the Illinois Bayou, halfway between Fort Smith and Little Rock. Believe me, I know every difficult mile of our new road between Cantonnement Gibson and Fort Smith, and Dwight is that far again --- even though we would go by river for the second leg of the trip. I'm afraid our only option is to write to Cephus Washburn and ask him to come here to marry us, or if he insists, we will go there. Two trips are entirely out of the question, but I promise you will like him." Pierce looked extremely uncomfortable and fidgeted throughout this whole explanation.

"Heavens, I am sure I shall if you recommend him," she agreed, "and I am not sorry to forego traveling again. I am quite content to stay in one place for the moment."

He looked greatly relieved. "Wonderful! But I still would

like to whisk you away for a ride today, far from prying eyes," he winked at her. "Could you meet me at the stables after Guard Mounting?"

"Of course, that sounds perfect." She watched him run off with his hat still in his hand. His attitude was comforting but she wondered how on earth she would convince her brothers to agree to the marriage.

Donning her riding habit, Julia observed Walela's quiet demeanor while she dressed. The girl was always polite but she seemed to have lost her sparkle, to be a muted version of the former person. When Julia joined Pierce at the stables, she asked to ride Cinder, a black mare she particularly liked. She almost mentioned Walela to him, but then decided she didn't want to color their morning with anything gloomy.

Her sidesaddle still had not arrived from Maryland, but since Mrs. Arbuckle never seemed to ride, it had not been a problem so far. All of a sudden, Pierce stopped saddling Cinder, put his arm around her and gave her a light kiss on the mouth, right smack in front of several privates busy currying the horses. This generated a few whistles and ooh's and aah's, but Pierce just smiled while Julia imagined she blushed.

"I think an engagement gives me some liberties," Pierce bragged.

"I think I agree." She returned his grin, loving the gleam in his brown eyes. Sometimes, on the prairie, she had noticed his eyes were filled with so much light, they became more amber than brown. "But you are going to ruin my reputation!"

Once they were mounted and walking their horses northeastward, Julia dared to ask Pierce his impression of her brothers' reception of the news.

"It's funny. It seems like they expected it but still were unprepared. As you know, they suggested we wait, at least a few months. Or at least until the court- martial is over. Would you prefer that, Julia?"

"Not at all. In fact, ever since you suggested we marry

immediately, it has seemed entirely the best idea to me. My only regret is that Mother cannot be here for the ceremony, but I am sure she would not make the trip out here at any time. It is just too difficult at this stage in her life. On the other hand, I know she would prefer that we return there for the wedding celebration."

"I understand, but that's impossible. My tour of duty here lasts for at least another year and a half, and I don't think it would be a good idea for me to desert --- even for you, my love."

So intense was the gold of the fields in the bright morning light, Julia sensed the flavor of metal on her tongue. The glowing grass spiked the broad blue horizon like golden arrows and bird-calls bounced in the light breezes. A windy night had swept the sky clean of any haze allowing them to spot a prairie falcon high in the unlimited cerulean firmament.

Deeply breathing in the pure air, Julia exhaled audibly, "What a relief to be out here with you! I was certain Edward would agree, but I fear William still might make trouble. He is just so discontented now, his unhappy attitude sometimes spills over to others."

"I think I convinced them the court-martial will come to nothing serious and that I always will be able to take care of you."

"Hmmm. I am not so optimistic. They are quite serious about our waiting and are more worried about the court-martial than you seem to realize. Pierce, darling, we really know so little about one another. Here we are talking of marriage and I haven't even the faintest idea what your religion is. I must tell you I am a little embarrassed about mine, only in the sense that it is fairly neglected. Our family attends a Huguenot church in Frederick Town but it has always been more a social event for me than a pious one."

Her fiancé chuckled in the manner Julia found so appealing. It was always a surprising sound, coming from someone who generally appeared very serious. "That pretty well describes it for me as well, my Julia. But I have always taken it for granted that religion was part of my life. For the important moments of my stay on earth, that is."

"Yes, that is true for me too. And I do pray, always remembering to thank God for all my blessings, including you!"

"My family are Irish Protestants," he explained, "who came over to the New World very early on, from the North of Ireland, County Armagh, to be exact. I think the family name came from the fact that our ancestors were butlers to the King and the family crest even has cups on it."

"Tipplers, eh?" she teased.

"I expect so," he laughed. What a wonderful sound she thought that chortle was, rather like a happy birdcall. "Julia, I just had an idea. Perhaps the Nicks would like Reverend Washburn to baptize their baby if he comes over for our wedding."

"What a fine idea! And I am sure there must be other pastoral needs as well. I'll check with the CO's Adjutant as soon as we return today."

"Ah, Julia, what will the CO think now? He already allowed one party partly in your honor and now you are requesting a wedding on the Parade Ground! You are certainly making an impact around here."

"But Pierce, it is you, not I, who will be requesting a wedding of Colonel Arbuckle!"

"I guess you are right," he grinned. "And I shall draft a letter to send to Reverend Washburn asking him to select a date for a ceremony, at Cantonnement Gibson, if at all possible." When they parted at her room, she barely resisted caressing his cheek. He wasn't as successful with his restraint as he reached over and tucked a stray lock behind her ear.

CHAPTER TWENTY-TWO
QUANDARY

IN FRUSTRATION Edward ran his fingers through his already scrambled hair. Abruptly pushing his chair back, he heaved both feet on top of his desk and gazed out the window. The Osage were a constant problem, like a sharp thistle underfoot. This particular situation would have had a wry humor about it were it not equally sad. More importantly, he had to make a decision about what to do in order to avoid serious trouble.

An Osage chief's son had been killed in a bizarre accident, and to make it worse, it had happened in a ball game organized for the amusement of some officers and other gentlemen from Cantonnement Gibson. The chief had come to the Fort, demanding a hundred dollars as compensation for the death of his son. In answer to a remonstrance that a hundred dollars was too much, he had justified the demand by pleading the dead young man was the best horse thief in the Osage nation. An inferior man might be worth no more than ten or twenty dollars, but his son was worth a hundred.[19]

Edward sighed out loud. Sometimes the most ridiculous matters seemed the most difficult. Of course the death wasn't ridiculous but he just couldn't fathom the Indian's thought process. He pushed the paper requesting his signature aside and reverted to looking out the window. Maybe Walela would have a suggestion as to how to deal with this; perhaps she would have a sense of what an Osage chief would consider fair. His boots hit the floor with a thud. How ludicrous and obvious he was, trying to invent a reason to see her at every turn. She was such a wisp of a girl, his arms would wrap several times around her. Her breathy voice softened every word and her dark eyes expressed such honesty. He almost upended his chair as he pushed it back further in his hurry to get away. Grabbing his hat, he clattered down the wooden steps to the parade ground, strode across it in his usual lanky loping gait and headed toward Julia's. If he were lucky, Walela would still be there.

Sure enough, the two women were engaged in some kind of project, sitting together in the grass, Julia cross-legged with her long skirt poofed around her, and Walela on her knees leaning back upon her heels. A book lay in the grass between them and Julia held a paper and pen. Upon seeing Edward approach, Julia waved the paper at him.

"Edward, look, look." She began chattering before he could even say hello. "Abigail sent me a letter ---- remember, I told you about my friend on the boat --- she included some of her lesson plans. They are so helpful. It will be much easier to get started now. I have felt so inept and awkward, wondering if I would be presenting the right things in the right way."

"That's terrific, Julia. I'm proud of you. I really am. Now we have just got to get you over there."

"Perhaps the children could all come here for our school," Julia suggested.

Edward guffawed. "Julia, I am the Indian Agent but Colonel Arbuckle will tell you he is running an Army here, not the Department of Indian Affairs. Which reminds me, I'm here on business and need to confer with Walela."

Walela had been quietly listening to the Du Vals' conversation and so far had not tried to join in. "Good afternoon, Agent Du Val," she replied.

"And I thought you had come to see me," Julia joked, then immediately considered it ill spoken when no one smiled. How insensitive she had been.

"Listen, Walela, what do you think about this?" Like a folding yardstick, he bent his angular frame down to the ground to join them, and proceeded to recount the tale of the death of the Osage boy and the requested compensation. "What do you think I should do?"

Walela shook her head. "I truly do not know. Except I would counsel you to remember this is primarily a matter of pride for the chief. It was an accident, not a battle and so he does not feel he needs to seek revenge. But you must honor him and his clan and not demean him."

"Yes, I can see that," Edward said, pausing. "That is helpful. And how are your mother and your clan members?" he politely inquired, understanding this question must include Red Fox.

"All are well," she answered seriously.

Julia watched the stiff politeness of the two and impulsively said, "Edward, I have an idea. Perhaps on Monday, for my first visit, you could take me over to the village with all my materials. We could even take the donkey cart since I will have a lot to carry. Walela can help us set up the class."

Edward grinned. "You are persistent! I have work to do here, Julia and I would be wise not to be seen as my sister's lackey." He paused and appeared to reconsider. "On the other hand, perhaps we can stretch this venture to be considered Indian Agent related. After all, I am assuming the school will improve Indian/ White relations."

Julia jumped up to give Edward a hug and felt Walela would certainly have liked to do the same. Julia suspected her own present lovesick state had sensitized her to recognizing the symptoms in others.

SUMMER WHIRLWIND

CHAPTER TWENTY-THREE
SCHOOL

EDWARD AND Julia set out together in the buckboard on Monday morning heading toward Walela's village. The donkey's tail swished sassily in front of them making Julia laugh. It was sunny and bright, albeit muddy as there had been a mighty grist of rain overnight.

"I hope we don't get stuck," Julia worried. "What's this silly animal's name?"

"He goes by the imaginative tag of 'Brownie', and he won't let us bog down," Edward replied, apparently sharing the donkey's optimistic outlook for the day.

Julia had been busy sharpening quills for the children to write with and also had brought some of her own store of charcoal and paper. Her lesson plan swirled in her head and seemed to contain more questions than answers. How many children would show up? What ages would they be? Would they truly want to learn? Would they like her? Would they pay attention in the English lesson or only laugh at her? They could simply use sticks for learning adding and subtraction, and she would order more supplies from John Nicks when she had a clearer idea of what she would like to do. She had also brought some hard candy to give to each student at the end of the day. Perhaps they would enjoy learning a song, but which one should it be? Maybe "Yankee Doodle." The words wouldn't make sense to the children, but then it didn't make much sense to an English speaking person either. But the music would help them learn the sounds.

"Edward, it is just not logical," she said, seemingly from out of nowhere. Supposedly we want to teach the Indians our ways and encourage their assimilation. Yet we build the high walls of the fort to keep them separate."

"You are forgetting, Julia, that not everyone agrees they can learn our ways or even want to. And you must admit it's more complicated than you are allowing."

"I know." Julia sighed. "But I cannot help but wonder if the Army is not going about this in the wrong way. For instance, it would help a great deal if the Army thought about helping the native women as well as the men. They want to learn too, and also, I think it would be well worthwhile for the Army to hire some agricultural specialists to help the Indians in the I.T. I know there was a lot I had to learn at the farm when you and William left."

Edward suddenly began fidgeting beside her, seeming almost as nervous as she. Having removed his hat, his hair stuck out in its usual unruly fashion and his eyes, as blue and friendly as the sky, squinted into the sun.

"Julia, I just cannot stop thinking about her," he confessed. "What am I to do?" He rolled the reins around in his fingers like worry beads.

"I honestly cannot imagine," Julia shook her head. "But I do think Walela cares for you, Eddie. Something is bothering her; I know that."

In agitation Edward stomped his feet on the buckboards, knocking off some dried mud. Considering what she had said, he brightened. "Do you really think so? Like me, I mean."

"Yes, I do, but Edward, that is only half the problem."

"No, it's all that matters, because if she feels the way I do, I am sure we can solve the rest."

Julia burst out laughing. "Oh, Edward, that is crazy! You know it. Like you just said to me, it's a little more complicated than that. Oh my Lord, love does make us crazy, doesn't it?" Brother and sister spontaneously hugged side-by-side, glad to have this moment of understanding. Then Edward sobered.

"I am going to have to talk to her, Julia. I cannot go on with this polite charade much longer. I have to know how she feels."

Brownie waved his tail at them again, the scraggly black hair on the tip flicking flies away.

"I truly wish you good luck," Julia said. Worrying that the sun was burning her nose, though still early, she pulled her bonnet closer around her face. She would have to remember more often to apply buttermilk and lemon juice to her skin, fortunately still flawless but no longer fashionably pale. "Since you can understand how I feel about Pierce, I don't know why you want to obstruct our marriage, Edward," she interjected, sensing the leverage she needed to swing him to her side.

"Yes, I understand how you feel, but it's different for a girl. There are all the problems living in the I.T. would bring, and I don't think you appreciate what it would be like to be a military wife. I am sure Mother would agree with William and me."

This last point actually bothered Julia more than she wanted to admit, but somehow she expected she would be able to convince Jemina that Pierce made her life make more sense. "We will have to talk about it more later," she said. As they neared the village, they glimpsed Walela awaiting them in the trees by the path. Edward stood up in the wagon and waved, then pulling on the reins, brought Brownie to a halt. He held out his hand to her. "Would you like to come aboard?" He smiled.

Walela considered for a moment. "I would. Thank you." She forgot the "Sir" for once and gave him her hand to climb up.

"We have been having a fine time," he announced. "Glad to have you join us."

"Thank you, Sir." She looked straight at him. "We should go to the summer house," she suggested, pointing the way. "If we have the school there, everyone can see and perhaps more will join us."

Julia knew this was a good idea, but the thought of being out in the open for all to stare made her extremely nervous. But Walela would be there to assist her.

Edward helped them unload the wagon and mentioned he would pay his respects to Chief Jolly before continuing upriver a bit further to pay a visit to the Creeks and Chief MacIntosh. "I'll come back for you after lunch," he promised.

The children began arriving as Julia and Walela set their articles out on the benches. The sun had risen to an angle of about 45 degrees and cast light over the treetops onto their schoolroom floor. Most of the little ones were naked, and Julia knew they would not begin to wear clothing until about age eight. She must learn to ignore such a striking difference in dress code.

As each child stepped or climbed upon the raised platform, Julia handed them a slate and chalk. All of the children were silent, their eyes looking up to her with curiosity and some with apprehension. Offering her friendliest smile, she wrote her name on her slate. "My name is Miss Du Val." She pointed to herself and then to the name on the slate. Walela then said the same thing to them in Cherokee. Julia asked, "Will you please tell me your names?"

One little boy immediately spoke up and Walela translated, giving them English names. Julia wrote each one on their slate while they stared at her. There was Little Foot, a tiny girl with very long shiny black hair, and a fellow with the endearing name of Cricket, whom she would soon discover could be quite noisy. The children learned easily and quickly on this first day, their hunger to please and to know astounding her. The morning flew by and before she knew it, it was lunchtime. Walela invited Julia to eat with her and her mother. Julia gladly accepted though she had brought a meatloaf "sandwich," a relatively new invention. She would share with them.

The two young women passed by a very sick young Cherokee man who was lying on a pallet by his door. Smallpox pustules had erupted all over his face and looked to become one suppurating oozing blister. Julia looked away, unable to bear the sight and Walela made no comment.

Attempting a distraction, Julia asked, "What is your mother's name?"

Walela gave a little laugh. "She is called 'Black Cloud' because there was a terrible storm the day she was born. Her father wanted a bow and instead he got a sifter, which angered him so much, he called her Black Cloud. It is best that you call her Mrs. Bushyhead."

"A bow and a sifter?" Julia looked confused and Walela laughed.

"That's what we say for a boy or a girl when a baby is born."

They walked by one house where some cooking, hunter's style was progressing. Several small four-legged bodies were arranged on tapering spits of dogwood thrust perpendicularly into the earth so as to reveal it to the flaming fire below. The scent, however, was particularly overpowering, and Julia asked what was roasting.

"Pole cat," Walela answered. "It's a particular delicacy of the Cherokee."

Julia hoped that she contained her horror when she suddenly identified the strange scent as skunk. She heartily prayed none would be offered for lunch.

When they entered the house, Mrs. Bushyhead came forward to greet them. Julia thought her a very striking woman, with charcoal gray hair and black eyes. Walela must be the youngest, Julia surmised, because though handsome, this woman's skin exhibited numerous shallow creases, like winter twigs against an evening sky.

Walela led Julia to the table where three tin plates were set. In the center of the table lay a dish of fried prickly pears and a bowl of hominy. Julia brought out her sandwich, placing it in the middle, as well. "If you would like some," she offered rather nervously. The two women smiled with genuine pleasure and hospitality and equal portions were served of each dish.

Julia forced down the hominy with the acute realization she must acquire a taste for this ubiquitous dish, but she loved the tasty prickly pear. Walela explained that they boiled the joints of young cactus so the skin and needles could be easily removed, and then the soft interior was fried. Both the Indians and the Whites had learned this plant warded off scurvy. [20]

Edward appeared for the drive home, and somehow Julia

knew she would not have a problem many days finding a ride to her school. She thanked Mrs. Bushyhead for the lunch and when Walela agreed to come to the post as usual the next day, it felt like a comfortable pattern had just been established.

CHAPTER TWENTY- FOUR
PLANS

TWO RABBITS foraged in the clover near Julia's room, their puffy white tails and quivering pink noses making her smile. How vulnerable they looked, to an Indian's arrow, a coyote, or a white man's gun. She expected Edward to come prowling around, looking for Walela, but surprisingly, he didn't show up. Walela, however, arrived as usual, performing her tasks willingly enough but without much spunk. When Julia mentioned she hoped Walela and Edward would help her again at the school later in the week, she received a warmer smile and agreement. How tender and fragile we all are she couldn't help but think.

She wondered when her mother would receive her letter. Sometimes she felt so totally cut off from her former life, as though she had walked on stage, not just in the second act, but in a completely different drama. With so much time and space between Jemina and herself now, she wondered if their lives could really and truly intersect again. Several times a day she would dream of Pierce holding her so tightly she couldn't breathe and then, embarrassed at her longings, she would marvel at the thought that he yearned equally for her.

Since she was feeling a little lonely, she was glad to see William striding up the hill to her barrack. He waved when he caught sight of her sitting in the clover.

"How's my beautiful sister?" he asked.

"Just fine, Willie. And you?"

"I am in fine fettle today because I had a long letter from Harriet telling me the girls are doing well in school and keeping their health. Maybe they should all come out here for a visit in the summer, but I worry so about the travel conditions. And they could not stay very long. What a lousy life this military service can be! And by the way, I'm more convinced than ever that you shouldn't marry Pierce. Believe me, I know from experience that the army is not the life for you."

"I know you mean well, William, but I have decided to go ahead."

"Absolutely not, Julia! If father were alive, I know he would not allow it, and Edward and I are stepping in for him. You can tell your Captain Butler that I challenge him to a duel if he is determined to carry you off."

Julia gasped. "He is not 'carrying me off', William. We would be married here by a chaplain, hopefully with you and Edward giving me away. Don't be ridiculous about a duel! What has gotten into you? And I'm not sure Edward is so much against it."

"What do I have to do to talk some sense into you, Julia? WHY did Mr. Paddington leave you here? WHY did Mother let you come? This is not a place for well-bred women! I am going to talk to Edward." And with that as his final word, he stalked off, leaving Julia angry and agitated.

ABOUT A week later Pierce received a note from Reverend Cephus Washburn, saying he would be most honored to officiate at a marriage ceremony on June 22, 1826 at Cantonnement Gibson and he would also take care of any baptisms or other needs on the same day. When Pierce relayed the news to Julia, her hands fluttered up to her cheeks. "Oh, Pierce, I have been delinquent in not telling you about William's strong objections. I have been hoping Edward would make him cool off or he would just give up. He even threatened you with a duel, but I cannot believe he really meant it."

"Well, that's not something to be taken lightly. I fear your brother can be a bit of a hotheaded at times, and I'm not sure how far he will go with his challenge," Pierce replied, shaking his head.

"I agree. But there is nothing more I can say to appease him. I think we just have to go ahead with our plans. Let's announce our engagement tomorrow," she suggested.

"Oh, no," said Pierce. "Tomorrow is Friday."

"I do not understand." Julia appeared bemused.

"In the Army it is considered bad luck to become engaged on a Friday."

When she burst out laughing, Pierce looked a little chagrined. Then he laughed too. "How about tonight?" he prompted. "Why wait? Your brothers already know and I will alert two of my men to watch William if he should become contentious."

Everything seemed to be happening so fast. She longed for her mother or a sister to share this with, at least a friend of similar background. Even though she could think of no real reason to refuse, she felt terribly alone at that moment. Pierce stood watching her and waiting, obviously becoming perplexed about her hesitancy. She smiled at him, "Yes, you are right, of course. Why wait? I wish we could offer champagne and a special treat at dinner tonight," she said rather wistfully.

"Remember, sweetheart, this is the army, on the frontier, and I doubt if we can find any champagne on short notice. But just by chance, I have a special cache of wine --- just a taste for everyone --- and I'll visit the cook to request a dessert. The men, of course, would prefer liquor, but for you, I shall open my wine."

Julia threw her arms around his neck, burying her damp face in the crook of his neck, hoping to hide tears springing from a sudden riptide of overwhelming emotion. When he left, Julia thought again of her need for a woman friend, as well as someone who would know something about the practical matters of a frontier army wedding. She had not warmed to the CO's wife particularly, though she seemed the obvious choice. She had liked John Nicks very much and she imagined his wife would be nice

Sarah Nicks

General John Nicks

too. Besides, she wanted to talk to her about a possible baptism for baby Eliza. How to find Mrs. Nicks? She hurried over to the sutler's to find out. Finding something concrete to do would probably help calm her down.

Sarah and John Nicks lived about three miles away, and when Capt. Nicks assured her Sarah would be at home, Julia decided on the spur of the moment she could ride out that way this very afternoon. Rushing to change into her riding habit, she thought a moment about venturing out without a chaperone. Surely it would be all right as it was not so far, and she certainly could handle Cinder.

At the stable the young man recognized her and without being asked, rushed to take down Mrs. Arbuckle's saddle for her. He asked no questions and helped her upon the mare. When she inquired about the road to Sarah Nicks' house, he looked confused momentarily and said, "Do you need accompaniment, Miss Du Val?"

"No, thank you, I shall be fine," and off she went, on a lovely afternoon, feeling for the moment like she belonged to this prairie, with its teeming wildlife, multiple rivers and wide sky. She followed the Neosho north as Captain Nicks had directed her and after about forty-five minutes, she spotted a crude signpost pointing "To Captain Nicks' House". When she turned away from the river, she began to become a little apprehensive as everything began to look the same and the grass grew very tall, up to her horse's shoulders in some places.

The path remained clear, however, which restored her peace somewhat. Giving Cinder a little kick with her heel, she cued the mare into a trot and posted in good form for about ten minutes. Perhaps Sarah would not want an unannounced visitor out here in the middle of nowhere, Julia suddenly thought. Had she been too impetuous? But the sutler had believed it a fine idea. Mrs. Nicks must be lonely too, Julia surmised.

The grasses parted then, like long golden hair divided at the nape of a woman's neck, opening onto a round back of meadow cleared for a simple house to Julia's right. There was a tiny vege-table garden to one side and a few flowers planted by the doorway. Julia dismounted and tied Cinder to a low fence protecting the little plot. She noted carefully chosen stones edging the flowerbed and a straw mat before the door.

"Hello?" she called, tapping at the door which already stood somewhat ajar. "Anybody home?"

A tall, dark haired woman with a baby in her arms came rushing from a second room. "Hello! Come in," she welcomed Julia.

"Hello, I am Julia Du Val. I hope your husband has told you who I am and that I have not disturbed you."

"Not at all, and yes, of course. I'm very glad to know you," said Sarah Nicks. "Please, do come in and make yourself comfort-able," Mrs. Nicks offered a friendly smile.

"Thank you. May I see little Eliza? Is she sleeping?"

"Yes, I just fed her." With obvious pride, Mrs. Nicks pulled back a soft blanket swaddling the little girl, who had a cloud of black hair and soft lashes lying in little scallops upon her cheeks.

"Don't wake her," Julia whispered. "She is so lovely."

"She truly is," breathed her mother. "You must be thirsty. May I get you something to drink? Here, you can hold her while I prepare us some tea." She thrust the baby into Julia's arms and pulled out a chair for her next to the table. There seemed to be only two rooms, the one where they stood, which served as kitch-en/dining room/living room and a separate bedroom, all neatly swept with Indian rugs on hardwood floors and cheerful cotton curtains at the windows.

Julia watched Mrs. Nicks bustle around her kitchen. The home was certainly small but it was *theirs* and quite cozy. The woman's warm manner countered her rather prim façade of dark hair severely parted in the middle of a high forehead and pulled back into a bun. She had a long straight nose, wide brown eyes and full lips pursed over nearly protruding teeth.

"I'm so glad you have come to see me," she chatted. "John has talked about you and I have met your brothers, of course. Are you happy you came west? Do you miss the east coast?"

Julia laughed. "Yes, I'm glad I came and no, I don't think I miss the East so much, but I came to find you because I do miss my sisters and friends. They should call it the Men's Territory, not the Indian Territory."

"You're right!" Mrs. Nicks displayed a high giggle. "We're definitely in the minority which can be a problem. Lordy Mercy, when Eliza was born, how I wished for a good midwife. There is an Indian woman who helps at these events and the post's doctor, but we didn't have time. Eliza was in a hurry, but as you can see, she's a healthy girl. At least now she is. She had us very worried for a few days last week with the flux. I must admit to being quite frightened as I didn't know what to do. John suggested giving her some dock seed, it's a sort of sorrel that grows amongst the wheat. You pound it and put it in some broth. It seemed to help and the looseness finally ceased."

"I have tried panic, a type of corn," Julia replied. "You pound it like the dock seed and drink it with wine or boil it with goat's milk and eat it twice a day, morning and evening. I don't imagine this would do for a baby though."

The two women became immediately comfortable with one another, and Julia watched her hostess place tea in real china cups on the table along with some freshly baked oatmeal raisin cookies, which looked and smelled absolutely delicious. Having the sutler for a husband would definitely come in handy, Julia realized.

"When did you come here, Mrs. Nicks?" she wanted to know everything about her new friend.

"My family has been out here for a very long time. When we were just children, my brother, Constantine, and I were brought to the Arkansas Territory by our cousins, Mr. and Mrs. Benjamin Moore of Chelsea, Virginia. Mr. Moore had received warrants for land for his service in the Revolution. My own family, the Perkins, originally came from Russia and we have been in Virginia since 1641. I have two other brothers, named Peter and Nicholas and they still live in Virginia.[21] And my name is Sarah. You must call me Sarah and I will call you Julia. No sense standing on formality out here."

"Wonderful!" responded Julia. "Sarah is not a Russian name too, is it?"

"I don't think so," Sarah giggled again. "I was living near Fort Smith with my cousins when John came as sutler with the 7th Infantry to the new post."

"Were you married at the post?"

"No, but nearby at our family home. On July 13, already almost two years ago! The Reverend William F. Vaill, who was then the head of Union Mission on Grand River in the Osage country, came over to Crawford County in the Arkansas Territory to perform the ceremony."[22]

"So you will have a second anniversary soon," Julia observed. "I am about to be married," she happily confessed, "and one reason I came by today is that I'm hoping you will help me plan the wedding. Pierce Mason Butler and I are planning to announce our engagement tonight. Everything has happened so quickly and I am feeling somewhat over the barrel. Reverend Washburn has agreed to come to the Post to officiate --- and of course you and Capt. Nicks are invited to the wedding, and we wondered if perhaps you would like to employ his services either before or after to baptize Eliza." She paused for breath. "Perhaps I am being presumptuous in making such a suggestion but please believe me, I am only trying to be helpful and friendly."

"Oh, heavens, my dear, don't worry about that and I think it's a wonderful idea. But what tremendous news about you! Tell me about your young man. By the way, my John is not so young. He was fifty when we married but he is as strong as an ox as I'm sure you can see. He hasn't slowed down at all and that's amazing, considering the life he's led, a very hard army life all over the country. You should get him to tell you sometime. Goodness, listen to me, rattling on, now go ahead and tell me about your Pierce Butler."

"Well, I think he is very handsome. He is a captain and his

family lives in South Carolina. I am sure you must have noticed him."

"I'm sure I have and just was not introduced. And you caught him. Good for you! Some of these hard-boiled army men never want to get married. Look at my John, waiting so long. He says the right one hadn't come along until he met me, but I think he just was not paying attention. Never mind. Now, we must think about your wedding."

At this moment Eliza chose to wake up, drawing up her legs and letting out a squeal as she demonstrated a frog kick, startling Julia who had been enjoying the warm quiet bundle in her lap. Sarah jumped up and retrieved Eliza, "Time for tea, is it, my precious? I thought it might be." Without ado, she unbuttoned her blouse and set the little one to her breast.

"You seem very capable," said Julia admiringly, "and I am afraid I have taken too much of your time. But it is very comforting for me to know I have found a woman friend nearby. Do you come to the post often?"

"Not since Eliza was born, but I'll make an effort now that I know you are there and you can come and visit me anytime. We'll plan a bang-up party, my dear. Don't you worry about a thing."

"I can see myself out and thank you so much, Sarah, for your kind reception."

"Oh, pshaw, don't be silly. I'm just glad you came."

Julia unhitched Cinder, adjusted her bonnet and settled herself in the saddle. It was a bit later than she had expected to begin her return trip, but it had been so pleasant having tea with Sarah and holding little Eliza. How friendly and expressive Sarah was! Indeed, she found most westerners more spontaneous, more genial and frank than the usually practiced and studied manners of the east coast.

The shadows from the tall waving grass were much darker than before as she made her way along the path and the weather had turned refreshingly cooler. Perhaps she had left it till too late and there would be coyotes about. Don't worry, she told herself, I

shall be home soon. But she was afraid to let Cinder go too quickly because she couldn't see the trace as clearly as before and she
certainly did not want the mare to stumble. It seemed like forever
before she finally saw the river in front of her and then could turn
south toward the fort. She shivered a bit, probably more from
anxiety than any chill. Unlike Sarah Nicks, who had made a permanent life here, she herself planned to return to the East. This
was only temporary, was it not? Oh Lordy, if anyone had noticed
her absence, she was going to have a lot of explaining to do.

Suddenly a varmint dashed out from the brush along the
trail and spooked Cinder. Julia was so deep in thought she wasn't
ready when the horse reared and her foot slid from the stirrup.
When Cinder rose again on her hind legs, Julia found herself
rudely upon the hard ground. Tears came to her eyes, more out of
fright and anger with herself than from injury.

Fortunately, Cinder seemed to have completed her display of
panic and Julia, coming quickly to her senses, grabbed the reins.
At least, no one had witnessed her momentary loss of control and
she really wasn't too much the worse for wear. However, as she
brushed off her riding skirt, she saw a tear near the bottom. Hopefully, no one would notice until she had repaired the damage. She
would have skinned her hands badly if she hadn't been wearing
her riding gloves. Quickly, she mounted again, stroking Cinder's
neck while cooing soothing sounds.

The familiar trail along the Neosho was a welcome sight and
giving Cinder her head, the mare headed for home on her own.
Julia found herself beginning to tremble, probably from the shock
from her tumble, and sorely wished for someone to comfort her.
But she would have to manage this on her own. After leaving Cinder at the stable, when she spotted Pierce and Edward pacing in
front of the long low log building containing her room, she hurried
toward them. She told herself she had no real reason to feel guilty,
simultaneously hoping to stave off any unpleasant scene.

"Where have you been?" they chorused. "We were worried
about you!"

"You need not have been. I am just fine. I'll quickly change for dinner."

"But where *were* you, Julia?" Pierce asked again, pointing to her riding habit. "I hope not out riding alone. We never thought to ask about you at the stable."

"Yes, actually I was. I rode over to see Sarah Nicks and we had a delightful visit. You know I wanted to talk to her about Reverend Washburn."

"Julia," Edward exploded, "You can *not* go riding around the countryside by yourself. You were extremely foolish to do such a thing!"

"As you can see," Julia fumed, "I am fine. I cannot continue to behave like an east coast matron. It is simply not practical; common sense should tell you that."

Edward threw up his hands. "Pierce, I leave her to you. I give up." He stalked off, grumbling to himself.

"Julia," Pierce said, "Perhaps you have a point, but you should at least have told someone what you were doing."

"Then 'someone' would just have told me not to do it. I can see now that just by coming out here I acted more unconventionally than most young women, and in order to survive here and not be a burden to everyone, I really must continue to be more independent. You must understand that."

Pierce regarded her with amazement. "Heaven help us! You sound just like my mother, the infamous "Behethelund!" and they both started to laugh. "Just hurry, my love. Tonight is our big announcement --- as long as my independent fiancé is still willing."

"More than willing," she said. "I'm counting on it for the rest of my life." He raised her hand to his and kissed the palm. Thank heavens he didn't notice the bruises because she had not removed her gloves.

"Be quick," he advised, rushing off.

CHAPTER TWENTY-FIVE
THE RACETRACK

AFTER DINNER to the surprise of everyone, Captain Pierce Mason Butler tapped on his metal cup and stood up at his place. All eyes turned to him with curiosity. Julia's heart expanded with pride as she knew this man to be hers. He appeared handsome above all others to her, so bright and well spoken. She liked the way he looked around the table to take in everyone before he began to speak.

"I have some very good news to announce tonight," he began. "I would like to ask the subaltern to fill everyone's cup with a little wine for the occasion and ask you to all raise your glasses to toast the beautiful girl, Miss Julia Du Val, who has agreed to be my wife."

Boots began to beat on the floor, spoons on plates and the words "Hear, hear" loudly echoed around the room. All raised their cups to be filled as Pierce spoke again.

"It was my lucky day when the sister of the Du Val brothers arrived at Cantonnement Gibson." Julia could feel her cheeks burn when many eyes turned to look at her, some openly smiling and others staring. "We plan to be married on June 22, here at the Post, and invite you all to join us at the ceremony and reception. The commanding officer has agreed to this plan as long as all rules and regulations, including curfew, are observed." At this point many raised their cups to Colonel Arbuckle at his usual place at the end of the table. "Also, in celebration, there will be a horse race this weekend. I shall ride and pledge my winnings for the wedding party."

Again, general hooting and hollering filled the room and then all jumped up, pumping the hand of Pierce and some kissed Julia's hand in mock cavalier style. Her heart sank when she saw William leave the room, his face suffused with the blush of anger. Edward also witnessed their brother's departure and hurried over to embrace her. "Don't worry, Sis," he said softly, "he'll come around." But she was not so sure. At least he hadn't made an ugly scene.

With all the commotion she was glad when Pierce's arm slipped around her waist and supported her against the crush. As usual there were duties to be performed after supper and everyone quickly disappeared. Pierce gave her a public kiss on the cheek and she retired to her room. How odd it seemed, so intense and then over so quickly. No friends to rally around her and discuss the happy news. A silent subdued evening stretched out before her. It was just a fact of army life she would have to get used to and one she would tolerate because it meant having Pierce in her life.

LIFE COULD become extremely monotonous for a regular soldier at the post. Every day army drums marked exactly the same hour to perform exactly the same functions. A day's work generally involved hard manual labor at the mercy of Mother Nature. No matter that there existed a hierarchy among the trades, --- ditch digging, carpentry, or hauling --- outdoor construction was exhausting whatever the task. No nearby town beckoned with pleasure at the end of a long day. No cozy home-fire comforted aching muscles. Although the food was sufficient and healthy in the main, little variety and few surprises existed. Day after day, week after week, even if a man had some imagination, neither much fun nor much trouble could be found.

When one clever soldier dreamed up building a racetrack

at Cantonnement Gibson, the idea provoked an enormously positive response. Everyone gladly pitched in during their spare time when there was nothing else to do anyway. Good riders suddenly became heroes, and the smallest men, formerly at the bottom of the pecking order, found undreamed of repute as jockeys. The competitive spirit among the officers who owned the best horses reached a feverish pitch, and other enlisted men, who formerly had no chance of earning extra money, were unexpectedly in demand as strikers to curry and comb the swiftest mounts. Horseracing became an obsession at the garrison.

All the soldiers were constantly on the alert to find a pack of wild horses. Nothing would give them more pleasure than capturing one of these regal beasts and breaking him for their own. One method used was a grand hunting maneuver called "ringing the horse." Julia had never seen it but one soldier explained it this way. A pack of about twenty-five men quietly and secretly stationed themselves about fifty yards apart in a ring about three miles in circumference, so as to surround the game. They must take incredible care because the horses would be easily spooked by scent or movement. Two or three hunters then would ride toward the wild animals, causing them to bound away in the opposite direction. Then a soldier would present himself on the other side, turning the horses back, again and again. They were continuously checked at every point, running in circles until they tired, and it became possible for the men to lasso them. It would only take two or three days to subdue the free running creatures and tame them to the docility the men required. This had become the favored way of increasing the herd at the garrison, but having witnessed the horses' wild liberty on the prairie, it made Julia rather sad to think about the process of crushing their exuberant spirit.

On Saturday afternoon at two o'clock the owners led their steeds to the starting line of the racetrack. Already, the drum and bugle corps were performing a little set of songs to get everyone in a jolly mood, but few needed much help. The horses wore decorations in the favorite colors of their masters in whatever form could be mustered together --- yarn braided in the tail, cotton pompoms in the bridles or felt wrapped around the halter.

Since army regulations didn't cover horseracing, uniforms were few and far between; instead, the men's hats and shirts in all shapes and hues, like a ragtag assortment for a quilting bee. Some sported the colors of their state flag, which Julia observed generally meant a lot of blue. South Carolina's flag displayed a palmetto emblem on a background of blue and white, and today Pierce and his horse both sported blue and white cockades.

A picnic would follow the race, and so the few women present arrived with hampers full of pies, cakes and muffins. The army kitchen had set up a long buffet table under the trees and already the scent of roasting venison wafted from a charcoal fire. Several privates with notebooks and bulging pockets blatantly worked the crowd organizing a flurry of casual wagering. Catching sight of the Nicks family's arrival in a buckboard, Julia jumped up and waved them over to join her picnic. Sarah wandered in her direction while her husband headed for the stable.

A bay, a sorrel and a chestnut pranced by, all beautifully turned out for the day. Cavalry officers took great pride in their riding style and their mounts. A new cavalryman would draw a lot of ridicule until he could ride properly, which meant an erect carriage, a perfect seat and an ease and grace where a lithe form swayed with every motion of the horse.[23]

Every day after breakfast the cavalrymen donned their white malodorous stable rig to tend their animals while the infantry busied themselves cleaning muddy boots, weapons or other odd jobs until guard mounting. Julia wondered why white was the chosen color for such a filthy job. The horses were lashed tight to a heavy picket rope outside the stalls while the men wielded stiff brushes and currycombs until the animals' coats gleamed. In the winter they would take good care to leave the heavy undercoat of fur as protection against the harsh cold prairie winds. Some of the officers chose to hire strikers to take care of this messy work, but Pierce and others enjoyed the chore. It was often a favorite time of day, a time of comraderie for men and animals. And today provided an occasion to trot out their hard work.

"I don't know which is more handsome," Julia exclaimed, "the men or the horses."

"They certainly all look beautiful today," Sarah agreed, "but I do worry at the races. These fellows are all so competitive!"

"I expect Pierce and John will be careful. After all, they have us to return to."

"Or to show off for!" Sarah countered.

"Pierce wants me to learn to ride tight in the saddle, the army way, he calls it," Julia said. "He thinks it is easier to ride for a longer distance in that style. But so far, I cannot break the habit of posting."

"It sounds like you're a good horsewoman. You should give me riding lessons and I'll give you shooting lessons," Sarah offered.

"Good heavens, whoever said I wanted to learn to shoot?"

"Believe me, you do," Sarah warned. "It's generally safe around here but everyone will feel more comfortable if you know how to handle a gun."

Sarah had placed Eliza on a blanket spread upon the clover, and the little girl kicked her legs freely, cooing at the branches and sky above. Sarah pulled down the baby's sunbonnet to cover more of her little pink face and stroked the chubby thighs.

Julia pulled a handkerchief from her pocket and wiped perspiration from her brow. "Walela is bringing us some water soon, I hope. I am already parched."

Indeed, the day was warm and beads of perspiration showed on Sarah's upper lip. As summertime wore on, the humidity became more and more uncomfortable. The two women moved their blanket further into the umbrageous canopy of the tree and watched the growing crowd. Standing close to the track, Pierce held Chester's reins loosely in his fingers and talked to another officer, whom Julia didn't recognize. William, who was competing also, dropped by their cool oasis to show off his horse, Calhoun, named after President Monroe's Secretary of War. Somehow he had found red, white and yellow feathers, which he had attached to Calhoun's mane, to represent Maryland's colors. Calhoun stood about fifteen hands high and towered over their group below.

"I'm feeling lucky today, Julia," William bragged. "You should bet on me." Having apparently lost the battle over her marriage to Pierce, for the moment at least, he seemed to want to remain a part of the family.

"I shall leave the wagers to the men," she said, "but I shall wish you luck. You and that big animal certainly make a handsome pair."

"Thank you. I wish Harriet and the girls were here today," he lamented, gazing down at Eliza. "They would enjoy this too."

"I am sure you do," Julia sympathized. "Perhaps we could arrange for them to visit this summer."

"I've been thinking more about that," he grinned. "But there is probably not enough time. Well, I'm off." He grabbed Calhoun's mane with his left hand, put his left foot in the stirrup and swung his right leg over the tall horse's back as though it were one graceful movement.

John Nick's was the next to stop by to receive their good wishes for the race. He and his horse were both stocky types and presented more muscle than sinew. The broad chest of his black steed, Warrior, glistened in the sunlight, and John had cleverly woven some little sparkling Mexican silver coins along the top of the animal's neck.

"Isn't he a beauty?" he asked the women, stroking Warrior's nose.

"He is gorgeous," Julia admitted. "There are so many worthy candidates, I can't imagine who will win." She happened to glance down at Eliza. "Oh, do be careful! There's a wasp." She waved her hand at the insect threatening the baby.

"Oh, I know," moaned Sarah. "It's a constant worry. They seem to know she tastes sweet. Gallanippers too."

The bugles called the horses and onlookers to the starting line where momentary chaos reigned as all jostled for their places.

A gunshot in the air startled Eliza who began screaming as the steeds thundered away. Sarah immediately put the babe to her breast to calm her.

The course included a straightaway toward a clump of trees, then a longer country portion with a few jumps over a stile and across a stream, a length along a dirt road usually used by everyone, and eventually back to the straightaway where the starting line doubled as the finish line. The entire race took about ten minutes and everyone stood around waiting until the horsemen reappeared down the road.

On they came, the horses' broad chests looming larger and larger and a thicket of spindly knobby legs moving rapidly below. The noise became deafening as all hooted and hollered for their favorite. Julia found herself jumping up and down, waving her hat in the air, and yelling for Pierce to Run, Run, Run. Edward appeared next to her and poked her with his elbow, grinned, and began yelling for William.

Suddenly Edward picked up Walela, who was standing next to him. Clearly she couldn't see over the men in front of her and though she hadn't complained, he leant a helping boost. Her hands involuntarily closed over his large ones encircling her small waist. He held her up in the air for a moment, then slowly lowered her to the ground in front of him. He wanted to continue holding her, but she stepped lightly aside. "Thank you," she smiled up into his eyes. Julia had not been too distracted by the oncoming racers to miss the poignancy of this moment but she hurriedly turned her eyes back to the track.

Julia realized she very much wanted Walela at her wedding. In fact, the Indian girl had become her closest female friend and constant companion at Cantonnement Gibson. Even though they came from such different cultures, they chatted so comfortably and Julia's intuition told her she could always depend on Walela. No wonder Edward was so drawn to her. Perhaps it was going too far to ask her to be her maid of honor, but she would like to invite Walela, her mother, brother and Chief Jolly to the wedding if Pierce agreed.

When she spied Pierce among the leading pack, the tumult and furor became intoxicating. So much horseflesh barreling towards them, so much noise, so much color and heat and dust. She thought she might swoon. And suddenly it was over, the winner unknown to her, Pierce second and William third. John Nicks and Warrior, his sweating flanks shining like black lacquer, thundered by in the second pack and Julia rushed over to Pierce as he dismounted. Pulling a blue and white cockade from Calhoun's bridle, he presented it to Julia.

"Oh, darling, this is extraordinary," she trilled. "I don't know when I've enjoyed a race so much. You know, we're serious about our horses in Maryland, but this was so exciting!"

"Doggone, I wanted first for you," he grumbled.

"You are first for me!" Indeed, her cheeks were red with heat and thrill and her eyes gleamed. Pierce laughed and gave her a bear hug. Everything seemed to be more impromptu and less formal today. The fillies were being called for their race, and all crowded to the starting line again. Julia, of course, rooted for Cinder though she didn't know her rider well, and none of the winners were even acquaintances. The fort was a big place.

Wandering over to their picnic spot, Julia and Pierce found Sarah, John, Edward and Walela already there. The men swigged from canteens, and Julia suspected they contained plenty of heavy wet[24] and even spirits. Walela had brought two jugs of cool water for the women. William strolled over and tied up Calhoun before joining the others under the tree.

Julia observed Edward doing little nice things for Walela all afternoon. He offered to go and get water for everyone and suggested she relax on the blanket with the other women. Walela actually remained on her knees, never "relaxing" and always helping to serve the food. She invariably jumped up to pass dishes and remove trash out of the way. When Julia told everyone about the Cherokee village school, she included Walela in the conversation, and the girl graciously joined in.

"Yes," she said, "it's true, the children want to learn English very much, and Miss Du Val has won their hearts."

"I don't know about that, but they are all bright and adorable. I wish I could teach them every day but it is too far. And there is more to present than I ever have time for."

"Perhaps you should give them more to do at home," Walela suggested. "I am sure they will work hard."

"Beats me why you're bothering," William said, rather rudely, taking another swig from his canteen. From the color of his face and the perspiration on his forehead, Julia suspected the canteen did not hold water. "It won't do any good."

"I don't know what you mean," Julia chided. "Of course it will. You have to be able to speak to one another to understand each other, and I doubt if the Whites are going to learn Cherokee."

"Just my point," William sniped. "Their days are numbered."

Julia was mortified for Walela and furious with her brother, but for once she chose to ignore him rather than argue. This conversation would be better in private. Edward, however, could not restrain a comment.

"William you would do well, I think, to remember Jefferson's admonition: 'In all your intercourse with the natives, treat them in the most friendly and conciliatory manner which their own conduct will permit'[25] is how he phrased it, I think."

William guffawed. "I think it's rather hypocritical for you to take the high tone with me, Edward."

Pierce intervened. "Well, William, I thought our work at Cantonnement Gibson was meant to assure that the Cherokee's days aren't numbered, as you put it."

Mercifully, Eliza gurgled providing a welcome distraction, and Julia asked if she could hold her.

"Of course," Sarah smiled.

"Isn't she a bonny wee lass?" Eliza's proud father asked of his friends.

"Indeed," Pierce replied. "You are a lucky man, John, and I am too," he nuzzled Julia a little behind her ear until she swatted him gently.

The entire afternoon passed in a lazy blissful haze except for William's outburst. At dusk the gallanippers made their presence known with a vengeance and everyone packed up to retreat indoors. Pierce accompanied Julia home and with some malaise, she watched Edward accompany Walela away from the post. How on earth would he solve his emotional predicament?

CHAPTER TWENTY-SIX
WAITING

FOR THE next two weeks Julia had the strange sensation that she was waiting for her life to begin, absurd in that she had thought of herself as a busy complete person all of her life. Still, beginning again with a partner changed her outlook on the world to such an extent that it made her reconsider her life up until this moment. Of course it didn't make sense to negate her past because now she would be married, but she had to acknowledge she felt whole in a way she never had been conscious of before. Every day she felt somewhat anxious until her eyes beheld Pierce beside her.

Twice each week before the wedding, she managed to catch a ride with Edward to instruct the Cherokee children. Every time she arrived, their faces turned up like bright sunflowers, would be waiting for her at the summer-house platform. As she came to know them individually, she delighted in their achievements, yet her concern over particular health issues increased. One little fellow clearly had an infected foot, which had not been cleaned properly. After school Julia talked him into letting her wash the wound, but then his mother rushed over and grabbed him away from her. She could not afford to alienate the parents but then again, she ought not to allow such a glaring danger to go unattended. Encouraging Walela to make the boy soak the foot in water as hot as he could stand, she let the matter be for the moment.

Then health problems at the fort overwhelmed her concerns

at the Indian village. One of Pierce's Company B was diagnosed with typhoid fever and the chill of fear gripped the garrison. Typhoid was a known scourge of the military, where people living in close proximity to one another were often careless with sanitary practices. A number of others in the company began to complain of headache, constipation, and myalgia and all were immediately clapped in the infirmary.

When William dropped by one evening, Julia was delighted until he too began to complain of a certain malaise, and she asked if he felt feverish.

"Could be," he admitted. "You know, one of the worst outbreaks of typhoid in the history of the world took place in Athens during their war with Sparta. The Athenian leader, Pericles, died of typhoid, as did about one-third of the Athenian city population, tipping the balance of power to the Spartans. Now that's a powerful disease," he quipped.

"It's not a joking matter, William," Julia snapped. "I'm very glad you came to see me, but please, get yourself over to the infirmary right away!"

"Will do. I must admit I'm feeling worse by the minute."

When he left, Julia tried not to panic. She knew the disease could be fatal, but she didn't know much else. It must be very contagious though because the doctor had quarantined the ill soldiers immediately. She routinely boiled all the water she drank and stored it in a jar in her room, but she doubted if the kitchen were so careful. Perhaps they would be now!

When Edward arrived to drive her to the Indian village the next morning, he had not heard of William's illness and didn't know if he had been kept overnight at the hospital.

"I shall go and see when we return this evening," he promised.

The children found the scissors Julia brought over that morning as fascinating as she did their tweezers. To an Indian, a hairless body epitomized the height of beauty, and they spent hours pulling out hair with beautiful tweezers made from clamshells, brought from the east coast. She also enjoyed observing the women dye wool with various vegetable dyes, bloodroot and pokeberries for red, walnut bark for black and *indigofera* for blue. She asked one old lady whom she particularly liked to make a red, black and white rug for her and Pierce's new home. The woman seemed delighted with the commission.

Watching several of the children frolicking around, letting off steam after school, Julia noticed a few of the older ones had been put to work helping their mothers. One of the older boys called Blowing Wind, probably about age 10, with whom she had experienced some bullying problems, pushed a younger boy to the ground. Julia rushed over to the little one to help him up and spoke severely to Blowing Wind. As soon as she turned around, Blowing Wind gave the smaller boy another shove.

Edward, having arrived in time to witness the entire sequence, grabbed Blowing Wind by the arm and raised his hand as though to strike the boy on the bottom. The boy cowered. Edward's hand stopped in mid-air when he heard Walela shout "No!" She ran over and grabbed Edward's arm. Edward let go of Blowing Wind as though the boy were a burning ember and the child skittered away.

"You must not strike him," she said quietly, pulling Edward aside and nervously looking around to see if anyone else had seen. Fortunately, only Julia appeared to be aware of what had occurred.

"You must never whip a Cherokee in public because it will be too humiliating," she explained. "Even when an adult commits an offensive act, the punishment is exile or death. A public lashing would be thought worse, the shame unbearable for the offender and his family."

Edward's huge hands hung at his sides and he looked like a guilty child. "I am sorry, Walela." He shook his head in some confusion. "I did know that, and I've been here long enough to remember. I guess sometimes my society's instincts take the upper hand. I'm really sorry."

"I understand," she said and started to take his hand to console him. Then she too pulled her hand back quickly. Instead, Julia took her brother's hand and together they walked away, heading toward their horses for the ride home.

"I see how difficult this all is, Eddie. Now I am the one worried about you. You slink around looking like you're carrying the willow for Walela.[26]

"No," he muttered, in a thoroughly bad humor. "You cannot say I'm carrying the willow because I have not been rejected. And that's because I have not declared myself yet."

"Maybe that's just as well, Edward," Julia surmised.

"I doubt if I can let it be, Sis. And by the way, I've been meaning to say, just let me know what you need to help make your wedding a happy occasion."

"Oh, Eddie, thank you, thank you." She gave him a one-armed hug around his waist. "Of course I wish you could bring William around, but at least I am grateful he didn't carry out his duel threat. He really frightened me. But now he's scaring me more with this sickness. How bad can it be?"

"Pretty bad. You get a very high fever that can last for weeks. I know the death rate for typhoid is alarmingly high, but perhaps only for those who are not properly taken care of. Unfortunately, I think we're going to learn more about it soon."

They rode on home in an anxious but companionable silence.

THE NEXT day, after a breakfast of beef hash, dry bread and coffee, Colonel Arbuckle called the usual daily conference for the old and new officers of the day and invited the Indian Agent to attend. The officers never objected to these meetings because it offered a chance for an after-breakfast smoke. A few of the officers used long clay pipes to keep the smoke further from their faces but most of them, like the enlisted men, chewed their tobacco and spat on the floor. Two outstanding issues were on the agenda for Capt. Du

Val's attention, the murder of Red Hawk being the most pressing.

Having worked feverishly with the knotty problem for weeks, Edward intensely hoped the Cherokee would be satisfied with the settlement over the demise of their kinsman. He realized he was motivated by more than wanting to do a good job--- he needed the approval of Chief Jolly and Red Fox. The Quarter Master had been holding the prisoner at Cantonnement Gibson now for more than two weeks, still awaiting word from President John Quincy Adams for a resolution to the issue.

Edward informed the assembled officers that everyone in Washington City agreed it was critical to stop the feuding between the Osage and the Cherokee. The consensus was that peace on the frontier would facilitate persuading other eastern tribes to vacate their lands and move west. Neither Monroe before him nor Adams, who had become President in 1825, wished to force the Indians off their land but rather hoped to convince them of the benefits of life in the Indian Territory. Still, this continued to be a difficult idea to sell.

Colonel Arbuckle entertained another theory which he proceeded to put forth. He believed that continued strife had some value. He saw it as an escape valve for the many restless spirits among the different tribes on the frontier who would be employed in war or mischief of some kind no matter what. Furthermore, he argues, the arrival of large numbers of eastern Indians would eventually compel the plains tribes to seek peace.

Indian Agent Du Val asked to speak again. "For some reason I remembered today and want to remind you all of the words of Tatschaga, a leader of the Osage, a tribe, which, you know, once occupied vast stretches of grassland west of the Mississippi. Tatschaga was summoned to Washington in 1806 and then taken on a tour of the East. Addressing the senate chamber of Massachusetts that year, he said something like this, 'Our complexions differ from yours, but our hearts are the same color, and you ought to love us for we are the original true Americans.' Two years later the Americans took by treaty all Osage land between the Missouri and Arkansas rivers.[27] I certainly can understand their continuing anger. That, my good men, is what we have to deal with."

After some discussion Colonel Arbuckle summed up at the end of the meeting with what was obvious to everyone --- there was nothing they could do even if they totally agreed with one another until they heard from the President. "There is one additional matter," Arbuckle added, "which I would like to address. There are rumors among the Indian population about the typhoid fever at Cantonnement Gibson. We should not try and hide it or deny it. However, the Cherokee are saying our Great White Father has turned his face from us and we are not so powerful after all. We must be vigilant and strictly enforce the quarantine. We must take every measure not to appear weakened. Company dismissed."

Edward grimaced inwardly. *They may be right that we are not so powerful after all if this disease gained a foothold inside the fort.*

JULIA HURRIED over to a free-standing small stone building, which served as the infirmary, to visit William. She wanted to do something to nurse him back to health, and she had been dissatisfied with the scant information Edward had obtained from the hospital. A nurse met her at the door and refused her entry. "Everyone here is quarantined," she affirmed.

"But I am a close member of Captain Butler's family," Julia informed the nurse.

"That doesn't matter. Only medical personnel may enter."

Julia felt frightened and useless. If many soldiers were sick, she worried that William would receive little personal care and suffer more than necessary. She understood the rules, but questioned if such draconian measures were really called for. So many sick soldiers made it impossible for the nurses to issue personal bulletins, and Julia was impatient, simply having to wait until her brother was released from the infirmary. She wiped away a frustrated worried tear as she headed back home. And what of

Pierce? He was exposed daily to his men building the road and they didn't know how the disease was spread from one person to another. What lurking dangers was her fiancé exposed to out on the worksite? She felt like she would explode with so many questions fraught with alarm.

CHAPTER TWENTY-SEVEN
CELEBRATION

THE NIGHT before her wedding Julia fought off fleeting feelings of sadness, then shame for such weakness. At home in Mt. Pleasant this would have been an evening of gaiety with friends and family, she would have dressed up and been the center of attention, she and her mother and sister would have been in a happy frenzy of preparation and delighted anticipation. She would be introducing Pierce to people she had known forever, showing him off with pride and unfettered happiness. Also, she admitted to herself she would have welcomed standing with him before the neighbors who had considered her an old maid when she left.

Instead, this evening unfurled silently except for the trill of a flying friend or two outside. She smiled thinking of one of her favorite little Indian students whose name was Talks With Birds. Well, there were worse things to do. True, Pierce would come by just before tattoo after tending to a delivery of timber that had arrived all wet. Edward was too busy, and William, although better, was still too weak to socialize.

What a relief that had been! He had been laid low, as had many, but the garrison appeared to have avoided an epidemic. For that blessing, she thanked God daily. Also, William's sickness seemed to have subdued some of his anger, and he even said he was resting up so he could attend the wedding. Lying in bed, dependent on others had clearly knocked some of the arrogance out of him, and he must have come to understand he truly did not want to risk estrangement from his sister.

She knew it was extraordinary that Colonel Arbuckle had agreed to relieve everyone of duty tomorrow, --- except, of course, the post guard --- for the ceremony and party afterwards. The minister would arrive tomorrow in the morning, and Sarah would come over early to help her dress. Indeed, she would wear Sarah's wedding dress, which the two women had worked on feverishly this past week, altering it for Julia. Sarah stood at least four inches taller than Julia, but the two women shared slim frames and long waists, so after all, it proved not too complicated. Since there had not been time to order a gown from the East, Julia felt extremely grateful to find a genuine wedding dress so close by.

All that matters really is Pierce, she told herself, yet the absence of her family, especially her mother, left an extraordinary hollow which just would not be ignored. Pierce admitted he would miss his family too, primarily his brother, Andrew Pickens, who also could not make such a long trip for the occasion. Julia knew she shouldn't whine at all with Edward and William here, but everything was so different from what she had always imagined. Still, she knew this marriage was right for her.

When Pierce did arrive, she clung to him like moss to a rock. "Hey, little one," he said, "I'm not going anywhere."

"I know. I'm just feeling a little lonely."

"Don't worry, Julia. I shall always be with you," he promised, holding her close and stroking her hair. He pulled away and looked down at her. "But of course the groom can't see the bride until the ceremony, and we are very careful to observe our superstitions in the army."

Julia laughed which helped dispel her nervous butterflies. "How well I know! Like not announcing your engagement on a Friday. That is the silliest yet!"

Just the sight of his honest, serious and loving face calmed her tremendously, enabling her to go to bed looking forward to the morrow rather than concentrating on the regrets.

The next morning, carrying the dress and the baby, Sarah arrived all bustling and flustered. Placing Eliza on a blanket on the floor, the two women embraced and giggled with excitement. Sarah and the baby had made an effort over the past weeks to come and visit the fort and Julia had reciprocated whenever possible. The growing closeness obviously pleased both women.

"Oh, my dear, you sure have brightened up this drab place." Sarah began to unbutton the many, many, tiny buttons running down the back of the white silk dress. More little buttons at the wrists of the tapered long sleeves occupied her while Julia pulled on a petticoat. When the long dress whispered over her head and slid down her side, Julia felt it a transforming moment. She couldn't see her whole self in the little mirror above her dressing table but she popped up and down, turned around and around, seeing the bodice, which came to a V-shape at the small of the back and then with a bit of a flare and flounce, fell all the way to the floor in a modified train. Walela appeared at the door, asking shyly if she might help too.

"Of course," Julia happily agreed. "Otherwise we shall never get all these buttons done."

"You look so beautiful," Walela murmured.

Since any city where one might order special flowers and hats was far too distant, Julia had woven a crown of wild white and yellow daisies for her hair, and she would carry a bouquet of long stalks of soap weed tied with a ribbon of white silk, which they had cut off the bottom of the gown. The huge white blossoms lacked perfume, but arranged with a few other wild flowers, looked both dramatic and sweet.

"Oh, my dear, if you only knew how gorgeous you look," Sarah sighed, her eyes tearing a little. Eliza apparently thought so too as she gazed with rapture at the white apparition floating above her. Julia dabbed her eyes too, hugging Sarah, then Walela. "I cannot thank you both enough."

"I know. I know. Now we just have to wait for that infernal bugle call," Sarah said, picking up Eliza. "I'll wait until later to put on her Christening dress. She'll make a mess of it in two shakes of a lamb's tail."

The bugle made them jump when it finally blared, and Edward and William arrived on cue as Walela faded into the background. Suddenly feeling extremely nervous, Julia held on to one hand of both men as they made their way across the grass to the Parade Ground inside the fort. Almost immediately she had to release her hands in order to hold her wedding dress above the burrs and grasshoppers.

All the guests stood waiting in the stockade square. As Julia and her brothers approached the gates and waited at the opening, the bugles announced her entry. The sun glinted off gold buttons and epaulettes, blinding the bride for a moment. A sea of soldiers' blue coats parted to make the aisle wider and Julia beheld Pierce standing straight with Reverend Cephus Washburn next to him. On his other side stood John Nicks who professed himself most honored to be the best man. When it came to choosing someone for this job, Julia understood for the first time that her husband-to-be was somewhat of a loner and had no really close friends at the garrison.

Pierce stood as straight as the fort's pickets. In 1821 blue had been decreed the national color and the army dress coat was a single breasted blue coatee with silver lace loops down the front. The jacket fastened with ten white metal buttons with black twist loops, and the blue collar edged with white stood high, touching his jaw bones. Julia passed sergeants wearing a yellow epaulette on the right shoulder and corporals with their epaulettes on the left, all wearing *chacos* blazing with a yellow metal eagle plate in the center, with a white plume and white cords and chin scales. She was so accustomed to seeing the soldiers in their work clothes, the shifting scene appeared both startling and touching.

Rev. Washburn held an open Prayer Book but there was no altar, just the blue sky above and a runner of white canvas on the bare ground. Someone, bless them, thought Julia, had scattered a few wild daisy petals up the makeshift aisle. Sarah, serving as matron of honor, stood opposite John Nicks. Julia placed her hands through each brother's arm as Pierce's eyes drew her forward. She almost reached out to him upon arriving beside him, but caught herself to wait for Edward and William to give her away.

The familiar words of the ceremony were comforting as was the earnestness of her groom's expression as he promised to love her "In sickness and in health". Just when she felt she had recovered her emotional balance, Pierce slipped the ring on her finger, and it was almost over. "I now pronounce you man and wife," the Reverend announced. "You may now kiss the bride."

The drums rolled and the couple turned around to find an arch of crossed sabers while the bugles chortled happily and everyone clapped and clapped. Everything seemed to be happening at high speed in a blur, and Julia held Pierce's hand tightly as they moved together under their unique sword canopy. As they made the return trip down the aisle, she spotted her colorful Cherokee friends and felt a rush of joy that they had come. For Walela, Julia had a special smile.

When they reached the wedding cake, Pierce unsheathed his saber and handed it to her, handle first, then guided her hand as the saber's blade sliced through the fluffy icing and moist sweet cake. It was only a sheet cake, but it tasted amazingly good, and Julia expected the cook must have added extra eggs and taken special care. When man and wife were handed glasses of champagne, only recently arrived at William's store, Pierce handed the saber to Edward. As they hooked their arms together to offer the first sips to one another, Julia felt like she was in a dream.

What a glorious afternoon! The weather cooperated completely, offering occasional soft breezes and fluffy clouds like the icing on the cake. Though Julia didn't know most of the people at her wedding, they all joined in wishing her and Pierce a world of happiness. The momentous ceremony recalled family for everyone and the party offered fun and good spirits to the assembled guests while also providing an occasion to cement good will and peace with their neighboring Indian tribes. Pierce liked her idea of inviting the Cherokee, but only if she would also extend her hospitality to include the Osage and Creek chiefs. Perfect, she thought, and Edward and Colonel Arbuckle thought so too.

If only she could have a picture of the Indian costumes to preserve this memory! She regretted not finding an artist to record the color on this day. Some of the Osage men wore trade cloth shirts instead of suede. The shirts were appliquéd with bright silk ribbons, making the Indian men much flashier than the women, as in the bird kingdom, Julia thought. The Creek finery was altogether different, with floral designs cutout of trade cloth and sewn on a solid background to make a shirt or dress resemble a veritable garden.

When the fiddler picked up his instrument and called for a Grand March, everyone hollered for Pierce and Julia to come to the front and then all paraded around after them feeling silly and joyful. The musicians followed with a Virginia Reel, a polka and then unleashed a Scottish and a gallop. Julia had to pick up her dress and launch forth hoping for the best. When a caller came forward, he instructed everyone they would do a new square dance based on the European Quadrille. After much awkwardness at first, soon everyone wanted to participate.

> *Swing the other gal,*
> *Swing her sweet!*
> *Paw dirt, doggies,*
> *Stomp your feet.*
> *Ladies in the center,*
> *Gents round 'em run.*
> *Swing her rope, cowboy*
> *And get yo' one!*

Pierce handed over his bride to each brother for a dance and she felt so proud of all of them. The Indians stood around gaping but Julia noticed Chief Jolly's foot tapping. Edward bowed in front of Walela and asked Red Fox if he might dance with her. The Indian brave broke his stony stance to nod his head, and Edward led Walela out to the floor. He wanted to weep with happiness having her small hand in his. She seemed to move naturally and instinctively with him, and he silently thanked Red Fox for the generous gift of this moment. The open spirit of the day must have prompted this singular acquiescence.

Walela's dress of soft and supple doeskin exhibited intricate colorful quillwork which must have taken many moons to make. Edward had watched the work in her village, awed at the dexterity necessary to achieve the flat geometric designs from the dyed and unflattened quills. The artisans used awls as they inserted the quills into the material at both sharp ends, then pressed them flat with a heavy iron, instead of pulling the quill with a needle like a thread. The intricate finished product truly amazed him.

At one point late in the party the threat of a brawl between two drunken soldiers marred the mood, but the officers managed to break it up quickly and benevolent humors again prevailed. The dancing had become so popular that it had spread beyond the dance floor and all too quickly a fair amount of dust was kicked up by the drumming boots. The bottom of Julia's dress acquired a dark brown stripe at the edge, but she cheerfully decided not to worry about it.

After the festivities, Sarah escorted Julia back to her little room to help her change. She began unbuttoning all the tiny buttons down the back while Julia stood quietly.

"What an overwhelming day," Julia finally voiced. "It doesn't seem real yet."

"I know," Sarah said. "It will seem strange for awhile. I presume you know about the birds and the bees, Julia, having lived on a farm and all." Sarah looked uncommonly uncomfortable. "I hesitate to bring it up, but you are without any of your family here."

Julia tittered nervously, glad she wasn't face-to-face with her friend. "Yes, I do, and you are sweet to try and fill the breach."

Sarah looked relieved not to have to continue the subject. "Well, if you love one another, everything else always works out, I think," she declared in her usual matter-of-fact tone. "Now, let's get you dressed. That husband of yours isn't going to wait half the night!"

"And I cannot wait to see him!" Julia laughed gaily, hurrying to pull on a suit skirt of yellow cotton with a lace blouse under the fitted jacket. Somehow Pierce had managed to hire a carriage drawn by four horses to take them to a home nearby where they would spend a week. The house belonged to an officer presently on leave, and they hoped he would stay away longer than now planned. It was only a little over a half-hour's ride from the Fort, and Pierce could travel daily. Colonel Arbuckle thought he had done enough with the wedding on the Parade Ground and refused the groom more than one day's leave.

The wagon horses were decorated with white daisies in their manes, and when everyone waved goodbye, Julia felt truly like a Queen. And she also couldn't believe their good luck with the house. "I cannot imagine a more perfect wedding," she murmured, snuggling closer to Pierce on the buggy's bench.

"Nor I," he said. "You are positively enchanting."

Before her experience at the fort, this abode, which would be their honeymoon cottage, would have seemed abysmally lacking. But as they pulled up to the humble door, Julia thought it looked charming. They had three rooms all their own: a "parlor," a bedroom and a kitchen, which was really just an alcove off the parlor with a wide fireplace for cooking. Life would center around the fireplace equipped with heavy wrought andirons to support the logs and a lug pole with an assortment of hooks, chains and trammels hanging from it. A shovel to remove ashes, tongs to shift logs and a pair of bellows to fan the embers were piled at one end of the hearth, and an odd assemblage of darkened dented pots and pans and a cauldron were scattered around the hearth. There was even an outdoor privy and curtains at the windows – one in every room – and Indian rugs on the floor. Julia poked about in the larder, finding a few staples laid in. Having looked around the cookery and parlor about all she could, she realized with chagrin that she was avoiding the bedroom. Don't be a ninny, she chided herself and headed immediately toward the chamber.

A double bed, a chair and a dresser almost filled the small

room, but a hooked rug on the floor, a blue cotton coverlet and a flowered cushion on the chair cheered the place considerably. She turned to her husband. "Oh, darling, this is perfect. Listen to me! That is the second time I remember saying 'perfect' today."

"Well, let's see if you can say it again." Pierce pulled her to him, enfolding her in a deep kiss. When they came up for air, she said softly, "Perfect."

Feeling very warm, she removed her jacket and hung it upon the back of the chair. She knew her lace blouse suited her figure and was more revealing that what she usually wore. Pierce's admiring and longing look confirmed her thought and excited and emboldened her. When he took her in his arms again and his hand slipped down over her breast, she crushed her body against him, forgetting her modesty. At long last she could run her hands through his hair. He pulled her even closer and then they were undressing one another gently but hurriedly. "My precious wife," he said.

"My beautiful husband," she answered. The night enclosed the little house and embraced the loving couple. It didn't matter where on the earth she was, Julia thought, as long as she was with Pierce.

CHAPTER TWENTY-EIGHT
LONELY

EVER SINCE the wedding Walela felt strangely disquieted, experiencing an odd sense of dislocation. She knew Julia and Pierce to be honeymooning, and the thought made her uncomfortable. Even if Miss Du Val, --- she must remember it was Mrs. Butler now --- were back in her old room at the fort, she knew she wouldn't feel like going to work. It seemed like she had been left behind, abandoned, in some way, but of course that was ridiculous.

How exhilarating the marriage celebration had been --- and she had been such an intimate part of it, helping Julia dress, (in her own mind, she often thought of them as Edward and Julia and needed to censor their given names from her speech), and standing close by when Rev. Washburn read the vows, even swaying to the music when everyone danced afterward. How much she had secretly longed for Edward to dance with her, and then suddenly, there he was, standing before her asking permission of Red Fox. She had been so nervous, not knowing the steps of some of the western dances, she couldn't think of anything else but the dance. Since then, she had relived the experience one hundred times, trying to dredge up every detail from her startled memory.

Walela wandered around her village aimlessly for a week, lonely in the midst of her community and greatly worrying her mother. She should probably send a note to Julia at the cottage, but she wasn't really sure Julia expected her. She would pretend to be busy making corn cakes, but suddenly her hands would become still and she would gaze blankly toward the river. Finally Mrs. Bushyhead could bear it no longer and asked her daughter if she would not welcome a visit from the shaman. Surely an evil spirit must have entered her daughter's body for the light had disappeared from her eyes.

"No, kind mother, truly, I am not sick," Walela answered. But Mrs. Bushyhead did not believe her.

THE SUMMER wore on, with dry hot days and long evenings accompanied by noisy cicadas strumming in the trees. Julia loved the late daylight because it meant more hours for the men to work on their house. Also, it meant dinners outside watching for the first stars to appear. Not knowing much about the heavens, Pierce enchanted her as he whispered the names of constellations, outlining them with his finger. She brought a lantern out to the table and lazy conversation continued as the shadows lengthened and darkened. Mosquitoes could be a problem and so she hung strips of sarsaparilla from the trees and put sweet woodruff on the table.

Julia made a trip up to the fort the following week, accompanied by Pierce, in order to shop at Sutler Nicks' and to gather vegetables from the garden. She spied Walela's aunt on Colonel Arbuckle's porch and hurried over to talk to her. When Julia pressed about when she thought Walela would return to work, the woman, polite but equivocating, said Mrs. Bushyhead needed her to help at home right now.

"Well, please tell her to hurry back," Julia urged. "We all miss her." Oh dear, she thought, perhaps she shouldn't have said "we." What she had meant to be a warm conversation felt strained and awkward. "Well, goodbye," she ended dispiritedly.

As Julia headed home with her purchases, she smiled to herself. She loved the Indian beaded saddlebag she had purchased at Chouteau's store. No one made much of a fuss anymore about her riding alone to and from the fort. It was just too impractical to chaperone her everywhere, and she had proven she could get along fine on her own. Women were treated too much like children, she thought. If they only had the opportunity to show others (and themselves!) how capable they could be, many would be surprised. Yet, at times, she must admit she didn't feel so much bravado. But she liked being given a chance. As soon as she returned home, who should turn up on her doorstep but Edward.

"Well, Julia, I guess we should be happy you are safely married and you are Pierce's responsibility now, but I sure miss having you right underfoot at the Cantonnement."

"Thank you Edward. I rather miss it too," she admitted, "but here we have some privacy and at last, I can cook. In fact, why don't you stay for supper. I'm making prairie hen and spinach I picked from Lt. Munro's garden. He says I am always welcome to take what I need."

"My, aren't you the privileged gal. And what other favors have you finagled by flirting with the officers?"

Julia swatted him and he dodged the gentle blow with a laugh. "So, where's Walela? I thought she would be helping you here."

"I thought so too, but when I saw her aunt today, she said something about Walela needing to help her mother, who seems like a perfectly capable, healthy woman to me. Whoops! I guess the same thing could be said about me." Julia paused, pondering the obvious.

"Hmm," said Edward.

"Look!" Julia led him to the hearth. "Sarah gave me a good skillet and a kettle, and I have written mother with a request for her to send me a few more kitchen implements." As Edward regarded a large heavy pot astride the andirons heating the contents in the fireplace, he immediately became aware of a lovely aroma wafting from the hearth, a scent of onions and herbs making his mouth water.

"Isn't Pierce the lucky man! Certainly. I'd be most glad to."

"Good, he's due back from the road site soon. Why don't you sit outside where it's cooler while I stir things a bit and I'll bring us some refreshments."

Edward noticed the couple had set up a little table with a few rickety chairs under the biggest tree, a linden that spread sheltering branches over a wide circle. Taking off his cap, he wiped his forehead with his handkerchief. Christ, it was humid. No ice out here in the summertime. At least in the East, they could buy ice from a fellow in Boston, who would ship it downriver, wrapped in sawdust. They would lose about 15% during the trip, but hell, that was nothing, when you could have a cold drink. How wonderful an iced lemonade would taste right now. But out here there was no such luxury. He wiped his forehead again, marveling that his sister didn't complain more about the heat, dust and flies. At least she was away from the noxious odors of too many men living together at the Post.

Julia emerged from the cottage with three glasses and some tinned pate with crackers. "I have been saving this since my arrival," she said, proudly pointing to the hors d'oeuvre, "and now seems like the right time. When Pierce arrives, we shall open the whisky too."

"A real party," said her brother. "Are you getting along all right, Julia? I do worry about you."

"Of course I am. But I do miss Walela. I'm finding it almost impossible to get everything done, gathering wood, pumping and carrying water, washing, and cleaning, but I want everything to be perfect for Pierce. I'm becoming a real drudge. I know I cannot make it as nice for him as I could at Mt. Pleasant, but . . .

"Listen, don't knock yourself out. You're not used to doing this kind of heavy work, and I am sure he doesn't expect it to be like back east."

"Still, I want to make a comfortable home for him. I guess the standards of social conduct I learned growing up have stuck. We are hoping the owner won't return right away and we shall be able to stay here a while longer."

"I know. By the way, I miss Walela too." Edward fidgeted with his cap on the table. "I have decided I am going to talk to her."

Julia regarded her brother. "Do you remember the novel *Rob Roy?*" she asked.

"I think so. That's the one by Sir Walter Scott about a Presbyterian young man falling in love with a Catholic girl in Scotland?"

"Exactly. A forbidden love, and it seemed totally hopeless. I have thought about it recently because, as in your situation, it was not only the religious difference, the Papists and the Presbyterians, but two nations in conflict, England and Scotland. Admittedly, it took several years, but eventually the two lovers married. I don't want to encourage you or give you false hope, but it's not unknown to happen."

Edward squinted at the sun sinking on the horizon. "Yes, but that was just a made up story. And the man and woman at least shared a similar background."

Julia nodded. "That is true. Still, I have noticed how well you and Walela seem to understand one another." She began to lather a few crackers with pate. "I hope Pierce arrives soon," she fretted.

"He will. I know I shouldn't keep on about it," Edward said. "But will you let me know when Walela comes back?"

"Of course I shall," Julia smiled and got up to give him a kiss on the cheek just as Pierce's horse emerged from the trees. As Edward watched the newlyweds tightly embrace, he felt glad for his sister but the all too familiar longing in his own heart outweighed his first altruistic impulse. He muttered an old Scots' saying under his breath, "Aye, every path has its puddle."

Julia was shocked at her husband's appearance every evening when he returned from work. She had realized immediately after their marriage that she had never seen him except all cleaned and slicked up --- never fresh from the job. He had always been careful at the fort to wash away the evidence from the roadwork site before presenting himself to her. The dust powdered his clothes and face, and the fine grit worked its way into his hair, behind his ears and stuck in his chest hair. When he would discard his grimy clothes, a walking and talking gray mummy emerged. Keeping the house clean proved nigh impossible as Pierce seemed to bring in more dirt than a furry animal when he arrived. Even with removing his boots before entering the house, Julia swept up after him, easily tracking his dusty trail.

Besides the dirt, Pierce complained of his problems with the enlisted men. Overseeing the surveyors and civil engineers had become the more interesting aspect of the project. The difficulty lay in procuring a good day's work from the bored, illiterate, and all too frequently drunken louts assigned to building the road. A few of the crew were strong men and inherently good workers, people who took pleasure in getting a job done. Pierce was extremely grateful for every fellow who exhibited these characteristics, one less he had to prod, cajole and threaten lest they knock off early or laze around the site instead of wielding a pickax, rake or shovel. One crew cleared brush and trees as soon as the surveyors determined the projected route. Another dislodged rocks and stones from the hardened flinty ground while others prepared the road the way the clever Mr. MacAdam had invented of making pavement from ground up stones.

Boredom and booze were constant enemies but health problems could also plague the project. Indeed, many men vowed they drank whisky because they couldn't trust the water, and they were probably right. Now that summer was upon them, there were mosquitoes to deal with, black flies, bees and heat prostration. The men's bodies, hard and strong from daily physical labor, could still be vulnerable to the occasional work related accident. A saw, ax or sharp shovel could be a lethal weapon, not to mention quick tempers from the heat. A snakebite could be fatal and malaria totally debilitating. The area around the fort was becoming known for its malarial pestilence. Pierce told Julia he dreaded all these things much more than a "wild" Indian.

Most days she would pump water to be ready for Pierce's bath when he returned. At least she didn't have to do the heavy laundry which he would take over to Clementine at the fort, but it seemed she never had enough water to do all she needed to do, water for drinking, bathing, cooking, washing dishes, and cleaning house. She found herself skipping baths when she really needed one because she was too tired to haul more water. When they built their own home, she would hope to find a place by a stream. It would be nice to find time to go teach again at the village and get away from all this drudgery, she thought.

About mid afternoon every day Julia began to long for Pierce's company. Having finished her major chores, she wished for his voice and conversation. When he was delayed, she began to worry; perhaps there had been an accident. Was he all right? He really was extremely late. This happened about three times a week and so she should have been used to it. But when she heard his horse's hooves, she would run out the door to greet him if she weren't already pacing in the yard. She knew it was silly to worry but he had become the most important thing in the world to her, and she needed constant assurance he was well and in good spirits.

If he seemed especially tired or worried or distraught in any way, she hastened to soothe his mind with comfort and distraction. She wanted to take care of him and if truth be told, just to look at him. She found it amazing to awake next to him at dawn, to see his thick dark hair on the white pillow and hear his quiet breathing. When she moved closer to him, the warmth and calm of his sleeping body would soothe her to sleep for another blissful hour.

Everyone had left the newlyweds alone for several weeks and tonight both Julia and Pierce found themselves greatly enjoying Edward's company. Much to Julia's relief, the fact of the marriage seemed to have changed the character of the men's relationship, and with pleasure, she watched them chatting comfortably together. She expected William would be the more prickly brother, but she hadn't predicted that Edward would be so relaxed and warmly engaged with Pierce as they discussed fort-related issues. When she suddenly laughed the two looked at her with surprise.

"I was just recalling my life in Maryland," she explained. "Where in town the streets are cobbled and lit, the houses stand close together and there are a number of well dressed people in the streets. Now these grassy plains, rude hamlets and fertile fields of corn appear more familiar to me. Instead of attending a program at the music hall, I have my own personal concert of insects. And how happy I am here!"

Edward and Pierce regarded her beaming face with some amazement and Pierce rose to go over and kiss the top of his wife's head.

"It does seem rather odd, does it not" Edward asked, "that life has united the three of us in this unlikely spot? Come to think of it, when I was a youngster, I guess I expected to become a farmer like Father. We probably all did. Then the War of 1812 changed that idea. All of a sudden soldiering took on a new importance, and I realized I might make more of a contribution to our country in the military."

"I can see that," Pierce replied. "I was only fourteen years old then, but it certainly made a difference in my family too. I remember my mother saying she would like to have just one meal without talk of defending our shores."

Edward tilted his chair back like he always did and Julia, not wanting to break the mood of quiet and open conversation, had to restrain herself from scolding him. "But when I joined the army," Edward continued, "I certainly didn't plan on becoming Indian Agent. I backed into that, you might say, and now look where it's led me. I'd say we make our choices in life but there is equal serendipity along the way. Then it is up to us what we make of it."

They all say in silence for a bit, enjoying the cicada chorus behind them.

"I imagine a lot depends on what others expect of us too,"

Pierce ruminated. A comfortable silence fell. "I think it's very important work the Indian Agents are doing out here, Edward. Even though I know the Indians will tell you their life doesn't need improving."

"That's correct," Edward agreed. "But they could rightfully argue more bad befalls them for any ounce of good we bring."

"Can't say I blame them."

"I forgot to mention. We finally heard from President Adams about his decision regarding the fate of our Osage prisoner who apparently killed a Cherokee, and it seems all are ready to be done with worrying about it. The Osage have agreed to pay a hefty fine and the Cherokee have agreed to this penalty. But it took a great deal of time for tempers to cool down from the automatic revenge killing response."

"I think your intervention surely saved the day," Pierce complimented Edward.

"I've already told Julia you're a lucky man," Edward said. "Now I truly think she's a lucky girl."

"Thank you, Edward. That means a lot to me," Pierce replied.

The twilight deepened and Edward rose to leave, needing to reach the fort before tattoo and curfew. "Much obliged for the tasty meal, Sis," he waved goodbye.

AUTUMN CHILL

CHAPTER TWENTY-NINE
IT CAN'T BE

ANOTHER WEEK passed before Walela showed up at Julia's cottage, and Julia was ashamed she had not made it over to the Cherokee village in all this time to instruct the children. She had been too overwhelmed by housekeeping and too proud to let anything go undone for her new husband. The cottage owner had not shown up yet, and so at least they had a place to live for the time being. Whoever he was, perhaps he would be content with Pierce's room at the fort until his own family showed up. They were all like the birds who shared one another's nests, she thought, and there seemed to be a rigid pecking order, called "ranking out," which Pierce had explained to her.

Apparently, any officer of higher rank or seniority had the privilege to assume the quarters of any officer who was below him in the military scale. A single move could have the domino effect of causing everyone down the ladder to move also, and a senior new arrival had his choice of all the quarters occupied by the junior officers. In the military, she had learned, the rules mattered.

"How wonderful you are to come, Walela!" Julia exclaimed. "I am so sorry I haven't come to teach the children. Life just seems so complicated right now. I am very glad you are here!"

"And I am glad to see you too. I've missed you," a subdued Walela added rather shyly.

"And I you," Julia answered. She showed off her new cookware to Walela and proudly pointed out how neatly she was keeping the cottage. The girl generously admired it all before asking what Mrs. Butler would like her to do.

"The most important thing, as always," Julia replied, "is to carry in some water from the pump out back. We have been eating outside whenever possible and I just wash the dishes out there. It saves me some steps with the bucket!"

Walela finally really smiled.

"Come and have some coffee before we set to work. There is a little left still on the fire."

Once the two young women were settled, a moment of awkward silence intruded. They had not sat across from one another socially exactly like this before, and it felt a little strange. Walela broke the silence after looking around the room.

"You have made it so warm and cozy," she offered, complementing Julia with a smile.

"Do you think so? I have tried but it seems to take me all day just to prepare the evening meal. Sarah and I have started trading baking days. She makes bread on Tuesday and I do it on Saturday. That helps a lot and we share other cookery items as well. It makes for more variety and less work. And her cottage is not too far away. "

"That's nice," Walela replied. "When and where will Captain Butler build you a house? Or can you continue to stay here?"

"He plans to start this weekend. It is very near, so we shall be close to the fort and to the Nicks. I won't have a stream close by, but we shall manage. Pierce has employed several enlisted men to help and a few local laborers too. Also, he is expecting several slaves to come from his family's plantation, but not for a another few weeks. Hopefully, it will go fast. It better! Because we can stay here only for another six to eight weeks."

"Perhaps a few Cherokee might help too," Walela tentatively suggested.

"What a good idea! I'll tell Pierce," Julia, said, finding she was glad to have an audience to talk about her home. "He wanted to build us a frame house, but he says the workmanship would be too long and complicated. So, it will be a log house, much like this one. We shall have a stone hearth and chimney and he promises two glass windows on the front. Oh, and I forgot. A puncheon floor. No more dirt floors for me."

As soon as the words left her mouth, she wished them back. She wouldn't insult Walela for the world. How could she have said such a stupid thing. But she feared apologizing would only make it worse.

As they chatted a bit more, Julia realized they both were avoiding the subject of Edward. Another delicate silence lengthened until Walela said, "Time to beat the blankets. Dust must be the enemy here too."

"Amen," Julia said.

They worked side by side throughout the afternoon, talking about the wedding, about baby Eliza's christening and Pierce's work on the road, most of the earlier awkwardness having evaporated with the afternoon light. When several hours had ticked by without a word about Edward, Julia offered the information that he had come over for dinner recently. Walela looked like she was about to say something but then decided against it and continued cutting pole beans for their supper. Neither one seemed to be able to find a way to talk about what was on both of their minds.

"Will you come back tomorrow?" Julia asked when Walela got ready to leave. Julia handed her the soiled sheets to give to Clementine on her way home.

"Perhaps the day after tomorrow," Walela agreed.

Julia could hardly wait to get word to Edward but decided she would have to let Pierce tell him the next morning at Guard Mounting. It made no sense for her to jump on her horse and ride a half hour there, a half hour back, and not even know where to find him. How easy it was out here to think a union between Edward and Walela might be possible. Yet she knew any of her friends or family at home would consider it barbaric, if not insanity. She should not have encouraged him at all, she told herself, but having been exposed to Walela's intelligence and charm, she could fully understand the attraction. Perhaps Edward would make a life for himself out here dealing with Indian affairs. She could see that more as a possibility for him than for herself for she was still struggling to find her niche.

In spite of her happiness with her new home and husband, she frequently felt lonely in the late afternoons, thinking of Sarah with her baby, her mother in Mount Pleasant and all the activity at the fort. The peace and quiet here when Pierce shared it delighted her, but without him, the buzz of the insects and occasional bird-call made the same space seem vacuous. She brought a book outside to read awhile but found she soon put it down to wander restlessly about. She picked up her trowel, preferring the busy work of the garden right now to descriptions of the remote world of Sir Walter Scott.

When Pierce arrived and rolled up his sleeves to wash in the basin she set before him, the sight of his strong hands and tanned arms made her heart leap. How perfect now to have the privacy to put her arms around his neck and press her face against his shirt, breathing in his particular scent.

"I'll hurry with your dinner," she said, pulling away.

"No hurry," he held her more tightly. Knowing they wouldn't eat at all if she gave in, she twirled away and headed to the kitchen to fetch the cold venison and beans. Having decided it was time he knew about Edward's wayward affections, she asked, "Have you noticed my brother pining about lately?"

"Not really. Who's the lucky girl?"

"Walela."

Pierce stared at his wife in shock. "No! That would be impossible."

"I'm afraid he has other ideas," she answered. "And I think Walela may return his feelings, but he has yet to speak to her."

"Well, he should not! I shall try and talk some sense into him."

"It's too late," Julia replied. "He talks of nothing else."

Pierce shook his head in disbelief. "I expect she has more sense than he does then."

"I would not be so sure. Edward tells me Red Fox is very

angry about his attentions to her, and I imagine he is making life difficult for Walela."

"This could be dangerous for more than just Edward and Walela. I'm sure Edward realizes that. For Christ's sake, as a military man, he must have studied the Trojan War. We don't want an American "Helen of Troy" story on our hands."

"He must realize it but he hasn't talked much about that aspect to me. He is momentarily blind to everything but his feelings for her."

EDWARD FELT like a young boy sneaking behind the barn to see his girl. How ludicrous it seemed to be rushing to his sister's house for a clandestine rendezvous with a much younger woman and from a culture so different from his own. Admittedly, he was relatively old not to have married, but he'd never thought he had found the right woman. Now when he saw Walela, he felt like a bull in clover and like an enraged bull when kept away from her. He smiled. How apt that her brother was called *Red* Fox.

Relief and joy overtook him when he spied her in the garden with Julia. The two young women appeared to be on their knees pulling weeds. He had been somewhat surprised to find his sister so obsessed with her garden, but he suspected it was her appetite for vegetables rather than flowers which kindled such activity. Walela jumped up when she saw him approaching and flushed from head to foot. When he slid off his horse, it was all he could do keep from reaching out for her. Instead he said, "You two are always busy. I would employ you both with no questions asked."

He won a smile with his praise and was grateful to Julia when she announced she would go inside and make coffee for them, requesting that Walela stay outside and keep Edward company while she prepared their collation. Even though it felt like they were teenagers, he knew this was as serious a moment for him as he would ever meet again.

Walela knelt again bending her head to work. He knelt down

near her and gently put his hand over hers. "Walela, may I talk seriously to you?"

When she looked up at him, he knew immediately that she returned his affection but she also looked like a frightened doe. As their eyes continued to speak to one another, he dared go on.

"You must know that I care deeply for you. In fact, I can think of nothing but you. I honor and respect you and wonder if you might share these feelings." He began to tremble slightly, suddenly terrified he had gone too far too fast. Her silence increased his apprehension, but then she answered him.

"Captain Du Val, you have guessed correctly. I do share these feelings, but they are unwise."

"Oh, Walela, thank God, thank God! How wondrous you are. But silly girl, you must call me Edward from now on. And yes, they may be unwise, but we shall overcome the difficulties."

"Silly man," she dared to joke. "How on earth is that possible?"

"We shall, I just know it!" He pulled her up from the earth and embraced her as he had longed to do for months. She was so slim that when he held her tight, he picked her whole body up from the ground and whirled her around with him. "Trust me, Walela, we shall."

Hearing the door bang, he quickly put her down so as not to embarrass her, but held on to her hand.

"Julia, I am a happy man. This gorgeous girl says she cares for me."

Her brother, who had resembled a stooped old man for weeks, now pranced like a Minotaur. Glad for him but afraid for their future, she pushed fears aside and joined in their elation, for Walela also appeared transformed. She left her hand in his and smiled from brother to sister, her radiance enveloping the trio.

Julia placed her tray with coffee and biscuits on the table under the tree and proposed a toast to the happy morning. After the refreshments Edward, seized with ecstatic energy, asked Julia if he couldn't help her with something. "Anything," he offered.

Laughing, she said, "Another day, dear brother, I would welcome some help. But today I think you and Walela should talk." And again she disappeared into the cottage.

A sudden shyness descended on both of them and Walela began to brush crumbs off the table. Edward looked up at the cloudless sky and finding nothing to comment upon, looked down again. A soft breeze delivered the delicious scent of wild sweet peas to them, and Edward spied their fuchsia blossoms twined around a bush at the edge of the scraggly lawn.

"Walela, you do understand, do you not, that I wish to marry you?"

A tear slowly tracked down her cheek which she wiped away. "I believed so," she answered, "and I wish it also."

Edward breathed a sigh of gratification.

"But I am afraid it will be impossible," she said.

"No," he answered. "It will not be impossible. Not if we love one another. And we certainly will not be the first Indian and White to marry."

"I have thought of that," she admitted. "But you do not know Red Fox. In theory, a Cherokee woman may decide who her husband will be. The man must build a house for her and the house is considered her property. But this is so far beyond the usual choice, I am sure he will do everything he can to stop me. Also, my mother will be shocked. I don't even know how to tell her. Although I think she must suspect something."

"I shall go with you," Edward suggested. "I would do anything to help you. We are together now." So happy was he to learn of her returned affection, he felt strong enough to ward off any danger or to manage any objection.

"Oh, Edward," she cried, "How did this happen?"

He took her in his arms and held her, her head only coming to the middle of his chest. "I feel it was meant to be," he mused. "How else can we explain it?"

Lifting her off her feet again, he hugged her tight and bent low to kiss her lips. He whispered, "Your lips are sweeter than molasses." Walela threw her arms tightly around his neck and kissed him back until breathless. Edward swung her around and around holding her waist tightly, finally setting her back upon the ground.

"I will try and talk to mother and Red Fox," she promised, "but I cannot imagine anyone accepting this."

"I understand, dear one, I really do. It is so frustrating because the army is here to help and yet, I see we bring as many problems as we solve. I know that, but our intent is good."

"Because of all the bad things that have been brought upon us by the White Man, a great sadness has come over our people. I do not have much hope for our future." Walela's voice began to tremble. "But you bring me hope," she murmured and began to cry. Edward crushed her to his chest and stroked her hair until her agitation subsided. They separated when Julia emerged from the house. Squeezing her hand, Edward kissed Walela's cheek and said, "Send for me as soon as you can.

Julia expected Walela to chatter happily after Edward departed, but instead she seemed quiet and distraught. She worked quite willingly, probably relieved with the diversion. Yet when she left, she answered evasively about when she would return. Julia didn't press her, unsure herself how to break the girl's reserve. It had been so easy making friends with Sarah Nicks, but the cultural barrier seemed to add layers of difficulty. Julia promised to come one day soon for English school and couldn't resist giving Walela a quick hug when it was time for her to go.

TWO DAYS dragged by and Edward heard nothing from Walela. He worried not only about their future together but about her welfare as well. He doubted Red Fox would hurt her, but perhaps he would send her away. The thought frightened him and persisted like a sharp toothache. Try as he may, he could not drive it away.

On the third day, unable to bear his fears any longer, he easily invented an excuse to visit Walela's village. He couldn't wait to get there, simultaneously understanding that this state of hope was better than an absolute "no". Still, he believed his love strong enough to make it happen. Did she not love him enough? Of course she did. He was being a simpleton. The problem must be with her family and the tribe.

As he neared the village, laced with its usual wood smoke perfume, he saw several young Cherokee planting crops of corn, using the shoulder blade of the deer instead of a plough or hoe. Some Indians immediately accepted the White Man's inventions and others resisted, preferring the old ways, which Edward could appreciate, viewing it as he did today in the quiet of the morning far away from the pressures of civilization. He knew many tribes felt that succumbing to White Man's culture was worse than death, and of course, most Whites simply ignored the Indians' repugnance, cognizant only of their own sense of superiority.

As usual, the scout system was working for Red Fox awaited him upon his entry into the village. The Indian brave's fierce bearing and dark eyes radiated fearless hostility, causing Edward to wonder if he had been naïve to come alone, even on such a personal matter. He found it encouraging, however, that Red Fox was alone instead of surrounded by more young braves. He dropped his reins and slid off his roan.

"Good Morning, Red Fox," Edward greeted the implacable figure blocking his way. "I believe you know why I have come, and I ask permission to speak with you."

Red Fox nodded but refused to speak. Growing more uncomfortable, Edward said, "May I then please see Walela?" wondering what he would do if the response were negative.

Red Fox answered. "This is a matter not only for our family but for Chief Jolly." Turning, he ordered Edward, "Come with me."

Edward found this news reassuring rather than daunting for he had always found Jolly to be forward-looking and fair. Perhaps he would be less emotional than Red Fox. And he was ashamed to admit, it was fortunate for him that Red Fox's father was dead. It helped Edward immensely that he and Jolly had worked together in the past and, he believed, respected one another. Also, he had served as Indian Agent long enough for Jolly to understand Edward held the Cherokee's best interests at heart. At least he thought he understood their best interests. As they walked through the village, he cast his eyes in every direction looking for Walela but found no sign of her.

Chief Jolly rose when they entered his lodge, welcomed Edward and motioned to rugs around a low fire where they would sit. Edward noticed the Chief had draped a ceremonial red blanket around himself for the council rather than appearing bare-chested like Red Fox. The high planes of the Chief's face were still as smooth as a pecan but the high forehead was creased with the burdens of a lifetime of decision-making.

"I am honored you have received me on this most personal and important matter, Chief Jolly," Edward began, again heartened he would be dealing with the Chief as well as Red Fox. "I am assuming Walela has told you of our wish to be married. We love and respect one another and see no reason our union should be prohibited."

Red Fox apparently could contain himself no longer. It was considered extremely bad manners in Indian discourse to interrupt. One must always pause before speaking to be sure the former speaker had completed all his thoughts. Nevertheless, Red Fox broke in rudely, accompanied by an interpreter. Edward had learned a lot of Cherokee but he was relieved to have someone more fluent on hand.

"The White Man has moved our people from Georgia to west of the Mississippi. You have caused us to enter into a competition with you that we have no possibility of winning. You have isolated us in our own land. You have made of our proud race a little colony of troublesome strangers in the midst of a numerous and dominant people.[28] Now you want to steal our daughters and sisters." His face, hot with anger, glowed like a bright red sky at sunset.

Edward waited. Jolly raised his hand to quiet Red Fox and

turned to Edward for a response. Edward was always struck by the eloquence of these people and certainly what Walela's brother expressed was heartfelt. Indeed, Red Fox's speech rang with poignant truth. The White Man had consistently abused his power with these people, simply because they could.

"I listen to your words with respect and understanding," Edward answered. "Indeed, I think much of what you say is true and I am sorry. Still, my hope is that our peoples will learn to live together. Furthermore, I believe we are on that path. It is not my desire to steal Walela but rather that she will come to me happily and willingly and that our union might be a symbol of the future way for our peoples to live together."

Chief Jolly shook his head, perhaps in agreement with this last concept. When he was sure Edward had spoken his piece, Jolly said, "What you both say has truth. Yet it is difficult to find the right way when on a new path. I know that Walela's mother is distraught. She is afraid of losing her daughter. She has already lost a husband." He paused, waiting for this to sink in. "I understand Walela has informed you that a Cherokee woman may choose her husband. This is true. But perhaps she has not told you that if you have children, they belong to her. Also, to obtain a divorce, all she needs to do is pack her husband's clothes in a bag beside the door. Then both are free to marry someone else.[29] I know this is not consistent with your ways, nor does it sound agreeable to you. Yet it is what Walela would expect." He carefully watched Edward.

Edward spoke again. "You are correct. These concepts are foreign to me. But I believe Walela and I, because we love one another, would find our way together."

Red Fox spoke again, spitting out the words like hard seeds. "This would not be good for my sister. She is happy here. Perhaps the Indian Agent does not know that when there have been marriages between Cherokee and Whites, the Cherokee people welcome the White Man if he is willing to adopt Indian ways and live amongst us. Has Walela asked you if you will do this?"

Frankly startled, Edward considered how to reply. "No, she

has not," he answered honestly. "We have not discussed this." He assumed she would be content with the life he offered, even welcome it, but he didn't dare say this for fear of antagonizing his audience, also painfully aware he truly didn't know Walela's feelings on the matter.

Chief Jolly rose. "I think this is enough for today. We will all consider what has been said this day and meet again in seven suns."

Edward rose also and nodded in agreement. "Please, Chief, may I see Walela?" he asked.

"No, not today. She must think all this over as well."

Edward decided not to argue but felt at a terrible disadvantage, not knowing what she would be told about today's meeting and worried that he could not encourage her with his love.

THE FIRST day and night of the prescribed seven days of waiting crawled by, seeming as long as a whole week itself. Julia reported to Edward after going to the village to teach that Walela looked sad and worried, not at all her usual vibrant self. Moreover, she had again said she did not know when she could come to help Julia as she was very busy at this time of year assisting her mother and the entire community working in the corn fields. Julia chose not to mention to Edward that she found the girl's remote manner discouraging but did agree to deliver a note to Walela the next time she saw her, either at her house or in the village, a promise which calmed him somewhat.

At least he could write to tell her how much he loved her and to reiterate his desire to share his life with her. He discovered, however, that he could not promise to renounce White Man's ways nor consent to live in an Indian village. The idea absolutely appalled him. Although he greatly admired individual Cherokee and fine men from other tribes, he found their way of life raw, difficult, and if he were honest with himself, primitive. Some men had done

this, Chouteau, for example. But he would not trade his civilization for a simpler life; he could not. So, why should he expect her
to give up her traditions? He just had so much more to offer, he
told himself, and had she not been attracted to his way of life? He
thought so. After all, she had learned his language and seemed
more receptive to the outside world than most of her tribe, like
Chief Jolly. They must find a way to talk. In his note he begged
her to come to Julia's so they might discuss their future.

But Walela did not answer his note before the week was out
and the day dawned for his second trip to talk to Chief Jolly and
Red Fox. Had she deserted him? Given up? Edward told himself
he would have heard if she didn't wish him to pursue the matter.
Perhaps this was a test for him. If so, he would see it through.
Indeed, he had no choice given his obsession with her.

An overnight storm had washed the sky until it shone a lim-
pid blue, and Edward wished he could feel the optimism the clear
day promised. Instead he boiled with anger. What he would really
like to do was to punch Red Fox in the nose, settle his hash once
and for all. But of course, that really wasn't an option. Once
again Red Fox awaited him at the south end of the village and
wordlessly escorted him into the presence of Chief Jolly. Looking
around the simple room, he could not imagine choosing this for a
home. It was too much for them to ask of him.

"Have you pondered our questions?" the Chief inquired.

"I have done little else," Edward answered with a grim smile.
"You brought up some difficult matters but I refuse to abandon
my hopes. I intend to pursue Walela until we are married." Red
Fox made a sound something like a bark, but Edward continued.
"Again, I beg you to allow me to talk with her. I believe we are
meant for one another and that I would make her happy."

"I admire your persistence," Chief Jolly acknowledged. "I
think you have earned an audience with her if she wishes it." He
smiled. "And I believe she does."

Edward's face visibly relaxed as Red Fox's tightened. The
Indian jumped up. "This is a mistake, Chief Jolly! With all due

respect, this is a mistake!"

"We shall see," the older man replied. "Red Fox, go and find your sister and tell her Captain Du Val wishes to meet her here and speak with her in private."

Agitated but obeying, Red Fox departed, his moccasins usually so silent now pounding the ground. At this moment Edward greatly appreciated this culture that so strongly demanded respect for one's elders and especially the Chief of the tribe.

"I, too, will leave you," Chief Jolly said, his eyes kind though framed in a halo of wrinkles.

"Thank you, Chief." Edward's gratitude was so great it made his voice tremble. With total concentration, he watched the door, not even aware he was holding his breath. When Walela appeared in the frame, backlit by the morning sun, she looked like the Madonna to him. As always, in a simple straight deerskin dress, rubbed soft and supple with constant use, she could not be more elegant. The glowing copper skin and black eyes made his heart overflow with love and admiration. Rushing to her, he enfolded her in his arms as though to capture her for his own. As her arms encircled his waist, he stroked her hair.

"Oh, my precious," he murmured. "I cannot endure being without you."

Looking up at him with tears in her eyes, she said, "I know, but you must understand how difficult it is for my mother and brother. She has always expected that I would be close by all her life. Red Fox is concerned for her too."

Edward held her hand and led her to sit down with him.

"I understand, Walela, at least I think I do. Our mother hated to see Julia leave, I know. Our father, passed away many years ago and she is alone. At least your mother lives in a close community."

Fear and concern nearly overpowered Edward as tears again filled her eyes. "I don't know if I can desert my mother," she cried. "It is so difficult. She needs me. The entire clan needs me."

The despair in her face and voice frightened Edward more

than the objections of Red Fox. "I love you, Walela, and I believe you love me. We must find a way to be together," he argued with conviction and fervor.

Walela stroked his cheek, melting his heart. "I hope it will be so," she said, "but I must think about it further." She disappeared so quickly Edward had no time to capture her in his arms again, and he wiped his eyes in anger and desperation. What else could he do but wait?

CHAPTER THIRTY
WALELA'S CHOICE

EVERY SMALL task Walela shared with her mother now became precious. Living and working together they had established a comfortable rhythm, a daily dance of life choreographed to suit them both. Pounding corn, sweeping their house, beating dust from the rough blankets, and especially weaving baskets and deciding upon the designs all brought her pleasure because of sharing the activity.

Walela realized she had essentially already deserted her mother by going to work with Julia. She had traded her ordinary life for the excitement of the new environment, for the opportunity to learn English and to watch from the inside the life of the White People. She had been seduced by their charm, their talk, and especially by Edward's kindness. His sapphirine eyes, his long lanky form, his wayward hair, and especially his love for her, thrilled her. She could think of little else.

How strange that she felt so comfortable with Edward and Julia. She knew she was usually quiet around them, but still, she felt their acceptance and kind regard for her. Their life at the fort didn't seem so different from her village life, but she knew she should not deceive herself. One day Edward would want to return to the East. She could not expect him to be Indian Agent forever, or even for many more seasons. And of course he would expect his wife to accompany him. How on earth would she cope with the complicated life of the east coast? And why would he want her for his wife? It all seemed a mystery and an impasse.

Wrestling with the complex issues was making her ill. She was tugged every which way with confounding emotions and could see no way to a resolution. Not only did she worry about her ability to enjoy, even survive, such a new life and question Edward's desire to marry her, but even more she agonized about leaving her mother alone. How could she ask such a sacrifice of her mother who had always believed her daughter would be by her side? Such a defection would be considered a tragedy in her community.

Deserting Julia also made her uncomfortable, and she missed seeing her employer and friend. To be honest, going over to help Julia might afford an opportunity to see Edward. With this rationale, the next morning, she borrowed her uncle's horse and headed for the Butler's temporary home.

ALL ALONE every day, Julia still couldn't find time for the Indian school, and she missed the children's eager faces. William had come over for dinner a few times but said it made him miss Harriet even more. Life had been easier at the fort where she could run over to Sutler Nicks' when she needed something, where she could eat in the officers' mess hall and take care of only her little room. Some days the chores here appeared daunting, like a heavy stream she must cross; but the knowledge she was doing it to forge a future for her and Pierce delighted her and made the work worthwhile.

The sight of Walela coming through the trees again early one morning brought both relief and pleasure. Running to greet her, she threw her arms around her merrily. Like a cedar waxwing tipsy on a berry bush, Julia chirped with welcomes over and over again.

The labor of housework occupied them for a while, and they recovered their old rhythm of working together. The familiar pattern made them both more comfortable and Julia considered raising the subject of Edward. Perhaps it would be rude, but she couldn't stop herself.

"Walela, is there anything I can do to help? About Edward, I mean." She blushed scarlet once the words were out, fearing she had overstepped the bounds of their friendship. She had sensed the Indians were rather reticent, particularly vis-à-vis the White Man and now, most likely, she had committed a cultural taboo. To make things worse, tears sprang to Walela's eyes and she fiercely brushed them away.

"Oh, Walela, I'm so sorry," Julia blurted. "I should not have said anything. Please forgive me."

"No, no, it's all right. I just don't know what to do."

Both at a loss for words momentarily, they stared at one another. Finally Julia spoke. "Of course. It is very difficult, but I am sure Edward does not want you to be unhappy."

Edward's name only made her tears resurface. Quickly turning, Walela called over her shoulder, "I'll try and come again the day after tomorrow."

Julia sank down in the nearest chair. That probably was another message for her brother, she realized. She would ask Pierce to tell Edward tomorrow at the fort, and she would try not to meddle next time. It probably would have been better if these two had never met, if the Indians and Whites had never met for that matter. But it was too late now, water over the dam. They were unwelcome neighbors now, both wanting the same land.

Two days later early in the morning, Walela carefully avoided being seen by either her mother or her brother. Unless it proved absolutely necessary, she wanted to dodge any explanations. She led her horse far into the trees before mounting and in order to tease any prying eyes, she headed at first for the tribal cornfields before turning towards Julia's house.

Her heart pounded in her chest, whether from fear of being

caught or from the excitement of seeing Edward, she knew not which. As she moved through the brush, feeling both cowardly and ashamed, she slumped lower and lower over the mare's neck. Riding bareback as usual, she twined her fingers in the mane and worried the coarse hair. What was she doing? What was she thinking? She could not live her life hiding behind bushes and lying to people she loved and who trusted her. Yet she did not turn back.

Just as she expected, having received Julia's message, there stood Edward in the clearing near the cottage waiting for a glimpse of her. If she turned back now, he would probably see her flee and take "no" for her answer. Pulling the horse's head up slightly, Walela stopped before her approach would alert him. She watched him pace and fidget and repeatedly glance toward the woods. Kicking her mount gently, Walela emerged from the trees into the yard. Edward bounded forward and as she slid down, he caught her tightly in his arms. "Walela, Walela," he murmured, stroking her smooth jet hair. "Oh my dearest one, at last I can put my arms around you."

Walela let her cheek rest against his rough vest, soaking up the comfort of his holding her. When they slowly separated, he led her over to the table and chairs under the linden tree. Walela looked toward the house but saw no sign of Julia. Brother and sister must have agreed on privacy for the lovers, she imagined.

"I was so relieved when Pierce brought me your message," Edward said. Walela didn't contradict him that it had been a direct message for she had to be honest with herself. She granted him a warm smile.

"You look very handsome," she offered but hung her head momentarily when he guffawed.

"Love IS blind," he covered her hands with his. "We must find a way, Walela. I cannot be without you."

His intensity frightened her somewhat, yet believing him, it seduced her. His eyes reminded her of cornflowers in the spring, almost purple with their depth. Of course, one never saw blue eye color among her people, and so she suspected she must be attracted by this exotic trait. Yet how clear and honest his eyes appeared. Pulling her shoulders up, she answered him. "Edward, my feelings for you are as strong as a mighty storm, but I do not know how I can desert my family."

"I know, Walela, I know. And I do not see how I could live like an Indian and support you as I believe I must. Surely you can see that. I must be able to do the work I am trained to do so we might live the way you deserve."

Walela shook her head. "I do not need or want much," she honestly declared. "You must know that. To be with you all my life would make me as happy as a bear in a honey tree."

Gathering hope like flowers from her words, he encouraged her. "Perhaps if your mother understands your feelings, she will want you to be happy and will not forbid our marriage. I understand Red Fox is another issue, but I sense your worries are primarily for your mother."

"This is true," Walela agreed, "but I am not so sure she will be as understanding as you predict. Rather she will see it as my duty to stay."

Edward grew silent while Walela stared at his strong arms with a light cloak of golden hair. How handsome, rugged and unique he was. He looked up and asked, "Again, I would like to offer to talk with either Red Fox or your mother. Do you want me to do that? Perhaps they expect it."

"No. I must do it."

"Will you try and persuade her, Walela? Will you try?"

"I think I must. For both of us," she declared before going inside to find out what Julia wanted her to do today. After the young women discussed housework, Julia wandered outside to find her brother staring into space. She put her hand on his shoulder wishing to give him some small comfort.

"How did we get so mixed up in this Indian business?" he asked her. She heard no bitterness in his tone but a hint of confusion and even apprehension. "And look at me. I'm apparently looking for more problems!" He gave his sister a quirky smile. "Mom always said I was hardheaded."

"I wouldn't worry about that. Mother said that about all of us, especially William."

"Well, maybe she was right."

As JULIA came to know her husband better, she marveled at his intelligence and gentleness. He could be irritable and a little sharp when tired, but in general, she found him good natured and optimistic. Julia began to feel very tired herself and attributed her fatigue to the hard labor of housekeeping on the frontier

"You should put me to work building our house," she quipped to Pierce. "I'm becoming as strong as your men."

"But much easier on the eyes," he replied.

As the weeks slid by in a blur of domestic activity, Julia began to worry that she didn't feel herself. Perhaps she should prepare of brew of horsetail, the rushes with a bushy top that grew everywhere,. She'd been told a decoction of the herb helped various stomach problems, but she couldn't really say what was bothering her. Sarah invited her to a preserving party, warning her that they must set in a store of fruits and vegetables while the garden was bountiful in order to ward off scurvy in the winter. She enjoyed the day but found herself overly weary afterward. Where was all her usual hummingbird energy? Indeed, laughing one day, Walela had pointed to a hummingbird; this is the little bird which carries my name in Cherokee, "Walela" and she had observed, Julia deserved this name more than she.

But not these hot stifling days. Julia dragged her feet and sat down whenever possible. One day when the smell of river perch for dinner made her queasy, she finally understood. Of course, she must be pregnant! Relieved to discover an explanation for her fatigue and upset stomach she experienced a flash of fear as well. How would she manage? She didn't know much about babies at all. At least Sarah would be nearby.

Planning to tell Pierce that night, she worked especially hard on the evening meal. But he arrived so late and so worn out, having labored on their new house after work as long as the light would afford, she put it off until tomorrow. The next night a special officers' meeting at the fort kept him late again. Feeling hot and irritable, Julia wished for a cool bath with water pumped and poured by the servants. Don't be spoiled, she chided herself, but the gathering grays of evening suddenly made her nervous and lonely. Sarah, with her hands so full, visited seldom, and Pierce was absent all day. She could not just hang around the fort, talking to whoever happened by, like she did before they were married. How she longed for a friend to chat with! And she felt too tired to consider going to the Indian village to teach.

Rubbing her lower back which ached a little, she gathered paper and pen together to write the happy news to her mother. She had to tell someone! Again, it didn't seem right for Jemina to miss such an important event in her life, but having several grandchildren already close by probably would soften the disappointment for her mother. It was Julia who would miss having female family near by the most. Her eyelids drooped before she could finish, and she was ashamed to be already asleep when Pierce came home. Oh, dear, this would not do at all.

AT BREAKFAST the next morning Julia couldn't stand keeping her secret any longer. As soon as she had poured their coffee, she blurted out, "Pierce, darling, I have some important news." He looked up at her expectantly, albeit still a little sleepy eyed. How she loved that look, thought Julia, still a bit of innocence lurking before full awareness of the day.

"I am almost sure . . . I mean, I think we're going to have a baby."

His reaction was all she could have hoped for, immediate and spontaneous. Whooping and jumping up, he knocked his chair over backward and squeezed her tightly in a bear hug. "Ju-liette, Juliette, what wonderful news!"

"I think so too. I imagine that's why I have been so tired lately."

"Why sure! We have to make you rest more. And now I shall really have to hurry with that house. I feel as frustrated as a trout swimming upstream because I can't move the work along as quickly as I would like. I can't get as many carpenters as I need. They're all tired after a long day on army jobs."

"How about the Cherokee? Walela suggested it, and I know many need work."

"That's a fine idea," he agreed. She loved him for not calling the Indians lazy or dirty like some of the Whites did, including her brother William.

"The not-so-good news is that Walela clearly hasn't made up her mind yet and Edward is moping around like a young lad in his teens. I can understand her point of view. It would be hard to give up everything she has always known and adopt his way of life."

"Well, there certainly are many differences between our so-cieties. One of the greatest, I think, --- and it is a subtle one --- is that she comes from a matriarchal clan and our structure is pa-triarchal. They won't ever be able to figure out who is the head of the family. I really don't know how it can work." He paused when Julia regarded him quizzically. "But it sure is clear they are in love with one another!" he blurted.

Julia laughed. "Do you think we were so obvious?"

"I imagine so. I don't remember anyone being very sur-prised."

"Pierce, please tell Edward that Walela will be here tomor-row."

"I am glad to hear it. You need more help. No more water carrying for you."

We shall see about that, Julia thought. There would be no way around it.

As THE days shortened and the mornings dawned cold and crisp, Julia noticed the coyotes coming closer to the cottage, skinny and shivering and hungry. And it was only early October. Pierce told her not to feed them; the wild had to care for themselves and she would attract more savage creatures if she were not careful. Still, she began to appreciate the vulnerability of all things in a way she had not before.

Perhaps it was because she felt so fragile herself. She'd begun to worry about the pregnancy a little. A nagging pressure and pull in her lower abdomen bothered her frequently, and she wondered if it were normal. She did not want to concern Pierce, and she doubted Sarah's experience was that extensive. The doctor at the post certainly would not know much about women's ailments.

Of course staying busy was never a problem and that usually had fixed whatever bothered her. But now she always felt behind, too much to carry, cook or clean. She called them the three "c's", all for CARE. Some days her usual energy would return, and she would skitter through her chores like the squirrel busy in the yard burying acorns and nuts. What a relief that was, and she would believe all was well.

She realized now she could not have remained at the post once it got cold. Without a fire in her room she would have frozen to death, and she wondered how the enlisted men stood it. On especially chilly nights she would remember the servants at the farm in Mt. Pleasant, who would put long handled bed warmers filled with hot coals between the sheets before she jumped in. But now she had Pierce to keep her warm, she thought, and to hold her and love her. She should be ashamed of herself for being the least bit homesick.

How blasé and cavalier she had been, she marveled, at taking on life out here. At times the isolation seemed like a greater barrier than the walls of the fort had been. Some nights when she could not sleep, she would wander to the window and peer out toward the silhouette of trees near the cabin. A long eared owl stared back at her with round yellow eyes. At first she was startled, then decided he was a friendly soul watching over her.

Julia didn't tell Pierce when she began to notice a little vaginal spotting of blood. What could he do? And she would only worry him. At least since the corn harvest, she had a good supply of soft silken cornhusks for her intimate needs. The lack of newspapers and magazines out on the frontier provoked a shortage as important to hygiene as to intellect. She tried to rest every afternoon but the long list of things to do for lunch, supper, cleaning, etc. rarely allowed such leisure.

One morning shortly after Pierce departed, after much cramping, a gush of blood confirmed her fears. She must have lost the baby. Wadding up a scrap of sheeting, she pressed it between her legs and lay down. Weak and numbed, she thought she must rest no matter what needed to be done. How could she have let this happen?

Turning her face to the wall, she let tears steam down her cheeks. How inadequate she was. Why had she failed? The cramping began to subside around noon, and Julia made herself rise to heat some soup. She thought of all her young friends back home who were successful and prolific mothers. Having married late, she had never thought about problems with child bearing. Finding she had not the heart for anything else, she lay down again.

When Pierce returned, mercifully earlier than usual, he found the cottage shadowed and quiet. Pushing open the door, he called Julia's name just as he saw her form upon the bed.

"Dearest, dearest, what has happened?" he cried, kneeling beside the bed.

"Oh, Pierce, I'm so sorry. I lost our baby. I'm so sorry," she wailed.

"Julia, it's not your fault. Are you all right?" She looked pale and he noticed blood on the sheets under her.

"I think so," she replied. "I am just very tired."

He helped her up and into a chair so that he could clean the bed, much to her consternation. He brought her clean cool water from the well which revived her considerably, and when he tucked her back in and brought her some eggs and toast for supper, she admittedly felt better, physically at least.

Upon awakening the next morning Julia discovered that Pierce had already left but a note for her was propped against the sugar bowl.

> *Darling, I am so sorry. You must take care of*
> *yourself today. I will send Edward to fetch Walela*
> *for you. Drink some tea and go back to bed. Walela*
> *will bring your lunch. You are my dearest love, Pierce*

Tears ran down her cheeks as she prepared her tea. She didn't feel all that bad really, only drained, but sadness robbed her of a will to do anything. Taking her tea back to bed as Pierce had instructed, she drank it before sliding back down between the covers. The baby had become a part of her so quickly. Now that she had lost it, she realized how much she had already planned around their life together, being a mother, being a young family. She stared at the wall, wondering what she would do with herself for the rest of her life, even for the next week. All sense of purpose seemed to have leaked out of her with the birth fluids.

She had pictured herself showing off the baby to Sarah, had imagined their children playing together and cherished the image of nursing her baby by the fire in their cozy cottage. She felt so ashamed at her failure. She was a healthy, well cared for young woman, and yet she could not even manage such a basic human feat. She must have dozed off, for when she turned over, there stood Walela by her bed.

"I have brought you some soup," she said. "How are you feeling?"

Julia tried to say "Fine," but tears again filled her eyes. Walela sat down on Julia's bed and stroked her shoulder. "I know it must hurt, but you know it is nature's way of taking care of us. You will soon be ready to have another."

To Julia the Indian girl's words sounded both harsh and comforting. She didn't admit her feelings of shame but finally mustered up a wan smile. "Perhaps you are right, Walela."

"I am sure I am. Here, let me help you up and then we shall eat together. Captain Butler and Edward are concerned about you and I want to be able to take them a good report this afternoon."

Walela would not allow Julia to do anything, sending her back to rest after lunch. She then prepared an evening meal for Julia and Pierce, swept the floor, washed the dishes and pumped and carried water for Julia to bathe.

"Oh, Walela, you are an angel. This bath feels better than anything I could imagine," cooed Julia, sinking down in the warm water. She allowed Walela to brush her hair and admitted to feeling much better.

"I am sure Sarah will hear about this tonight and come over tomorrow," Walela guessed.

"I feel so useless," Julia blurted.

"Don't be silly," chided Walela. "This happens when all is not as it should be. You did nothing wrong and by tomorrow you will be back on your feet."

"Of course I will be," Julia said, but then she had no other choice. Then again, perhaps that was a good thing. A niggling thought persisted that perhaps this would not have happened if she had been coddled and cared for back home. Everything was so much harder here. Well, she would never know the answer to that and so she had better just get on with what she needed to do.

RED FOX intercepted Walela when she returned from Julia's. Grabbing her arm rather roughly he demanded, "Why won't you stay in your own village?"

Walela pulled her arms away. "You know I work for Mrs. Butler, Red Fox, and have done so for months."

"We should never have allowed you to go to the fort for work. Now your own kind aren't good enough for you." His words wounded her like an arrow.

"That is not true and you know it," she answered.

Changing his tone, he said, "Come, Walela, let us talk a little." He waved her toward their house. "I think our mother is out for awhile."

As they entered the log house, he dropped the softer approach. "How can you think of living with those people? They are not like us!"

"Oh, yes they are! In the ways that matter. You are quite wrong, Red Fox. I have just come from tending Julia because she lost her baby after carrying it only three months. She wept as any Indian woman would. But you are right in that she doesn't understand as we do the ways of nature. I think I was able to help her somewhat," she recounted with some pride.

"Walela, that is just what I mean. You have more to give them than they do you. And you are becoming too involved with their family."

"I do not think so. I have learned a great deal from them." And Edward loves me, she thought.

"Sister, these people are against us, not with us. Their brother sold liquor to our people! Do I need to remind you of that? How can you marry into a family bent on destroying us?" His voice rose with vehemence.

Knowing this was a valid point, she could not argue otherwise. Still, she warded off his obstruction. "Yes, I have to agree one of them was wrong. But every clan has its difficult individuals; I've heard them called their 'black sheep.' That doesn't make the entire clan evil. Julia and Edward and Captain Butler too, are extremely upset with William Du Val. Edward especially feels like it is a betrayal of his work as Indian Agent."

"And well he should! I find it a sorry and pitiful state that he can't control his own brother."

Walela sighed. Apparently he did not see the irony in his remark. He couldn't dominate her and his opposition was only making her dig her heels in all the more. "So, is that what you think, that a brother can command his brothers and sisters? Well, you can't control me!" And out she went, nearly knocking over her mother, who was returning home, as she blew out of the cabin.

Mrs. Bushyhead looked worriedly after her. "What is the matter, Red Fox?" she asked.

He exploded. "Your daughter is headed down a dangerous path, and I cannot convince her how wrong headed she is."

"Well, Red Fox, you are perhaps looking at this only from your point of view. Perhaps Walela sees and understands things about the White Man that we do not."

"I can tell you what she doesn't see. She does not see that they want to take over our land, our minds and our women." He sat down at the table, looking as though the wind had been knocked out of him.

PROPELLED BY fury, Walela hurried over the hard packed earth to the Chief's lodge. Not finding him there, she headed to the "hot house" where often the elders sat for hours sweating and pondering upon the immense problems and difficulties of life. She saw the mockery of her present state, steaming and fuming, on her way to the hothouse and smiled. Amazing how far humor could go in turning down the heat.

Instead of barging in as she had almost done, she sat down on a rock outside to gather her thoughts. After all, the Chief would not respond well to anger. Better that she appear collected and resolved. The afternoon chill quickly penetrated her moccasins and her leggings as she had run off without a proper wrap.

When a villager finally left the lodge, she asked him if he would tell Chief Jolly she would like to speak to him in private. She did not wait long before the Chief came out to find her. Almost losing her nerve but then understanding full well all that was at stake, she plunged ahead albeit with a bit of a stammer.

"Chief Jolly, I have considered the problem from many sides and for many moons and beg you to allow my marriage to Captain Edward Butler." The wind soughed in the trees and leaves rained down on them carpeting the ground in red and yellow. "I feel this to be the right path for me and seek your assent for a traditional Cherokee ceremony here in my village. My union with Edward does not mean I leave my duties as a daughter. I will always try and care for our mother."

Chief Jolly nodded in approval. "Whether that will prove possible or not Walela, we must wait and see. But I welcome your concern for your esteemed mother. Such a marriage will not be easy. This I can promise you. Still, since you persist and seem certain, I shall grant my permission. Does your family now agree?"

Walela's shoulders slumped. She knew she must be honest with him.

"No, Chief. At least I know Red Fox does not. He still is angry and I will need your support. Somehow I believe I shall be able to win over my mother." She failed to mention she had not asked Edward if he would marry in the Cherokee way, having only just decided herself, but she was positive he would accept her wishes.

"Very well, Walela. We will talk more tomorrow about your plans."

It seemed like the falling leaves had created a glowing golden path for her as she skittered back home.

CHAPTER THIRTY-ONE
RESOLUTION

WHEN WILLIAM came thundering up at full speed on Calhoun early the next morning, Julia was already feeling much stronger and more optimistic about the world. He rushed in as though he were arriving mid-crisis, almost destroying her fragile equanimity with hugs and expressions of sympathy. Staving off her sense of failure, she managed to welcome his attentions. Pierce too seemed glad her brother had come for a visit. Apparently, Edward was not far behind, and entering more quietly than William had done, he hugged Julia.

"I am so sorry, Juliette. I don't want you to be sad. But I remember that mother had this happen several times. Since you were the youngest, you probably might not even know."

"No, I didn't know. Thank you for telling me." With Edward, Julia couldn't hold back the tears and let him gently hold her for a time. Gathering her composure, she thanked them both for coming right away, as did Pierce who busied himself producing coffee and toast for everyone.

"Walela says it is nature's way of telling me all was not as it should be. I imagine she is right," Julia conceded.

"And there is plenty of time for more babies," Pierce interjected. "The important thing now is to get Julia feeling better."

"Hey, that's right," William boomed. "Now listen everyone, I have some good news!"

"Well, let's hear it," Pierce rejoined.

"I have just received notice that the Secretary of War, John Eaton, has commanded Arbuckle to return my confiscated property. You will remember, we argued to Eaton that the liquor they found at our store did not constitute a violation of the Intercourse Act."

"What a relief!" Julia exclaimed. "I am so glad, William."

"Well, I am too," Edward added, "but I think you had better be more careful from here on. I suspect it was political pressure in the East from our powerful friends which allowed you to violate the Intercourse Laws with impunity."

"I am afraid I agree, William," Pierce said. "Colonel Arbuckle told me if the case came to trial, he would be able to prove your guilt regarding selling liquor to the Indians. Although I am happy for you and your family, this outcome is only going to multiply the enforcement problem of the Army in the Indian Territory."

"You all are such a dreary bunch," William complained.

"Don't mean to be," Edward replied. "We just want you to obey the laws more stringently next time. Promise me, William. I am very serious. Maybe if you set an example now, some of the damage can be undone."

"Now listen, I've already taken the high road and except for the return of the merchandise he seized, I have released Arbuckle from any liability for damages from his accusation"

"Good," Pierce said, but Julia witnessed a "can-you-believe-it" look pass between her husband and Edward. "Now I must be off for work. Will you two keep my wife company a little while?"

"Glad to," Edward said. "We won't be as much help as Walela would be, but we shall see what we can do around here. Wait a minute, can you, Pierce?" Edward added. "I have some good news too that I would like you all to hear." His face radiated joy like the candles on a Christmas tree. "Walela has accepted my proposal. Chief Jolly sent me a letter last night, saying I may visit her later today."

Everyone spoke at once, Julia and Pierce with congratulations, Julia with an added hug and Pierce with a slap on the back. William looked stunned.

"Aw no, Edward, you can't do that! It is a mistake! You have taken leave of your senses! I admit she is pretty but my God, she's still a primitive!"

"Don't say that, William." Edward's lips stretched tight and thin, like a wolf bearing its teeth. "I won't abide any aspersions about her or her people. Ever again. I mean it. From now on. Do you understand?"

"You will only bring shame on our family, Edward. DO NOT DO THIS."

"I have made up my mind, William, and I hope to see you at the wedding."

William's face turned beet red with emotion. His answer was to turn away, grab his cap and rush for the door.

"Oh, Edward, I'm so sorry. He will get over it," Julia tried to comfort him.

"Let's all hope so," Pierce added. "In the meantime, I am late for work. Again, my felicitations, Edward." Shaking hands with his brother-in-law, he grabbed his hat and gun as he headed again for the door. "I don't imagine it will be easy, but what is? And by the by, I'm sure your company is the best medicine for Julia." The door slammed behind him too.

As soon as everyone left, Edward pulled a letter out of his pocket.

"I almost forgot with so much going on. A letter for you from Mother."

"How is she always near when I most need her?" she marveled as she opened the flimsy pages.

My dear girl,

How much I miss you! It is such wonderful news about your expecting. I remember how nervous I was with my first, and I hope you are getting a lot of rest. Probably not (you see, I am a realist) but a mother can hope.

I just cannot get used to this big house without your chatter and light step. Mr. Paddington comes in several times a day to check on me and chat with his wife. He clumps around so loudly, I think one of the horses must have come inside. He assures me you are fine out there (It seems so very far away!) because you have such a strong constitution. I hope he's right! He tells me it has been a good harvest this year and I trust him. I have had a touch of the lumbago and find it hard to climb the stairs. But generally, I am in fine health.

Your sister's baby arrived last week. Another strapping healthy boy. She will have her hands full.

I am so looking forward to meeting your Pierce. He sounds like a fine man. He must be if you have chosen him to love.

In any event, I sincerely hope you will not stay away from home too long. Write often and tell me about my boys as well. They rarely put pen to paper but I know they are busy.

You are always in my thoughts and prayers, dearest Julia.

Your loving mother
October 5, 1826

In the envelope with the letter was a tiny baby spoon, which Julia knew must have been her own. Now her mother was sending it to her for her new baby. She handed the letter to Edward and retired to her bedroom for a little while to pull herself together. Indeed, it helped Julia greatly to have her brother around for a while during the morning and then, late that afternoon, Sarah came over too, bringing a stew she had made for their dinner.

"John will come too and we'll all cheer you up. Eliza is good at that, aren't you, my poppet?" she said, nuzzling her little girl's ear and causing Julia a pang of jealousy and grief. Of course she didn't begrudge Sarah her happiness, but the presence of the healthy radiant baby renewed her disappointment. However, when Pierce and John arrived later, bringing the dust of the day and their vibrant energy, Julia felt such a burst of gratitude for this loving husband and exuberant friend, she reprimanded herself for too much sorrow. How lucky she was to have so much to look forward to. The warmth and noise of the evening took her away from contemplating her loss too heavily and Pierce's arms around her at night soothed much of the remaining ache.

EDWARD THOUGHT he should seek out William to try and make him understand his feelings. Surely he could bring him around. As expected, he found his brother at his store stocking shelves for the month. They always ran out of the popular items quickly --- sugar, coffee and jerky. The flour would just gather weevils for a while. William turned back to his business when he saw Edward approaching.

"Look, William, we have to resolve this. I am determined to marry Walela and I want your good wishes."

William whirled around and exploded. "Well, let me say, Big Brother, you don't give us any choice, do you? This whole idea is crazy! Damned crazy! What will mother think when you bring a wild woman into her home and call her your wife. I'll allow Walela is a likely[30] enough girl, but I laugh, no I cry, to think how she will behave at our formal dinners."

"William, I trust Jemina to be more open and welcoming than you have been. You have watched Walela. She is quiet and gentle and lovely and intelligent. She will learn quickly but I hope she will keep her soft manners, which are more pleasing to me than the often rude and abrupt ways of the Whites."

"Love has clouded your mind, Edward. The Indians are nowhere near our level of civilization, and I see no great strides in their changing their slovenly ways."

Edward seethed. "Sure, I see lazy Indians and I see lazy Whites. And I see the Whites mistreating the Indians. But if you witness a White Man mistreat another White, you would not stand for it. You would not behave that way with a child who misbehaved because he didn't understand. You would try and teach the youth. That is what must happen! Open your eyes, William. The Indians are not too primitive to learn as you have clearly seen in Walela's case."

William looked Edward square in the face. "You are whistling in the wind, Eddie. It's a lost cause. Sure, we can help curb the violence and try and make things easier for everyone out here in this God forsaken I.T., but mark my words, it's a lost cause."

"We don't have to solve the grand scheme today, William. I only hope you will be at my wedding."

"We shall see," William said.

DURING HER lying-in (Julia wondered if you would call it that if there were no child), she became unusually depressed because of Pierce's absence during the day and her enforced inactivity. She tried to hide these low moments from her husband, but he was too sensitive not to notice. After dinner one night he made a suggestion. "Perhaps, dear one, we should ask Paddington to send us out a slave or two to help us. Walela will have her own home now and I know you won't enjoy anyone else's help as much as hers. We could cultivate a little more land for a vegetable garden, and you would have company and much needed assistance about the house."

Her first response was defensive. "Sarah doesn't need servants. She manages on her own, and so once I regain my energy, I should be able to also."

"I am sure you can, but I doubt if Sarah tries to do as much as you do or plans such a fine house."

"But Sarah is busy with a child."

"Let us not distract ourselves with the way the Nicks live, sweetheart. I want you to be happy here, and I am only thinking of what I can do to make your life easier," Pierce said. "Just think about it a little while," he suggested, kissing the top of her head as he rose from the table.

Julia waited a week before writing to her mother. She was afraid her sadness would creep into the letter and wanted to allow some time for recovery. However, when she finally dipped her quill into the ink, she had to wipe away a tear with her other hand.

Dearest Mother,

I am very upset at this moment because I recently miscarried a child. I am up and about and everyone has been loving and kind. Still, it is a blow and I am trying to recover my equilibrium. I realize now that being the youngest of ten children, I didn't know that you had experienced this particular loss, and it is more draining than I understood before enduring it myself. I have missed your presence greatly during the ordeal and just thinking of your strength in times of despair has helped me get through this. Pierce has been especially dear and keeps saying there is plenty of time for more children and he is sure we will have others. I am sure he is right but when your hopes and expectations are knocked down so suddenly, it is a shock. Funny, I feel better already, just writing to you and thinking more about all the joys and sorrows in your full life.

Edward has told me that he has written to you about Walela. You will love her. Admittedly, it is an unusual union that must bear unusual stresses. But they appear to love each other greatly, and both are determined to be together. William is having a particularly hard time with the idea but I think Walela will charm him out of his objections. She truly is an extraordinary young woman and I am proud of Edward for following his heart with such determination. This will be a challenge for the Cherokee as well, but we are blessed with a forward thinking Chief --- Chief Jolly by name --- who is willing to envision a new future for his tribe in many ways.

Please, mother, do not worry about us. I am regain-

ing my strength and we are helping one another. I miss you greatly but take comfort in knowing we will be together again, hopefully in the not too distant future.

Your daughter who loves you, Juliette

FIRST WINTER

CHAPTER THIRTY-TWO
CHRISTMAS

EDWARD WAS extremely tired, trying to balance the demands of his job and the demands of his heart. So preoccupied was he with his deskwork that he did not hear three Indian braves come up behind him in his office. One, whom he immediately recognized as Red Fox despite the war paint, grabbed both arms, yanking him up from his chair. One seized his hair and another kicked the chair away. Fortunately, two guards, who evidently had been asleep on duty, heard the commotion and stormed up the stairs with their guns at the ready. They pushed the attacking Indians against one wall, holding their guns on the marauders.

"I think I only need to talk to this one," Edward told the guards, pointing to Red Fox. "Take the others outside the fort and send them home."

When everyone had left, Edward motioned Red Fox to a chair and picked up the other which had been tossed by the attackers. Red Fox's eyes glinted with fury and the muscles in his arms rippled with nervous energy.

"You have no right to take my sister," he exploded, speaking better English than Edward knew he could.

"I do not take her, Red Fox. She comes to me of her own choice. I regret your anger but shall not change my determination," Edward replied. "And what did you plan to do? Kidnap me? Kill me? Walela would hate you if you did either one." Edward's anger was increasing as he talked to her brother. "Your Chief has given his consent. You cannot stop us!"

Red Fox jumped up from his chair but his tomahawk hung at his side. Even in his anger and frustration, he understood it was no match for Edward's gun.

"You do not understand, White Man. You do more harm than good. You should leave our women alone."

"I did not plan to fall in love with your sister, Red Fox. Believe me, I understand the problems it creates. But your world is changing and so is ours. We must make peace. I do not want to arrest you although I could and perhaps should for this attack. Now leave and tell no one of this incident. Especially Walela. And I shall do the same."

Red Fox spun on his soft moccasins and fled down the stairs to the courtyard. Edward strode out to the verandah overlooking the parade ground and shouted to the guards to let him go untouched. How had the brave gotten past these guards in the first place, he wondered, but he would not investigate in order to keep the whole thing quiet.

IT HAD been a month since the miscarriage. Julia still felt somewhat subdued, but on the whole, her usual composure had returned and her confidence and hopes for having another child expanded daily. She had so much to be grateful for, especially Pierce, whose strong and obvious concern for her health had somehow surprised her. Usually so solid and unflappable, he had clearly been shaken by her brief bout of physical and emotional illness.

Now she needed to show her support for him. He was clearly worried about the pending court-martial, although he tried to hide it. She had put it aside in her mind as she had been so overwhelmed by her own trouble. He sat up late many nights in a row, writing his defense. When she asked him if he could possibly be incarcerated or expelled from the Army, he would only say, "Not if there's any true justice." He had told her not to fret but it was hard not to, watching him write, scratch out and write again, night after night.

Also, they both worried about the slow progress on their house. The cottage owners could show up any day and the building didn't seem to be going fast enough. Pierce couldn't pull Army workers off their jobs for his personal needs, and sometimes the Cherokee volunteers showed up and sometimes they did not. Still, Julia had decided she did not want slaves from Maryland or the Butler plantation in South Carolina to help her out here. The Cherokee needed the work, and she would find someone from the reservation to assist her. Walela could guide her with that.

When Julia visited the fort for vegetables and other supplies a few weeks before Christmas, a group of enlisted men huddled together and whispered as she walked by. One particularly ornery fellow dared holler, "Your boyfriend is guilty, ya know!" He earned some snickers from his pals as she held up her head and ignored him. The taunting grew louder and more daring as the date of the court- martial neared, although those doing the harassing had to be careful not to speak out when an officer was nearby. It seemed to Julia that the number of Newell supporters was growing and she wondered why. Did they know something she did not?

She longed to talk to Edward or William in order to probe whether there were really something she ought to worry about. But she didn't want them to have the chance to say, "See, we warned you," or even worse, "We were right." Any officer would have been able to stop the taunting immediately, but again, she did not want to risk more awareness of the issue. She ventured to speak with Lt. Monroe about it, but when he said, "Not to worry," she sensed his heart didn't back the encouraging words.

The fact that Pierce's court-martial had been scheduled for the day after Christmas put somewhat of a pall upon Julia's first Christmas at Cantonnement Gibson. Though fairly confident of a good outcome at the trial, an occasional nip of fear nibbled at the edge of her mind like termites weakening wood. What if she should have waited longer to know Pierce better --- at least until the court-martial was over? Why had she so stubbornly raced ahead when she had been so conservative before? She had been right to show her loyalty, had she not? But had it been at the expense of reason? She would stand by him, whatever the outcome, she told herself.

The giant machine of the Army, plowing forward on the frontier with supreme confidence in its rituals, its courts-martial, bugles, and orders sometimes overwhelmed her. What chance did an individual have against such a behemoth? What chance did the Indians have? But had she not, only recently, told Pierce how much good he and the Army were doing? All the furtive doubts were taking a toll on her energy and spirit, but she hid all this thrashing of her mind from her husband, trying to be jolly and festive as summoned by the season.

The atmosphere at the fort helped her in this endeavor as everyone appeared to have entered into a holiday frame of mind. A huge tree was dragged into the middle of the fortress yard and all helped in decorating with dyed walnut and sweet gum husks and garlands of winterberries and dried apples, interspersed with red bows. Julia wondered where the ribbon had come from.

On Christmas Eve afternoon, gifts, which had been accumulating for weeks under the tree, were distributed to all the children from near and far. There was a package for Eliza Nicks, something for all the laundress's children, and Edward had seen to it that Julia's students from Walela's village were invited to open small gifts. There were dolls, handmade of straw or cloth, animal figures carved by some clever wood whittler at the post, and a little sleigh made of twigs. Apparently many folks had been hard at work for weeks preparing for this day. At the gift giving, the fort kitchen liberally distributed dough nuts, balls of sweetened dough fried in hogs' fat. The children and adults couldn't seem to get enough of them.

There would be a special dinner with all the fixings and entertainment on Christmas Day at the cantonnement, but Julia and Pierce elected to cook at home, inviting the Nicks and Edward and Walela over to share the afternoon. William, of course, had been asked as well, but Julia feared he would not come because he still could not bring himself to accept the idea of Edward's marriage to Walela. Just thinking about it made her slam her pots around the kitchen a bit harder than usual. Then remembering she didn't want to upset Pierce, she advised herself to quiet down. She hoped her stubborn brother would surprise her and that the season's symbol of love and giving would soften his attitude.

Knowing Pierce worried more than he disclosed, she welcomed all the distractions of the holiday. A big Cherokee basket she had bought at Chouteau's for her husband especially delighted her. She found the shape appealing, a twelve inch cone, open at the top, rising from three slightly raised points. A complicated geometric design encircled the container, and she knew he would like it. Perhaps he would put it next to his desk to hold important documents. In the evenings she loved spreading out their drawing of the new house and imagining where she would put their furniture and household items. She tried to involve Pierce in order to get his mind off the court-martial, and he seemed to enjoy the planning as much as she did.

About one o'clock on Christmas Day William did appear, raising everyone's spirits. Apparently the tug of family at Christmas had proven stronger than his negative feelings about Walela. He even seemed on especially good behavior, being careful not to make any derogatory remarks about anyone. Hallelujah, thought Julia.

After dinner Walela entertained them with one of the Cherokee's stories which Edward could not seem to get enough of. Every time they were all together, he would press her to tell another. When the shadows drew around their windows, as they all sat warmly around the fire, replete after all the good food, it seemed like a perfect time. Eliza, too, seemed to understand the special aspect of the day, smiling and gurgling for all the company. Now she lay in her basket watching the firelight on the ceiling. Walela, not being used to such a large group, seemed a little shy at first and spoke softly, but in a short time caught the excitement of entertaining her audience.

"The bluebird is very blue," she began. "As blue as a brilliant lake. Many moons ago the bluebird used to be white. One day he was flying and came upon a lake and saw how blue and beautiful it was. He stopped and asked Grandfather, "Grandfather, can I be as blue as that lake?" So Grandfather gave him a song to sing. He told him what to do. Every morning for five mornings the bluebird would dive down into the lake singing the song taught to him by Grandfather, then come back up. The whole time he was doing this the coyote was watching him. On the fifth day, the bird dove into the lake, and when he came back out, he was as blue as he is today.

"The coyote saw this and thought to himself, "Hmm. . . I'd like to be as blue as that bluebird." He said to the bluebird, "Teach me your song." So every morning for the next five days the coyote would take a bath and sing the song from Grandfather. And on the fifth day the coyote came out and was just as blue as the bluebird. The coyote looked at himself in the reflection of the water and thought, "My, I'm the prettiest coyote there is. There is none prettier than me." So he strutted down the road, not unlike a rooster, looking around to make sure all the other animals could see him and see how truly beautiful was his color. He was so intent on having everyone know how colorful and beautiful he was that he paid no attention to where he was going in the road. He ran into a tree, fell down on a dirt road, rolled around and came up. That's why, when you look today, he's brown and dirty. That's how he got the color of his fur."

Everyone laughed and clapped, thanking Walela for the entertainment with pleasure. Julia wasn't sure if Walela believed her stories and was always a little worried how other people would react. But no one laughed *at* her and with the charm of the telling, the response invariably was delight. As everyone had a far way to go to reach home, all departed as the shades of dusk darkened the cozy interior.

CHAPTER THIRTY-THREE
Court-Martial

THE NEXT morning they arose especially early. Julia shivered as she cracked the thin layer of ice in the pitcher for her morning ablutions. Fortunately, the courts-martial for this time period would be held here at Cantonnement Gibson and not at Fort Smith, or at some Army site even further away. Julia would be permitted to sit in the room to listen to the proceedings, and she hoped her presence would help her husband rather than hinder him. He said it would.

Pierce gathered his papers and put them in the saddlebag before they set out together. Julia gave him an especially strong embrace before mounting Cinder. "I know all will be well. No one will believe Neville instead of you."

"I'm counting on it," he said in a rather grim tone.

When they arrived, the solemnity of the occasion again struck a sharp chime of fear in Julia. She found all the dark dress uniforms and stern serious faces daunting and prayed Pierce was not as affected as she.

Colonel Arbuckle called the court to order and named the officers presiding. Each one nodded without changing expression as their name was intoned. Then he commanded the Quartermaster General to read the charges against Captain Pierce Mason Butler as brought by Lieutenant Newell. Julia glanced over at her husband's accuser and was surprised to see a rather mild but cocky looking individual, not at all the threatening ogre she had imagined. Still, as reading the charges took a very long time, she became quite worried and sitting forward, locked her fingers tightly together in her lap. The room grew colder and colder as the morning wore on, and it didn't help that the fire at one end of the room was blocked by the row of presiding judges sitting comfortably in front of it.

The court adjourned for lunch with the instructions that Pierce would be called for the defense immediately afterward. He was led away like a common prisoner at this juncture, which surprised Julia because he had been a free man until now. Too upset and nervous to eat, she managed to drink some tea at Sutler Nick's and paced until the Adjutant recalled the court into session.

When Pierce stood up before the assembled judges, she felt her heart pound in her chest like an Indian drum. She hated being this frightened and tried to calm herself. When William and Edward slid into seats next to her, it helped immensely.

Captain Pierce Mason Butler was directed to stand before the court. As he began to read from his defense statement, Julia noticed a slight tremor of his papers, but his voice rang clear and firm.

Mr. President and Gentlemen of the Court

After eighteen months suspense, I am called to answer charges implicating my character as an officer and a gentleman. Need I say that disquietude and anxiety have been my inseparable companions. I know the characters of the individuals composing the court. I believe in their integrity. I believe in their intelligence. I go to trial in the absence of many material witnesses . . . .. But I seek, I court investigation, privileges I waive, advantages I forego. I bring before you no supplement imploring mercy. And in the proud consciousness of innocence, I ask, I demand justice at your hands. I shall raise no unnecessary difficulties. . . .

I am arraigned on three charges with numerous specifications under the first two.

The specifications of the charges, nine in number, per-
tain to the same subject – they are blended and merged in
each other ---the guilt imputed to me is common. The charge
is "mutinous and unofficer like conduct" imputed to me on
the 4ᵗʰ May 1826.

As Pierce recounted the specifications against him, Julia stole looks around the room to see how people seemed to be receiving his remarks. She thought his stance straight and confident and his cadence rang strong and true. He did not have an especially deep voice but she believed it carried well with a pleasant tone. He did not sound arrogant or gruff or angry, rather resolute and full of conviction. Everyone appeared to be listening earnestly and with concentration which she took to be a good sign. They must believe him, she thought, so honest did he sound. Her attention returned to her husband's words.

On the evening of the day in question there was disor-
derly and riotous conduct among the men of Company B, of
which I was the officer. The accuser was loose, incoherent,
disjointed in testifying to the disorderly conduct. . . . I was
not at my quarters. I was sent for; on my arrival, I enquired
of the accuser, the officer of the day, in what consisted the
misconduct of the men.
I received no satisfactory answer, but was met by the
abrupt declaration, "I know, I will have the man at the ex-
pense of my life or blood". He was in search it seems of a
private of that company, named Peasly, an alleged rioter...

Pierce went on to explain how his accuser had already broken into the chest "where it was utterly impossible Peasley could have been concealed", show he had threatened Pierce with words and by priming and picking the flint of his pistol. Newell had drawn his sword and threatened another soldier with "direct violence."

These and similar extravagances induced me to cease to re-
gard him in a character, the duties and dignity of which, he seemed
entirely to have forgotten. ..... . I arrested him and ordered him to
his quarters.. . . . Pierce continued his defense statement for
the better part of an hour, his voice growing stronger through his
speech. He came to the end of the specifications of the first charge
of disorderly conduct.

Thus have I gone through the specifications to the first
charge, to each of which I have pleaded not guilty, To the
charge generally I have also pleaded not guilty. I submit to
the court with a firm belief, that I have a right to ask a ver-
dict of acquittal. With an entire conviction that if any facts
are found to have been committed, it will be a finding of the
naked immaterial facts, a finding carrying with it no guilt or
criminality.

Julia hoped he had not gone on too long. But he had to cover all the points. Still, it seemed overly detailed and long-winded
when usually his style was terse. She shouldn't let her mind
wander. Perhaps he was making some headway because when
she stole a glance at Lt. Newell, he seemed to have slumped a
little lower in his seat. Pierce then turned to the second charge of
"Unofficerlike and ungentlemanly conduct", listing all the specifications against him, including "degrading familiarity with a Negro"
and "enlisting an alleged Army deserter." Finally, he came to the
end.

Acknowledging the frailties and confessing the weaknesses
to which our nature is incident, I proudly spurn the idea of
intentional crime or designed culpability. A soldier of seven
years standing, I trust I appreciate the chivalry of the insti-
tution that regards a stain as a wound. I have told you I ask
not mercy, sustained by innocence and integrity of purpose.

The defense statement was found in its entirety in Captain Butler's handwriting in the National Archive in Washington D.C. His military record resides there as well, dates of service,
promotions, and names of fellow officers.

*I commit myself to your impartiality, confidently expecting
an <u>Honorable Acquittal.</u>*

Cantonnement Gibson
Pierce M. Butler
Dec. 26th, 1826
Capt, 7th

When Pierce sat down, Julia discovered she was holding her
breath and tightly grasping William's hand. Again the court was
recessed and Pierce led away. Hopefully, they would know the
result before evening.

"Why is it necessary to go through this?" she asked her
brothers in frustration and fear for the hundredth time. "He is
clearly innocent!"

They reassured her that all would be well, but she knew
they were putting a good face on a nerve-racking situation. Julia
looked around to discover how Pierce's remarks had affected others and everyone seemed to avoid looking at her. That could not
be a good sign.

Trying to divert herself, she began a conversation with Edward. "How are you and Walela faring with all the strain over the
pending wedding?"

"There is no question that we are very worried about how
her family feels about our marriage. But we can not believe how
happy we are when we are together," he mused. "Of course we
have a lot to learn about one another, and no doubt, it will be an
interesting life! I'm beginning to think I whine a lot because she
never complains, even when to my mind, she is deprived."

Julia was too preoccupied to answer. The wait lengthened
interminably. What could they be discussing? Surely there must
be a clear and unequivocal answer; it should be an open and shut
case. The hours crept by as they all sat in the bitterly cold room.
Julia wished she could see Pierce to encourage him, or to be honest, so he could encourage her.

The wind whistled through the one window and clattered the frame. Looking out she viewed the vast plain extending beyond the fort. This afternoon it looked so empty and frigid with a leaden sky casting no shadows. Barren trees webbed the horizon making her shiver inside her coat. She looked down at her hands in her lap, all red and raw from the cold and hard work. What on earth was she doing here in this God forsaken place? She had cast her fate with a man now on trial by his peers and being held like a common criminal. She must have looked terrified because Edward reached over and put his arm around her.

"Don't worry, Sis. It will be all right." How many times had they said that to one another? Oh, Dear God, she thought, she could get through these difficult times as long as they were together, and now they were going to withhold him from her.

The presiding judges trooped in followed by the guard with Pierce walking next to him.

"Will the defendant stand before the court?"

Pierce stood as straight and unbowed as a pin oak and looked directly at his accuser before turning to the judges.

"Captain Butler, the court has reviewed your case and finds as follows. You are reprimanded by the court for any intemperate behavior exhibited by you toward your accuser. But in no specification does the court find you guilty, in any sense, of criminality or serious wrongdoing."

The reading of the findings continued in some detail but Julia could no longer listen attentively. Of course! She had not really doubted the outcome. Pierce smiled at her from across the room when, unable to hide her jubilation, she jumped up from her seat. How much she wanted to be with him, wherever that might be!

So many wives didn't last long in the I.T. but she would not want to leave now! How confining it would feel to be chaperoned everywhere; she was not about to give up a shred of the freedom and independence she had won. Besides, such important work was going on here, and surely she could make a contribution. She felt a responsibility for her Indian students and Walela would need a lot of help. She smiled to herself with some chagrin. And she needed them too. Well, she would muster the courage to do what she needed to do. Had she not coped so far?

"Now let us go home and prepare a celebratory dinner!" she exalted.

CHAPTER THIRTY-FOUR
TOGETHER

ALL THE nuts from the sweet gum trees had long since fallen to the ground and their prickly exteriors been trampled underfoot. Still, under a few trees far from the house, Julia gathered enough to enhance her dinner table decorations. She planned a party for Edward and Walela to be held a few nights before the wedding. Dropping the dark spheres into her basket, she decided she could dye them red with pokeberry juice and scatter them upon a bed of red oak and yellow birch leaves which she had saved, strewn the length of her table. Her spirits rose with gladness over the coming festivities and her brother's obvious happiness. Candles on her table would make everything glow.

William had promised to bring Julia a brace of rabbits, skinned and cleaned, this morning for the pre-wedding feast, showing he might give in to Edward's appeals. Julia knew his refusal to come to the wedding had caused both pain and embarrassment for Edward, but his arguments and pleas must have finally gotten through to William, especially the comparison that Red Fox, although he objected, would stand up with Walela. If William joined them this evening, Julia felt it would be a signal he would accompany them to the ceremony.

Lt. Munro had already filled her larder with fresh thyme, onions, potatoes and winter squash. She and Sarah planned to make apple pies this morning, and Julia would begin the rabbit stew about three o'clock. She looked forward to the spicy aromas filling her home and seeing the house decorated for this festive family occasion. Walela had explained that none of her family would come; it would be better to wait for the ceremony, she said. This would be just a Butler/Du Val family send off.

WALELA KNEW she should be thankful --- and she was, for all the attention and kindness her White "family" gave her. But the comfort this acceptance brought failed to mask the gnawing worry over her own family. Would the wedding really take place? Certainly, Chief Jolly had given his permission, but would Red Fox control his anger? Would her mother break down? She was much more anxious about Red Fox's behavior but more disturbed about her mother's emotions.

Did her brother not see that things were settling down, that the Indian Agents were really here to protect them and help them? She had only recently heard about a new treaty between the Osage and the Delaware prohibiting all parties from hunting in the territory of the others. The new law imposed a $1000 penalty on any tribe whose warriors took the lives of members of other tribes. Hopefully this would prevent situations like the Red Hawk incident. But she understood that it was not a political or moral issue for Red Fox. He simply did not want a white man for a brother-in-law --- just as she sensed William did not want an Indian girl for a sister-in-law.

She shared none of this with Edward when she arrived at the fort to ride over to Julia's with him. She had made her decision and she would cope with the outcome. Smiling to herself, she mused about how Julia would be someone she could talk to in the future. And tonight she would enjoy the luxuries of the Butler's table and the incredible joy of knowing Edward loved her.

When they crowded into the little Butler's house, Sarah and John Nicks and William were already there. Edward strongly clasped his brother's hand and clapped him on the back with relief and affection. There was barely room for all the people, not to mention the pile of coats and hats, making Julia wish again for their larger home to accommodate friends and family. William brought out a bottle of bourbon, saying they should all drink a toast on this momentous occasion and suggested Pierce do the honors. He raised his glass to the union of Edward and Walela and added he also would like to celebrate the loyalty of friends and family. Julia, her face pink from the cooking fire and sweet exhilaration, could not believe her brother's transformation. Isolation within his family was evidently more that he could bear. At last everything seemed to be going more smoothly.

THE DAY of the wedding dawned cloudy and cold with the scent of snow, the air a white pillow ready to burst with feathery flakes. As planned, Julia and Pierce collected Edward and William in the wagon pulled by Brownie. All three soldiers wore their dress uniforms with long underwear, Pierce and William in winter blue and as the groom, despite the weather, Edward had chosen his summer whites. Julia laid her dress in the back of the wagon so she could wear warm clothes for the long ride to the village. The four huddled close under a blanket to ward off the descending damp chill, and Edward, usually temperate, passed around a flask of whisky. Given the nature of the occasion, all seemed a little subdued, perhaps from the apprehensiveness of not knowing what to expect.

"You should probably tell us what we need to do, Edward," Julia suggested, unable to mask the shivering in her voice.

"I would if I could, Sis. Walela explained it all to me, but honestly, I couldn't pay that much attention. All I wanted to do was look at her."

His family laughed. "You're beyond rescue, my friend," Pierce kidded. "Just follow directions from the Priest and Red Fox, and you all will do fine. I don't imagine it's all that complicated."

"You would be surprised," Edward said. "But Walela told me she will show you anything you need to do. I remember she informed me that after the ceremony, dancers will perform."

When the groom and his family arrived at the village, general awkwardness prevailed. No official greeter appeared, there apparently being no precedent for such an event, and so they stood around at a loss as to where to go or what to do. Walela, as might be expected, was nowhere in sight, and the village center was quiet and empty, hardly a welcoming or festive beginning. The others ignored William when he complained that this treatment was an insult. Finally, the sound of a squeaking door broke the silence and Chief Jolly, bedecked in his red blanket, approached their little circle.

"Come," he offered. "You may warm yourselves by my fire until time for the ceremony." They were all shivering as the wind whipping across the plain pulled the few remaining leaves from the trees and scraped their dry sharp edges against the hard ground, making a sound like skittering mice. Julia, Edward, William and Pierce gratefully followed him indoors. While Julia changed her dress behind a screen, Chief Jolly answered Edward's queries about the procedures, and mercifully, it was not long before he led them to the Council House.

THE SACRED spot for the ceremony had been blessed several times over the past several days and at last, the time for the nervously awaited event arrived. Early that morning the officiating Shaman had gathered special roots together and laid them a little apart upon the ground. He then turned his face to the east and prayed. If, during his prayer, the roots moved together the marriage would be happy. If they did not, the marriage would not be completed. If one of the roots wilted faster than the other, this also was a bad sign. In case two signs were bad, the priest would forbid the marriage. If the signs were good, and apparently they had been today, the people concerned would assemble in the wooden Council House.

Edward waited at one end of the Council House before entering and the bride stood alone at the other end. At the proper signal, they both stepped inside and walked toward one another, meeting in the center by the sacred fire. Walela wore a traditional "tear dress," so called because, since the Cherokee didn't have scissors, it was made by tearing trade material into squares or rectangles to make the garment. White doeskin moccasins with fringe on one side bedecked her feet. Edward appeared tall and proud in his army dress uniform.

The Shaman raised his hands and spoke in a sonorous voice, "The fire is and was sacred to the Cherokee, and is a living memorial. It has been with the people from the beginning of time." He then turned to face east as does one door of the Council House. Except for the older men who took the higher seats on one side of the Council House and the older women who occupied the higher seats on the other side, he called all guests to move toward the fire.

The bride's mother stood beside Walela and Red Fox stood on her other side, symbolizing his responsibility for his sister and her children. Mrs. Bushyhead wore an "elk tooth" dress of soft antelope hide yoked with rows of elk's teeth. These dresses could weigh up to ten pounds and were meant to show off the prowess of the woman's husband.

Walela held the bride's gifts of corn bread and a blanket, representing her promise to nurture and support her husband. Traditionally, the groom's mother would stand beside him and the bride beside her. Today, Julia stood next to Edward, who held a basket filled with venison, representing his ability to provide for his wife. The couple then moved close to one another as Red Fox and Julia draped them in blue blankets, symbolizing their old ways and loneliness before finding one another.

The Shaman blessed the fire and the union of the two, asking for a long and happy life for them. He told them to be faithful to each other and then nodded to Walela that the moment had come for her to give her groom the gift of a red and black belt which she had made. When Edward held out his hands to receive the offering, he thought he would weep from joy and terror. How fragile this girl looked in her dress of flimsy trade fabric and the gorgeous white moccasins on her feet. He would only be making life more difficult for her in so many ways.

The couple joined their blankets, symbolizing their mutual support within the marriage and each drank a corn drink from a double-sided wedding vase. They drank from east to west, then from north to south, giving their blessings and respect to other creatures. As together they threw the vase down upon the earth to seal their wedding vow, the Priest intoned that the broken fragments had returned to our mother the earth. Julia and Red Fox moved forward in unison to place a white blanket around the shoulders of the couple representing their new life of happiness and peace. Walela and Edward then turned to face their wedding party, holding out their baskets to offer a piece of bread and meat to everyone as a sign that following the ceremony, a feast would take place for the entire gathering.

Julia could not imagine what her brother was feeling during this strange and exotic ritual. Knowing what a dream state her own wedding had been, she thought perhaps it really wasn't so different after all. She didn't want to commit a *faux pas* and so she refrained from rushing to them, as was her first instinct, which was fortunate because Mrs. Bushyhead, as mother of the bride, moved forward to escort them into their new world. When Julia took her turn to embrace the new couple, they both felt as stiff as puppets. They would need some help pulling the strings to help them at first, she thought.

With pantomime gestures a group of young Indian maidens gestured for all the guests to sit in a wide circle around the fire with an opening at the east end. All the Indian males sat cross-legged and all the females sat with their knees bent, leaning back upon their ankles. For Julia, this was not such an easy posture to assume and gladly accepted Pierce's hand while finding the appropriate position.

A haunting beat of drums began outside the Council House and then a stream of alternating male and female dancers entered, the women wearing turtle shell shakers, three strapped on both sides of each leg. The shakers were filled with small rocks and punched with holes so that the stomping of the female dancers marked the beat. The dancers formed a circle around the fire alternating male-female-male-female and moving in a counterclockwise direction   Each male dancer held a turtle rattled in his right hand, the turtle a sacred creature symbolizing longevity. The rattles were made with the oval of the patterned turtle shell wrapped in deerskin leather and mounted on a wooden handle, which was either carved or wrapped in suede adorned with seed beads and rabbit fur. The female dancers held two twigs of the spruce that they waved up and down like pigeon wings. The beat held the onlookers rapt, and then like a rush of birds the dancers swooped out as quickly as they had come in.

"How thrilling!" Julia exclaimed.

"Indeed," echoed Pierce. "How lucky we are to see your dancers."

After the performance, Walela explained that the dance had been adapted for her wedding day from the traditional Cherokee stomp dance. The cultural tension had been mitigated by the prescribed ceremony, but now, with no pageantry, awkwardness crept back. Julia imagined Edward and Walela's tightly clasped hands were what held the afternoon together.

At first none of the Cherokee moved forward to speak to the groom's family, but finally, the mothers of Cricket and Blowing Wind, whom Julia taught, came over to them with their children. The little boys' excitement at seeing their teacher erased some of the constraint, and gradually, others who knew Julia or Edward came to offer good wishes. The community must have known of Chief Jolly's respect for Edward, and his presentation to the newlyweds of a beautiful blanket added to the nascent feeling of good will. At that moment, one of the children let several of the village dogs inside the Council House and sensing the excitement, they chased first the little children and then each other, their barking adding to the confusion but breaking some of the tension.

Julia and Pierce asked Walela if she would translate for them with Mrs. Bushyhead, and the newly married couple accompanied the Butlers, including William who remained quiet, over to where she stood with Red Fox beside her. Though Walela's brother's stance was rigid, his manners were acceptable. The gentlemen inclined at the waist to Mrs. Bushyhead and Julia gave a little curtsy, not knowing what else to do. She began, "Mrs. Bushyhead, we would like to welcome you into our family and congratulate your daughter and our brother. We hope they will have a happy life together and we pledge to do everything we can to help them."

Mrs. Bushyhead granted her a wan smile and responded in a similar vein according to Walela, that she appreciated their kindness. "Thank you," Julia answered, "and I hope that Edward and Walela will bring you to our cottage one afternoon for tea. I would be very happy to welcome you in my home." Red Fox looked like he might be thawing a little but remained quiet until Pierce turned to him.

"Red Fox, I noticed this morning when we arrived that your tribe appears to have more fields for sowing than I last observed. This is wonderful progress. What do you expect to plant in the spring?"

"Farming is not my expertise. I am a warrior and a builder. But I understand we will harvest more corn and add various kinds of beans for our tables."

"If the garrison can help you, please let Edward know," Pierce offered. Red Fox inclined his head in agreement.

The couple had decided to stay in the village for their wedding night at Mrs. Bushyhead's request. The next morning Edward and his bride would ride to Cantonnement Gibson where they would live in his quarters until he could find married accommodations. After they had tasted the smoked meats, primarily venison, pumpkin stew, tapioca pudding made from the manioc root, and some kind of dry cake with peanuts, the Butlers decided it was time to leave. Julia, Pierce and William changed back into their warmer clothes for the buckboard journey back to Fort Gibson, leaving their brother among the Indians with whom he was now so intimately bound.

"What a lovely new sister we all have," Julia commented.

"That she is," William agreed. "And though you well know, I have my concerns, I wish them well on the bumpy road ahead."

When the buckboard jounced, they all laughed and snuggled closer for the long ride home.

EPILOGUE

IT WOULD be another two years before Julia and Pierce could leave Cantonnement Gibson. Julia probably lost another child by miscarriage during that time because there was no means of birth control, and we know she had many children once she reached South Carolina. In the Winter of 1827-28, it's likely she stayed behind at the fort with Walela when a group of the western Cherokee's most prominent men, including Sequoyah, accompanied by Captains Edward Du Val and Pierce Mason Butler, journeyed to Washington D.C. Their purpose was to express the tribe's concern over the violation of government promises, particularly those regarding a piece of land called Lovely's Purchase. It must have been difficult from Julia's point of view living near the Indians to understand why Washingon remained so unsympathetic to the Indians' plight.

When tribal representatives rejected President John Quincy Adam's offer for a settlement, Adams railed that the tribe "had already more than they have any right to claim."[31] If the tribe refused to move from Arkansas, the government might actually reclaim land already given the tribe. The government's strategy was successful, and the Cherokee delegation did not long resist presidential pressure and other inducements. Acceding to the wishes of President Adams, the delegates on May 6, 1828, concluded a treaty by which the Western Cherokees agreed to give up their Arkansas lands and accept a tract beyond the western boundary of that territory. Although the treaty required the Arkansas Cherokees to again abandon their homes, it did give them seven million acres that included several million acres of choice land in Lovely's Purchase.

On October 1, 1829, Captain Pierce Mason Butler resigned his commission and the couple returned to South Carolina, establishing a permanent residence near Columbia. They built their home, "Dogwood Plantation," upon a land tract of 154 acres that Pierce had inherited in 1818 from a maternal uncle, William Moore.[32] The *Federal Census Report of 1840* indicates that Dogwood Plantation was a middle-sized farming operation with twenty-seven slave workers. As open as Pierce and Julia were to improving the lot of the Indians, they evidently maintained a blind spot regarding slavery.

Julia's friends at Fort Gibson clearly missed her as Sarah Nick's letter below poignantly indicates.

Letter from Sarah Nicks to Julia Du Val Butler[33]

The spelling and grammatical errors are exhibited here as found in the original document. This letter was probably sent about six months after Julia's departure from Cantonnement Gibson.

Arkansas Territory, Cant *Gibson*
April 18th 1830

Dear Julia
Your letter came to hand the first of December and I feel almost ashamed that I have not answered it before now --- the only excuse I can make I have bin very much ingaged and I shall do better for the future. I was not hear at the time Dr. Towns was but I met him on the River. I told him you wished him to take on your things he said it was impossible that he in tended returning imedeatly in a skift.

I requested Mrs. Carter if he should come in my absence to get him to take all of your things she could and particularly your Trunk marked letters she gave him your spoons it was the only thing he could cary, your things have been packed up for some time but there has bin no opportunity of shiping of them, the River has bin very low this winter and spring so much so that it has bin with great difficulty Keels could get up as high as this --- untill a few Days past, the Steem Boat left hear on Monday last she brought up the publick supplies, your things were shipped on her for New Orleans --- what house they were shipped to I do not know but I expect you will be informed by this mail by John (Nicks) --- your Negroes are not yet sold Genl. Nicks has bin trying to make sale has bin in bad health for some time, Mr. Vail wishes to purchase them --- has bin down twice I believe on that business he is down now and I am of the opinion it will be closed this time.

I sent Sucky your Domestick frock agreeable to your directions --- Mrs Carter and my self like wise received the things you directed Col. Arbuckle to give us for which I feel great ful for --- Dear Julia you do not know what painful feelings it gave me when I saw your things opened some of them looked so familiar to me, it made me think of past events --- which would never again be realized ---

I believe there is very little news about Camp that will be interesting to you there is not much alterations since you left hear Mrs. Dawson has a fine sun, and Mrs. Carter is pretty far advanced again in the family way --- I herd from your Brothers family a few days ago they were quite well. Mrs. Du Val has a fine daughter[34] and Capt Du Val at Fort Smith has a fine sun[35] it is about three months old ---

You wished me to write you what has become of Lieut. Macnamara ---he left hear six Weeks ago he said he intended returning to Virginia ---

Dear Julia I do not know whether we will ever see each other again but if we do not I wish you great happiness and prosperity --- kiss your too little children for me and believe me to be your devoted friend
--- Sarah Nicks
And give my best respects to (paper torn) Butler

Sarah must be mistaken about "too" children, because Julia's second child was not born until 1831. It's difficult to explain the confusion.

Pierce and Julia welcomed their first child, Behethelund, into the world shortly after their return to South Carolina in 1829. Another girl, Emmala was born in 1831, and four boys followed, William Louden (1835), Pierce Mason, Jr. (1837), Andrew Pickens (1839) and Edward Julian (1841), whom they called "Ebbie". In order to supplement the farm income and support this growing family, Pierce embarked upon a new career in banking.

Julia received very sad news in September 1830, that her beloved brother Edward had died at his residence Spring Valley, Pope County, Arkansas, of typhoid fever contracted on the reservation,[36] an ironic demise after he had successfully avoided the earlier threat at Fort Gibson.

Pierce's brother, Judge Andrew Pickens Butler, was a member of the South Carolina General Assembly c. 1824-1833 and a U.S. Senator from South Carolina c.1847-1857. He drew Pierce into politics as well and they both became ardent supporters of the nullification movement in 1832, to the extent of representing the county at the Nullification Convention in Washington. Fortunately, for the good of the Union, the Nullifiers lost.

In 1836 Pierce formally entered the world of politics becoming Governor of South Carolina where he served two terms. Then in 1841 at the request of President Tyler, Pierce accepted the position of Indian Agent at Fort Gibson and returned there, leaving Julia at home. Many of their letters to one another reside in the Butler Papers Collection at the Library at the University of South Carolina.

As Indian Agent, Pierce Mason Butler organized an Indian Council at Tehuacana Creek on March 28, 1843. His speech at this council is evidence of his empathy for the indian cause. A painting of this event featuring Pierce Mason Butler by John Mix Stanley belongs to the Pierce Mason Butler IV family. *(Seen at right.)*

Again, in 1846, Ex-Governor Butler and a cousin of Julia's, Isaac Du Val, were sent out to the Indian Territory to solicit the Indians to sign another treaty with the government now headed by Andrew Jackson. Butler negotiated in good faith, but of course, his promises would later be broken by Washington.

Because of health problems, especially severe arthritis, Agent Butler resigned this commission in 1845, but then one year later, could not turn down a request by his President, Andrew Jackson, to lead the Palmetto Regiment from South Carolina in the Mexican War. Pierce Mason Butler was killed on August 20, 1847 in a bloody fight at the Battle of Chiarubusco in Mexico. Julia drew an army widow's pension of $30 per month until she died in 1864 at the age of 62. Her two daughters preceded her in death, Behethelund at age 23 and Emmalala at age 31. She also lost two sons in the Civil War, Edward (Ebbie), at age 19, and William Louden. Andrew Pickens and Pierce Mason, Jr. survived to marry. Pierce Jr. fathered Julian Du Val Butler, a doctor by profession and my mother's father.

The scene of the death of Col. Pierce Mason Butler at the battle Churubusco, Mexico is etched on a sword presented to his son, William Louden Butler, in 1849 by the State of South Carolina to commemorate Butler's death. (Etching seen at right.)

DEATH OF COL. PIERCE IN BATTLE.

ILLUSTRATION ATTRIBUTIONS

Cover: Art: Portrait of a Woman by Thomas Sully, 1830. Private Collection. ArtCyclopedia Image Archives. The Atheneum online works by Thomas Sully: Mrs. C. Ford. Image use allowed.

1. The Du Val Family Tree
2. Map of Julia Du Val's Journey, p. 25. Map by Nelda Hirsh.
3. Photo by N. Hirsh at Fort Gibson, p. 41. A National Heritage Site since 1943.
4. Map of Fort Gibson, c. 1835, p.45. From a drawing by Lt. Arnold Harris, Seventh Infantry. Original at Smithsonian Institute. Copy at Fort Gibson.
5. Portrait, Colonel Pierce M. Butler, p. 56. Appeared in The Chronicles of Oklahoma, Vol. XXX, Number 1, Spring, 1952.
6. Western Territory, c.1840, showing Indian Tribes around Fort Gibson, p. 58. D.W. Meinig, The Shaping of America, Vol.2, The Gallatin Plan, Plate 43.
7. Portrait of General John Nicks, p. 182. Courtesy Arkansas History Commission, Department of Archives and History, Little Rock, AK. Appeared in Chronicles of Oklahoma, Vol. 8, No.4, Dec. 1930.
8. Portrait of Mrs. Sarah Perkins Nicks-Gibson, p. 182. Courtesy of Dr. and Mrs. Collier Cobb, Chapel Hill, North Carolina, Appeared in Chronicles of Oklahoma, Vol. 8, No. 4, Dec. 1930.
9. Painting by John Mix Stanley, March 20, 1849 of Tehuacana Creek Indian Council (1843), featuring Pierce Mason Butler, p. 293. Courtesy of the Pierce Mason Butler IV Family.
10. Death of Col. Pierce M. Butler at the Battle of Churubusco, Mexico. p. 295. Scene etched on the sword given to William Louden Butler to commemorate the death of his father. Pierce Mason Butler III made a bequest of the sword to the state of South Carolina.

ENDNOTES

Chapter Four:
1   Thomas Loraine McKenney, History of the Indian Tribes of North
         America, with Biographical Sketches and Anecdotes of the Princi
         pal Chiefs, Embellished with One Hundred and Twenty Portraits, from
         the Indian Gallery in the Department of War, at Washington, Philadel
         phia, F.W. Greenough, 1838-44.
2   Mason Sister Letter, Detroit Public Library
3   Mason Sister Letter, Detroit Public Library
4   Letters were charged according to the distance they would travel, with
         a maximum of 25 cents for 500 miles or more.

Chapter Six:
5   Socially accepted euphemism for "I swear", which was considered rude.
6   Fort Gibson National Site Museum
7   Westering Women and the Frontier Experience 1800-1915, Sandra L.
         Myres, p.152.

Chapter Eleven:
8   A mixture of tobacco, sumac leaves and dogwood bark smoked in a
         pipe by the Indians.
9   John Ehle, Trail of Tears, p.203
10   Ed. Kent Netburn, The Wisdom of the Native Americans, p.63.

Chapter Sixteen:
11   Expression of the period, meaning to accomplish one's ends in a
         roundabout way. Random House Historical Dictionary of American
         Slang.

Chapter Eighteen:
12   Ortiz, American Indian Myths and Legends, pp 154-155.
13   Lewis Spence, North American Indian Myths and Legends, p. 111.
14   The paper's first edition was on Feb.   1828. Grant Foreman, Sequoia,
         p. 14

Chapter Nineteen:
15   Agnew, Fort Gibson, p.44.
16   The election of 1824 was the first to go to the House of Representa
         tives because of a deadlock. Adams was the eventual winner when
         Clay threw his support to him, and Adams, in appreciation made Clay
         his Sec   retary of State.

Chapter Twenty:
17   Myers, Westering Women, p.157
18   Adapted from Red Jacket's Speech in 1805 to a missionary's request
         to build a mission along the Seneca on the Buffalo Creek Reservation.

Chapter Twenty-two:
19   Event recounted later by Gov. Butler in a letter dating 1841. Reported
         by Grant Foreman (ed) A Traveler in Indian Territory (Cedar Rapids,
         1930) From Chronicles of Oklahoma, Pierce Mason Butler by Carolyn
         Thomas Foreman p. 10 Volume XXX, No. 1.
20   Peavey and Smith, Pioneering Women, p. 35

Chapter Twenty-Four:
21   Chronicles of Oklahoma, Vol. 8, p.400.
22   Arkansas Gazette, Little Rock, Aug.3, 1824, p.3, col.1.

Chapter Twenty-Five:
23   Oliver Knight, Life and Manners in the Frontier Army, p. 97.
24   Random House Historical Dictionary of American Slang, Vol.II, "a well
        known appellation for beer and ale". 1820's.
25   Thomas Jefferson, Instructions to Merriweather Lewis, 1803, before
        they set out on the Lewis and Clarke Expedition.

Chapter Twenty-Six:
26   On the frontier in 1826, the expression "carrying the willow" meant
        "carrying the torch" for a lover who has rejected you. Oliver Knight,
        Life and Manners in the Frontier Army
27   The North American Indians, A Sourcebook, Roger C. Owen, James
        J.F. Deetz, Anthony D. Fisher, Macmillan Co., NY 1967, p.150

Chapter Twenty-Nine:
28   John Ehle, Trail of Tears, The Rise and Fall of the Cherokee Nation,
        p.170
29   John Ehle, Trail of Tears, The Rise and Fall of the Cherokee Nation

Chapter Thirty-One:
30   Attractive

Epilogue:
31   Brad Agnew, Fort Gibson, Terminal on the Trail of Tears, p.61
32   Miles Richard, Pierce Mason Butler, The South Carolina Years 1830-
        1841
33   This letter was given to the Oklahoma Historical Society by Mr. Pierce
        Mason Butler IV of Nashville, Tennessee and was addressed to Mrs.
        M.J. Butler, Columbia, South Carolina. It was published in the
        Chronicles of Oklahoma, Carolyn Foreman, "Pierce Mason Butler",
        Spring, 1952.
34   Another girl for William
35   A boy for Edward and Walela
36   Pioneers and Makers of Arkansas, by Josias Shinn, 1908, p.141.

BIBLIOGRAPHY

AGNEW, Brad, <u>Fort Gibson, Terminal on the Trail of Tears</u>, University
    of Oklahoma Press, Norman, 1939.

BALL, Edward, <u>Slaves in the Family,</u> Ballantine Books, New York, 1998

BODIE, John B., <u>Historical Southern Families</u>

BRUCHAC, Joseph, <u>Sacajawea,</u> Silver Whistle, Harcourt, Inc. NY, 2000

DILLON, Richard H., <u>Texas Argonauts: Isaac H. Duval and the</u>
    <u>California Gold Rush</u>, Illus: Charles Shaw, Wind River Press,
    Austin, TX 1987

DOANE, Nancy Locke, <u>Indian Doctor Book</u>, Distr. By Aerial Photogra-
    phy Services, Inc., Charlotte, NC

DUVALL, Deborah L, <u>Images of America, The Cherokee Nation and</u>
    <u>Tahlequah,</u> Arcadia Publishing, Charleston, S.C. 1999

EHLE, John, <u>Trail of Tears, The Rise and Fall of the Cherokee Nation,</u>
    Doubleday, Anchor Books, New York, 1988

ERDOES, Richard, and ORTIZ, Alfonso, Eds. <u>American Indian Myths</u>
    <u>and Legends,</u> Pantheon Books, New York, 1984

FEEST, Christian F., <u>The Cultures of Native North Americans,</u> Kone-
    mann, Germany, 2000

FEEST, Christian F., <u>Native Arts of North America</u>, Thames and Hud-
    son, Ltd., London, 1992

FLORIN, Lambert, <u>Western Wagon Wheels</u>, Superior Publishing Co.,
    Seattle, 1970.

FOREMAN, Carolyn Thomas, <u>Park Hill</u>, Star Printery Press, Muskogee,
    OK, 1948

FOREMAN, Carolyn Thomas, <u>Indian Women Chiefs</u>, Zenger Publishing
    Co., Inc. 1976, 1st ed. 1954

FOREMAN, Grant, <u>The Five Civilized Tribes, Cherokee, Chickasaw,</u>
    <u>Choctaw, Creek, Seminole,</u> The Civilization of the American
    Indian Series, University of Oklahoma Press, Norman, 1934

FOREMAN, Grant, <u>Sequoyah,</u> Civilization of the American Indian Se-
    ries, University of Oklahoma Press, Norman, 1938

GRIERSON, Alice Kirk, <u>The Colonel's Lady on the Western Frontier</u>,
    University of Nebraska Press, 1989

HAWKE, David Freeman, <u>Everyday Life in Early America,</u> Harper &
    Row, New York, 1988.

HUTTON, Paul Andrew, Editor, <u>Soldiers West</u>, Biographies from the
    Military Frontier, University of Nebraska Press, 1987

JACKSON, Donald, <u>Voyages of the Steamboat Yellowstone</u>, Ticknor and
    Fields, NY 1985

JOHNSON, Diane, <u>Lesser Lives</u>, The True History of the First Mrs. Mer-
    edith and Other Lesser Lives, Heinemann, London, 1972

KEMBLE, Frances Anne, Journal of a Residence on a Georgian Planta
    tion in 1838-1839, Edited by John A. Scott, University of
    Georgia Press, Athens, 1984
KING, Charles, An Army Wife, 1896, Colonel's Daughter, 1883, A
    Daughter of the Sioux, 1903, The Hobart Co., New York
KNIGHT, Oliver, Life and Manners in The Frontier Army, University of
    Oklahoma Press, 1978
KNOTEL, Herbert and SIEG, Herbert, Uniforms of the World, A com-
    pendium of Army, Navy and Air Force Uniforms 1700-1937,
    Charles Scriber & Sons, New York, 1937.
LANDER, Ernest M., Reluctant Imperialists, Calhoun, The South Caro-
    linians, and the Mexican War, Louisiana State University
    Press, Baton Rouge, 1980
LARKIN, Jack, The Reshaping of Everyday Life, 1790-1840, Harper Pe-
    rennial, New York, 1988
LECKIE, Shirley Anne, Editor, The Colonel's Lady on the Western
    Frontier, The Correspondence of Alice Kirk Grierson, Univer-
    sity of Nebraska Press, 1989
MATTHEWS, Sallie Reynolds, Interwoven, A Pioneer Chronicle, Texas
    A & M Press, 1936
McCUTCHEON, Marc, Everyday Life in the 1800's, Writer's Digest
    Books, Cincinnati, Ohio, 1993
MCKENNEY, Thomas Loraine, History of the Indian Tribes of North
    America, with Biographical Sketches and Anecdotes of the
    Principal Chiefs, Philadelphia, FW Greenough, 1838-44.
MEINIG, D.W., The Shaping of America, A Geographical Perspective
    on 500 Years of History, Vol. 2, Continental America 1800-
    1867, Yale University Press, 1993
MEINIG, D. W. The Shaping of America., Vol.1, Atlantic America
MYRES, Sandra L. Westering Women and The Frontier Experience,
    1800-1915,University of New Mexico Press, 1982
NERBURN, Kent, Editor, The Wisdom of the Native Americans, New
    World Library, Novato, CA, 1999
NEWMAN, Harry Wright, Mareen Duvall of Middle Plantation, 1952
    Random House Historical Dictionary of American Slang, Vol. I
    & II., Random House, 2002.
O'BRIEN,MICHAEL, ed. An Evening When Alone, Four Journals of Sin-
    gle Women in the South, 1827-67, University Press of Virginia,
    Charlottesville, 1993.
OWEN, Roger C., James Deetz, Anthony D. Fisher, The North Ameri-
    can Indians, A Sourcebook, MacMillan Co., NY 1967
PEAVY, Linda and SMITH, Ursula, Pioneer Women, The Lives of Wom-
    en on the Frontier, University of Oklahoma Press, Norman,

1996

RONDA, James P., <u>Lewis and Clark Among the Indians</u>, University of Nebraska Press, 1984

SCHERER, Joanne Cohan, <u>The Great Photographs That Reveal North American Indian Life 1847-1929,</u> The Smithsonian Institution, Bonanza Books, NY 1973

SNYDER, Gerald, <u>In the Footsteps of Lewis and Clark</u>, National Geographic Society, 1970

SPEAKE, Jennifer, ed. <u>Oxford Dictionary of Idioms,</u> Oxford University Press, 1999

STRATTON, Joanna L., Pioneer Women, <u>Voices from the Kansas Frontier</u>, Simon & Schuster, New York 1981

TOMER, John. S., and BRODHEAD, Michael J., Eds., <u>A Naturalist in Indian Territory, The Journals of S. W. Wodehouse, 1849-50,</u> University of Oklahoma Press, Norman, 1992

TOMKINS, Calvin, <u>The Lewis and Clark Trail</u>, Harper & Row, NY 1965

UTLEY, Robert M., <u>Indian Frontier, American West 1846-1890</u>, University of New Mexico Pres, 1984

WARFIELD, J.D., <u>The Founders of Anne Arundel and Howard Counties, MD,</u> Baltimore, 1967

ARTICLES AND BROCHURES

THE BUTLER SOCIETY, North America News Bulletin, Nov. 1998

HERSHBERGER, Mary, The Journal of American History, The Struggle Against Indian Removal in the 1830's, June 1999

MILES, Richard S., <u>Pierce Mason Butler, The South Carolina Years, 1830-41,</u> The South Caroliniana Library, The Butler Papers

THE CHRONICLES OF OKLAHOMA, Summer, 1952, Vol. XXX, No. 2 Carolyn T. Foreman, pp. 160-173

THE CHRONICLES OF OKLAHOMA, Spring, 1952, Vol, XXX, No. 1, Carolyn T. Foreman, pp. 6-26, "Pierce Mason Butler"

THE CHRONICLES OF OKLAHOMA, Vol.8, No.4, 1930, Carolyn Thomas Foreman, "General John Nicks and his Wife, Sarah Perkins Nicks"

THE CHRONICLES OF OKLAHOMA, Vol. L, #4, Winter 1972, Carol B. Broemeling, "Cherokee Indian Agents"

SOUTHWESTERN HISTORICAL QUARTERLY, Vol. XCVII, No. 4, April 1994,Cover: John Mix Stanley photograph, courtesy of Susan and Pierce Butler

TEXAS INDIAN PAPERS 1825-1843, No.123, Minutes of Indian Council
    at Tehuacana Creek, March 28, 1843
TIGNER-WISE, Lori F, "Army Laundresses and Officers; Wives: Simi-
    lar?," Courtesy of Fort Gibson Archives, December 1986
ZIMPEL, Christi, "Separate Lives: The Lives of Women on a Frontier
    Military Post",Courtesy of Fort Gibson Archives, December
    1986
THE MASON SISTER LETTERS, 1844-45, Courtesy of Fort Gibson Ar-
    chives, reprint from Detroit Public Library

WORLD WIDE WEB

Archive.scsa.edu, Technology, About Steamboats
Geocities.com, Cherokee wedding
IMH.org, Stage Travel in America, The Overland Stage, Native Ameri-
cans and the Horse, Women's Riding Attire
Providenceri.com, Paddle Wheels and Steam
Southernpride.com, Stories as told by a Cherokee, by Gail Lang, 1997
Wickipedia, Cherokee Dances

ACKNOWLEDGEMENTS

Researching and writing this book brought me tremendous pleasure, first because I learned so much about Julia's life and the time in which she lived, but also because I met many interesting people, who helped with the project. The University of South Carolina Library (called the South Caroliniana Library) holds the Butler Family Papers, and their librarians were an essential resource. Fascinating information about the so-called Five Civilized Tribes (Cherokee, Creeks, Choctaw, Chicksaw, and Seminole) resides in a beautiful modern library in Tahlequah, Oklahoma, the capitol of the Cherokee Nation. The talented librarians in Tahlequah located interesting material for me regarding the Bushyhead clan. The Museum of the Five Civilized Tribes in Muskogee, OK also held numerous treasures that enlivened my understanding of the differences among tribes.

I extend my appreciation to Chris Morgan, the head of the National Historic Site at Fort Gibson, the docent at the Historical Society in Frederick, Maryland, and to the librarians at the National Archive in Washington DC, who all provided excellent help and direction. I owe a special thanks to Pierce Mason Butler IV for his research on the early Butlers and their heraldry, and to the Butler family for their access to the John Mix Stanley painting of Capt. Butler with the Indian Council.

I am grateful to each of my readers --- David Hirsh, Jewel McCullough, and Judy Reilly --- who all provided invaluable suggestions. It was a pleasure to work with my editor, Melanie Fleishman, who brought experience and much insightful counsel to the table. Nick Pirog came up with a fresh format, layout and an imaginative cover design, Daniel Hirsh of Westend Photography offered his technical expertise with the photography, and Aaron Hirsh generously shared his book savvy. Many thanks to all of you.

I am blessed to have such a talented and supportive family – David, Daniel and Aaron Hirsh – who encouraged my endeavor. And of course, my thanks to my mother, Jewel Du Val Butler McCullough, who is a direct descendant and the model for Julia.